AF192440

LISA KRÄMER

Half the World Away From Home

novum ◢ premium

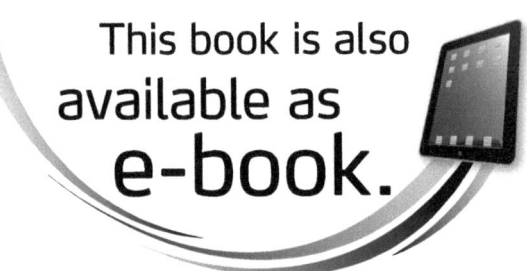

This book is also available as e-book.

www.novum-publishing.co.uk

© 2022 novum publishing

ISBN 978-3-99130-166-0
Editing: Hugo Chandler, BA
Cover photos: Lenapix,
Yura Gridnev, Alena Ohneva,
Forplayday | Dreamstime.com
Cover design, layout & typesetting:
novum publishing

www.novum-publishing.co.uk

Climate neutral
Print product
ClimatePartner.com/16547-2201-1002

To the person
I love and miss the most
this one's for you

Acknowledgement

Before I start, there are a few people that I need to thank because this book would be nowhere and nothing without them and their help. First of all, my biggest thank you goes to the team of Novum Publishing who has supported me in this journey and has made the once impossible possible and made my biggest dream come true. Because dreams really do come true. Thank you to Bianca Bendra, my editor, for spending hours on coordinating and helping me with all my questions. Thank you to Brenda van Rensburg and Hugo Chandler for editing my manuscript and writing me a few words that will always have a special place in my heart. Thank you to my French teacher (who's an English teacher as well) Marianne Dambach who has helped me with my vocabulary and grammar before submitting my work. You are amazing. There are so many more people that have worked on it in the background and I thank you with everything I have.

My next thank you goes to my best friend and soulmate Natalie for being the best person I know on this planet, for caring about me and being the first one to read my book. Thank you to my family and friends who have supported this project, every following one and me in my illnesses and darkest times. You were and continue to be my source of light. I love you all to the end of the universe and back. As you might imagine there aren't only positive aspects from human beings whenever doing something unusual. But despite it all, I would like to thank every person who has told me to give up on my dream and not to set my hopes too high. I hope, dear reader, that this is an example that people's opinions are not always true and that you should never stop fighting for what is yours and right.

A massive thank you to you for choosing this book to read out of all the millions of options. You have made a huge impact on my life.

I'm very proud and scared at the same time because this book holds a place very dear to my heart and thinking about giving it to the world has been a terrifying thought. However, if there's even the slightest possibility to give someone out there that ray of hope and understanding that I ached for in my darkest times overtakes that fear by far. So please know that it is okay to be broken. It is okay if you can't handle daily life like society tells you you need to. I have been there, I and others still are there and you are never ever alone. Please speak up, please write about it, please listen more than you assume and please always search that light in the dark even if it might be unrecognisable at first, it's always there. It will get better, I pinky promise you it will get better, there's always a way out. I'm not going to tell you that life is all glorious, happy and sparkly because it's not. As simple as that. Life is a bitch, but you are the strongest and bravest warrior in your story. Your past and your future might be someone else's source of light. Keep fighting and always keep on dreaming.

HALF THE WORLD AWAY FROM HOME

Chapter One

She loved reading. It allowed her to cry over someone else's sadness when she could no longer identify her own.

Standing here feels so weird. I wouldn't have ever thought of actually ending up here.

My own apartment in London only for myself, where I am all by myself and only for myself. If you had told me I'd end up here three years ago I would have asked you if you were freaking insane.

I'm taking the rest of my stuff out of the taxi that drove me here from the airport. I'm taking my stuff and the key and I'm opening the door to my own place for the first time. Jesus Christ who am I and how in God's name did they convince me to actually do this? My best friend in the whole world, Abby, made me do this. She knows me better than anyone else, even myself, so she knows what's best for me, I guess.

I'm not a person who often steps out of her comfort zone or more likely never at all. This whole thing, moving somewhere all by myself, especially here in London, was always a huge dream. Whenever I think of this place or this country I kinda feel safe and at home. It's a charming place to be sure but the feelings I get are just unbelievably hard to explain. All people say the same; London is like New York but just on another continent. People come here to finally put their dreams into reality, to live and to enjoy. I came here to find out who I am, I suppose.

I walk into the small hallway, taking off my shoes and smelling the fresh paint in my nose. I put the rest of my stuff on the floor and walk my way through the apartment. It's like I have always dreamed about, it's gentle and open. It is really inviting indeed. She surely would've liked that as well…

After having spent the whole rest of the day and the next as well, running around, trying to organize the things I've brought with me and decorating everything. I lie down on the floor and pick up my black guitar for the first time in a while. The instrument lay on top of my chest, as I repeated the same cords over and over again that have stuck in my mind for some time now. I silently hum a melody as I try to come to terms with where I am. *This is so unreal. Why am I even doing this?*

My phone starts to vibrate, so I force myself to get up and take the call.

"Hello?"

"Oh my gosh you're still alive!" a well-known voice shouts into my hear, causing me to take the phone away from my ear.

"Hah, you're so funny Abby." I respond, sarcastically.

"Well, it's not my fault. You've been literally ignoring my texts and calls for the last 48 hours. I thought about you dying in at least fifteen different ways."

"I am sorry, I didn't mean to, I just needed to take some time and accept all this. I can't believe that you made me move to a different country without you," I reply more seriously now.

She sighs before I hear her soft voice again. "You're doing this for you Liv and not anyone else. I might have pushed you a little but we both know you've been annoying me with this since you were like fifteen years old."

"Convincing me to move somewhere completely alone, if I might add again, is not a little push. That's like throwing someone out of a plane and you know exactly how much I hate planes and all that stuff, so thank you Abby for that. This is such a bad idea it can only get worse I'm telling you. I can't even talk to someone except you and my family, and it will not take ten minutes when I step out of that pretty door until I embarrass the shit out of myself." My voice starts to shake again. Please no, I've been over this, why can't this little shit called anxiety just stay home and not come with me all the time? I'm twenty-two years old and I shouldn't be dealing with such things the whole time.

"Olivia shut up right now you're just talking nonsense. We both know how much you wanted that. You're just afraid. Do not let this wash the biggest opportunity in your whole life away or I swear I will come there and throw boiling tea over your whole body until you stop talking like this!" She always had her special way of threatening me. Not that I ever took that too serious.

I told you, she knows me better than anyone else even though she sometimes can be a pain in someone's ass. No names here.

"Listen, I know this is difficult for you, but it will eventually help you. I mean you can write your songs there, you will get new inspirations, you can take those lovely photos and you can skate wherever you want. It will take some time but one day you will be thankful I made you do this and for that you owe me something huge. Just letting you know."

I know she is trying to give me confidence but that's not really helping and one day I hope someone will tell her. I'm not going to be the one because I can gladly live without a fist in my face.

"Well today is not that day. I am just scared… that she wouldn't want me to do any of this like the rest of my family ya know …"

"L, if I can tell you one thing you should be proud of yourself. Like hell. I know you and I know that this, won't make you feel better so just write about it. Write a song and go out tonight. Go and have some fun, but not too much do you hear me?" she laughs as she starts to tease me again.

"Yeah, as if that's gonna happen. But I think you're right for once. I mean the exploring thing not anything else!" I tell her.

She laughs again before replying. "I love you to L. Now go and enjoy, find out who you are and do the things you want to, not because you should or because someone else wants you to, okay?"

"I'll try, I love you too, I'll text you soon. Bye Abby."

"Bye, love you and wear protection!" she says. Before I could say anything she hangs up.

Yeah, she's got a special sense of humour, but I adore it. Abby always does this, first she tries to make me comfortable and in the end she pulls that weird humour of hers out of somewhere to make me laugh. She's a really good person, the best that I know if I'm being honest here. A little smile takes over my face. I'm missing her already.

I sit on the floor leaning against my grey and brand-new couch as I try to turn my thoughts into words along with the same melody from before. As always after I have written my feelings down I feel a huge relief in my chest. This is good, this is what I need to do.

The thing with writing or making music is that you can put into words, what you might not be able to explain or share with anyone. I've been writing serious music for about seven years now but over time, I've tried to become more professional. Writing music is something that I cannot go without otherwise I'll bottle things up deep in me. I know many young people feel this way and I sometimes feel the urge to help these people; to tell them that they're not alone. I mean, I wish I could …

Abby's right. I landed here in my favorite city, more or less by myself, so I need to enjoy it. I need to go and walk through the city and take photos. I need to try not to be freaked out by the thought of being around people. Oh, good Lord help me…

I walk back into my bedroom that I decorated today, and I let myself sink onto the clean sheets on my bed. "What have I got myself into?" I murmur.

Calm down Olivia, you've got to do this. You love London, you love taking pictures and you especially love music. Go out and do it.

I get up and I approach the closet which goes into the wall. Everyone wants to live here so I guess they thought they had to make the place look smart. I open the cupboard doors and stare at all the different colours and materials, as I wonder what would fit best. After about ten minutes trying on and thinking about different outfits as well as all my insecurities, I had finally found something to wear. It's not too much but it is still kind of stylish. The baggy jeans fit my waist perfectly and combined with my top and my denim jacket it looks as if I have a sense of fashion. Which I definitely don't.

Funny, because that's my everyday outfit, but at least I'm wearing something.

Nevertheless, I braise myself at the thought of going outside but for now I will think about the clothing thing, okay? I wonder what she would have said, would she have done the same?

I grab my camera, keys, purse and my phone. I lock my front door breathing in the air. This is beautiful, this is good, and I need this.

The sun starts to set which causes a beautiful pink and orange sky and I see so many people as they try to find their way in the chaotic traffic which I definitely do not want to be in. I really, really hate being near so many people. It just gives me a weird feeling in my stomach besides all the scared thoughts of course.

I put my earphones into my ears, and shuffle through the songs that I've written and recorded by myself, pulling the camera up I start to take the first pictures. I start to make my way to the subway station to head into the city. Taking pictures is also one of the things that calms me. If you watch a chaotic situation, it would probably make you feel uneasy as you cannot apprehend what is happening so fast. If you take a picture of it instead, it still has a sense of calmness through the chaotic mess. You just need to search for it.

I walk for about ten minutes before I finally reach the entrance to the subway. I take my purse out to buy a long-term ticket. If I really want to live here I will need one at some point, so why not now? Standing in the moving train I can see all the people and it makes me so nervous. When I'm in a crowd I always feel as if everyone's watching me and it drives me absolutely crazy. The only good thing I can think about when it comes to crowds is that you see all those faces. Everyone goes through something different, they feel things differently but they still don't realize that they're not alone. It's crazy, isn't it?

I make my way out of the subway and onto the city streets. After some time walking around and taking pictures of different places with different perspectives I find myself wanting something to eat, because I literally only have bread and water at home. Maybe that's a plan for tomorrow, to buy groceries. I look through the photos that I've taken, and they actually didn't turn out too bad.

I was concentrating so hard not watching where I was going until I bumped into something. Because of the unexpected stop, my purse falls to the ground and my camera slips out of my hands. Luckily, it does not fall onto the ground thanks to the unknown person I've run into.

"Oh my gosh I'm so sorry I wasn't watching where I was going."

I look at the person in front of me. It's a tall man with brown curly hair and brown eyes. If I had bumped into him on a different occasion, I would've admitted that he was handsome. Not this again Olivia just shut up before you talk.

He looks at me and the camera and smiles slightly. "Don't worry I wasn't watching where I was going either. Those pictures are very good, did you take them?"

I nod giving him an awkward smile when he hands me my camera. "Thanks... uhm... for catching it." Why can't I just talk like a normal person? Use your damn words! English language? Never heard of it.

"No problem, I'm glad I did. Sorry for bumping into you. Have a good evening." He smiles and hands me my purse.

"Yeah, you too, bye." I said walking away.

What the actual fuck? I take my phone and open a chat with Abby. See I told you I've already embarrassed myself. After I texted her I put my phone away again to watch where I was going this time.

I'm in for a fun evening.

Chapter Two

After walking for twenty more minutes, I finally finding a take-away place which wasn't full of people.

This is actually a tempting take-away place, they have all kinds of delicious things that you could imagine. I stare through the glass, which I guess keeps the food safe from people like me. I am not saying that I would eat all of it but after what has happened I needed something to calm my nerves down.

"Are you all right?" I hear a deep voice to my right which that causes me to flinch and hold my chest. Please not again, is once not enough for one day?

"I am sorry. I didn't want to scare you, but you've been staring at the food for quite long time, the stranger says laughing a bit. He is tall and has long black hair, which is in a bun. I suppose that's in now, but it actually looks better than what I previously thought about men with buns.

"Yeah, no, I mean, I couldn't really decide, and I got lost in a song," I replied. Still out of breath I pointed to my earphones, before taking them off to continue the conversation. Please send help.

H smiles again. "Oh, I know that is too good, which song is it?"

"It's… uh… actually my song, so, uhm… nothing too special," I confess. This is awkward and it is the exact reason why I hate talking. Well, except to Abby.

He lifted his eyebrows and stared at me, as if he's just seen a flying cat. Great. "I'm Jacob, what's your name?"

"It's Olivia," I nod awkwardly.

"You can come and sit with my friends and me Olivia, I'm sure you would like to meet them," he finally says.

Please don't be a psychopath. I nod as he leads me through the small room to the end where there is a little sitting area. There are two women and another man seated. They all look absolutely stunning, is this a thing in England?

"Hey guys, look who I just met. This is Olivia. Olivia, these are Emma", he points to a redhaired girl, "Mary", a brunette, "And this is Ben." Everyone gave a polite hello smiling. He indicates for me to sit down on an empty chair with my back to the rest of the place. The yellow lights give the brick wall a soft and welcoming colour.

"So, Olivia is a songwriter." He tells everyone while I frown at his words.

"Well, it's Liv actually. Olivia is the name my parents gave me so, uhm yeah, and also I'm not a songwriter." I tell them honestly feeling my nerves explode. So much about quickly grabbing something to eat.

Mary looks at me and says, "So song writing isn't your profession but your hobby, right? What's your profession then?" She seems to be very kind and confidant.

I realize that everyone's attention is on me again. I hate this so much. "Yeah, I'm on a mission to find out so I can't give you any further information."

They laugh at my words. "You're funny but not one for many words, are you?" Jacob said taking the lead again.

My eyes move to the ground. "I am not one for crowds and I don't have much to say, so no."

"Well, that's too bad, because you got yourself into something. Hey guys, we're all hanging out tomorrow so why don't you just drop by Liv? I'm sure Ethan wouldn't mind either and maybe you can help us out?" Emma suggests.

Am I supposed to get what they're talking about?

Jacob sees my confused facial impression. "What she was saying is that we're actually all working with a more or less talented artist and that you could help us out with your music."

"I don't think that's a good idea, I'm really not that good and I don't want to interrupt anything."

"You're not, we invited you. And besides that, I'm sure your music is better than you like to admit, believe me. I'm good at reading people and you, dear Liv are lying." Jacob says.

It's the first time I hear Ben speaking. "Yes we'll send you the address and we will just hang out tomorrow, nothing big."

I sigh, is this really good? I like to stay in my own bubble because it's silent and safe but if Abby were here, she would kick my ass and shout at me to do it. Would she think that this was a good idea?

Jacob holds his hand out to me raising an eyebrow. I hand him my phone and he types something handing it back a few moments later.

"It was really nice to meet all of you, but I should really get going now." I say breaking the conversation.

Mary smiles at me and says, "It was a pleasure, and we'll see you tomorrow then."

I nod, saying goodbye. I make my way back to my apartment. On the way I get a tight feeling in my chest and my pulse starts to race again. I can't do this again not here, not now.

This is a terrible idea, I cannot meet them. This is too much for me. Why have I even agreed to this whole thing anyway?

I arrive at my new home, and put my stuff away. I lay down on my bed and I try to calm down and forget about all this. Eventually my fatigue overcomes the panic in my body and I actually fall asleep. We'll not talk about the quality of the sleep, okay?

The next morning I get up and I motivate myself to actually go out to do some shopping. Well, I have nothing to eat so I kinda have to but that's not important.

On the way back to my apartment, bags in my hands, I start to wonder again if I should actually go there. After Jacob had texted me the address and time I should be there, I got my nerves together to tell Abby. Oh, of course she shouted at me that I should go. She's very motivational but has a hard time actually listening and understanding why I doubt my decisions. That's the reason I write the song in the way I do and why I keep them to myself. In seven years of writing, I can only remember having shown my songs to people three times. The first one was for Abby, she started to sob and she hugged me tightly before buying me fast food. Yeah, I know. The second time was to someone in my family and the third time was a huge accident and I definitely regret it. I had stayed at my ex boyfriend's house and he while he played it I was getting something. That was the first time I remember getting upset and angry. When it comes to my songs, which are about my personal emotions and about what I've lived through, I wouldn't want anyone to know that. I'm good, I need to be.

I pack the stuff away into my fridge and cabinets. I sit down on the floor again. I'm not really in the mood to write, I just want to calm my nerves down before it's too late.

What are you going to wear for a 'hangout'? What's that even supposed to mean? I don't care, my jeans will have to fit again. I'm new to this city I know nothing about fashion or hangouts or even song writing. Why have I agreed to do this? Funny I haven't. Whenever someone in my life actually leaves it is the moment I can die in peace. I'm telling you.

The baggy shirt doesn't look stylish either but if we're honest, who cares? Except me and all the people there, right? Nevertheless, I don't have time anyway because I should be there in thirty minutes and I still need to do my hair, pack my things and get there.

I take my old skateboard for the first time since I got here and make my way through the city. The place, Jacob suggested, is outside the city, so taking the subway wouldn't help me. The summer is beginning to end, so it gets colder in the evening. I start to feel the cold. I should have taken a thicker jacket with me- dammit.

I eventually reach the address standing before a huge and old brick building. It kind of reminds me of New York again, I've told you this is basically a second New York. I pick my skateboard up and take my phone out and- shit I'm late. Great start, well done Olivia.

I step up to the black door in front of me and I get my shit together to ring the bell. I stepped back to look around the neighbourhood. This is actually a very nice place, I definitely need to explore this place more. Added to my list.

The door opens and I look into Jacobs' smiling face. "Hello," I say smiling.

"Well, hello there. We didn't think you'd actually show up," he replied and we both laugh.

"I am sorry, it took me longer to find this place than I thought but it's really nice here." Do not mention the fifteen minutes 'what-to-wear' decision.

"No problem, have you skated the whole way here?" His deep voice asks me.

"Yeah, I have."

"All right, come in then. We're all waiting for you." His smile grows again. He steps back into the building, making space for me. This is going to be nerve wrecking and I'm so in for a very long day. Oh crap!

Chapter Three

Please send me some help.

I followed Jacob through plenty hallways it felt like a freaking labyrinth here. When we finally came to the end and into a little open garden space where everyone's eyes were on me again. But that wasn't the biggest problem. The biggest problem, and I'm talking about a massive one, is that he sat just in front of me. The guy I bumped into not even twenty-four hours ago.

So, that brings me to where I am right now, confused as everyone stares between him and me.

"You," he says shocked. Jacob walks a little further to the couple of chairs where everyone's seated.

"You guys know each other?" Ben asks while running his fingers through his hair.

"Well knowing is not the right word. We bumped into each other after I had left yesterday," he tells everyone and gestures to the free chair nodding.

Maya's sits up a bit and says, "Well then Liv this is Ethan, the dipshit artist we make music for. Ethan, this is Olivia."

"I'm not a dipshit Mary," he says offended.

"Oh, shut up before you start Ethan. So, Liv, have you got your music with you for us?" Emma asks, and they all chuckle a little while I stare at them.

"You write songs? I thought you took pictures?" is the first thing Ethan says to me. He keeps his eyes locked on mine which makes me want to run away. Why are they all so intimidating?

"No one asked me to bring anything with me… uhm…," is the only thing I can say to this.

Jacob chuckles before he tells me: "Yeah, if we had asked you, you definitely wouldn't have shown up here. Besides that, I kinda feel offended that you didn't tell me that you're a photographer as well."

"That is true, but I am neither a photographer nor a songwriter. And I won't show you anything, if it's not good enough." I'm tell him raising my hands up.

"Oh, stop talking and give me your phone right now," Jacob replies.

"Jacob, stop pushing her. She doesn't want to show us," Ethan says attacking him.

"Of course, she does. I swear I can smell that she has got some stuff we can use. It's like God gave me the task to find someone to help you with writing so no offence Ethan but stop talking. You will thank me one day anyway." I only watch swearing that they're like two five-year-old children.

"I swear you're already getting on my nerves. Why do you need to be like this the whole time J? Leave her alone, she doesn't feel comfortable around someone like you," he blurts out putting his hands on his head as if he has a headache.

"Could you both just stop acting like this and maybe consider asking her what she wants you two idiots!" Emma shouted at them which caused everyone to laugh except for the two of them. She turns to me and asks, "So, what do you think?"

I chuckle before replying. "I think my best friend is totally like you Jacob. She is literally you in female form." Everyone starts to laugh again.

"Why don't you want others to listen to your music?" Ben asks more seriously now.

I feel my pulse racing faster and my chest beats faster. Not this again, just calm down, no one's going to die.

"I... uhm... I've actually played my songs to only three people in my life and it's just... It is like giving a part of me away. The stuff I write, I write with honest vulnerability. So, I guess I don't want to be vulnerable in front of someone else." I admit, more honest now.

"Honest vulnerability? You are at least going to have to explain that to us darling," Jacob states. He's like the gay best friend that everyone wants to have I can feel it..

I take a deep breath. "You can write down what you feel, honest and vulnerable but you hide it behind the music and in the lyrics, so it means something different to everyone else. It's like mentioning a place, and everyone thinks of a different sight or view of it even though it's the same subject."

"Wow, she's also smart. I like her, she can stay." Ben tells everyone and they all chuckle. Me on the other hand, I start to feel more nervous again.

A new conversation's starts, which is a huge relief to me, and everyone seems to be involved except for Ethan. He's constantly staring at his phone. What is he even doing?

"Okay, so Olivia will you come to the studio with us tomorrow? If you don't want to show us your music now you could send it to Jacob or Ethan if you want to," Mary asks me and now even Ethan's looking at me. Wow, not this again.

"I don't think that…," I start to say but no one else other than Ethan himself interrupts me.

"Leave it guys she won't do it."

Everyone frowns at him.

"Dis someone shit in your coffee today, mate?" Jacob asks.

Before they even get a chance to have a fight I should go right? It's my fault he's pissed. What have I done? "I think I should go now. Thanks for inviting me it was nice to see all of you, but this is… I should just go."

"No, Olivia wait he didn't mean it like that he's sometimes just kind of a dork don't listen to him." Emma tries to make it all sound better and less hurting but that does not help. I'm definitely not welcome here anymore. Now they're all starting to discuss it again. I decided to just vanish out of here. This was a freaking bad idea, and I should've listened to my doubts. You see, they're there for a good reason.

I pick up my backpack and my jacket, and make my way through this whole labyrinth again. Did we take a right or a left here? Who even came up with such a stupid idea? I eventually reach the door and taking my skateboard I open the door. It's already dark outside, which means to find the way home will be a fucking lot harder this time.

"Olivia, wait. Please!" Ben shouts from behind me.

As I turn around, he's already reached me and the look in his eyes makes me want to cry even more. That's why I only hang out with Abby because she does not hurt me or embarrass me when I'm alone. Well, she does hurt me but not in that way.

"Ben, I can't do this, and we all know that. I really need to leave with the rest of my dignity I have left because I feel fucking embarrassed now. Please don't try to make me stay because you will only waste your time."

"I won't, I promise. I'll take you home, it's late and dark and you said you didn't know the way."

I nod as he leads me to a white car. With my skateboard in one hand, I open the door and climb in to the car.
"I am sorry about what happened. He's not always like that," he calmly says.

"It is okay. I shouldn't have come any way. I don't know why I agreed to even show up." I admit looking out the window. The last thing I want to see now is the pity-look from him or anyone else.

"Don't say that, you're very welcome with us. He just doesn't know what's good for him and as far as I know you don't know what's good for you either. Just come to the studio or send Jacob just one song, you won't be judged."

"We both know it's not a good idea. I should just stay in my place, in my one bubble and you guys do what you do." I murmur. Don't you dare to fucking cry in front of a stranger Olivia Jones, or I'll murder you afterwards.

He doesn't say anything. We're both staying quite except for when I give him directions. After some time, we reached my home. I grabbed all my stuff and opened the car door. "Thanks for the ride Ben, it was nice to see you."

"The pleasure was ours, Liv. I'll see you." He smirks and I can't do anything else but roll my eyes and chuckle.

I entered my apartment and put all my stuff away. I sit down at my piano. It's time to write. Don't think, just write Olivia. I always do this, letting it out in the way of a melody, before I give it the power to make me drown in all of it.

Chapter Four

As I open my eyes, I can see the ceiling in my living room. How did I even end up on the coach last night? At least no nightmares this time, we're making progress here.

I end up eating some toast, scrambled eggs and tea of course. We're in England, I just have to have tea.

After I took a shower I recorded some more music. I thought about telling Abby everything. Writing songs helps me with my feelings but it doesn't give me advice or talk to me; just like you.

I pick up my phone to call her.

"Hey Abby."

"Hello Liv, why are you calling me? It's like six in the morning. Don't get me wrong, I really appreciate hearing anything from you," she says. Yup, time zones are usually not nice, unless you want to avoid someone, who lives half the world away from you.

"I've just missed you and I want to hear your voice. Besides that, it's nearly noon sleepyhead." (I'm lying.)

"You're still a shit when it comes to lying. Now again, why are you calling me so early in the morning?" she asks. And again, she knows me too well.

"It was horrible. They wanted me to play music, but I couldn't do it, and you know why. It got worse when the guy, I had bumped into, suddenly sat in front of me and wasn't too happy with me being there and my not wanting to show them my music."

"Damn Olivia. I know you're scared but maybe this is the right time to open up and to take new opportunities. And the guy's just an ass when he doesn't realize how perfect you and your music are. Don't you dare let anyone else question you about yourself or talk you down."

"It's just so difficult without her and you and…," I am interrupted by the ringing of my front doorbell. "Give me a second Abby, I need to open the door really quickly." I walk towards my front door and I open it. The second I see who's standing there I feel as if my eyes are falling straight out of my head. "What the actual fuck? Abby, I'll call you back later." I tell her before hanging up. The devil himself stands before me and he looks as if he has just climbed out of bed. Brown curls hanging messily in his face and his eyes still have a light glimmer.

"Hi," he says.

"What are you doing here and how do you know where I live?" I ask, as I start to feel a little angry. I never get angry, what is he doing to me?

"Ben told me where your apartment was after he had driven you home. I came to apologize and to take you to the studio."

"Well, that's not gonna happen. Sorry but you have wasted your time coming here. Have a good day now Ethan and tell the others a hi from me." I'm about to close the door in his face when he holds his big hands against it to keep it open. Shit, he's got some muscles.

"Olivia, wait," he murmurs. I turn around to face him. "Can I come in?"

I sigh and step aside to make place for him. "It's really… nice here. Haven't pictured you as a minimalist though," he says.

"Considering I've moved here three days ago I didn't really have the time to buy something fancy."

"You've just moved here?" He seems surprised. Yeah, I told you that five seconds ago Sherlock Holmes. I nod putting on a tiny fake smile.

"Jacob made me come here. He basically yelled at me for thirty minutes to apologize for being an ass and to make you come to the studio today... with your music."

Are you fucking serious now? "At least he's got some sort of morals. Maybe you should really consider, listening to him. You can tell him that *she* said no thank you." Give it to him Olivia! I'm really not in the mood to talk to him, considering how he acted yesterday. I had hoped he was actually nice... guess I was wrong. Not the first time and it probably won't be the last.

He starts to chuckle. This was supposed to offend him, what the fuck? "I didn't know you were that feisty, but I like it."

"You know nothing about me Ethan." I tell him sending him some provocative looks.

"So do you. Listen, I'm admitting I wasn't too nice last night and I'm kind of sorry for that, but I really haven't got the nerve or the time to deal with this for much longer. I have got some things to do today. So, would you please stop provoking me and get in the damn car?" he says very directly and intimidating. He's kind of sorry? What the hell is wrong with him?

"Give me one good reason to come with you right now." I'm so tired of people just wanting things from me without giving me something back. I don't care whether he has no time or something to do, I literally do not care anymore.

He sighs, looking at the floor and back to me. "Because I've asked you to." Now I'm the one who's sighing.

"You won't leave, will you?" I ask and he shakes his head with a little smirk on his face.

"I'll be out in five minutes. You can wait outside." I see a little relief in his face before he leaves through the front door. I turn around to go to my room to get changed.

I grabbed my computer. When I got outside, he was already sitting in his black car in the parking lot.

"Jacob is gonna finally stop yelling at me because I got you to come." He jokes. It's not really a funny joke, you idiot.

"Good for you then."

He looks at me and starts to drive. We were both silent even when we reached the studio. I did not feel the need to talk to him, as he is getting on my nerves. It's a relief that he hasn't caused me more anxiety. I don't even know what he's making me feel.

I'm going to walk into the studio for the first time and I'm scared as shit. What if I'm not enough or what if I don't even like being here? I never could've pictured myself being here after what happened to me and what he did to me...

I'm so lost in my thoughts, that I do not realize we are going into the building, until I hear a couple of voices chatting. We went into the studio room and took a seat. This place is huge, it's got several instruments, a computer space for all the smart guys who work with the music..., the producers, you know what I mean, right? The floor is laid with vintage carpets which matches perfectly with the wooden walls and ceilings.

After a quick hello and Jacob picking on Ethan for actually getting me here, they started to have a conversation about some songs they're currently working on. My thoughts drift off to something different again, while I text Abby about what has happened. The coughing pulls me out of my daydream. I lift my head to see everyone else staring at me again. I should get used to this, right?

"Sorry, what did you say?" This is so embarrassing.

"You get lost quite a lot, don't you?" Ethan is picking on me now. I was just about to calm down from our meeting this morning.

"Shut it, Ethan." Jacob asks if I am willing to show them some of my music.
"If you don't want dipshit here to listen, we'll just send him out. Don't worry about him." Mary tells me. Ethan opens his mouth and lifts his hands with a pissed look. He deserved that, let's be honest.

"Yeah, I'll show you if you want to, of course. I also don't care whether Ethan is listening or not. That's not my problem."

"Yes, go on Olivia."

Jacob stands up to give me high-five. I'm telling you, he's just like Abby. I take my computer out of my bag and start to find one of my better songs I can play for them without losing more of my dignity. My hands start to shake again, and I am sweating and become more nervous again.

"It is okay, you don't need to be nervous." Ethan tells me. Is he pregnant or why is he having these mood swings?

In the end, I choose the song 'Light Stick', which is about her, to show them. At least that's what everyone thinks, who knows about my mother. As most songs are, but this one is a rough, touching and still beautiful song. I wrote it about six months ago when I had another one of my episodes.

I take a deep breath in and out before turning up the volume and clicking on the song. She would've wanted that, right?

I hear the intro and the soft piano chord and immediately I get a shiver down my spine maybe this wasn't a good idea. I have only listened to this one twice after having recorded it and every time I end up having a breakdown and calling Abby.

After hearing the first chorus my eyes start to tear up and my chest tightens. Olivia Jones you cannot start to cry in front of all these people again. It's just a damn song about one person. It's gone, it's over, so stop acting like a child.

Maybe it's because I felt like a child back then when she did, what she had to...

Chapter Five

The song slowly fades and everyone is silent, not looking at me. Is it seriously that bad? I know I'm not a professional, but this is one of the better songs. I think… so at least.

"This is…," Jacob begins but doesn't say anything more.

Ethan turns his head towards me and says, "It's absolutely brilliant. It's rough and heavy and still full of emotions at the same time. It makes you think of lying on the street in the rain and not stopping to think of this person. It's like you turned something dark into a piece of music that is utterly incredible." His eyes are a little swollen and red. Is this man seriously that emotional?

"Liv this is great seriously you have to work with us. It would be so much better with your words and that brilliant brain you've got in your pretty head. You should really release this song. I'm serious this is… I can't describe it in words." Mary says and now they are all looking at me.

"I can't release it, it's nothing special and I'm not a professional. No one would want to hear it and besides that I have no people I work with." I admit.

"You have us now," Ben says, and it makes me smile. "No seriously, think about it, this could blow up, I can feel it. We've worked with dipshit here for a few years and I just feel you have potential. Maybe you'll even become better than him and we can finally work with someone nice. No offence Ethan." Everyone laughs except for him. If looks could kill, he would be dead. "This is fun, you need this Olivia, you need people in your life."

"If you guys despise working with me so much then you should maybe consider backing the fuck off before we finish this whole thing. You could finally work with someone like *her*, and I'll have one pain less in my ass and focus on this album. Which we need, if I may say again, to finish very fucking soon. I don't need any distractions anymore so Olivia, either you're in it or you should go." As I said, he's a dick but this time he won't humiliate me again.

"Maybe Ethan, you should be glad that someone like *her* has actually agreed to work with someone as nice as you." I retort giving him an innocent smile.

"Oooh, she's getting feisty now. I swear to whoever is up there Liv, you have saved us," Jacob says.

I raise one eyebrow at Ethan. He sits with his jaw tight and his hands made into fists. His knuckles are already going white… he doesn't hit women, does he? Maybe I shouldn't have? Oh shut up now he deserved it. If you can't take it, you shouldn't be so rude to others Mister Happy.

"So, what's this whole project about?" I ask to change the subject and to focus on being productive for once.

After they introduce me to their new project, which is absolutely amazing to be honest, I decide to pack my things and make my way back home to get some rest. About their project, they're planning an amazing album and a huge tour, which will take about five months. Along with some music videos of the songs they've already got, they still need about six more songs to complete the whole thing. Don't get me wrong but I didn't pick Ethan as such a well-known singer. I really need to Google him when I get home. The thought of him actually being in front of so many people trying to be nice is really scary… he's so confusing. Sometimes his nice and sometimes his just a dick. You never know when his mood changes.

I leave the studio, as quietly as possible, putting the backpack over my shoulder and my headphones in my ears. I make my way through the dark city. I keep walking for about five minutes when I hear a car driving next to me slowly. I turn to my left just to see the devil himself in the car, staring at me with amusement. I raise my eyebrows confused taking my headphones off.

"Ran away quickly, didn't ya? Not so brave anymore now huh?" I roll my eyes at his statement and walk faster. Just ignore him and walk home. He speeds up a bit still following me. Why is this so funny, you dork?

"Seriously, what do you want Ethan?" I ask aloud, which scares me but obviously not him. He just finds it even funnier.

"Right now? I want to know where you're going."

"See, I have this thing and it's called an apartment and I can actually live there." I keep on walking while he laughs out loud. At least he knows what sarcasm is. We're taking baby steps here.

"I'll take you home. Get in the car," he's saying monotonously. You're ripping my nerves apart seriously.

"Thanks, but no thanks. I told you I won't get into your car more than once and if I'm able to count this once has already happened." Yes, give it to him!

"This wasn't a request, Olivia." Who do you think you are? I stop walking and look into his eyes. He stares at me with his deathly eyes, and I get into the vehicle.

"Didn't pick you as someone with a sense of humour, not after I heard your song," he admits. Mood swings, again.

"What has my song got to do with all of this?" I ask bringing my hands to my head. I swear if this keeps going on, my head will definitely explode before his damn tour is even being announced.

"Dunno, just trying to figure you out. What was it called again? Light Stick?"

I look at him and then out of the window. "Believe me, there's nothing interesting you would want to find out about me."

"Well, I'd like to find out on my own if you're lying to me right now."

"Just don't, please. You'll be disappointed. Besides that, didn't you wanna drive me home so badly?" I ask him. He nods slightly. "Then why aren't you driving?" He drives me fucking crazy. That's what he does.

"Why are you so... closed up? What are you so afraid of that you won't open up. If you work with us you will have to open eve..", he says as I interrupt him because I cannot take this interrogation any longer.

"Because I'm fucking scared of that!" I shout at him and I turn away so that he can't see my face.

"Of telling me...?" He doesn't get it, does he?

"I'm fucking scared of being vulnerable in front of people. I hate the thought of someone knowing everything about me because no one does. So, Ethan, please just let it be." My eyes fill with tears, I didn't wanna cry before him. That's not the plan.

"You're scared of people leaving you, aren't you?"

"I'm scared of losing people I care about." I turn my face towards him letting him see how much this hurts me, maybe then he'll finally stop.

"And the song is about that…? Sorry, you're just really difficult to read."

"Have you actually considered that I don't wanna be read, especially not by you? You know for someone who writes songs, you're freaking shit at finding the emotions in others' songs." I tell him making him smirk, which makes me smile for a small second.

"I must admit, I deserved that. Never been good at things with emotions and stuff. I usually write from actions and not from special emotions." Wow, that's the first thing I know about him. I don't even know his last name, which is a little weird, considering that I'm going to work with him. Or for him?

"If you don't want to tell me, fine. But don't worry, I'll find out anyway whether you like it or not. Take it as a promise."

"You won't stop, will you?" I ask.

"Nope," he replies smirking.

"Great, then I'm in for a super exhausting time."

"Probably, but you're not the only one. The others are often a pain in someone's ass."

"Does that include you?" Now I'm the one grinning.

"For someone who's kinda shy you actually do have a lot to say when it comes to talking me down." He smiles.

"Believe me, I'm not saying half of the things I'd like to. Say thank you, accept it and drive me home so I can finally get out of this car." He laughs, shaking his head and starts the car.

Abby will definitely freak out about this. But what would you say?

Chapter Six

After fifteen minutes of awkward silence, we finally arrive at my apartment. I get out of the car with a small goodbye.

It has been three days. Three days of me organizing the rest of my stuff, exploring London, writing some music and three days of absolutely no Ethan-incidents. It actually felt absolutely great to be on my own, although I did speak to Abby a few times but nothing more.

Okay, I lied. Who are we kidding here?

It's been three days of nightmares, mental breakdowns and me ignoring all calls. You happy now? I told the truth, just the way you always wanted me to. But today's different, it has to be. I am going to make it stop by going out and not crying. I have this kind of often actually. I just spend days at home, ignoring everyone, as I try to focus on becoming a little more mentally stable.

The truth is, I've been hiding these things for years and I've become very good at doing so. Most of the time I can even hide it from Abby, which is a great achievement after what I told you. No one should worry about me. I can't bother anyone after what happened in my life. Besides that, I don't even have a reason to be sad when so many people are fighting to stay alive. I shouldn't feel this way. I have Abby and myself. I don't need anything else. Maybe I need you more than I thought I would, but who even cares? You left me like everyone else.

Just get over it and move on, seriously Olivia, you're not in school anymore.

"Hi Dad. I'm sorry I didn't call earlier. I've just been busy with moving." I realize now that it was a bad idea to call him.

"I was very worried Olivia. Besides that, you knew that I didn't want you to move to another country." He sounds angry again. He always does, since you know what happened.

"It's not your decision. I'm an adult, I'm my own person and I need to go my own way, no matter how much you like it or not. I'm sorry that I'm not what you wanted me to be and I'm sorry if that makes you feel disappointed, but this is my goddamn life and I don't need to make all of you happy anymore. I did that for way too long," I tell him honestly holding on tighter to the phone in my hand.

"What happened to you? You've only been there for a week now and you're already so different. You need to be careful."

"I grew up. That's what happened, I had time and I can very much live on my own without any of you telling me what to do." I lie. I can't really live on my own. Well, unless you want a freaking mess, which you already have.

"I'm worried because I care about you. You don't know if *they* are still out there Olivia." Oh God, not this again, seriously, we've been over this.

I pace up and down in my living room to be less stressed and to sound more... mature than usual. "Dad when are you going to stop harassing me for something that will never happen? That's pathetic and you know it. I'm done with this shit and all of you coming at me. If you're gonna continue to fill my life with lies and false excuses because I'm not good enough for you... then please say it Dad. I'm done doing this shit and if you all won't stop then... I must be done with you too." So much for sounding mature. I'm more likely to sound like a little child while

43

crying... maybe because I'm crying? Anyway, that's what you would've wanted me to do just like Abby still does and for once, it's what I want.

"We're all in danger and you moving away doesn't make it all better. These men are dangerous and you're unknowing and innocent and...," he starts, but I cut him off and scream into the phone.

"Maybe I wouldn't be unknowing if you'd actually tell me what happened to my mom, your goddamn wife. I feel as if I don't know myself, but her and all of you too. You need to trust me instead of trying to lock me away. Why are you doing this to me?"

"We're doing something to you. God, Olivia, we are keeping you safe from these people who actually want to hurt us for what she did, even though she did it in good faith."

"You are not keeping me safe; you want to keep me hidden from all of this. And I'm so beyond done with all of this shit. It's over, she won't come back, and neither will these people, you're constantly talking about. I'm done talking to you until you can actually find it in your heart to treat me like a normal person, like a daughter. I hate to break it to you, but you've never been a father to me, and you never will be. You fucked up the only job you had, and I'm done waiting for the person I wanted you to be. I am done with waiting desperately for all those things I will never get. This is my life and I do not intend to waste it anymore. Forgive me or forgive yourself, I do not care but I'm ending this conversation now. Bye Dad." I hang up the call and start sobbing more and more. It's a relief.

You did it. After all those fucking years. I'm so beyond proud of you Olivia, holy shit.

This is the perfect time to write music, right? Do your thing and you will stop feeling this way, eventually. It will settle, once the storm is over, it has to. I've learned to deal with it on my own, I don't need anyone else now.

After about an hour of sitting, writing, recording and listening to music, I finally took a shower and grabbed my camera. I mean, I live here now but I'll have to work eventually, and I'm not sure if I can stand working with Ethan... no, I'm sure I can't. He doesn't like me. I don't like him and all of this is too new for me... I guess.

When I arrive at home from taking photos, I start to edit them to upload them onto the website I created about a year ago. It doesn't bring me a lot of money, but it's better than nothing and maybe someone will book me for an event, when they see my pictures. Again, I am not a professional but they could be worse. I actually had a few little jobs through this website, so, I'm not too hopeless when it comes to that.

When it got darker, I ordered a pizza, because I was starving... no I was hungry, very hungry. I don't like to use terms like starving or depressed instead of words that actually mean sad or hungry. They're half the world apart from each other and still, people misuse these words. I shouldn't be this way. People are suffering, people are dying and others just mistreat their illness for something which is common. It is like: 'Oh, I have migraine' instead of 'Oh, I have a headache'. They're not the same and we really shouldn't let anyone say such things. It's just not right.

I've been waiting for around thirty minutes when the doorbell finally rang, and the pizza guy finally brought me my dinner. I left him the change and got back to my couch, to watch a movie.

So, here I am, eating a pizza like a five-year-old child. How I love it. Maybe that's another reason I despise eating in public. I just look like a toddler. To be completely fair with you, I might look uglier, because I'm still half crying but I guess you'll never know. I'm just really sensitive... I hate to know that people are suffering and that I can't do anything about it. Pizza and music will fix that.

While I cut the rest of the pizza up with my scissors (Yes, that is the only right way to do it. Besides; I don't have a pizza cutter, so don't come after me please.) the doorbell rings again. I get up from the couch and walk towards my front door. Just wipe the tears away Liv, before someone sees them. Why do people always interrupt me when I'm having these… weak moments.

I wipe my eyes with my sweatshirt and open the front door. Standing there are Jacob, Mary and Ethan. Please kill me now.

I stare at them in shock.

"It's nice to see you too Liv," Jacob says pulling me into a hug before stepping in. Oh yes sure, just come on in and make yourself at home. Whatever.

"Hey Liv, can we come in for a second?" Mar asks waiting for my reply, and after a small nod she also steps in giving me a hug.

"Hi."

"Hi Ethan." I say as he walks into my apartment and follows the others. I close the door and go back into my living room.

They all sit down on my couch and look weirdly at the TV, the pizza, the tissues and then back to me. They are all frown at me. Jacob is the first to say something. "Have you been crying while eating a pizza and watching *this* movie?"

I frown trying to think of a good answer, but to be honest, nothing I could say would make this less awkward than it already is.

"I... uhm might have but that is a good movie," I say, trying to defend myself.

"No it is not. They both die in the end," Ethan says, looking back at me.

"Yeah, that's like the whole point. We all die in the end." I say standing in front of the couch, picking-up the remote control and switching the TV off. "What are you all doing here and where are the others? You already decided to show up without telling me?" It's a mix of confusion, being pissed, embarrassed, tired and sad. Just like everything else, I can't understand it.

Maybe someday I will.

Chapter Seven

Beauty is in the eye of the beholder, but, sadly, the eye of the beholder is tainted by the hallucinations of reality itself.

It was a rainy Tuesday morning and if I think about it now, I wish I hadn't woken up that day.

I manage to dragged myself out of bed to eat breakfast. I can hear the rain beating against the window making streaks all the way down. It looks as if the sky is crying. Why would it be crying though? What has changed in the sky that the clouds opened up?

The voices all around me are the same as always. Dad is drinking coffee and reading his paper. You, are sitting there drinking your tea. I guess it's just kind of your thing, isn't it? but this morning is different. I head straight to the bathroom and then back to the dining room. I pick up my mug of chocolate milk and drink it slowly, while listening to your conversation.

"You cannot go there!" Dad says.

"Yes, I can, and I will. I need to do this for all the others who have suffered. Someone needs to stop them, and I will not sit here and watch him do all these things Mark." Mom never talks to you like that Dad, and I realize that it would maybe be best not to ask too many questions; but maybe I'm not smart enough, am I?

"What are you talking about?" I ask my dad quietly, but they ignore me again.

"These people are dangerous, and I want you to be safe. Safe with your family."

"I will be careful, and they won't do anything, not while I hold their secrets in my hand. Nothing will happen to us. We're safe but please just trust me that I am doing the right thing." Mum tells Dad but she is looking at me this time. "Olivia, please go into your room. We need to talk and then I'll go to work. I'll see you for dinner and I love you very much, I always will." She is close to tears smiling at me, God she is the strongest person I know. Hopefully, I'll be like her when I'm older.

"I love you too Mum, just be careful, okay?" I tell her, giving her a huge hug.

"I always am honey. Now go."

"See you later. You too, Dad." I whisper and go into my room. The only thing that I can hear now are loud voices. I immediately turn up my music. It's always like that and I really hope it will stop soon.

✶✶✶

"Sorry guys, I didn't mean to sound rude, I am just not in the mood right now." I say looking at Mary, Jacob and Ethan again.

"Don't worry, it's our fault. We would've called you, but you ignored us for a solid seventy-two hours," Ethan says with a sarcastic tone in his voice.

"Ethan, we've been over this, now shut it. Ben and Emma are on a date, that's why they're not here." Jacob chuckles and I frown.

"They're dating?"

"Kind of, I would say. But back to you, why have you been ignoring us? We're working together and we have been waiting for you the whole time," Mary admits.

"Yeah, I uhm... I felt kinda sick, so I thought I'd just skip the session... or sessions in this case, but I'm better now and fully ready to write. *I guess*." Yeah, finding excuses is not really my big strength either.

Ethan laughs and looks straight into my eyes now. "You're really shit at lying Olivia."

"And you're shit at remembering. I told you I don't want anyone to call me that." I bluster out.

"And why not? What is your problem now?" He provokes me again, great. Mary and Jacob are about to say something but I'm faster than them.

"Because it's not your place to call me that or to act the way you do around me! No one calls me that anymore and you should be the last one to do that! And if you have a fucking problem then get the fuck out of here, I'm not in the mood for your games Ethan!" I yell at him and the other two are sit gaping, but he smiles. "I have enough to worry about and that does not include you at all."

"The matter is settled then, great now I can go. See you tomorrow Olivia. Bye guys. I'll be in the studio at about noon," he calmly says and leaves.

"What the fuck." Is the only thing I'm able to say now.

"You're lucky he didn't punch you. He never lets anyone yell at him so easily Liv, and I have known him for a long time now," Jacob tells me looking at the door. Ethan just got up and left my apartment.

"I've never yelled at someone before. Should I feel bad or worried?" I ask them honestly and they both start to laugh. I let myself fall onto the couch.

"You should feel good as hell for yelling at him. That was literally the best thing I've seen for a while now. This deserves a freaking Oscar or even a reality show." Jacob chuckles as a smile come to my face.

"Why did you come here?" They still haven't told me and I'm tired of this... whatever this was. Maybe they just want to laugh at me, or they want something from me, or they want...

Mary turns to look at me before she says, "We came because we were worried. You didn't answer our calls and we just wanted to make sure you're okay and to get you outta here. Sorry to say, this apartment is gorgeous, but you need to see the world from outside."

"Now again, are you okay Liv?" Jacob seems the most serious, I've ever seen him in this short time.

I sigh. "I wasn't, but I'm okay now." I have to be.

"Are you sure? You know, you can always talk to us, we're good listeners." Mary says. Why are they so nice to me? I don't even really know them.

"Yeah, the way Ethan would. I don't want to be rude again, but I barely know you and I'm more of a silent suffering person, if you know what I mean." I look down at my lap trying to avoid eye contact until someone touches my hand. I look up and I can see their worried expressions. They really must think I'm weak now.

"It's okay, we understand, you need time to trust us but whatever you say stays between us, you know that, right?" Jacob says and I look away. Don't cry again now Olivia...

"Hey, Liv, look at us. Please." Mary's voice is soft and gentle but still really comforting. "It's okay that you want to be alone once in a while, we all do, but what's not okay is the feeling that you need to suffer alone, because you don't. Don't bottle everything up. The people around you are there for a reason, because they care about you and they want to help you."

I sigh nodding, she's right and I know it. But accepting is still a lot more difficult. But if I died tomorrow the sun would still rise. The earth would still rotate. The stars would still shine through the night. The seasons would still change. And time, time would heal the pain. Nothing would change.

I may be around for others but when I get home and close the door, the only person who knows me a bit and is there for me, is me. I lost myself, trying to please everyone for years, and I know it. I really do.

After some time, we ended up laughing and smiling again. They do have a good impact sometimes. Well, leaving Ethan out of this, besides, I'm really glad he left. What I am not glad about is, that he again made a promise to me. If I didn't show up tomorrow, he sure as hell would come here and that's the last thing I wanted.

They end up going home at about nine and I'm really glad they did. Not that I don't like them, because I do, but this whole socializing thing makes me extremely exhausted. So, I'm really not complaining about going to bed this early. Maybe I'll be able to sleep a bit more this time. Hope dies last.

Chapter Eight

Sometimes, when things feel like they are falling apart, they might just be falling into place.

I don't remember a lot of what happened afterwards, but what I do remember is that Dad ended up drinking way too much, and Mom never came home. I sat in my room because he yelled at me to stay away.

I've never seen him cry before this moment, and never after. But in this moment, I felt as bad as never before. His eyes were lost in the pain and they looked as if they were drowning in tears and no one seemed to help him out of it. Maybe they didn't because drowning people can pull you down with them because of their panic, but maybe, maybe no one wanted to.

I, on the other hand wanted to but didn't know how. Since the funeral of my mom, which I also barely remember, Dad shut me out and tried to avoid me most of the time. He didn't tell me where she went, why she went, or when she would be coming home. Every time I asked him, he just yelled at me to go away. Since then, we have barely had a conversation longer than fifteen minutes and he never hugged me again. I was still in my room, with the music playing and I wondered, when she would come home.

She never did, and I found myself still clinging to the sound of her voice, her soft lips, her touches and even her look. In the end, if someone dies, the second they're really dead is when everyone forgets them and I feel like I know her less every single day.

I realized that for the first time after about two years. Since then, I haven't tried to talk to Dad or anyone else anymore. I've been quite lonely, except for the music. It might have come from there. Who knows.

And from then on, Dad and the rest of my family kept telling me that we needed to be safe and that they will try as long as they'll have to, to more or less keep me hidden from the thing my mother had done before she died.

I have tried to get along with all of this, but it's hard to live one's life for the two of us.

★★★

One more flashback to then, a couple of tears and two cups of coffee later, I'm sitting in front of my closet and again I don't have a fucking clue what to wear. I feel as if I do this shit every time I'm about to meet someone. Maybe I should just stop doing it then?

Anyway, I grab a blue dress because it's supposed to be warm today, according to Mary and Emma. The navy blue matches my dark brown curly hair very well. I end up putting on a tiny bit of mascara and some lipstick. I am not someone for fussing about makeup considering that no one has ever shown me how to use it.

I pull the charger out of my phone to check it. It's only nine in the morning, so Abby won't be awake yet. However, she had sent me a text to say that she'll be in London for the next few days for some business. Apparently, she's also decided to stay with me. Yeah, thanks for asking, but sure, you can stay. I still love her. I always have and I always will. Even though she deserves better than me.

After another twenty minutes according to the address of the studio they had sent me I finally arrive at the front door. It's nearly ten, so I open the huge wooden door and walk in. I think it was the Abby Road studio? No, I'm pretty sure, but what I'm not sure of, is how long I'll have to stay here. I'm supposed to be fucking asleep right now. In my bed. At home. Alone in peace.

When I arrive everyone is already there, well except for Ethan. They are all sitting around talking or playing some instruments. Jacob says something nice about my look, which boosts my confidence.

"Jacob, how long are we going to stay in this studio?" I ask turning around with the guitar in my hand, and drumsticks in his.

He tucks his long, brown, curly hair behind his ear rubbing his nose. "As far as I know Liv, I have no fucking clue. I would guess the whole day and the next ones as well."

"You're kidding me, right?" I ask him freezing in motion.

"Wish I could darling, but no, I'm deathly serious," he replies chuckling after he's seen my face.

I slowly roll down onto the floor, which is covered by several beautiful vintage carpets and stare at the ceiling. "I swear I will commit murder if I have to stay in this room for the whole day. Unfortunately, I'm busy the next few days. My best friend decided to come to London tomorrow and she'll be staying at my place." I tell them and we all start to laugh.

"I already like her then. What's her name and how long do you know each other?" Mary asks sitting on a piano chair, but I doubt, that she really plays it though.

I look at her and then back to the others. "Her name's Abby Winston and I have known her for, well technically nineteen years. We basically grew up together." As I speak the words, I can see their faces turning white. Please don't tell me that this is going to happen again…

"Excuse me but have you just said Abby Winston as in Abby Winston the fucking model is your best friend?" Emma says and I roll my eyes as a joke.

"I might have left out that detail but yes, she is."

"Holy fucking shit, why in God's good name didn't you tell me earlier? You need to get me an autograph, there will be no excuses young lady. No, wait, shit, you can introduce us to her when she arrives," Jacob says thrilled as he gets up from the chair behind the drums and starts to walk up to me. He looks down at me running his fingers through his hair in shock.

"Who will introduce who to whom?" I hear a voice coming from the door of the studio.

"Oh Ethan, nice you decided to show up as well. Liv just told us that her friend is Abby Winston and she'll be visiting her, and good Jacob here may have let the little stupid fangirl in him slip out." Emma explains with a huge smile on her face.

I turn around and look into his brown eyes, just to see a big fat smirk in his face. So, I turn back looking to the wall. It doesn't really work if some ass decides to stand right in front of it. He kneels down to my level and looks at me with an amused kind of smile.

"So, little Olivia here has got some grade-A celebrities in her list of friends. How amusing. Are you doing better now sweet-heart?"

"Maybe if I just punch you, I'll feel better. Shall I try, what do you guys think?" I smirk to myself and I turn around to see everyone's excited faces.

"Watch your words, you're working for me Olivia."

"Well, technically I work *with* you because Jacob asked me to do the job and not you. Anyway, have you calmed down a little Ethan? Let me quote you here: '*I really haven't got the nerves or the time to deal with this for much longer, I got some things to do today. So, would you please stop provoking me and go on singing?*'" God he gets on my bloody nerves and it's not even noon. The thing that actually amazes me, is that I've actually said what I thought.

I hear laughter from behind me. Ethan closes his eyes, and runs his fingers through his hair sending them a killing-expression and they immediately stop.

"I must admit, you're a lot more interesting than I thought at first." He whispers in my direction so that the others can't hear us. I frown at him and he says with a normal voice. "We should really get going guys. Also, *Olivia,* why don't you bring your friend here tomorrow afternoon when we have finished the session. We could grab some drinks."

"She doesn't really work with crowds, so I think it would…" I start to say but Jacob cuts me off.

"No fucking excuses young Lady!"

"Then we'll go to my place and get drinks there. A nice little talk-hangout is always good, right?" Ethan says getting up. It would not help me to say something. Hopefully, Abby doesn't want to go, for both our sakes.

After about six hours I finally got to go home and I'll tell you, I've never been more excited to go to sleep than now. We recorded some vocals and instruments along with a whole song we had written, but of course Mister Perfect wasn't happy enough. He has a very strange way of writing songs though… much to tell *you* when the time's right. Right now, I am back at home and in my bed, I just want to fall into a long sleep and stay there. A world, where everything is right, but we're half the world away...

Maybe at another place or a different time everything would've been the way we wanted it to be. I guess we never get what we want or deserve.

Chapter Nine

It's fucking morning and I didn't even have a single cup of coffee. Abby decided to take the earliest possible flight so that we could spend the whole day doing something. She knows nothing about the others having made plans for us. Anyway, I've been standing at the airport for twenty minutes and it's only eight in the morning. If this keeps going on I swear I won't make it 'till the end of this month. At least I'm not the only person who seems to be freaking tired here. They all look like zombies.

After another ten minutes and the hundreds of texts I have sent her, saying she should get her ass here, I finally spot her dark black curly hair in the crowd. Of course, I'm not the only one who has spotted her, since I can barely see her through the flashlights from the photographers. The second she spots me, her face lights up in a huge smile and she starts to walk faster in my direction until she is finally close enough to give me a huge hug.

"Oh God Liv I've missed you so, so much!"

"I missed you too Abby, though you could have hurried a bit more, my feet killing me right now. Maybe we should get away from these people and go to my place first." I say into her hair taking a deep breath of her perfume. She still smells the same and sometimes I just want to drown myself in a bottle of her perfume. She really is my comfortable space. She nods as we make our way to one of the taxis, since I do not have a car here. I'm actually really glad about it. The traffic here is the worst I've ever seen and I'm not really good at staying calm in such situations.

I open my front door and I show her every part that I created on my own and she seems to really like it. "This is exactly what I thought it was going to look like. I just know you too well. She would really have loved it and you, to see you doing this on your own. God, I'm so fucking proud of you. I will start crying right here and now."

I turn to her and see tears welling up in her eyes. I give her a small smile as I try to hold back my own tears. I lead her into the kitchen, to make us both a cup of coffee. "I do not care what people in this country drink because I freaking need something to wake me up. How was your flight?"

"Oh, you know flights and I don't really mix well. It was fucking long and exhausting and I slept most of the time, which means I'm really excited for today. What have you planned for us Miss Guide?" she says as she jumps around the counter to look into my fridge. You won't find anything because I haven't had the time to buy anything. Thanks to Mister Perfect.

"Yeah… well, about that… I kind of haven't planned much because… some people might have planned for us to go to a hangout and yeah… You really don't need to go, they will be totally fine with … you know not coming, considering the long flight and…"

"Jones, you really will not start to make me your excuse again to not go there, will you?" She laughs and I just stand there pouring the coffee into two mugs. Fuck.

"I really don't want to go there. I told them that I wasn't going to come to the studio to record and write because we were going to see… something I guess." I admitted trying to avoid her eyes until she turns me around taking one of the mugs from my hand.

"You're recording in a studio… with people? The people you just met?. Who are you and what have you done with my best friend?"

"You might just have missed some parts while you were gone …
I showed them my song and then they asked me to work with
them and that they will help me to publish something if I want
to. I'm not sure if I want to and then… there's the guy I told
you about and he's literally driving me freaking insane. He's
so difficult and he has these massive mood swings and yeah…
that's about it. Oh, no wait, the other guy, he's called Jacob
and he's really nice and funny, I think you'll like him. But an-
yways, he went insane when he found out you were coming,
and he said we needed to meet." I'm telling her everything
I've kinda missed out to tell… or maybe on purpose, but that's
not important.

"Damn. Your life deserves a reality show, more than mine now.
Something else on that pure heart of yours, that you need to
tell me?"

"Uhm, well see, I spoke to my dad and I basically told him to
back off but no, nothing special here. Normal stuff. Nope, that's
it. You're here for the fashion week, right?"

"No, nothing about my career, today is about you. Nothing
more. When are we going to meet them and where?" she asks
smirking. I'm so beyond done.

"We're going to meet them, are you sure?" Please say no, please
say no.

"Of course, I need to know who you're hanging around with,
when I'm gone." And here comes her devilish smile, I did not
miss that.

"Great. You can bury me at the end of the day." I say and she
shakes her head laughing. "Okay, I got it. You can stop making
fun of me now. We're going to the studio this afternoon and then
we will go with them to someone's place."

She smiles as if she has just won a freaking race while sipping her coffee. I'm in for a super long day.

We went to do some sightseeing… discreetly of course, and she also forced me to get some groceries. We went to this super nice restaurant where they sell the most amazing kinds of salads and all the healthy stuff. Sometimes it drives me crazy that she's such a healthy eating person but sometimes she pushes me to get out of my comfort zone. Once in a while I actually like it, well, not as much as making me move here but those are details now, and I'm quoting Abby here.

So, here we are, getting ready to leave my place and to go to the studio. Jacob texted me that they were going to be finished soon and that they would wait for us. I hope that something will come in between because I really, really do not want to go there at all. Maybe I should take something to calm my nerves. I reach into my closet and grab a plastic bag with joints in them taking one out. I usually don't smoke, I promise but I really need to get rid of my anxiety. Abby gave me these, not my fault, it's hers. I put them into my bag making sure they are covered by all the other things. Abby's already calling me, so I put on my Convers, and I take my flannel jacket in case I get cold. Better be prepared for everything with jackets, useful stuff… and a joint – okay stop it. I know you wouldn't like it but it's my decision. My life. My decision.

We climbed into the taxi that Abby had ordered half an hour before. We drive past the center of town and in the direction of the studio. She seems to realize how on edge I am and tries to calm me down.

Problem is, if I'm too deep inside my head you'll probably won't get me out of there. She knows, I know it and you know it. The only thing that helps me is silence… or a joint maybe…? However, she doesn't know I've packed it and she probably wouldn't like it as well, so just leaving me alone for the rest of the drive is the option. Why did she give me the joints anyway?

We arrive in front of the Abby Roads studio at three p.m. The name is kind of ironic, right? I lead her into the room we had worked in yesterday and the closer we get, the more voices I could hear. I stop in the doorway looking at Abby. She gives me a reassuring nod. I nod to myself opening the door.

The second we stepped into the room all eyes were on us, or more likely on Abby. She smiles at everyone and gives them a kind, "hello."

Jacob's seems like a little child who had too many sweets, as he is actually flipping out because he finally got to meet her. I sometimes forget how well-known she actually is and I'm really glad I have known her for so long. We just kids who lived their lives not caring about anything else.

"We were afraid you weren't going to show up here," Emma says standing next to Ben. He puts his arm around her waist and places a soft kiss on top of her red hair. They're cute.

"Well, Liv here has tried to convince me not to come but I'm very stubborn." She smiles looking at me. I'm stretch my arms in front of me frowning.

"You're supposed to be on my side as well Abby." They all laugh, and with all, I mean all. Even Ethan. "How was today's session by the way?" I ask to change the subject.

"We definitely missed your good ideas and Ethan was very... difficult today." Mary pipes up from across the room where she is sitting on the piano bench.

The next thing is Ethan explains to them why he is as he is today. Abby seemed to enjoy watching all of it, but I just want get going. This whole kid thing is going on for a bit until Ethan tells everyone to shut up and that we should be going to his place now. I agree with him there. Wow, first time I ever did. We all piled into two different cars, one is Ben's and the other is Ethan's. Jacob decides that he has had enough of Ethan's 'shitty attitude' and he's gets into Ben's car. Since Ben and Emma are a thing, she goes with them and all three of them want to have Abby as well. So, I end up in Ethan's car with Mary. Luckily, she gets into the front seat when she realizes I'm not too happy with all of it. I really need to remember to thank her for that. And here we are now, all three of us sitting in the car with an awkward silence with I don't even know how many minutes left to drive. Would it be all right if I just quickly pulled out my joint and—no? That's not good? Okay, I'm damned.

"How long is it 'till we're there?" I ask and they both look at me confused. Can't I just ask a simple question?

"Why? You don't want to be in a car with me alone again? Don't worry sweetheart, Mary's right here." He says smirking to himself while Mary opens her mouth frowning in my direction.

"Olivia whatever your last name is, you definitely will have to sit down with me and talk after today." Mary says making it clear.

I pull my knees closer and I cover my face with my sweating hands because this is freaking embarrassing. She keeps on staring at me while Ethan just laughs.

"It's Jones. Olivia Jones and I'd really appreciate it if you just kept driving and stop that ugly laugh. You have already told her lies her and I swear if you keep on doing that, I will commit a murder. I am deathly serious Ethan." Mary starts to laugh now while Ethan tries to hold back a laugh staring at the streets in front of us. Abby, please come here or I will start to smoke in this damn car right now.

Chapter Ten

We arrive ten minutes later, and I have never been more relieved about anything. When we arrived, the others seemed to have already got there and are waiting in front of the black door. His apartment is also made of bricks and mostly decorated in a black and a modern style. I suppose that's another English thing I don't get. Well, not yet. We go into a living room area with sofas and a bar. It's really nice and comfy if you asked me. We all down on the two different black couches and Ethan goes straight to the bar to make us some drinks. I have literally no idea what he's mixing but it tastes sweet, sour and still amazing at the same time. Nevertheless, it's fucking strong.

"So, Abby, has Olivia ever showed you her music?" Emma asks into the round and the chatter stops. Abby looks straight at me smiling before she answers.

"A few times she has, though I could count them on one hand. She thinks that they're not good enough but everyone I heard went directly under my skin and into my heart if you know what I mean."

"Go on, explain it." Jacob encourages her.

"They're… they're all so different but vulnerable at the same way. I'm able to feel and hear the pain of emotions that leads to it. No matter how you're feeling, I'm sure that there is at least one song she wrote that will take you there. Her words are incredible, and they mean than one thing that she understands and cares about when no one else does. I can really see her doing something in this direction. She has never stopped talking about how much making and listening to music meant to her. I am always sad when the song ends." I really want to cry now, she's never been so honest about me and my songs in my presence.

"Every song ends, is that a reason not to enjoy the music?" I don't know why I said that, it just came to my mind. I should just shut up.

"You're incredibly wise and you know it Liv. I've known you for so many years and you never seemed so free to me, what changed?" No, no, no, no. No. Do not go down this road again.

"Does it have anything to do with why you were watching this senseless movie and were crying?" Another voice comes from my right. Thanks Ethan, really. I think I will kill you now in all honesty. Abby's opens her mouth and stares at me.

"Tell me you did not watch it again. What happened? Tell me now. The last time you watched it was when your dad did – wait a goddamn second. Have you spoken to him?" She knows exactly which one, because I barely watch any, and when I do and then exactly this one... there might be a good reason. It was her favorite movie and it just stuck when she... when she left.

I'm fucked. I'm officially fucked now. I was about to take a sip of my drink, but I stop looking at her. "I might have. I also might have told him not to call me again. Please Abby, just stop embarrassing me now, it's not a big deal."

"Not a big deal? It is as if you have finally started to release your music, Liv, this is amazing. He deserved it after all he did."

"Abby. I'm serious. Cut it now, I don't want them to know." I ask looking around to see them all staring at me in confusion again. She says nothing realizing that she's just kind of planted the bomb about how fucked up I really am. "Excuse me, I need to get some fresh air for a second." I run my fingers through my brown hair and taking my bag I make my way to the door. I sit on the few steps that lead to the door and I open my bag. I do not care what they'll say, I'll smoke this goddamn thing right now. I light it up and bring it to my mouth. The rough feeling in my throat reminds me of the last time I did this. Since then, nothing has changed because it still calms me more than anything. I let the smoke out taking a deep breath before I close my eyes and continue to smoke. This is good, I needed this.

"I've been looking for you. I Thought you had already left." I can hear someone speaking from behind me. I let out a small scream, flinching I turn around to see Ethan grinning before sitting next to me. I take my free hand to cover my heart, which had nearly stopped.

"Holy fucking shit Ethan. You've just scared the shit out of me. I nearly had a heart attack. What are you doing here?"

"I told I was searching for you. The more interesting question is what you are doing with this?" And he points to the joint between my fingers. "You probably shouldn't do that. You could get cancer and stuff." Did he just actually say that?

"I don't normally smoke, and it's supposed to be a metaphor but you're killing the vibes."

"A metaphor? Explain that to me?" He says running his fingers through his messy curls.

"Have you ever watched 'The fault in our stars'?" I wait until he shakes his head. Of course he hasn't, as if he had a sense for something like that. No front, but still a huge front though. "So, this boy had cancer and is about to bring a cigarette to his mouth while this other girl is going crazy and asking him why he would pay a company to give him cancer again even though he already had it. He then says that he puts the thing that can kill him between his teeth but he doesn't give it the power to actually kill him because he never lights them. A Metaphor. My metaphor on the other hand is, that I'm putting the thing that can kill me between my teeth, giving it the power to kill or hurt me and then don't die. A metaphor." I bring my hand up to make a funny but still an annoying gesture and I take another drag from the thing between my fingers.It reminds me of the videos I used to watch from a girl on the internet.

"That's about the most stupid thing I've ever heard and it's somehow still wise. Abby was right." I glance at him with a deathly stare and he laughs. "What is your problem? It's not like she told us your secret."

"No, but she mentioned something I would never want anyone to know besides her. And she knows that, but she just can't stop sometimes. Why does anyone want to rip information out of me anyway?" I look at him and see him becoming serious.

"Because spreading you open is the only way of knowing you. I didn't think, you were that interesting when I met you."

"Interesting?" I repeat, raising my eyebrows and laughing before I take another drag from my joint.

"If you had to decide which colour you were, what would you say?" He looks at me with interest and curiosity as he fiddles with his hair again. A colour?

"What kind of question is that? I don't know, I've never thought about it."

"Just answer what feels right to you. You won't be able to prepare every answer to every question people will ask you." He seems to be so… soft as if he actually cared.

"See, that was my plan, so I'm really sorry but I haven't…" I try to find an excuse but I get cut off immediately. Why can't he just let me finish a freaking sentence, it's not like I'm about to say something forbidden, right?

"Olivia, seriously just answer. There's no right or wrong."

"Okay, so… I think I'd be a green, but more like a forest green not that bright one. A pastel one from the forest. And before you're asking why, it's not too obvious, not too eye catching, I'm nothing of that sort. It's also the colour of my converses and… well something else." I reply directly into his brown eyes and saying nothing. Empty stares, here it comes again. I don't want to tell him what I referred to as the last reason. It's too personal and not even Abby knows it.

But as he listens to my words he looks confused. "You're wrong." Is all he murmurs in a calm but serious voice.

"I'm wrong?" I question frowning. "How could I be wrong about my own colour?"

"Because that's not you. It's what you think you are, but it's not who you truly are. I can see that now."

"And what are you seeing then?" Is all I can think about to say. How broken I am? Thanks, but I already know that. No need to tell me again.

"I can see you. You walk through this world as if you were the only person here even though you will not believe me. You're more than hidden or not eye catching, I caught your eyes the first time we met. I see so much more behind those pretty green eyes of yours, than you're willing to admit or to know. I'll just have to figure you out more and then, I'll let you know. I can promise you that."

What am I supposed to say now? Stay away from me for your own sake or please help me to figure it all out?

A part of me worries some days, that I'm weak. That I'm fragile and not strong enough to stay here. Sometimes I wish I could be more like Abby or you...

I'm trying so hard to find out where I fit in, where I belong. My own space, my own bubble with my apartment, guitar and piano. And a tiny part, but still one, is trying so goddamn hard every single day to get out of this prison. I'm scared as hell that this part will be outnumbered once. Sometimes I just want to stop time and just take a deep breath. But this all keeps going on.

I just want it to stop so badly... and I just want to breathe. Is that too much to ask after all I've done?

The truth is? I don't know, I really don't know. I am confused. I'm not numb but I often feel nothing. I'm not bad but I know I've never had a phase where I felt so low in general. I don't want to die but I sometimes don't want to live. I'm not happy but I smile a lot. I'm not angry but I get pissed quite easily. I am not okay but I am. I'm just kind of there.

Chapter Eleven

I'm broken, I tell you I'm fine. But you wouldn't believe me if you knew the things that crossed my mind.

I'm hurt, but I show no sign because I'm afraid to give in, break down and waste your time.

Now I'm waiting for you to come and pull me out of the fire. Come and save me like you did when we were young.

Oh please, come and bring me out from my lowest, take me higher. Can you see me through the ashes and the smoke?

I'm lonely. I tell you I'm all right but you wouldn't even realize how I felt in the darkest of times.

I'm trying, and trying and trying but I'm just so tired, I'm terrified to step into the light, I want to stay in the dark and cold.

Oh please, put some light in this hole, show me the end. I can't see clearly to the bottom where it crumbles.

I want to let you in but I still feel anxious in my skin. We've been living on a fine line and for a while, this was all mine. Take me back, take me half the world away.

★★★

"Oh, for God's sake!" I yell throwing my notebook onto the ground. I can't even write a fucking song these days and not feel as if... as if I'm about to freaking drown in this. I always thought that expressing the things I felt through songs, even though I didn't really understand them, was very helpful but something seems to... have changed. I don't know what to write next and it's literally driving me insane. Ever since the night I spoke to Ethan.

After we had sat a bit and talked about the world in general, we went back inside for another few hours. It was a bit weird afterwards because they seemed surprised that Ethan actually brought me back a lot happier. How are we calling this? I'm surprised as well. Abby was quieter with more information because she seemed to have realized that she had kind of overstepped.

It's been two days since that, and Abby and I spent the last day together. Well, we mostly sat on my couch, watched some films of her choice and ate way too much ice cream. But hey, everyone has these days once in a while. I guess I just needed a bit of time to process everything that had happened lately. My dad, Abby arriving here, all the new people, the whole music thing that I am new to and well, there's Ethan too.

I know I've never been a ray of sunshine and I don't think I can pretend to be, but I tried to be as good as I can for everyone around me and especially my mom. Do you know the feeling when the container, where you seemed to have everything bad in it explodes inside you and your chest feels as if all the splitters rips open your heart? Like you're screaming in a room full of people and no one seems to recognize it or to even bother to help? Then, welcome to the club.

Today's plan was not made by me, what a coincidence. Abby had to do some work and a casting for the upcoming fashion week and the others wanted to have another studio meeting. So, here I am, about an hour too early. I want to try and do something with a few songs and lyrics that I had in mind for some time now. Just trying some things and getting into this whole stuff. Maybe I'll try to record some of it, so that I can get a clearer version.

Seeing as this new project will not work today, I go through my list of songs and pick one out to record. Light Stick. This one always seems to kind of get back, like a person who comes and goes in and out of your life. You just know that you will meet them again and don't have to bother. I stand in front of the microphone trying to organize myself. I put the headphones onto my ears. I take a deep breath giving a thumbs up to show the guy who helps here with the technical stuff, that I am ready so that he'll start to play my track recording my voice.

The calming piano chords start to play while it builds up into a melody. Here it comes, this is my part, you can do this Olivia. I literally sang this all the time after I had finished writing. I can do this.

My voice is raspy in the beginning but slowly it turns into a mix of belting and keeping the normal tones and textures that come with this song. I can hear exactly every tone that I'm singing through the black headphones and it sounds fine. It's fine, you're doing okay. After another few different parts and lyrics the background music is quietly starting to fade, and I keep my eyes shut to just realize all of this. Every time I hear the lyrics it feels as if for the first time, I go through them, the emotions that inspired this song. Light Sticks need to break first before they can glow Olivia. The sentence she said always stuck in my head and I don't think I want it to leave. Maybe I'll keep her just a little longer.

It's like art. You don't always look at the things that you have created but if you do once in a while, you remember every little piece of colour you put on with your brush and the emotions you feel within it. I'd like to hang this song on my wall, so I can look at it for a little longer.

I put the headphones back on the top of the microphones just to hear clapping. My head shoots up and through my blurred vision I can see people looking at me through the window where the other guy stands. I open my mouth in shock covering my face with my hands.

"Don't get all shy on us now Liv." Mary says as she steps into the recording room. Her yellowish light tanned skin is even more brown now. I've loved her African hair since day one, when I met her and the way she styles it makes it even better. Behind her, everyone else is coming in and sitting around the room.

"You have just heard the whole thing, haven't you?" I ask looking at them in embarrassment. As they nod, I say. "Oh shit. Whoever is up there you need to help me, ugh!"

"Oh no, don't go down that road now. You need to develop some self-confidence my dear; this was bloody amazing." Ben takes the lead making me smile. He's nice, he has been the whole time. He seems to be rather a shy kind of person but with a good soul.

"I think we should work with it today. I can't hear another try from all of us on one of my songs, they're just kind of getting on my bloody nerves. We all need a break and something... different. Also, Jacob promised to help you with your own songs and if we do it together, we can get out of here faster." Ethan murmurs just loud enough for all of us to hear it.

"You guys... would do this?" No need to tell me, my questioning stuff is pretty annoying sometimes but that's just how I am.

"We would. Now get back and we'll record some harmonies if that's what you'd like of course. Ben and Emma, you two can add some bass of course and Jacob, you'll need to be careful that you do not add too much drumming stuff in order to still hear the focus on the piano, which Olivia will need to record again; again if that's okay for everyone." As everyone nods and looks around, he gives an approving nod back and says, "Then let's go, we got some work to do guys."

We did all the things Ethan suggested and even added a little more detail. My voice seemed to be on the edge of breaking because we had to record so many different versions of everything and change a line or two from what I wasn't totally happy with before. Now I am. Today's been a good day. Good, but fucking exhausting.

At around five I left the studio and took an uber home. I need to mention that several people asked me if they could drive me home but honestly, my barrel with socializing is way too filled for today. I want to be alone and cook myself a meal and take a bath but most importantly, just sleep. My sleep schedule has been turned upside down and I was being dragged through the mud ever since I arrived here. Before I left, to go back home, I had a routine that I kind of stick to. Guess with that nothing can possibly go wrong. Every time we moved, which was quite a lot, it took me about a week or two to get used to the time zone and then it just stayed in my routine until we moved again. I must say, I hated moving. Yes, the prospect of getting to know the world would have been great, but I never got to do that because my dad always wanted to somehow keep me hidden because of the thing that had happened to my mother. I was originally born in Australia but during the ensuing years I lived in Canada, France, Australia and Norway. Makes no sense, I know that. I didn't have much to say back then. My dad already flipped the fuck out when I told him that I was coming here but since I was an adult, he couldn't stop me either. But I don't need to tell you that, do I? I climb out of the uber, paying the driver. Taking my keys out to open my door I grab all my mail. I close the door behind me placing the mail on the counter before getting rid of all the unnecessary clothes I'm wearing. In the end, I decide to have a shower instead of a bath because then I'll have more time to sleep. Smart move, I know. I look through the envelopes while my hair dries in the towel, I wrapped it in. Next to some bills that I will need to pay tomorrow and some advertising, I find a blank envelope.

Picking it up I turn it around to see who it is from. Nothing, just a blank envelope. I open it and I start to feel as if I'm getting another panic and anxiety attack at the same time.

'We know who you are,' it said.

Chapter Twelve

I don't remember a lot about what happened. It's all a blur in my head, mixed with the sense of terror, anxiety and me nearly shitting my pants. I let myself sink against the counter until I am sitting on the ground, my face covered in my hands with tears of anger and fear streaming down my face. They've probably been waiting for the right moment when I lost control.

This can't be real. It cannot be true because it's supposed to be over. I have absolutely no fucking idea what kind of problem *they* have with me. I did absolutely nothing. I need to call my dad and talk to him about this, he finally fucking needs to tell me, what's going on. Not even Abby knows about this. She thinks that my dad made us move all these times because it never really worked the way he wanted it to. That's probably another reason, but not the main one. Over all these years Abby and I have always kept in touch and we met as often as we could. I suppose you can't tell your best friend face-to-face that someone is after you. They would ask you why, and I wouldn't be lying, saying that I absolutely have no fucking clue.

I didn't know what to do. I'm not able to be alone, and I don't want to be alone. I can't call Abby because she isn't close anyway and she would torture me until she got the answers that I cannot give her. So, who can I call? Yes, you're absolutely right about this one. Though, he's the last person I want to see me in this... way. I pick up my phone, my hands are shaking trying to touch the right buttons. The second I dialled, the phone starts to ring. Please pick it up. I for sure can't do this alone.

"Olivia, I didn't think you'd miss me so fast. What's going on?" At least he seems to find it amusing that I'm calling him. Well, he won't scream at me this time.

"E-Ethan?" I try to say a normal word, but my voice starts to break again. The water works are coming again. I absolutely did not miss it.

"Hey, are you crying? What's wrong? What's happened? Are you all right?" he asks with a lot of concern and a rush in his voice.

"I-I don't k-know. There's b-been a-a...," I can't get further because he doesn't let me finish that mess of a sentence. Just one sentence, is that too much to ask?

"Listen to me, just stay where you are, I'll be there in five minutes."

"N-no. Do not come here, I-I don't k-know why I-I called you. I am sorry." Do I really not want him to come here? I don't have a fucking clue. My brain's been in a freaking tsunami. I can't think right now. I just want it to end.

"Do you seriously think that I'll leave you alone? I am getting in the car. Just try to calm down and focus on your breathing. I'll hang up the call so I can reach you as soon as possible. Everything's going to be fine. It'll be okay, all right sweetheart?" How can he still be so calm and caring and an ass at the same time?

I only manage to give him a "mm" before the call is over. I try to stand up on my own. It must definitely look strange, but I can do it. I try to grab a glass to get some water. Just stay fucking calm. As I bring the glass to my lips, I start to think about it again. I shouldn't have come here, and I should have listened to what my dad said. This is so fucked up. I'm so fucked up. The anger's washes over me and I slam the glass onto the floor. I see it breaking into a million pieces like my hope for everything to be okay just did.

The second I'm doing this I realize what I have just done. I get onto the floor and I try to clean up the mess. This is not who I am. This is not what was supposed to happen. I should have had a fucking normal life with normal parents and a normal job and normal friends and not this shit.

While I try to find and collect all the pieces, I hear the doorbell ring. Since I was so lost in my thoughts and still terrified, I flinch cutting myself on one of the glass splinters. "For fuck's sake!" I shout at myself as I see the blood dripping down my hand and onto the kitchen floor. I grab a tissue from the counter and put it on the floor, so that the blood does not drip all over the rest of the floor. While I'm doing that, my tears are still running down my face and Ethan's ringing the doorbell again. I walk towards the door and look through the peephole to make sure that it's really him. I'm really getting pathetic. At least I have a good reason to.

I open the door and I see him standing there. Hair messy as always but with a fucking worried face which does not fade away when he sees my tears and the tissue which isn't really white anymore. "What the fuck happened Olivia?" he blurts out very directly. Why is he pissed now? The regret of calling him takes over the rest of my emotions and I start to cry even more now. He steps into the hallway, closing the door and... hugging me? "You're okay, I'm here now. Nothing will happen."

After a few more minutes in silence, I slowly start to calm down breathing normally. More or less normally. He doesn't stop hugging me though and I must admit it really helps. I am the one to break away from him. I turn around, so that he faces my back. You're all right this is... normal. My hands are moving up to wipe away the rest of my tears until I touch the open wound and let out a small noise. He seems to hear it and he steps in front of me.

"Where is your bathroom?" he asks me, as I look into his brown eyes. I like the fact that he doesn't ask me questions right now, knowing I can't answer any of them right now. They're looking so... lost?

"Third door in the hallway." As I speak the words, he takes my other hand and pulls me with him. When we reach the bathroom, he makes me sit down on the toilet. He opens a few cabinets until he finds a first aid kit. He opens it and takes away the tissue and looks at the cut.

"How did you do this?" he asks, staring into my face.

"A glass fell, and I wanted to collect the splitters and then… you can think of the rest, I guess."

He stays quiet cleaning my wound and putting a light bandage around my hand. After he has cleaned-up the mess he makes me stand up to go back into the kitchen. He follows me but stops when he sees the letter, I have just had a breakdown about. "What's this?" he asks, frowning, glancing at me and holding it in the air.

Shit, I should've thrown it away along with what was left over from the glass. "It's nothing." I try to sound more… assertive and I want to take it away from him but he doesn't hesitate to hold it higher, so I can't grab it.

"I will ask you again Olivia Jones. What the fuck is this?" He seems pissed and freaking serious.

"Do not fucking call me Olivia!" I shoot back and again I try to grab the letter from him. As I said, try… He takes hold of my wrists and keeps me from moving away. "Let go of me!"

"I need you to calm down and tell me what's going on. Is this why you're acting so weird about your past?" he wonders again. Mood swings. I knew it but I'll mention it again for you.

I shake my head looking down to my feet. "It does not matter. Nothing has happened. I'm okay."

"Yeah, you mean nothing as some psychos are stalking you, you having a breakdown and you call *me* and you cut yourself with whatever that was." He takes a pause to breath normally again. "Who is doing this?" he asks putting his huge hands around my jaw to make me look at him again. Why does he even care? No one cares about me in that way, that's why no one knows.

"I don't know." I reply letting out a huge sigh.

"What do you mean, you don't know? This isn't making any sense Olivia."

"I said, I don't fucking know Ethan. Do you want me to spell it out, or what? It has something to do with my family and that is the very reason I told my father to back the fuck out of my life. I'm so sick of it but now I'm their object to harass over God knows what." I had to let this out one way or another.

"I am sorry but I really don't understand," he admits.

"Yeah, welcome to the club then," I reply

"And you've been keeping all of this to yourself? Does Abby know?" he asks.

I shake my head and he pulls me into his chest for another hug. "I should've just listened to my dad I should never have come here; I shouldn't have left where I was safe. I shouldn't have called you or told you and I shouldn't be this fucking way. I'm so stupid and this is all my fault."

"Woah, woah, woah. Stop blaming yourself. You're allowed to care about yourself first, then about others. Start being selfish Olivia." We stand there for a while in silence. Though, it's not the awkward kind you would want to ignore. It's a comfortable silence.

After a while he's the first one to break it. "C'mon, we'll get you some rest now and tomorrow, you and I will have a talk." I look at him rolling my eyes in annoyance. "Hey! Watch it!" He threatens, pointing a finger at me laughing. A small smile's comes to my face before we walk towards my bedroom. I sit down on the edge of the bed, taking off my slippers before crawling under the sheets. He stops in front of the bed staring at the wall behind me, which is covered with the pictures I took.

"Did you take all of them yourself? They're very pretty."

"Don't tell me you're getting sentimental over some photographs Ethan." I joke turning to look at them and then back at him. He chuckles before sitting on the edge of the bed, where I am.

"You really should get some sleep. It was a long day. I'm going to leave you, but I'll pick you up in the morning." I don't answer and he turns around to stand up and leave. No, no, no. I can't have these nightmares again and I can't be lone I just…

"Ethan?" I whisper with a silent and exhausted voice.

He stops and turns back to me. "Yes?"

"Please don't leave." I mean, I can't be alone after today and I'm trying to explain myself but he interrupts me. It's kind of his thing.

"I won't. I'll stay if you want me to."

"Thank you. For all of this." I admit looking over at him.

"You don't need to thank me. Is there a place where I can stay the night? I highly doubt that you want me in the same bed as you." Well, he's not wrong. I liked him when I bumped into him, then I hated him and now. Now… Not sure yet.

"The next room on the right."

"Thanks. Good night then, oh and Olivia," he says.

"Yeah?"

"*It's not your fault sweetheart.*"

Chapter Thirteen

To begin with, I survived the night, had no nightmares and slept right through, which hadn't happened for quite some time now. Maybe my brain had had enough terror for one day. I woke up to the sun shining aggressively bright into my eyes because I hadn't thought of closing the blinds the night before. How could I?

However, it was a lovely morning and I got out of bed and had a shower. I had to be careful and redo my bandage because of what happened the day before. I get dressed into a pair of baggy jeans, a shirt and a flannel shirt on top. You can't go wrong with a flannel, never. I combine my green Converses with them and head out of my room, wet hair still hanging loose. I walk into the kitchen to see no one. Has he left or is he asleep? I open a cupboard above the sink taking a coffee mug out of it, brewing myself some coffee. Next to my coffee machine is a little paper with a note. *'Had to leave earlier. I'll meet you at the studio at twelve a.m.'* So, he left and I'm actually not too mad about it. He won't do an interrogation with me. Also, we avoided an awkward conversation that would have happened for sure.

I just don't get it. First, he's so cold, being an ass and closed up and the next second he's caring and wants to actually help me...? I still can't wrap my head around all of this, and I'm not even including what the people who sent me the letter did. The minutes go by with me cleaning my place and doing some paperwork. That's also a thing. Not one person likes to do it and we try to ignore it for as long as possible until we all still have to sit down and do it. It's like dealing with problems. You try to push them away and tell yourself there's nothing wrong until it gets so obvious that you cannot ignore it anymore.

We're going to continue working on my song. My song... that's sounding absolutely crazy. The plan was to figure out some parts of the lyrics to the song. *Lyrics, that say what I can't.* The thing with creating something in general (doesn't matter whether it's a book or a song or anything else), is that you need to find something that you would love to hear or read, but that has never been made. Then you need to stick to that and follow along with it. The biggest uncertainty is that you do not know whether you love or hate it, because it's not done. You don't know in which direction it's going to go because you're open and free. And that's the most amazing place to start working on something. I love working on anything like that. No one can tell you what you're supposed to do or when it's supposed to be done in this or that way. An absolutely great feeling.

Anyway, Abby said she'd come by to come and say hello before we grab some dinner together in the evening. In total the plan was all clear for today, but in all honesty, do you really think one single thing in my life follows the plan? Because I certainly do not. Not anymore.

After I've cleaned the mess from the past days and weeks, I grab all the stuff that I will need such as my purse, laptop and phone. Just the normal stuff, I suppose, putting all of it in one of my bags which kind of matches to the rest of my outfit, or so I hope. Also, I managed to actually do something with my hair for once, and it actually doesn't look too bad. Along with the rest I'm taking my skateboard and camera with me... you never know. I reflect on the things that I love doing; in all this mess that has happened. When I left home, I promised that I would not do that because these are the things that I can keep to myself, which no one will ever be able to take away from me. Those are also the things that make me the happiest (along with music) in this time. I also promised you not to let down who I really am... and unlike you, I will not break any promise I made.

I arrive at the studio five minutes late which is quite on time, considering all the traffic and how unsure I always am about leaving my place. I push myself against the huge heavy door to open it walking through the hallway to the room we usually rehearse and work in. The closer I get, the louder the voices get, and I find myself smiling about it. After all that has happened I really shouldn't be in the mood to have fun, but waking up to sunshine does really change your point of view. There were times where neither the weather nor anything could change the fact that I didn't feel present. Now I'm alive and I have everything I need. Well, most of it, and that's what counts.

I take a deep breath opening the door into the room to see everyone smiling in my direction. "Hey, guys!" I'm speaking up and finally realize that everyone's staring at me again. I turn my head to look over my shoulders and when I can see absolutely nothing unusual, I frowning and looking back at them. "Is something wrong?" Do I really look that bad? Oh, c'mon the day started so much better, and I've given everything not to look like a sobbing wreck.

Jacob hits Ethan slightly on his arm. He is dressed in brown baggy trousers with vans and a comfy looking cream-white t-shirt. His hair hangs messily in his face as always. The only difference is his face as I realize that he's been staring at me and I still don't know why. "You... uhm look... you look very different today that's all." He admits shifting from one foot to the other.

In a blink of an eye Mary stands up along with Emma. "That's fucking all? Are you freaking blind Ethan?" Emma asks him.

Mary says, "You look absolutely stunning darling! Like a goddess." And I smile the widest smile I have since... I can't even remember. No one normally compliments me... this is new but so, so incredible.

"Thank you, I'm feeling stunning today. Today's just a golden day," I say and turning around and laughing along with them before we start the work we have to do.

After another few hours and discussions, we finally finished recording the whole song. My song. How crazy does that sound to you? "So, when are you going to release it?" Emma asks sitting on Ben's lap. They're actually really cute together. He behaves absolutely amazing towards her and she deserves it. From what I've learnt so far, she's smart and extremely kind. She makes sure that everyone is happy and she never fails to make us laugh and smile. Her red hair matches perfectly with her freckles and ocean blue eyes. She's just the perfect image of happiness. And Ben, Ben makes a lot of nice comments when he's not picking on Ethan. I like him because he cares and he matters to the whole group.

"I never said I will," I reply and smile at her. "No one would listen to it and I don't want to put part of my heart out there, so it gets lost in the ocean of music."

"But you will never know, what could've happened if you don't release it," she says. "We'll talk about it another day. Take your time to think about it darling. Anyway guys, Ben and I will be leaving now as the air in here smells like ten dead rats."

"Perhaps it will get better when you have left." Jacob jokes and Emma just puts her tongue out before packing up and leaving. As they're leaving Abby comes into the room after saying hello to both of them.

All of us welcome her talking about the casting she's just had. She got the job, but I could have told you that before. She's just amazing at doing everything and once she's got something in her head, she will for sure reach that goal with no exceptions. Though it is a good thing she can because otherwise we would give her a hard time. Such things mostly have a positive but sometimes they also have negative effect.

"It's been a nice day with you. We'll get going now. I'll see you... sometime soon I guess." I chuckle. As we are about to leave, I feeling something warm and large holding tightly to my wrist turning me around. I see Ethan in front of me. I fucking knew it. He cannot leave things as they were. I had a nice day, instead of one blighted by mood swing things with far less fear of awkward conversations. I wish I could get him to forget that I had one of my weak episodes last night. He probably won't ever let go of it.

"Where do you think you're going?" he asks me with a smirk on his face. Abby sees the interaction and stands beside me.

"She is going to have a nice meal with her best friend. What do you think you're doing Ethan?" *Oh yes, don't mess with her.*

"She's not going anywhere." Excuse me? Why in God's name are they doing this 'acting-as-if-I'm-not-there' shit again?

"Woah guys chill for a second. Abby, I can handle this you don't need to fight him," I say letting out a quick laugh before trying to get my hand loose from his grip. It doesn't quite work, what a coincidence.

"Maybe I should, then he wouldn't dare to talk to you in that way," she says, fighting back and raising an eyebrow at him.

He quickly looks at me and then back at her. "At least she calls me when she needs help." Fuck. If he's going to tell her, I'll end him before she will end me and at least one person at least will die if we go down that road. Before she starts questioning him and me, I interrupt both of them.

"Fucking stop! Both of you. Now, Ethan, you'd better let go of my hands and tell me what your damn problem is." Normally I would never snap at anyone but he's just... making me feel so different than I have ever felt before. Whether it's good or bad, it just makes me feel different in a new way.

After my statement he lets go of my wrist, and rakes his fingers through his hair before answering me. "You and I need to talk; you know about what."

I sigh. "Can't we just do that tomorrow or something like that? We have plans now for the two of us."

"Then we'll have to make three out of it, I suppose," he replies smiling in a really disgusting way. He seems to always win but this will not happen. I will not let him fuck-up this time of my life up. That has happened enough and it hurt enough. *It hurt because it mattered.* And after all that happened and after everyone who broke my heart, there isn't enough left for him to break.

"You'll be the cause of my death. I swear my nerves are freaking shattered so don't come up with some shit like that again. Do you understand Ethan?" I lean forward so only he can hear it.

He does the same thing with me now and it drives me crazy. His raspy voice and his breath against my neck makes my hairs stand up. "Being bossy, I see. Though I adore that very much Olivia, I don't like being ignored. So, unless that happens again, my mouth will remain closed. But only for you." What?

My body's moves away from him and I look at Abby. God, she's pissed. "Let's go I really need to get out of here and I am very hungry. Please don't be mad at me Abby."

"L, please tell me that he will not bloody come with us!" she asks very directly, crossing her arms in front of her.

God, this is going to be an exhausting evening. Yayyy, Yayyy, or something like that.

Chapter Fourteen

I highly doubt that I have ever felt this uncomfortable in my entire life and I have felt that way very often. You can believe me. Also, I don't think that Abby has ever been this pissed. She's not pissed at me; she never is, but she is beyond angry at Ethan. That's why I am sitting between both of them kind of like a wall blocking their stares.

We got out of Abby Road quite quickly, and Ethan drove us to the restaurant we had planned on going to without him. But as I already said, nothing in my life follows the plan.

"I've heard a lot about this place. They say that the burgers here are absolutely incredible. What do you guys want to eat?" This is so awkward. However, this place is huge and very modern. I like it a lot in fact, but who is asking me? Right, no one.

Absolute silence. I murmur 'great' to myself and look at the menu again. The waitress comes and to ask for our orders. I politely ask for what I'd like, unlike the other two. They barely look up without glaring at each other. I hate this so, so much and I have never seen Abby… this awkward. She's the kindest person I know but at least I'm not the only one who can get freaking angry about him though.

"I hate to break it to you, but I really need to use the bathroom. So, if you could do me a favour, please don't kill each other while I am gone," I'm telling them and leave immediately. As I walk towards the restroom, I feel my body calming a bit. I hadn't realized how … tense this was for all of us, I suppose.

I'm open one of the doors and sit down. While sitting there, I check the few messages I received. Nothing fancy. What a wonder since I have like no friends at all and my family... yeah, that's something different again.

About five minutes later, I finally get up and walk towards the basin. I wash my hands taking a deep breath before exiting down the hallway. I take my phone out of my pocket to look at the time. It's only six and this is going to be so... and I hit something hard in front of me.

"Jesus Christ, what the fuck! Ethan you are going to give me a heart attack." I yell bringing my hands up to my chest.

"You never look where you are going do you sweetheart?" he asks me calmly but with a smile I can't identify yet.

"Let's quit this and go back, I don't want to leave my best friend alone. You were supposed to stay with her."

"Yeah, about that... she kind of left," he admits running his hands through his hair while I continue to stare up at him. I never really thought about the height difference, but he is freaking tall. Maybe I'm just small but those are details; small and unimportant details.

Now I'm confused. She wouldn't just leave; she never would do such a thing. "What do you mean she 'kind of left'? She wouldn't just go."

"I can be very convincing if I want to," he's assures me. I am going to murder him.

"What are you saying?" I ask very directly and angrily, wanting to hear it all over again.

"I asked her to leave in a more or less friendly way. I also made it clear that I can take very good care of you even if she doesn't send me those killing-glances." He takes his sunglasses out of his pocket before continuing. "Now, let's go. I've asked them to pack your food and I've already paid. You and I need to talk."

What? This is not how it's supposed to be. "Well, I don't want to talk to you, and I wouldn't know about what." Lie!

"Has no one ever told you that you're absolutely shit at lying? Anyway, I wasn't asking Olivia."

He basically pulled me out of there and put me into his black car. The drive was silent because he knew that I was really pissed. As always, I can't just stay silent. "Where are we going?"

"Somewhere," he replies without even looking at me and I sigh.

We drove for about an hour without talking until he finally stopped the car at the end of the world. So here we are, with him outside the car waiting for me. I shake my head in annoyance before opening the door to get out. I still don't get it.

My eyes open wide when I see the view. We're on top of the coast. The sky is tainted in many colours and even the ocean, we can clearly see, seems to dance with the sun. It's utterly and completely beautiful.

"I knew you'd like it," he says next to me with an ugly smile on his face.

I move a little closer punching him just a bit the arm. "Calm down Romeo."

"Though, I didn't pick you as a romantic kind of person.", He places his statement while getting some things out of his trunk including a blanket.

"I write songs. I have to be a romantic person. Although I am not the one who carries blankets and picnic stuff with me." Got you there, huh?

"Touché. But I'm not like that for everyone." Woah. I don't realize how direct he can be until he comes up with something like that. He lays the blanket on the grass and puts our food and a bottle of water on top of it.

I stare at the view while he sits down staring at me. This view has something of calmness and it is comforting me more than everything I know. And the ocean, I'm looking at the ocean in jealousy because of how free it seems to be boundless The ocean never changes for anyone, its independence is something I desire. It needs nothing but itself and it seems to be okay with that. Sometimes I want to be like the ocean, I want to be in the ocean. Forever. Maybe the voices around me will be silent then. The soft grass is even more welcoming and all of this, the masterpiece which is made of so many tiny details makes it feel like… *home.* I always believed home would be with people that you love and in one place, one place only. But now I know better. Moving here on my own showed me that home can be a feeling, a person or a place. It's whatever makes you happiest in this world. I wish people would understand that, and would understand me better.

I look at him sitting down next to him on top of the red blanket. "Why have you brought me here?"

"I figured it's a better place to have this kind of conversation. I like it better not to connect such feelings with my home. Maybe you don't want to either," he admits. That would depend on where my home is. I had never for once heard him speak so honestly, it's almost intimidating. From the outside Ethan seems like a cold, brutal and self-confident man; someone who does everything for a good reason and someone who will do everything to protect everyone they love. However, the closer I get to know him, the clearer it becomes. He's trying to protect his real and somewhat softer side and he does it so he doesn't appear weak. Like someone else I know.

"It is nice that you're thinking of something like this. Not everyone would, I appreciate it."

"I know I may seem cold on some occasions but I'm not stupid. Perhaps you don't understand but I know that you're hiding something, and I will find out what it is, for your sake," he tells me taking a deep breath before continuing.

He wouldn't understand the small hints that are left over after years of hiding and playing pretend if he hadn't known a feeling like that himself. *We're all broken in some way.*

"It took me some time, but I figured it out. You're kind of carrying it very well. Not everyone would notice."

"Just because I carry it well, doesn't mean it ain't heavy."

"I never wanted to say that. Many people suffer, you know that right?" he asks.

"People have it worse than me."

Besides that, I don't even know what the problem is. That is the whole point of my problem. I'm looking at him and seeing his eyes. You can get lost in them as you can get lost in the ocean. I haven't known him for very long, but one thing that I figured out today is that things feel... they feel so simple with him. He feels like the ocean. You might be scared to go into it in the beginning but once you did, you never want to leave it. At least he feels like that when his caring and nice side comes out of him.

"Just because the person next to you is in a full-body cast, that does not mean that your broken arm doesn't hurt. Feelings are valid and they are there for a reason," he says, taking another deep breath before continuing to speak. "So, what are you hiding?"

"Why do you care?" is the only thing on my mind I can tell him now. It's all so confusing and I can't look past the blurry mess of thoughts in my head.

"Don't get me wrong Olivia. I don't have to care. I choose to." Has he just said that?

"Why? No one cares. People don't care or they wouldn't be so..." I start, but he cuts me off.

"Because you're different than all the other people I have met. You see things differently, you're doing them differently and I know for sure that you think differently. *A mind and soul like that doesn't just pass by.* Maybe someone like me can help you. I know for sure that you're not okay, I can see it in your eyes. Those eyes don't lie, that's why they're green like the grass. You will immediately see if there are parasites on the ground or if it's too dry and I just feel these things. Let me in, so I can save you from yourself and everything else," he confesses.

"Some people are not supposed to be saved," I say, looking at him my eyes tainted by tears. Here we go again.

He looks at his laps doing movements with his fingers before he's gazing at the sunset in the distance. "Someone told me once that God lets all the artists who die paint the sky for one last time. The thing is that I don't believe in such stuff."

I frown watching the colourful sky and then back to him. He looks so honest and vulnerable. '*Honest vulnerability; you can write down what you feel, honest and vulnerable but you hide it behind the music and in the lyrics, so it means something different to everyone else.*

Ethan's not hiding his feelings in his songs. "Why are you telling me this?" I ask.

"Because sometimes people want to make you believe things are not true or that you don't want to believe in the truth," he says.

"Are you sure these things are not true?", I ask him, and stares right at me now. He's appearingHe appears very thoughtful and almost sad.

"I am sure of it. Just as I am sure that we can work this out, *to-gether*; but only, if you will let me, Olivia."

Chapter Fifteen

"Who made you believe that you had to be okay?"

"My family, myself and everyone I knew. I was just raised a bit differently," I confess.

"How were you raised then?" he asks with a lot of interest, while pulling food of a plastic pback.

"My mother... she always told me to treat people the way I wanted to be treated. I suppose that's why I never argued when my family wasn't... nice towards me."

"Being kind also means being kind to yourself. And that means also caring about yourself first. Sometimes saying 'no' is the best way of self-care. I'm sure she taught you that as well, right?"

I look at my lap answering him. "She didn't exactly have the possibility to teach me much."

"Oh,.", and watching the view in front of us.

"Yep." God, this is so awkward.

"Does this have to do something with those people?", He raises his suspicions towards me before taking a bite of his burger.

"Ethan, if I'm telling you this, do you promise to keep this to yourself?"

He looks into my eyes again before continuing. "Whatever you tell me will stay between us. You do not need to be afraid of me. Not you."

"All right, she died when I was about sixteen years old, and I never could say goodbye properly. She wasn't sick, at least that was what my dad told me. One of the only things in fact, that's the reason we barely talk, or more likely why we mostly scream at each other. Anyway, she was an author, a journalist. And God she loved reading and writing as they always gave her comfort. She had the same eyes as I do, but her hair was blonde and shorter than mine.

"The only thing I know was that the morning before she… left, my dad told her not to write or publish something about a person I didn't know. He said that it was dangerous, and he wanted to keep her safe. And, when she never came back, he felt guilty for not stopping her, but she would've done it anyway. She wanted justice no matter what and she always looked at the world in the way it could possibly be. Not the way it seemed to be, or what people said about it. In fact, she was the kindest person I have ever known and… I really don't know what these people could want from me. My plan was to call my dad tomorrow, but I'm scared of his reaction and… of bringing up memories that are buried deep down in me for good reason."

"I'm so sorry Oliv…", he's beginning but now I'm cutting him off while raising a hand.

"Don't be. Please, I neither want, nor need your pity."

"That wasn't my intention at all. I want to make you comfortable," he's clarifying.

"If someone's telling you something about their past, it's not because they want your pity. It's because they want you to understand them better as a person. Most people don't talk about what hurts them, but it's still the thing that made them who they are now. That is the exact reason why I've been told to be kind to everyone. You never know what someone has had to deal with," I admit.

"Well, I met her daughter, so I'm quite close to knowing her. And from what you've told me about her, she's just like you. You don't see the things I see in you, but they are still there."

"Well, Ethan, you can be glad I've talked to you about anything. That's rather rare." He smiles and I'm doing the same. Sometimes he's just easy to be around, when he's not behaving like an ass.

He brings one hand to his chest saying, "I am honoured Miss Jones."

He makes me smile even though the world seems to just want to mess with me. "I don't even know your last name. You're asking so much about me and I don't know one thing about you."

"That is a lie. You know what I do for a living and you know my friends, the only ones I've got. You know my music more than everyone else does just yet," he says. Why can't he just give me simple answers?

"That is not the same, you just don't…"

"It's Murphy. Ethan Murphy."

"Woah, hold on a second. That is an Irish name." I frown as he keeps on smiling to himself.

"It is. You should thank my parents for that."

The next few minutes is just about sitting, talking about nonsense and just accepting the other's presence. We ate all our food, well he ate half of mine as well, and just stared at the sunset which slowly began to fade. Never in my life had I been so comfortable around someone except Abby. His music is an exact copy of his personality. It seems bold and rough at the beginning, but the more you start to listen and understand those fine lines, it's actually very sensitive and calm. The true feelings, true pain, hurt and so much grace within it. He's hiding it. He's hiding that he can actually be a nice and caring person because he seems scared of people's reaction. He's protecting himself and he doesn't want to get hurt. He's not the only one, though.

"I know… I know I seem difficult to everyone. But I don't want to be like that around you because it's not who I am. This is who I am, and no one gets to see it. You make me feel so unusual and honest, and I don't know why, but It drives me absolutely crazy," he admits, speaking from his heart and not just his head.

"Yeah, I kind of have that impact on people." We both laugh and I move closer to him. My head rests on his huge, strong shoulders and he seems very surprised but calm at the same time. "I'll be serious. I didn't like you in the beginning and you can be very… rough towards people but I like the person you are when we are alone. Most of the time, I'm glad you feel this way though." First I liked him, then I hated him, and now? I have no idea what this feeling is called but overall, it's one of the best things I have ever felt in my entire life.

"Thank you."

"For what?" I ask turning around to get a glimpse of his face.

"You don't get to know that yet," he answers, smiling to himself. "I'll try to help you with everything, and I will take care of what I can. You're safe with me, nothing will happen to you as long as I am here, but you need to be honest with me."

"I'll try to. And I still don't know anything about you, but I will try to trust you if you will trust me. I won't try to dig up any information about you and I will not force you to tell me anything. If you don't want me to know something I'll respect that, and if you want to tell me something I'll listen and try my best to understand and help you." I know he's a good person even though he hides it. Most of the time people in general don't want help from all sides. *Because most of the time, the only wish we have is to be understood.*

"You're truly a shining person."

I chuckle as he lays down so that my head can rest on the top of his chest now. "A golden person?" I ask.

"Yes, you are. You shine as bright as the sun and you impact the people around you with your shine. You try to embrace their shining personality so much that you sometimes forget about yourself and care about them first."

"So, that's a bad thing then?"

"No, it's the opposite. But still, it can make you forget the most important thing in your life. Yourself," he says.

"Is that why you're so... so closed towards everyone?"

"I am not closed to everyone. I've opened up to you Olivia. The most I ever have in fact," he answers me and we are both resting as we are; enjoying the situation and the silence, the comfortable silence. As we do so, we gaze at the sky above us and at all our surroundings.

The sun's slowly fading in the horizon and the sky is getting darker and darker with time. As much as I adore the winter, I'm glad that it's summer now, well it's nearly over, but remember the details? It allows us to stay here without ending up as icebergs.

"I want to be a croissant." I spit out, and he chuckles. My head moves with his breaths and laughs, it's actually quite a comfortable feeling. I don't feel alone for once.

He frowns, laughing as he stares down at me. "Did you just say that you want to be a croissant?"

"I might have, who knows," I reply smiling to myself now. It's nice not having to keep your jokes to yourself.

"And why is that so Miss Jones?" he asks.

"They're nice, tasteful and pretty. They are never alone because you can't just eat one and stop. They make everyone addicted but in a cool way, ya know."

"You're something else, but I adore it," he replies laughing to himself. He can actually be cute when he's not being... yeah whatever he's pulling off most of the time.

"Please tell me that we will not be staying here. This is so awkward." God, I never... this is... what was I thinking? Abby hates him, I... do I even hate him anymore? This is so confusing, but I can't do this even though you would've wanted this right now. Sometimes I hate you for all of this. I suppose that's what you wanted, and you've got it. Happy now?

"Why not? The sky is beautiful, and it deserves more attention. Every little star you see is so far away, but we can still see it. It seems so normal for us to see these, but you never know what's happening closer to them. I've got more blankets in case it gets colder and to be honest, I am not in the mood to drive all the way back now. We can go tomorrow. We only need to be in the studio at eleven a.m. We've got enough time sweetheart," he says. Sweetheart, this makes my heart jump and I don't even know why.

"Why do we have to go to the studio again? We're there nearly every day now." I'm tired of being there. It's like it's the only thing I am doing in my life at the moment, and I need to call my dad.

"That is in fact a good point, but I've got some stuff I need to finish, and we need to discuss your song release."

"Woah, woah, woah, wait a diddly darn second. I never said that I was going to do it." I sit up in shock, looking at him with one finger pointing at his face.

"I know you did not, but I did." He sees the expression I give him and says, "Okay, I am sorry. It's just a very good song and it would be very sad if it got lost. You said you didn't want to throw a part of your heart away."

I don't want to give a part of my heart away, and be judged for it. I don't like someone judging me when they don't know what it means.

I feel a hand going softly up and down my back and his calm and comforting voice speaking. "I am not like Abby, no offence but I'm glad about it. I think she hates me. Also, I'm not pushing you to do things you cannot bring yourself to do. I'm just trying to get you to see over the wall you built in front of you to protect yourself. You think you got everything you deserve, that's why you don't search for more." I look up again at his face and he's smiling a bit. "Let's go to sleep love. We have some things to do tomorrow and it's late. Don't worry, I've got you and you're safe with me."

"She doesn't hate you. You're just on her bad side," I reassure him.

"Yeah, not that that would make any difference."

"Believe me, if she hated you, you would definitely feel it in some way." She can be quite tough protecting me; not that there would be any other people who would be like this towards me.

Chapter Sixteen

I hear a voice and I turn around to face someone next to me, Ethan. My legs are twisted with his and his arm's resting under my head. He lays there peacefully, breathing calmly and untroubled. The next thing my eyes catch is the grass we are lying on and our surroundings. We are still there. I take my phone out of my pocket to see that it's already half past nine in the morning. We slept next to each other, the whole night, under the sky, more or less on top of each other. This is so awkward. And holy shit we slept fucking long and I didn't have one single nightmare and I didn't wake up once. What the heck. Normally I avoid sharing a bed, Abby knows that as well, because I'm known to take-up quite a lot of space. Not only in bed but also on the person next to me. Whoopsie...?

The sun is already shining but this morning I don't care because we are going be late, and I don't have anything with me, and he is still asleep. I try to get my legs out of the position they are in. At the same time, I try to sit up and wake him. My hands shake his body gently and my morning voice doesn't really help. Christ, I didn't even brush my teeth. Do I have morning breath?

"Ethan! Christ, can't you just wake up? We are late!" I yell at him and he finally opens his eyes, looking around us, smiling and putting his head down again. "Get the fuck up sleepy head we need to go because you need to drive me home. I need to get changed and this is your fault, so you will have to make it up to me."

"Relax yourself. We're not going to be awfully late, just a little bit," he replies with an extremely raspy voice which actually sounds... interesting.

"We are going to be late, and I still need to go home first," I tell him again, and he finds this even more amusing than before, and he finally sits up.

"You're not going home. We'll head to the studio, just give me a few seconds to wake up. I am not a morning person."

"What do you mean I'm not going home. I need something to wear, I can't keep these on." I say to him pointing at my clothes. What will the others think?

"I've got some shirts in the back of my car; you can wear one of them."

"That will not happen."

"God, you can be a pain in the ass. Just wear one of these, then we can go directly there. Honestly, I don't care what the others say," he says.

"Yeah, well I do."

"You see Olivia, *that* is the problem." He fights back, getting up to pack away all the things. I know that he is right, but it's hard to just change that. I help him as we walk towards the trunk putting everything into it. I stand at the side of his car to breathe in once again and remember this spot; the best spot that I have ever been to. It reminds me of some things.

Ethan comes towards me and hands me a light blue shirt with a cheesy and still obvious smirk. I take it, roll my eyes at him and go behind the car again. I hope he doesn't see me. I pull my old shirt over my head putting his on as fast as I can.

I climb into the passenger seat, not looking at him. "Oh, come on, you're not seriously pissed now?" he asks still laughing a bit. Does no one ever take me seriously?

"I am not pissed at you, I'm pissed at myself."

"Does that mean, you're regretting the last day? It was a nice talk in my opinion. Or maybe it was the night? You seek to cling to the object next to you, I am glad that I wasn't born as a cushion." He provokes me. See, I told you before.

"Watch it!" I yell at him and we both start to laugh. We talked a bit about my photography and his music. What I learned is that he was a new artist and this would be his first whole album with a big tour. I'm glad he told me something and I tried to just listen and understand, as he did for me a few hours ago. It took us a lot longer on the way back because the traffic was horrible. Although, we arrived *only* half an hour too late, he did not feel bad at all, but I did. I hate the feeling when I know someone is waiting for me and I'm just not showing up on time.

I walk quicker than him into the room and see all of them there. Jacob with his man bun, Ben in his hoodies he wears to every occasion (I always wonder why he still hasn't died from overheating at this point), Mary in an exquisitely, long and dark red dress and Emma with her braids as always, still a calm and nice expression on her face.

Ethan comes up behind me and when they see the look on my face and my shirt and the fact that we both arrive at the same time, most of them smirk. I just roll my eyes and apologize for being late. They don't seem to actually listen, but instead Jacob makes the whole session a torture for Ethan with little hints and annoying facial expressions. I won't lie, I find it very amusing.

They actually convinced me to release it and I will most likely. I tell them that I wanted to have a bit of time before I would give them the go ahead sign and that they just should do their producer things with the two men who helped me on my private studio session a few days ago. Maybe a few days will develop into a few weeks and months? Who knows?

"So, how was the food yesterday?" Jacob asks with a huge smile on his lips.

"Cut that shit J."

"What? I was just asking my friend something. Normally the friend would give a normal answer back. Except for when he has something to hide..." He provokes him again. Here are the children coming out again.

"You two behave like freaking kindergarten kids and it's really getting on my bloody nerves." Ben pleads making us all turn our heads to him. He holds his bass in one hand, and a coffee in the other one.

"Maybe you should consider bloody shutting up then. It is not my fault that Jacob can't keep his mouth shut!"

"Woah buddy, calm down. You know, I've been taking some yoga classes and maybe you should swing by. Finding and embracing your soul and inner peace. It could help you, Hakuna Matata and all that stuff," he says and we all chuckle. We sit around currently taking a break from recording and writing.

Ethan turns his body towards Jacob and looks at him with a freaking angry facial expression. He said he was going to try to be... nicer. I mean, these are his friends after all.

"Hakuna Ma ... fuck off Jacob."

Suddenly Jacob bursts out in laughter and all of us are going along with it except for angry face himself. "I forgot how funny you actually could be when you don't have that stick shoved up in your ass."

As Ethan's about to fight back, I clear my throat, which causes him to look at me. I raise my eyebrows to make him understand and he looks at me for a brief moment before breaking eye contact.

"Yeah, whatever," he is murmurs loud enough for most of us to hear. Jacob suddenly stops laughing and he stares at me confused. Don't tell me he has seen a flying cat again.

"Have you just made him shut up? You gotta tell me how you have done this Liv, I am serious. Is there a way of eye reading or manipulation?"

"I haven't done anything. He decides to do whatever he wants to." I try to convince him and the others.

"I'll quote this dumbass. 'Yeah, whatever' you say darling. How's Abby by the way?"

Holy fucking shit. I forgot to fucking call her after what Ethan pulled of, she must be worried and angry, and God knows what. I'm a bad friend.

"Fuck," is all I can manage to say.

"That seems like the call to contact her." Mary says.

And that was the moment it hit me like a fucking rock from above. All this time she waited for me to call her while I was busy doing stuff for me, I never thought about giving something back to her. She made me do this, I have all of this only because of her and I haven't thanked her. I only cared about myself and not about her. She deserves so much better than this, I'm not good enough for her. She stood by my side all the time, it made me believe, that this is usual but it's not.

"I'm a horrible friend I haven't called her or texted her," I say out loud.

Jacob comes closer, putting a hand on my forehead and asks me, "Are you sick? You seem to be hallucinating."

"This is not fucking funny I'm a horrible person… I'm a horrible friend. I should've…" As I start to get it into my head again I am being cut off by Ben. Wait, am I really saying it's Ben? Yup, surprises me enough.

"Let me ask you a few questions. Do you care about her?"

"Well, of course I do."

He's going on. "Would you be upset if someone would hurt her or if she got hurt?" I nod. I would be fucking furious, she's my better half. Truly. "And would you try to protect her Liv?" Another nod. I would do anything for her. Literally anything. "Then you're in fact an incredible friend. Those are the qualities that make a friendship along with being vulnerable towards each other. Don't worry darling, I am not she is just fine," he states. I didn't see that he is actually a wise and caring person. Well, of course he's caring, otherwise Emma wouldn't want to be with him, but I mean in a different way. He cares in a more unrecognizable way. He sees the things that seem to be… normal and common, which we don't even recognize in normal life. In fact, I like him. How could you not? He's the kind of friend every person wants but no one deserves. Kind of like Abby.

"Thanks Ben, I appreciate your advice, but I still need to call her." I plead giving him a soft smile.

"You need to call someone else first. Let's make a deal, I'll call Abby and you will call this person." Ethan speaks from behind me making me turn my head in his direction.

"You? You want to call Abby?"

"Yeah, she will probably scream into my ear and make me deaf but according to all these people I can't make music with hearing. Doesn't matter," he jokes. I roll my eyes and smile.

"You don't have to do this."

"I meant what I said. I've got you. Call me if you need me, I'll be right outside," he states making my heart beat fast—woah. No, what is going on? I promised after what had happened in my past relationship not to do this shit all over again. *Love may fade at some point, but the lies always stay.* I give him a nod and a smile before he leaves the studio room.

"You're so in for it Liv," Mary says with a smirk.

"Yeah, I know. But not now." I leave the room during our little break and enter the hallway. My body walks on its own through the hallway and my head is lost in the terrifying thought in my mind. I don't know if he will tell me anything but the more I think about it, the more I am scared of what he could tell me. I take the phone out of my pocket the second I arrive in another empty room. I type in his number and let the phone ring. Once, twice, three times, until I hear his low and serious but still surprised voice.

"Olivia? I didn't expect to hear from you this soon."

Chapter Seventeen

"What happened to my mother and who are these people?" I ask directly, not being in the mood for his usual games. As I do so, I feel an unusual feeling coming up from my stomach into my whole body. Anger.

"Hello to you too."

"I'm not calling you for fun."

"Yes, I figured once I saw your name popping up on my phone. What happened to you in this time? You sound so angry. I told you this isn't a good idea, but you wouldn't listen to me, would you? What are you even doing there all day?" he questions, and I know from his voice that he is making fun of me.

"I'm making my own music and guess what? I will publish it soon enough." If he wants a fight, he will get it.

"Music? Are you pulling my leg? We both know that this is not enough to make a living. Who even got this dumb idea into your head?"

"I do not fucking care!" I scream into my phone because I am so tired of him talking to me that way. Ethan told me that I needed to be selfish and I fucking will in that case.

"Do not raise your voice at me. I raised you and I cared for you all my life. You made a decision when you went there, and you made the wrong one. It was clear as crystal that you would come crawling back to me," he states, still in a calm tone.

"No. You raised me the way you fucking wanted me to be. Well, I am not that person anymore, and I learned my lesson. Here are people that actually care about what I want. The song will be released because it fucking makes me happy in all of this bullshit." I take a break to collect my thoughts before I say what I always wanted to but never did. "And I just want to fucking do what I want because I do it with all of my heart. Why can't people just accept that?"

"Look, I only want what's best for you and I don't think you are old enough to know that yet,", he tells me.

He did not just say that. "You say I'm too young to know what I want and care about? And still, you think I am old enough to be kept away my whole life? I will not ask again. What happened to my mother? She would've wanted me to know."

"She trusted the fucking wrong people! She wanted to expose very dangerous people that I don't know much about. They went after her because the things she wanted the world to know would've ruined them. People like that see no line to keep what they have," he confesses.

"That did not answer a single question. What did they want from her?" I ask.

"It does not matter Olivia, not anymore."

"Yes, it does. It matters because this has always been a part of my life and apparently always will be. Why wouldn't you tell me? Unless there's something you're hiding." I'm daring him. I'm not one to do such things but after those years I certainly know how to press his buttons. *Paybacks a bitch.*

"She had a journal. It was green, an olive green one. She wrote everything down and she wanted to get more information before publishing it that morning, so she went to find it. You know the rest. I only tried to keep you safe, but if they come for this thing someday I won't be able to stop them because I don't freaking know where it is. She hid it somewhere and she did a great job doing that and many other aspects," he admitted. It's actually a miracle that I got anything out of him even though that does not really help me. Great, not one single step closer.

Let me quickly collect everything I know. Bad people wanting something, which is written in some journal, my mom disappearing that day and then there was- right, nothing more. Wow, I really feel like Sherlock Holmes now.

"Promise me that you won't go after them!" That would be the other way around actually...

"Doesn't she deserve it? To know what happened to her. Don't you want to know because she was your fucking wife? Because I think she does deserve this." I want to know because I loved her, and I lost her. I lost everything I had before I even knew I had everything I wanted. I don't know if he has a mortal heart as well but mine is missing a giant piece because of this shit.

"I do. But once I learned what these people are capable of, I needed to just accept it, and so do you,", he tells me.

"Yeah, whatever. It was *nice* talking to you as always but I gotta go now. Have a good one, bye Dad."

"Whatever you do, just be careful and don't trust anyone Olivia. I know you may hate me as of right now, but I care about you. More than you'll ever know," he says and I'm listening to his voice before ending the call once again. He does not or he wouldn't have done this. He would've told me everything, he would've been there for me as well and not only himself. He would have... I don't fucking know. He wouldn't have just done everything like that. I deserve an answer and I will get it one way or another.

It wasn't on purpose, but I have just realized something. I've felt like a shell of a person and I'm just starting to feel human again. Naturally, I still feel like that sometimes but at least I've realized it. Baby steps, remember?

I did what I had to. Because someone wanted me to do it. I can't remember exactly a moment or a memory where I was genuinely happy because I had achieved something. Yes, of course there were some things that I did, which were more or less special. Just as every kid does, good grades for once or something else, but all these people weren't okay with it. They always wanted more. It was 'yes, that's okay but why didn't you get all the questions right' instead of being proud of what I achieved. And I learned to be okay with it, it was normal and mostly still is. *People expect the things from you, they wish they could achieve on their own.* They want you to be who they will never be able to. They want you to believe things that they made up in their mind. And it is far away from being fair.

I wished so badly, every single day, that I would've had the courage to stand up for myself and tell them that they are so utterly wrong. But how do you stand up for yourself when you don't even know who or what you are? Despite from who and what you want to be. It's always the same, people told me that I couldn't become what I wanted to as a kid because it was just 'a stupid dream'. It doesn't give you enough money, or a 'safe lifestyle' or whatever. What if it had made me happy? Why wouldn't they care about what I wanted first? I just don't get it and I highly doubt that I ever will.

So, from time to time, they actually made me believe the things they put into my head. It began with not feeling happy about the things I used to. No feeling of proudness. No matter how much I got right, it was never enough. No matter how much I exercised, I was never skinny enough. No matter how much I tried, it was never right. Emptiness, sadness and lots of sleepless nights followed. It'd be that girl who said, 'I'm fine.' While walking out of the bathroom with dried tears on her face. I'd be that girl who loved like she had never been broken once before. I'd be that girl who was everyone's therapist but who needed it the most. I'd be that girl with the loudest laugh, but with tears that could fill the ocean. I'd be that girl telling everyone that things will get better but doesn't believe in it herself. I'd be that girl and I hated it so freaking much. That was the thing I despised the most about all of it, that I did not change anything. Honestly, if I think about it, I still don't have a clue about what I could've changed.

And now?

I'm half the world away from finding out.

That's the truth and it hurts, so, so much.

And all of that, all those things that are so fucked up in this world, I would give everything to change them. Everything that I have. But how do you make people listen to begin with, when your opinion has no voice or importance? How can you make people understand when they refuse to listen?

Our world is so fucked up.

Don't get me wrong, I do think that life can be worth living for some of us. The ones who are lucky. *I just refuse to believe that everyone is that lucky.*

After all of this, I came out more broken than I was before. On some occasions, I wished so deeply for it to stop, to just have a moment of silence. Just to stop the world for a small amount of time, to have enough time to breathe. To breathe and live. But as I already made it clear, not everyone is that lucky.

Sometimes I want to go back and tell the girl that it gets better and that I will stop one day. Though, one thing I learned as well is, that you shouldn't lie.

Not long after I collected my thoughts, and mostly myself, I told the guys that I needed to leave because I just... I just couldn't do it today. Doesn't matter what. So, I left the studio without seeing Ethan, because I know for sure that he would've wanted to know all about this conversation. Sometimes it's nice to keep something for myself, just so people in general don't know everything about you. Besides that, I also don't want people to worry about me. I'm doing... I'm just doing. Sometimes that has to be enough. I am not stupid, I know that I'm not perfectly sane or fine but I'm alive. Even though there were times where I certainly wouldn't have minded if a car would've accidentally hit me somehow.

However, I actually made it home somehow. I don't really remember how, but that's okay as long as I ended up here. Sometimes you arrive somewhere, and you don't remember how, right?

I walk towards my fridge, after taking off all my unnecessary clothes, and opening it I take a beer out. C'mon, I know what you would say now but, since you're not here, your opinion for once doesn't count. To be honest, I'm not mad about it this time.

After opening the bottle, I take it together with another things, such as my headphones to the balcony. I have not yet embraced it enough, because it gives an amazing view of a park which is quite close. Maybe I should swing by later. For a walk or something.

I sit down on a few grey cushions which are laid out on wooden pallets. It's giving me aesthetic vibes and I know Abby is a person who must have her place in perfect order and aesthetics. It's kind of psycho but addictive.

I play some songs on my phone while taking a few sips of my beer. I look down at my lap, where the other object is. The colour of the cover is marked in my mind and memories. It comes along everywhere I go. The green is similar to my colour and it reminds me of some woods with different shades of green.

I never thought that this could be the key to so many things. I could never bring myself to open it and I'm not sure yet if I ever will. The solution could be in there, but what if Dad's right and I don't want to know?

And still, the questions won't leave my head. What happened back then?

Chapter Eighteen

So, it's Friday now. Finally. The week has passed so slowly and as I did before it was kind of a me-time. I got into the studio with the guys once more but mostly I just had calls with the producers and the label, which was going to release my song. That's the important point. My first single would be released in less than twenty-four hours. And, as it turned out, people had plans for a party at some private club and I found out about five minutes ago. Gotta love it. Also, I have barely talked to Ethan and I'm glad that he accepted that. I just needed some time to get over everything. Well, mostly.

He told me that he would handle all the things that naturally come when publishing something. In all honesty, I have no fucking clue what that is. I feel relieved that he did this for me, it was the best way of trying to help me. Mostly getting some stress factors off my mind. He also made some advertising for me on his social media, as did the others. I suspect that Abby lied to me, because I told her that I didn't want her to do it. C'mon, she has about as many followers as humans have hair and I am not very fond of that. If I know one thing about her, is that she might have lied to me a few times, and her excuse was always that it's 'for my best' and that I will 'thank her one day'. When it comes to that, I'm about as happy as a Panda baby because I don't have any of these platforms... yet. Ben, Emma and Jacob tried to get me to download the platforms but that will take a lot more than not shutting up for ten minutes. They said it would be about time, since I would become more popular now. I then told them that there are thousands of songs in this world and the chance that this would happen was about as small as if I jumped out of a plane and went ski-diving. Just extremely close to never happening.

Besides that, I don't know what Ethan spoke about with Abby on the phone a few days ago. It couldn't have been that bad, considering that he is still alive and has all his body parts… as far as I know. Although Abby came to my place to talk a bit, but that all was the cover of her telling me that she would be going to France for some jobs. I then told her that my song would be released just a few days later, so she decided to stay until tomorrow to party a bit with us. One thing all of the people around me know, or should know by now, is that I am the opposite of a partying person. That is the particular reason why I'm seated before my closet and I, again, am not having any idea what I should wear. To be honest, there's not really a guide to what I should be wearing to my first party, in which by the way my song will come out. I mean, I could try to Google it? Will it work though? Probably not. Normally Google knows everything. Literally.

While I lay on my floor, staring at the ceiling and listening to Light Stick one last time, I wondered what my mom would say. Would she be proud? Would she have done the same? If we're on this subject, I also began to read a few pages of the book. It took me so long, because every part or new subject she had in there, I had to search the article or thing she published about it on the internet. Besides it took me some time to even open it. Seeing her hand-writing hits just differently, because I know that I will never be able to see her writing again. *But she loved reading so much.*

Believe me if I say that it took me a fucking while. I still have no idea how she did it, but she exposed people in a way, which is not to be made up. She only did it with people, who were doing something illegal or something that makes you want to throw up. I never thought that people could be so… disgusting. However, I'm not near to being done with this. There were men that abused teens, girls or important members of companies that did illegal stuff behind the legal things and trapped their customers into contracts.

My phone buzzes on my bed causing me to finally get up. I have about an hour left, before Ethan picks me up. Considering I have already showered, I have enough time to clean up the mess, that will surely happen, once I force myself to look at the options to wear. Maybe I should've bought something new...? Mary answered my text about what to wear. She just said, 'Wear whatever makes you feel the best. Today's about you, you can be whoever the hell you want to be.' I swear this girl is going to make me sob like a total wreck. But in a good way though. My courage is a bit built up now, but I still do not know what to wear. Should I just Google it...?

I decide to open the white doors to my closet and look around for something to wear. The only thing that would come close to a party outfit would be... shit. I take the outfit out shaking my head. The only thing I have is a skirt with a matching top and it's... it's very not me. It is not as if I would be naked or something, but it definitely shows more skin than I'm used to. The weather is hot so I will definitely not freeze, one point for it and many against it. However, as this is my only option and I still need time to do my hair and makeup as I don't have any options, I will need to wear it. I take the skirt out and look at the material. It's a dark red checkered one with a top that belongs to it. At least when I bought it, I thought I would be looking pretty and... cute. To be honest, I never wore it. Details, remember?

I ended up doing simple curls and a bit of eyeshadow and lip gloss, nothing fancy. Along with that, I matched some golden necklaces, earrings and rings to go with the outfit. Standing in front of my mirror, I look at the vision and I think... I think I'm looking good. I am feeling... weird, but in a good, weird. After a few more seconds of taking this all in, my hands grab my black purse and a black suit jacket, which I lay over my shoulder. Casual, but still a bit fancier than usual. As I hear the doorbell ring once again, I step into some high heels, which have laces to tie around your legs. In total, I am feel good, this is good. You got this Olivia. I open the front door to see a tall frame. Ethan in a… suit? The trousers are black, while the jacket on top of a basic white shirt is made of a very similar red satin and he looks freaking amazing. Aside from that, he's also got some necklaces, rings and fancy sunglasses. His hair is as messy as always, but I suppose that's kind of his thing. At least he knows, what looks good on him. That would make one out of the two of us.

"Hi." I greet him staring into his hazel eyes.

"Hello sweetheart. I don't think I need to tell you how freaking gorgeous you look?"

"I don't think that would give me enough confidence," I reply giving him an awkward smile.

"Today is about you and about having fun. It's okay to be who-ever you are, and we'll work on that confidence. We gotta go now, or we'll be late." He puts his large hand behind my back to guide me to his car.

"Funny, because Mary said the exact same thing," I add laughing. Once we reached his car, he turns around again.

"Have you locked your door?" he asks with a serious facial expression.

"Geeze don't be so dramatic. I always lock it, besides, who would want anything from in there?"

"I dunno, maybe the ones behind your family? Have you got anything they could want Olivia?"

Uhm… without my lawyer I can neither confirm, nor deny it. "Chill Ethan, I locked it. I always do." I reassure him to calm him down. Seems like he's the one who could use some drinks after all. Or maybe one of those presents Abby has given me…?

He gives me a smile continuing: "Then let's go." We both climb into the car and drive in more or less silence. "You're scared?" he asks me after about ten minutes.

I didn't quite recognize that I was playing with my hands, it's another bad habit I suppose. I consider my answer before giving it to him. "There are so many things I should figure out right now. I've got a lot of things I should handle first." Turning around, I catch a glimpse of him and he looks at me for a short second before concentrating on the traffic.

"It's okay to look out for yourself first. Besides that, will these things still bother you after this night?"

"Pretty sure they will." How could they not?

"Then why don't you take a break from them? If they are still there tomorrow, why don't we trick them and don't give them as much room as they would like to have?" he proposes smiling to himself. Cheeky but funny.

"Thank you," I add and he takes one of his hands off the steering wheel before taking mine in his and giving it a quick reassuring squeeze.

"It'll be fine. It's okay."

Sometimes I wish people would give this whole thing more room. People are suffering and dying, and it does not matter whether it's from a physical or a mental thing because they all suffer. They suffer *differently*, as everyone does. What matters is, that they suffer. People feel things, see things, understand, and comprehend them in other ways and still, it might be the same reason or emotion. Sometimes words aren't enough to explain that. In my case, that's what the music's for.

Anyway, we had arrived at the place where we were supposed to be about fifteen minutes ago. Never mind the thing about being punctual. We get out of the car and are immediately welcomed by a tone of light and people taking pictures of all the humans entering this place. It seems to be something nicer and well-known than the places I've been to. Oh, no, silly me, I've never been to a club. Nearly forgot that fact but yeah, chill out I would say. That fact is kind of embarrassing, since I'm past the drinking age and not a minor anymore. The friends I had, well there was just Abby. However, we would never do something big. We didn't have the opportunity to thanks to my dad and the fucking moving around part. If this evening should work, I really need something to calm my fucking nerves before I leave again.

I follow Ethan and tuck my head down, trying to avoid everyone there. We entered the club not long after escaping the paparazzies. The warm thick air hits me straight in the face. The dimmed neon lights make it hard to focus on something and it was at least twenty-five degrees in here. This place is hot, huge and filled with many people who seem to just want to let go of something. Not hard to understand if I'm being honest. We walk past the huge amount of people at throughout the room... you kind of get used to such things with time. To my surprise we climb up a couple of stairs reaching a sort of platform. There are couches and tables there, but most important there is enough air to fucking finally breathe. I close my eyes for a brief moment and try to focus on my breathing while Ethan lets go of my hand coming closer to me.

"Hey Olivia, just concentrate on your breathing. Everything's fine, we're all here." He reassures me causing me to open my eyes again to see everyone I know who I spend the most time. Along with everyone from the band there is also Abby, the producers and the manager I met a few times to discuss my release. I look at him and see him smiling at me. I nod, and he pulls me into a hug. It takes me a moment to realize it, before hugging him back.

I sit down on the couch after saying hello to everyone in the area who I know. Let me just say that they all look fucking stunning. I'm by far the worst dressed person here. It must have something to do with the genes of British people, I swear they can do everything. Abby's of course not British, but she always looks perfect.

"So, Olivia, are you ready for the first and probably best party of your life?" Abby asks from my left crackling into a laugh when she sees my face.

Oh crab.

Chapter Nineteen

I feel absolutely wasted. You probably won't be able to use me for the next few days either.

We started the evening off, or more likely the night, with a few drinks, which were in my case cocktails. I am not a shot kind of type. When I told them that and after they had offered me a shot, Abby of course had to throw the fact in, that I hadn't had one since my birthday two years ago. Full birthdays are just in a separate league. However, we all had enough drinks now that we finally got up to dance a bit to the music. Well, we girls did because the males in the room seemed to be 'bad dancers'. Yeah, whatever helps you sleep at night guys. The beats were actually pretty crazy and amazing. It is like jumping on a trampoline every time you hear the beat or the drums. I never danced that much before and that was bad, but that is the whole point of doing so, right? Emma tried to show me some steps, but I think she just made these moves up in her mind. Also, I'm really hopeless myself when it comes to dancing, the only difference is, that I don't take that as an excuse not to. Perhaps the alcohol helped me just a little bit to step out of my comfort zone though.

The good thing about this evening will most likely be, that we will not be able to remember a lot in the next morning. I definitely won't, because my body's already reacting to the liquids I've had, more than I hoped for. I feel kind of lightheaded and weird, but in a cool way. This might have caused us girls to dance more than we did anything else, but I like it. If you knew me, you'd know that I despise dancing and here I am. Maybe I won't the next morning, but as of right now I do. Our dancing session came to an end once the song was over. I don't really remember how many there were, but I suspect quite a few. We walked back to the others and kept on talking for a while until the topic came up that I had tried to drink away.

"Five minutes until your song comes out Liv. How do you feel about that one?" My manager called Ash asks me after checking the time and everyone seems to expect a serious answer.

"I am wasted right now, so I will probably cry later on." I admit and we are all laughing for a second until I start to get more serious again. "Now in all honesty, I would never have been able to do this without all of you. Whether it was pushing me or helping me, you guys are pretty much the only reason I am doing this. Thank you from the bottom of my heart. You welcomed me here and all of this is slowly starting to become normal to me. I'm really starting to feel more at home every day, around you and this place. I feel honoured to know you and to be with you every second." I tell them and they give me a group hug.

This feeling is quite new but still amazing to me and if I'm honest, I wouldn't want it to change right now. Because right now, all that matters is what my heart feels, all the music I have created with them and all the things I have got through to end up here. I haven't figured out many things in my life, but one thing is very clear now. Those are the humans I need to have around me, they make me the best version of myself and I hope that I can return this opportunity to them one day. I also learned that this world is pretty much a dark place most of the time. That is the particular reason why we need to be kind to one another. Every person has a different story and things that they had to go through, and everyone deserves compassion and kindness. It's the very thing that keeps people together and creates the most important bond. Friendship. People you know who will never leave you or betray you, people who are not afraid to stand up for you or to kick your ass once in a while, people who care about me the way that I care about them. *Because people who value you, will never ever put themselves in a position to lose you.* That's all I've ever wanted.

Light Stick will launch at midnight which is about thirty seconds away from now and I'm slowly get the urge to pee myself because I am fucking terrified. No matter how much I am scared, it will happen anyway, which means this damn fear could just disappear. Not that easy sometimes.

"Five... four... three... two... one... zero!" We are all screaming and jumping with each other. Once the countdown is done, I can slightly hear the song through the whole club, and I'm immediately glaring at them.

"Surprise I guess." Jacob yells over to me as I make my way towards him to punch him in the face because... well... I don't know. Once I reach him, he holds his hands up in surrender, but I hug him tightly and bury my face in his chest. He seems to be as confused by that as all the others are.

"Thank you Jacob, I would never have ended up here if we hadn't met."

"It was my pleasure. You're good for all of us and you deserve this more than everyone," He states. I let go of him to look into his brown eyes. He truly is a good friend.

We're all singing along with the lyrics and just enjoying what we have created... together. Nothing and no one could ever take that away from us, from me.

I take a step closer to Abby when I hear that the song will come to an end very soon. She gives me one of those bear hugs I love and I bury my face in her black curls. They smell like... like they always have and will, they smell like my best friend. "I hope you know that words couldn't express how much I love you Abby. You truly are the best thing that I have, and I never want to lose you." I admit to her letting a tear run down my face. As of right now, my heart is speaking again. Through all this time I forgot how sensitive alcohol makes me and I haven't missed it at all.

"L, I hope you know that I will always be here for you. I love you and I am beyond proud of you."

We didn't break the hug for another few moments and we just cherished each other's presence. I know that she will be gone soon, too soon and I am not ready to be without her. I doubt that I ever will be. However, she also has a job and a career and things she wants to achieve. It is not all about me. Sometimes I feel as if I am being too selfish with having her around but come on, who wouldn't want to have a golden person as her around all the time? I suspect that she still wouldn't admit it, if it actually was that way and I am a tiny bit glad for it.

After a bit of sitting and watching everyone enjoying themselves, I tell them that I need a moment and fresh air. So, I pass by the massive amount of young partying people and I go outside through the back entrance which leads to the top of the building. It has a great view, you can see the city lights and even to the centre of London. The last thing I would want is to see more people outside. Once outside the cooler air hits me straight in the face and I start to feel the amount of alcohol in my blood and body even more. Someone once warned me about not doing this, but in all honesty, you only learn from your mistakes. However, I sit down on the ground and observe everything around me. Once in a while it's just nice to feel your breathing and to remind yourself that you are alive and enjoy just the little things about life, being here. I mean the chances of us being alive or even here at this point is nearly zero. Most of us don't even realize that fact and it's really sad because many did not have the chance to do any of this or to be alive this long. I wish everyone on this planet could enjoy being alive and that no one would willingly have to die. It's a shame that our society is… this way and I deeply wish that I could change it.

"You do have a habit of sneaking away. Also, you should consider stopping it or one day I won't realize it and you will be gone." Ethan speaks behind me as he opens the back entrance, interrupting my thoughts. He crouches down next to me, before sitting down.

"Maybe that's my plan." I joke putting on a smile before concentrating on the view of the city in front of us.

"I hope you're joking because that would hurt my feelings." He admits and dramatically he holds a hand against his chest as if I had stabbed him.

"You will never know Ethan. But anyway, go and cry like a baby." I joke and he smirks.

"How does it feel to be a professional singer now?" he asks after a bit of silence. Comfortable silence.

"I don't know, you tell me." I reply. He doesn't reply and smiles.

"When I heard it for the first time I wanted to cry. For the fact that I lost her, that she will not see it or me ever again, that I finally found people like you, that I am fucking terrified of these people and just everything. It was just overwhelming."

"It's okay to feel this way. Feeling anything is better than feeling nothing at all. I didn't know your mother, but I am sure as hell that she would've been fucking proud of you just as everyone is. As I am." He confesses looking down at his lap, rather than at me.

"You are?" I question him.

"Yes I am. You have grown so much since you arrived here and so have I. Because you made me the best version of myself and showed me what was right for me. This is much more important, you made me a better man."

"So, you know what you want to do? You want to stop singing?"

"Not that, but something else. I'm just not sure how to do it yet," he tells me while I rest one of my hands against his cheek and he automatically turns towards me. And again, he seems so bold when he speaks of his emotions. I'm not sure if it makes any sense but right now he is just the image of softness. His features are calm, and he looks quite relaxed overall. I doubt that I have seen him this way in the time that I've been here. I suppose his noticed it as well and maybe that's the reason why he told me that I had made him a better man. But Ethan, you wouldn't want to know what you're doing to me. Not just my state of mind, but also my body because right now, I feel as if my stomach has been turned upside down and my cheeks glow like a fireball.

"You don't need to have it all figured out. Seriously Ethan, does it seem as if I have an idea what I'm doing? Because I have fucking zero clue. That's why you have people around you. Sometimes it's nice to know that someone else will do something so you can get your mind off it. Your friends are here for you, I am here for you. Just as you have been for me."

"I'm feel as if someday people will leave me. You will leave me just like everyone has and I am absolutely terrified of that thought."

"You're not scared to open up, are you?" I ask, and he shakes his head in response. I can puzzle all the informations that I get out of him, which is not much. "You're scared of people leaving you."

He hides his face in his hands. "I know it's so stupid but I can't make it…"

I am not stupid. Feelings are valid and they are there for a reason, don't hide them away from anyone, from me." I tell him as he always made me feel comfortable. Also, that's just the truth even though we sometimes forget about it and many other important things.

He looks up again smiling a bit. "You're not like everyone else, Olivia."

"I'll just take that as a compliment." I frown trying to make him smile, which actually works.

"You should take everything as a compliment," he pleads coming closer to me. He is driving me insane, literally.

"Ah, is it like that? And what about if someone insults me?" I dare him, and he smirks as he is now resting a hand on my cheek. See, fireballs.

"Then they're just jealous because they're not as good as you are," he adds with that smirk of his still on his face. That's kind of his thing, besides, he looks damn gorgeous in everything and while singing, it drives me insane but in a good way, and – what's the point of this?

I take my thoughts and feelings into action and lean closer to him until our lips slightly touch. He seems surprised but he leans closer. However, the second I actually realize what have I just done, I break away from it and get up. He looks confused and in some parts scared. I can't, I mean I don't really know him, and I haven't kissed someone for… let's just say very long.

"I am sorry, I shouldn't have done that. I am drunk, you are drunk and this… I uhm… I should just go now," I tell him or more likely myself and turning around while he calls me by my name. I ignore it until I hear movements from behind me. He gets up and dashes after me until he eventually grabs my wrist to stop me making me turn around. He is still being soft but more painful, bold and confused.

"Ethan... this is not a good idea. I... we...," to make up for it because this is my mistake.

He interrupts me coming closer and kisses me again. This time with more passion and more confusion from my side. He puts his arms around my lower back while mine are resting in his messy hair.

Once we stopped kissing, he still stands there while my arms are around his neck now. "That... that came unexpected." I admit and we're both laughing.

"Oh, I've been waiting for this way too long."

It's a twisted world, isn't it? But I'm not complaining. On the other hand, there is one thing to complain about. What does that mean now?

Chapter Twenty

I stagger out of my bedroom and into the kitchen, trying to adjust my eyes to this freaking brightness. A side effect of this was that I had sweated the whole night and now I am only wearing shorts and a loose shirt, although I am still hot as fuck. I open the kitchen cupboard to take two mugs out of it as I start to brew coffee. I know, I know, we're in England which means tea but after this hangover I need something much stronger than that.

So, here's the thing; after we had gone inside, we still had a little party with the guys, and it was amazing. Still, something changed. Maybe it's the way that he looked at me or the other way around, but something was different. I wasn't the only one to get that easily. As a matter of fact, I think everyone did, but Abby was the only one to point it out with her stares towards him. She is a little harder on this topic and I don't blame her, because it is theoretically a good thing. A friend keeping her friend safe, right? I can't blame her after what happened in my past relationship. That is the particular reason why I am awake this early, she basically made me. Well, when I got out of there a few hours later, Ethan and I decided it would be best if he just crushed at my place. He was pretty much wasted all over. However, when I left, she sent me a direct text, saying she would expect me to call her at eight in the morning. Funny enough, she isn't a morning person as well, but she will be leaving today. So, yeah, I am pretty much fucked.

I decided not to tell Ethan, he wouldn't have made it easier. Here I am, waiting for that call and thinking about how many different ways there are, in which she could kill me through the phone. In the end, when my coffee is done, I can think of five. Number one; she could do damage to my brain and ears by yelling at me. Number two; she could just end this friendship. (Better think of any ending that could possibly happen). Number three; she could just not fly away and just come over to kill me. Number four; she could kill me when she comes back. And finally, number five; she could just order someone to kill me. A little pathetic, I know. If I thought about it longer, I would possibly, no, definitely, have come up with more ways but the second I consider that, she calls.

"Hey Abby," I say with my morning voice.

"I am not in the mood. I am tired and I want answers now, because I have to be on the plane very fucking soon." God, she is definitely not a morning person.

"I would like to help you out with that, maybe you could just help my hangover mind a little and tell me what topic you're on about?" I ask her taking a sip of the hot drink in my hand.

"Ethan!" she clarifies.

"See, we might have kissed each other, but we were both drunk, so this isn't a big thing." I'm such a bad liar.

"You know that I don't like him, right? I want the best for you but I can hardly see that in him."

"I know you're worried, so am I. But it's been a long time since I felt like this… since I felt alive. Not just because of him but because I have met all these people and I really like them." I admit looking out of the window. "I'd rather not talk about that topic on the phone. We'll talk when you're back."

"I'm not sure yet when that will be. Job's just making me crazy," she adds sighing. She sounds exhausted and I don't like it. When she started doing all of that stuff, shows and shootings and everything, she fell in love with every single bit of it and I don't want her to lose that sort of feeling. She gave me the start to this journey by feeling and falling in love with something, and she deserves to keep hers until the day she dies.

"If it's too much you should consider taking a break. Get your head cleared, travel a bit, spend time with your family and friends. It's okay to be selfish once in a while. I want you to do whatever the hell makes you the happiest person on this planet and when that means you need a break from life, I am more than willing to have my spare bedroom open for you."

"Thank you L. I'll think about it on the plane. I got to go now but we will talk. Be careful, okay?"

"Yes, you too. Have a good flight and be safe," I tell her, and she hangs up the phone. I lean on the counter with my upper body so that I can rest and take a breath.

"Good morning," I hear from my left and I jump up immediately. Not this shit again.

"Holy fucking shit. Jesus Christ in heaven you scared the shit out of me." I state, my hand resting on my rising chest.

He comes around the counter placing his hands on my waist. I might have left out the fact that he crashed in my bed… because if I had told Abby she would have thought the worst. Which did not happen.

"Still a bit skittish, aren't you?" he says going towards the coffee machine.

"I didn't think you'd be awake this early," I say sighing.

"Why are you doing that?" he asks very seriously as he turns around. I frown laughing a bit to myself, but his facial expression doesn't change in the slightest..

"Doing what?" I ask.

"Why do you try and fix people's problems?" The second he asks, I turn around to avoid him.

"I don't," I state, knowing full well that this is all I did.

"Yes, you do. All the time. You listen to other people's problems and fix them. And when it's your turn no one is there to fix yours, but you don't care. You carry on 'fixing' people. It's annoying. Why do you do that?" He says stepping closer to rest against the counter next to me.

This hurts. I mean, I know that about myself, it is far from being new. But someone who points it out to me, that hurts. For as long as I can remember I was a people pleaser. I am not even sure where it came from, only that it never went away. He is right.

"I fix people, so I don't have to focus on how broken I am," I reply.

He takes a deep breath letting his head fall down onto his chest before looking at me. "So, when are you going to let me put the pieces back?"

"I… I don't know where the pieces went," I admit watching his motions. My vision is tainted by my tears. He hugs me tightly while he softly runs his fingers through my hair. "They always say that you need to follow your heart, but if your heart is in a million pieces, which one do you follow?"

"Remember how you said that you don't think everyone is lucky enough to have a happy life?" he asks. I frown in the hug nodding.

"I thought about this for a while. After you said that not everyone was supposed to be saved. I am pretty sure that no one deserves to feel the way you and others do, but I agree that some deserve to be saved more than others. If I would have to make a list of all of these human beings, I highly suspect that your name will be on the top."

"Why are you doing this?" I ask him again. This is just my way, I can't stop questioning every single thing that happens which is not bad, because with time you just kind of get used to only bad things happening all the time. Someone could be standing right in front of me, telling and screaming at me that they love me and I wouldn't understand nor believe it. It's hard to believe someone could love you when you see yourself as the worst person you know.

"I like you Olivia, there is something more to you and you make me feel, so different. A *good different* and I want to find out more about that, but I can't make you any promises. I learned that nothing in life is for sure and I don't want to cause you any more pain by promising things I don't know if I can keep." He takes a breath breaking our hug to take hold of my arms with his hands. "I can't promise you that I am the best for you and that I can make it go away. You cannot promise me that you won't leave me. What I can do, is that I'll be here for you for as long as I can and for as long as you want me to be here. We'll get through things together as best as we can."

"I would want to promise you something but after what happened to my mom and the damage of these people, I don't even know what is going to happen. I know that Abby will hate me for this but at least five hundred thousand of those pieces want me to go on with this," I admit and we're both smiling.

I like to talk to him about this stuff, serious stuff. It gets quite annoying at this point when you talk to someone and the say, 'Life is shitty', they always ask you for a reason and that it's 'not that bad'. With Ethan on the other hand, I found someone I can talk to and someone who will say 'yes, life is shitty, but we're in this together' and that's the most beautiful thing that I could have wished for. I mean, we all know that life doesn't only give you the sweets but, in our society more people feel less good. Frankly, they still expect us more than ever to be good and only have the sweets. They don't seem to understand that people rather say 'yes, I am doing so great' than 'I'm doing shitty, and I don't even know why'.

As a matter of fact, if it did happen or if you stood up to your family, you have already failed them. If you don't want the job or the grades that they want you to have, you have already failed. You won't get a good education, which means you don't get a job, it means you earn no money and that means you're already a failure. That's how it works.

Same thing with body images. If you don't have big enough boobs or an arse you need to put on weight. If you put on enough weight to have an arse and the boobs, then you don't have that stomach that everyone wants. In order to get this, you would have to go to the gym seven days a week and basically dedicate your life to never being happy with what you have. Now, if you go to the gym seven times a week, and you're too muscley it intimidates the guys. If you're skinny then you're weak and that is not attractive. So, what is it that you want from us? The thing is that most of the girls don't even do that for themselves. If we all ate the same things and worked out the same amount, we still would look different. This just makes everyone sick, and it made me sick as well.

This world makes us all so sick, that is why we need to be kind to each other and have someone who keeps us sane. Maybe he is the one. I guess you would have known that.

"I don't want to sound like a narcissistic," Ethan says, "but I'm highly recommending to follow the pieces you have. Maybe one day they'll all come together and tell you in detail, what they want. I'll wait for that."

"Thank you, Ethan. Thank you for just being you and pushing me every day to be the best; well most of the time," I say, and we both laugh before we lean into each other again.

"It's a pleasure Olivia," he answers, and I smile as he kisses me. "Though, I can only go on for as long as I can stand. My belly is asking me to put food into my system. Quite a lot actually, so, unless you have food for an army, I am offering to take you out."

"I'll gladly accept. Although, I need to take a shower first and take some pills to deal with this freaking headache."

I think I could get used to this.

Chapter Twenty-One

Growing up I've learnt many things, good things and things that really fucking suck. For starters, I learnt how to live on my own and how to become the most mature person in class. It can be a good thing to be sure, but for me it wasn't. I didn't get why the kids my age did the things they did. The things they did, I couldn't do. I was always more into real things, such as thinking about my future, drawing, reading, or making and listening to music. I'd rather do these things than hang out with them and play silly games; and that caused me to end up pretty much on my own. See, the thing about it ironically is, that every time you end up alone you get more mature because you have to care about things on your own, that others maybe don't have to. This whole maturity thing lets you end up alone again, and again, and again. *I didn't mature because of age. I matured due to pain.* So, growing up I've learnt how to be alone; how to be alone with myself and my thoughts, how to do things with and for myself, rather than having others do them for me instead.

I never really wanted to have many friends. I liked being alone, but I didn't want to be lonely, no one does. However, I felt so freaking lonely that it haunted me in my dreams. I have had these nightmares pretty much since my mom died and they were always the same. She was gone, she came back, all happy tears and stuff and then, then she either died, went away or I woke up in a lot of sweat, tears and confusion. Pretty messed up, right? Anyway, I always thought it was because I missed her, which I obviously do, don't get me wrong; but one day when I was alone outside sitting on a bench, watching the grass, and the flowers bowing to the wind, I finally figured it out. I had these dreams because I was and still am petrified of the thought that people will leave me. They come into my life to spend some time and they take what they want and eventually they make me happier for a certain amount of time, but in every case they just fuck me over and leave. Every time someone did this, it broke me more and more. And now there isn't much more to break anymore. As I said before, this is how fucking terrified I am.

Whenever someone intended to ask me why I would never reach out when I had a hard time or a panic or anxiety attack, I always said 'because I don't want to bother anyone'. Now, that is a reason as well, but not the most important one. The reason why I would rather suffer alone and wait until it's over, is that whenever I needed someone so desperately, whenever I sat there wanting to end things, wanting to resort to anything for the pain to end, I was alone. I was alone when I wanted to die four years ago. I was alone when I wanted to die three years ago. I was alone when I wanted to die two years ago, and I was fucking lonely when I wanted to die less than a month ago.

Surprisingly, I am still here. Mainly the reason for that is Abby. *She's the peak of my existence.* Mostly, it wasn't even the thought of 'I want to die' in that moment. It could be 'I want this to end so badly', or 'I don't want to be alive, but I don't want to be dead' or even a 'I want to stop feeling altogether'. About the not feeling thing though, when you're in so much pain, it can actually be a relief to feel numb.

The problem is how to start feeling again after that. At some point, I found myself wishing, desperately, to feel anything at all, to feel as if I was actually alive and breathing. *I wanted to just breathe so badly.* I wanted to be alive for myself, but not for everyone else. I wanted to care for once for myself first before others. You see, that is my whole point with my sad movie. *No matter how we choose to live, we die in the end.* I never told anyone this, but before I fell in love with music, I was deeply in love with reading and I read every book I could get. My mom always got me to read and we would sit by the fire on the couch, and we used to discuss books for hours. Yeah, we used to do many things together back then. When she died, I loved reading and listening to music because I didn't have to focus on my own sadness and numbness, but rather on the feelings of the author and artists. The problem with reading was, that at some point, even my most favourite characters of my most favourite book did the same and it took away the magic. *I love reading because I didn't have to focus on my own numbness until one day, even the most special characters turned numb as well.* Or they died. They say that even the authors don't know what they're doing, until they have created it. It really is a pity to see how many people feel this way. And music; music is a way of letting all one's feelings out and understanding them in a different way, I never felt numb while listening to music and making my own. Music was there, when no one else was.

Many don't understand that a mental illness can make someone suffer as much as if it were a physical thing. If you ask someone, they will probably tell you, that it's something you also feel in your body, rather than only in your head. The closest description I've heard was when I was about seventeen years old. A man said that living with depression feels like having another person inside you, who constantly tries to kill you. You don't need a professional to tell you that you have this person inside you. Believe me, if you do, you will not overlook or not feel it anymore. You just do and you just know.

Normally, I don't talk about this in any way with anyone. Hell, I even don't say the word 'depression' anymore. I hate it so goddamn much and I hate people using it as a 'label'. A 'label' doesn't make a person and just because no one has diagnosed you in any way, that doesn't mean that you're not suffering from it. Every illness was undiagnosed at some point. Besides that, if we all asked the right professional, we'd probably all have a 'label'.

That is the reason I am alone. That is the reason I have these nightmares and that is the reason why I fucking have trust issues.

All of this brings me back to the present, which is a total mess as well. I'm trying to figure that one out before it will turn into my past, like all the others.

We, which includes me and Ethan (weird, right?), spent the next few days trying to recover from the massive hangover and just kind of getting to know each other better; well, that's what he said, because I know fucking zero about him. That brings me to the reason why I'm slightly pissed-off right now. Come on, I am literally not asking for a lot, but I really know nothing about him, and it drives me crazy. I told him that I was scared of the thought that someone knew everything about me; and every day he comes a step closer to being that person, while I am stuck in whatever you want to call this. Frankly, he hasn't made me pissed off enough to confront him yet; despite me being a people pleaser and hiding from people, I know. What I don't know is how long I'm able to keep it that way.

So, this morning, when he is 'discussing something with some-one important' and going off about it, I take my time to invest in something which is actually important to me and is something I will learn something from. So, this is me revealing secrets out about my mother before my... what is he actually? A friend? No, friends don't do... what we do, do they? Doesn't matter now, because I have spent the last hour reading through a tiny green book, I found a few day ago. That's why I am a mess, and I hav-en't showered. My hair is in a ponytail, to keep it out of my face and allowing me to ignore the knots in it, I suppose. Her book is also a weird mess because it seems as if she just scribbled her thoughts in it, with no structure; as if she were in a hurry the whole time. I don't remember her that way. She was someone who always knew what she was doing. A person who knew a solution to every problem. Things change, though. There were notes from cases she published later on in everything that would get people's attention; no matter whether it was a newspaper, a magazine, an article or even on social media. Don't get me wrong; but at first, I was confused that these platforms even existed, about seven years ago. Crazy, I know. I'm not even halfway through it and if I'm being honest, I don't understand half of what she wrote. I was always aware that she was a lawyer before she became a writer, but I didn't know that it went that far.

Theoretically, I could just start to read from the back, which would be the last case, but where is the fun? I want to find out what happened to her. I want to know the full and bold truth for once. I am so sick of secrets, lies and people trying to protect me. Because of these things, the lies always stay even when the people are gone. If this affects my life, which it clearly does, I want to know what's going on. I deserve to know. I was about to fetch a glass of water while I continue to read and my phone vibrates from across the living room. I close the book and walk over. It's Ethan.

"Yes?" I ask while holding the phone against my ear.

"Hello to you too,", he says chuckling. He's still successful at making me smile and laugh at his corny jokes or anything stupid which is often not even the slightest bit funny. Sometimes, his reactions make the whole joke funny; but not the joke itself.

"Sorry, I was lost in thought. Watcha doing?"

"Oh, nothing important, I just had to talk to someone." He's lying and I know it.

"Someone I'm not allowed to know about?"

"Look, I would tell you. I just don't know how yet."

"Yeah, no problem, I'll just wait to add this to all the other things I want to know about you." I sigh; and I can hear through his breathing how difficult this is for him. "Ethan, I'm not asking you to open up about your whole life. It would just be nice to know some little things about you. I feel that you know me way too well already, and you know how scared I am about this sort of thing." No, he didn't make me pissed enough. He made me frustrated and as it turns out, that's also a very effective way to make me speak very directly.

"I should have thought about that. I'm sorry Olivia. I'll make up for it. What are you doing right now?"

"I was reading one of my mother's diaries I found a couple of weeks ago," I say walking back to the kitchen to take a sip of water.

"You are reading her... diary?" he asks, making me frown.

"Yes, why are you reacting... this way?" I reply.

"I'm just surprised, you didn't tell me you got anything from her. But I'm happy that you did, maybe you should stop now and get ready because we are going out later with the guys to celebrate you and your song." Not this again.

I might have left out two things... well, you see, it's a bit more complicated. Number one. I kind of forced myself not to look up my song or anything else up in the last few days but Jacob and Mary couldn't respect that, and they told me that it went great. I've no idea what that means, but I was right about the fact that Ethan and Abby couldn't resist making something bigger out of it than it was and they posted it all over their social media. It's like the strangest feeling that, even if I hadn't decided to release it; somehow it would have definitely ended up out there. And I am not sure if I would have found that amusing or if I should be scared. Great friends; most of the time at least. So, I denied every meeting with my manager and I told him that I wasn't ready to hear anything about it yet. I had to take some time to realize what I had done. It seems as if Ethan called him today, and the others, to plan a dinner. Wait a second! why do they plan events with me all the time without asking if I was willing to attend? Wicked things happen all the time.

Number two, I installed social media. I finally did it, well Jacob and Mary did it for me, but that's basically the same. They just downloaded Instagram and Twitter to start with, and I'm already struggling with that. I just don't get what the sense in looking at people's pictures is? It's just a new way of hating them and making them feel insecure; which is the reason I hadn't posted anything... yet. And I hoped that in the future I wouldn't do it either... never mind.

Here I am, not knowing what to wear again and Ethan should be here any second now. While I'm trying to open the closet after I have curled my hear and put on light makeup, I hear the door-bell ringing. I walk towards the end of my minimalistic hallway, since I still haven't found the time to decorate my apartment, and I pull the door open.

"Shut up before you start, I haven't decided what to wear and I need your help," I interrupt him before he could even adjust that I am too late. Instead of replying, he shakes his head smiling, and he pulls me closer to kiss me. God, I missed those kinds of touches so much in my past relationship. Both the guy and I weren't very physical. When looking back now, he was more of a status-boy-friend kind of person. Yes, we kissed here and there, but he refused to hold my hand in public or anything of that kind. He said it was 'inappropriate'. He was a classic daddy's boy. The thing that affected me most was that I basically had to say the three words. He said them to me when I wasn't even ready to think about it and I felt pressured to say it back. And all of that made me believe that it was love. That's why I'm so fucked up about that now. He did what he did until the love was gone; but the lies stayed.

"Then let's find you something to wear, shall we?" he tells me and I look at him. It should be a crime to look that good in every single piece of clothing you wear. He's wearing a pair of cloth trousers and suit jacket; both in grey, with a white shirt underneath and gold buttons which matched his rings and the necklace he always wears. I have never asked about it, but I noticed it. It's a small circle with a rose on it and it seems to mean a lot to him. I told him that I wouldn't ask about it. I would until he told me, but that information would actually interest me. He puts his arm around my waist while walking into my bedroom with me.

"Or you could just tell them that I got the flu, and so we don't have to go, did you consider that? Wait a second, the next time you could also tell me where we are going, so I might be able to prepare myself a bit more; that would be nice. You people never ask me if I want to come anywhere. You just make me come." He seems to find that amusing until he stops when we reach my wardrobe. He stands tall in front of me and he looks into my eyes smiling – Cheeky bugger.

"Olivia, would you like to go out with me and your friends today?" he asks.

"No," I answer him, and he bursts out laughing tilting his head backwards.

"See, that's the reason why we don't ask. We just want the best for you, and sometimes you need a little push to see what's best for you and what you deserve," he tells me while opening the closet.

They want the best for me. They are my friends. I am safe with them. It's going to be okay. It has to be.

Chapter Twenty-Two

See, I was always alone, and I got used to it. I got used to dealing with my own thoughts and feelings alone, rather than sharing them with anyone else other than via a piece of paper. I got used to more or less living with myself. Whenever I felt as if my emotions would overcome me, I would have liked to have let them out, but I couldn't. I couldn't because I didn't want to bother anyone, and I just couldn't tell anyone. I was ashamed of it.

Then I always remembered that I had to pull myself out of my current hole, over and over again, and I am okay with that. I am tired of it, but I am still here, right? Now, I would like to live every single day to the fullest, for everyone who didn't get the chance to. I'd like to spend the days with my friends and everyone I love, but things aren't always the way we want them to be; and that is okay. I still wish I could treat myself with as much kindness as I give to everyone around me but every time I look at myself, all I see are the things I couldn't achieve and everything I did wrong. I'm so used to all the bad things that I cannot believe when someone is being nice to me for no reason, or if something good happens once in a while.

I didn't understand and I couldn't comprehend why people would tell me that I'm strong and brave, because all the things that happened to me seemed normal. My point is that it wasn't. Life is not supposed to be this hard and I am still trying to accept it. I find it hard to accept my flaws and the fact that I have overcome so many things that most people never have to deal with. What I am saying is that recovering, and healing, is not a recipe. You can't follow any directions because there are none. Everyone feels differently and everyone heals differently because emotions are not the same for everyone. Healing isn't linear. It's a messy chaos of pain and the pleasure of getting back what you lost once; but emotions are valid, and they are important. They need to be dealt with and we cannot underestimate or ignore them.

Right now, I should pay more attention to my emotions, that tell me I should not be here; as if anyone would let them do that, right? Anxiety is a crazy thing. I know I said that I didn't like to talk about it explicitly, but right now I need to focus on something that will distract me. In fact, it's really hard to explain it to someone who has never had to deal with it. It's a constant fear of things that could happen, a fear that can take over your whole body. It's the fear of having all eyes on you. The fear of making mistakes in front of people; that people could make fun of you; the fear of having to ask yourself, Am I stuttering? Why is everyone watching me? Do I stink so much? What could they be thinking of me right now? Is the couple over there laughing about me? Am I walking normally? Is my hair still in place? It's a fear of all the things that could happen but most of the time they do not. And most of the time it's not even just in your head. Your body starts to shake, you're sweating and panicking all over again. Your head makes up things and that make you panic. Your whole body will act as if the world is crumbling. You will find yourself thinking that the situation is the problem, when in reality, it's the thought about what the situation will become rather than what it is at the moment. For people with anxiety, it's hard to feel like living in the present because it's filled with overthinking and fear. You have a hard time focusing on your breathing and getting out of your head, you feel like you're stuck and that it will only get worse. I wish there could be an easier way to get rid of all of this, but I haven't figured out a way yet.

Right now, I am in my head and it tells me a crazy number of things that could happen.

"Are you aware that you get this certain look on your face when you're anxious?" Ethan tells me while I try to pull my dress into the right position as it should have just stayed in place.

"You don't know what I'm thinking about right now," I say while walking next to him through the crowded streets. This makes me freaking terrified because of the clothes I'm wearing. For once I'm wearing my boots and it might get to be my new thing. My brown hair is curled again, half of it in a bun, but the dress is simply a bit much for me. It's black and it has nice, sweet red flowers on it. It's a bit much because it ends in the middle of my thigh and has quite an open back. The back is connected by laces of the same material and is the same colour as the rest. Ethan got it for me because he kind of knew that I didn't know what to wear and that I did not have much fashion sense nor many clothes. I stayed in my own lane, my little bubble, with my own clothes and stuff. Well, I used to…

But back to the point, my thoughts are about people staring because they seem to do that quite a lot. I normally don't walk in the streets at such a crowded hour, but of course he has to push me again. "Do you even realize how they are all staring at us? Do I look that bad?" I ask him and he immediately stops and turns me around so that we faced each other. I stare into his eyes while the whole crowd of people around us seem to fade.

"They are staring, and I also know why. You look absolutely… there's not even one word to describe it all," he says. "They could also be staring because you are famous. Have you even considered that?" I swear there will be pictures all over social media tomorrow. So much to staying in my own bubble.

"In a good way?" I ask again.

He takes hold of my chin with one of his hands nodding. "In a very good way." After saying so, he comes closer and kisses me softly on my lips. He lets go and takes hold of my hand and we continue to walk to the restaurant. Looks like he's different after all, right?

"Aren't you thinking about all of them taking pictures? Pictures of you and some girl? Aren't you thinking about what they could think of you?" I just have to know this time.

"Oh, Olivia. You're not just some girl. I'm well aware that they'll take pictures, but I don't care because no one can make me feel different about you. Not even you." If you only knew…

But as I said, I've never loved someone. My ex might have convinced me that I was in love with him but I didn't love him. That's like worlds apart. Oh yes, love is a crazy thing. If you believe in it and if you get to experience it, I'm sure it will make you crazy as hell. In a good way. However, for all the people who haven't, or who don't believe in it anymore, it is crazy as well. People talk about soulmates and love at first sight and all that stuff but what I believe is different. I know that this world is fucked up. Humans are fucked up, the earth is fucked up because of us humans and still we get to experience something greater. I'm far from being sure that love exists. Most of the time I doubt it, but I think if there is a chance someone important can make you feel as good as you deserve to, you should go for it. What I am sure of is that love isn't meant for everyone. Once again, you might have to be lucky, but what you need before you can love, is a person that can make you the best version of yourself. Hell yes, love can hurt you like a bitch. It might actually break you apart but once you have experienced it, it will never fade away completely. I learnt that from observing the ones around me and obviously from reading books. But falling apart, feeling your heart ache to a point you want to scream and it heals again afterwards, falling in love with something or someone and crying happy and sad tears. These are the things that are here to remind us that we are alive. Your heart will break maybe eight times, or maybe more, throughout your life, but what's more important is, that it's heals nine times. And feeling the good stuff and the bad, is what makes us human. We all die anyway, so what about a little bit of fun? *Because in the end we all become stories.*

We enter a pub about fifteen minutes later and it's not that full, so that is something good. When we walk towards the back of the pub, we can clearly see our group of friends. They're quite hard to overhear, considering you hear their elephant laugh through the whole place. Funny enough, it's very similar to where I first met Ethan and the others. Perhaps that was the best day of my life. It is open as well, with brick walls and black tables and chairs. Along with very fancy hanging light they have a bunch of plants. Playing it green, I see. I'd stay here if I could. I really love plants, but I don't have any because they always die and, in all honesty, I have no idea what I do wrong. Probably everything.

We greet everyone and sit down. The thing that makes me smile is that they always point out my style. Well, I'm paying a little more intention to it for once.

"So, how are you guys doing?" I ask around. Everyone's here, Mary, Emma, Ben, Jacob and my manager. Oh, I haven't mentioned, he's called Ash and he is an angel. Literally. He's someone who will take away as much of the stress as he can to help you and he obviously did this, or I wouldn't have been able to handle all the things about my song.

They tell us what has happened and doing some small talk while eating pizza, drinking a beer and laughing about silly stuff.

"Liv, we really need to go out tomorrow. Have quick a talk, you know." Jacob proposes.

"We definitely need to!" That will be fun. When I feel Ethan getting more... nervous next to me, I turn around to see his eyes locked with Jacobs.

"Oh, mate c'mon. It is not like I would take away your girl."

"His girl? Excuse me?" I state frowning while laughing a bit.

"Oh, don't worry. We all know. It's not like he would ever shut up about you when you're not around." Oh crap.

I turn around to look at Ethan again and he rolls eyes in annoyance. "Are you talking about me?"

"J, stop talking bullshit." Nice, back to as if I'm not around.

"Nope, just telling the truth. You don't need to get so furious about it though. Hakuna Matata, remember? If you want to, you can also come along with the yoga stuff tomorrow before I come and collect her. Don't worry, I'll bring her back before she needs to put you to bed big boy." This is not going to end up well.

I should have become a fortune teller instead. The second the last words leaves Jacobs mouth, Ethan gets up rapidly and stumbles towards him. I grab him by the arm trying with all my power to hold him back. God damn, someone has been working out a fucking lot. Everyone's attention is back on us now and I'm not sure yet whether I should like it or not. I hold him back, but he seems like a wild animal right now.

"What about we all take a second to fucking calm down and take a breath?"

"How about I will make him shut up?" Ethan asks me when the others seem to pay attention to their food again, rather than on this kindergarten fight.

"I think the fuck not. He is your friend, why do you get pissed about us hanging out anyway?" I ask raising my eyebrows. When says nothing and stares at his lap it all becomes clear now.

"Ethan are you jealous?" I ask chuckling a bit.

His eyes shoot to me immediately. "Maybe?"

"Are you trying to convince yourself or me now?" God, this is hilarious.

"Look , I am trying to warn you. Jacob can be very… exhausting sometimes. I don't want you to have to deal with it."

The only response he gets me bursting out laughing. The big bad Ethan is jealous of his best friend. How fucking ironic is this?

"Look, nothing can happen that will make me run away screaming. And if do, I will call you, I promise."

He laughs and puts his arm behind the back of my chair. "Then you clearly don't know the real Jacob. Mostly when we partied, then he was the worst."

"Excuse me, but were you partying with him? That's a lot for my brain to comprehend and imagine."

"Yup. He was the 'yee' to my 'haw' when we were wasted. Like really fucking wasted," he states taking a sip from his drink while focusing on a random point in the room. I burst into a bunch of laughter and he is soon joining me. He doesn't joke a lot but when he does, it's too stupid not to laugh. I could get used to this. But I'm not sure what to expect for tomorrow.

Chapter Twenty-Three

Hello, nice to have you back here. Missed me already? The thing you missed was the whole evening, which consisted of Jacob picking on Ethan for being jealous. I'm honest now, I thought it was quite hilarious and I had to try really hard not to laugh. Mostly it worked, as I said mostly. By the time we went home again Ethan tried to act pissed. No wonder he became a singer. He's shit at acting which makes it, in my view, even funnier.

Now back to being more serious. (At least trying to) Ethan headed home to his place after we arrived, which is understandable. What I don't understand yet is why every time we do something together, we stay at my apartment. It is not that I don't like being here but if I should get on with this, whatever this is, I should know him better. The only thing I know is that his last name is Murphy and that he is a singer. Oh, and I have been to his place once. That was the time I became high next to his front door... whoopsie? All of that brings me to the plan for today. Jacob and I are going to do something and he said I should bring stuff to make me comfortable. The way I am, I don't understand what that means. So, I put the bag of joints into my bag. Not that he would smoke, I mean I don't know that but in case it could be fun.

I haven't spoken to Ethan, nor have I seen him but it's good in some way. When you spend a lot of time with someone, especially when you're a person who is rather on their own, it can be nice to have a break. Let me tell you something, socializing is quite exhausting. You must worry about who will be there, what they think, what to wear, how to act and the list goes on. Points to me are that Jacob isn't the most fashionable guy I know. He's kind of the opposite to Ethan but still so similar on the second look. Anyway, that is why I decide to wear a normal pair of mom jeans and a loose shirt on top of it. I also pack a sweater because it slowly, but still is noticeable autumn. I don't know how the others see this season, but I hate it. I really do, because somehow, it's the season everything dies. Besides that, I don't like it if everything looks orange and yellow and it rains even more than at my hometown. Those colours are just too bright for my eyes, so happy and too noticeable. All the things I am not. Oh, and I dislike pumpkin soup, any kind of cake, salad, meals – the point is if you have a pumpkin, you should stay the fuck away from me. They even smell disgusting, and it makes me want to throw up. And they are orange. Now let's we stop talking about them or I'll get nightmares for sure. Wouldn't be the first one.

No, we need to even it out. I said that pumpkins are most likely the most disgusting vegetables on this planet, but we need to adjust what the best ones are. Hands down, baby corn and peas. I mean, come on they are tiny and cute and they are delicious, you can eat them along with almost everything. Yes, I know that baby corn is yellow but that is something else. Details, remember? Enough of this talk for now.

Jacob texted me, saying he had yoga until three and I am okay with it because I need to clean my shit. It looks like a bomb has exploded here and I feel bad about it, I am honest. Life can be busy sometimes. Thinking about it now, I'm having a hard time imagining Jacob, the Jacob of the band, doing yoga possess. Nope, he would need to show me before I would believe it.

Taking my keys I unplug my phone, the second I hear a cars horn. Stepping out of the door I can clearly see him with a wide smile in his car. His car is red by the way. Jesus Christ, I don't know anything about any of the guys.

"Hello sunshine, what has made you so happy today?" I ask laughing while I climb into the car.

"It's a beautiful day. I have a beautiful person in my car, I had yoga class and you are here." Cheeky bugger.

"I like that mood. What are we gonna do today?"

"We, dear Liv, are going to have a talk," he whispers while driving somewhere I don't know. Yeah, no shit Sherlock Holmes.

"You are about as open as Ethan when it comes to things like that. Another thing you have in common," I tell him, and he is immediately gives me a strange side look chuckling.

He shakes his head and continues to drive. "You won't find many things that we have in common.", he's pleading. Why would he say that?

"Is that the hint that you want to talk about him?"

"Nope. Today is about you and me. Actually, I wanted to talk to you about some things."

"Did you say things? With an 's' as in plural?" I question him calmly but frowning. I'm not a good help, all the advice that I could give someone is what, I should consider myself. It's not that easy sometimes.

"Wow, you can have the ability to listen and sing? I'm impressed," he jokes, and we are laughing. "No, seriously now. I want to talk to you because I think you can understand me. I don't need advice, I need someone who listens and understands."

"Well, I can't promise you that I will understand your problem, but I do understand the feeling."

"See? I knew you were the right person to talk to," he adds smiling again. He is like a huge ball of sunshine, and I'm adoring it.

We keep driving talking about normal stuff for a while. In the end, he stopped the car at a parking lot next to a park. Since we drove to a different city, more likely a village, there weren't that many people, and I was very happy about that. Wouldn't be something new. By the time we stopped he still didn't want to tell me where we were going and he just said that I should take all my stuff, get out of the car and follow him.

We entered the park walking towards a bench under a cherry blossom tree. He stops and sits down, on it observing our surroundings. I sit next to him doing the same.

"It's beautiful," I tell him trying to adjust to all of this around me. It's like when we were at the coast. It seems normal but if you take a closer look, it's probably one of the most special places you have ever seen. That is about how it works with humans. You see them all over the streets and it seems… normal. However, every person has a different story, a different feeling, and a different past. *Everyone is special in their own way.*

"It is. I come here a lot, when I need time to think about something and I have never shown this place to anyone."

"I should feel lucky then," I joke smiling, but he has become more serious now. He is being vulnerable and he shows me a part of him that others don't know.

"It looks even more stunning when you close your eyes and focus on the sound. We see everything with our eyes, and it becomes natural in some way. We don't appreciate it anymore, at least not in the way we should. When you close your eyes and just feel your body and everything around you, you somehow realize that there is so much more to this world than just us." Everyone has their own story and demons they fight with inside when no one's there to notice it.

"I love that. Sometimes it helps me realize that we are too deep in our own matters so that we forget about the world and the people around us," I admit, and he looks at me, but I don't.

"How's your song writing going?" he asks avoiding my further questions. It's okay, sometimes I would be glad if people didn't push me that much.

"I've stopped." The second I tell him that, his head immediately shoots in my direction and he wants to say something, but I am faster. "I still make music I just can't write music. I found a journal of my mom, who is dead, and she was a writer in any way you could think of. I found out this is a good way of coping with my feeling, letting it out and still feeling closer to her than ever. The sheets seem to be a pretty good listener to me when I get the feeling that ... when I somehow don't feel human anymore." At the moment I'm just too scared to sit down and write, because the honesty of writing is killing me.

Writing came closer again in the last few days, but I did it when no one noticed. However, he is the only one who knows. It's nothing special but it is something I do for myself. If I feel as if all the emotions will make me explode, I write them down. I can't talk about what I sense because it even scares me. I heard someone saying once that you should write what you're most scared about. And I'm doing that.

After a few seconds he says in a soft, calming, and comforting voice, *"Feeling human and being human are two completely different things."*

"Thank you but we are here to talk about you, not me." I don't need someone to tell me how fucking broken I am. I am aware of that fact.

"We're all broken in some way. I won't ask you any further if that's not what you want but I do want you to know that you shouldn't compare your pain to others' pain. You don't need to just look out for everyone else and let yourself down that much. In the end it is your life and you're the most important person in it. It's okay to be selfish," he tells me, and it warms my heart. He's like the tough guy who will cheer anyone up but this side of him, the soft one, has literally warmed my heart.

"Two to zero for me. That was another thing you have in common with Ethan," I add laughing a little bit.

He covers his face in his hands shaking it. "Please tell me that you will not continue to do that."

"I apologize, but lying isn't nice."

"Oh no. I will just pretend that I haven't heard any of that in case he asks," he adds.

"Do what you want. Now it is time to talk. Why have you brought me here?"

"I ... uhm... I know this probably might not be a big thing but... I'm feeling so... so numb at the moment. I see all the guys like Ben and Emma, and you and Ethan and I just wish not to be so alone. And when I see all of you this happy, I just want to stay at home so that it doesn't affect me. I just don't know why but there are days...," he begins but stops. I think he just doesn't know what to call them, but I do.

"Significant and initial bad days?" I ask him, and he nods.

"You don't affect our mood or destroy the vibes. You increase mine every single time. It's hard... it is hard sometimes especially if you feel as if you must keep up with the emotions of people around you. The thing I can tell you is that if they are your friends, they will help you no matter what you feel and you don't need to hide away. I hope you know that this is no point for me because I have these days as well and I'll always just hide away. Ethan likes you more than he would admit. You're important to him and I can see it.

"Have you spoken to Emma and Ben?"

"No they will be gone soon, so there is no point in speaking to them," he whispers just loud enough for me to hear. He is thinking out loud, and I have never seen him do that in all these weeks. Not that I would be better.

"Leaving the team and the band? Why would they do that?" I ask furrowing my brows. They belong and they are all friends… friends don't just leave.

"Yup. They wanted to do some… things which they knew they couldn't. Ethan had to basically kick them off and he didn't like it. We all have known each other for quite some time. He didn't want to, but he knew he had to."

If that's what he had to do. Why didn't he tell me?

"I mean, what did they even do? Why wouldn't he tell me to begin with?" One step forward, two steps backwards.

"It's not my position to answer you about these questions, Liv. I can just tell you that there were a few rules, but these ones were important. Ethan is not a control freak, he trusted them. He trusts us and they wanted to misuse that trust for something they believed was right."

"But if they wanted to do it for something good, why did he punish them in that way?" I ask.

"Because it wouldn't have ended up nice for all of us."

Chapter Twenty-Four

"What do you mean by that?" I keep asking. My head feels heavy from all the little pieces of information I'm getting. Not that I'm getting a lot, but when I do, they seem to overrun my brain.

"You cannot trust anyone blindly. People will make you trust them and then they will use you, that is how it works. What I am saying is that they wanted to let something out that Ethan didn't, and he told us about a thousand times." We're still sitting in the park that seems like a sweet melody and a distraction in the river. It is bold and beautiful.

"They wanted to release a song from him?" I murmur.

"Yes, but let's not talk about this anymore. If he wants to tell you he surely will," he states. But what if he doesn't? It's not that I know many things about him.

A sudden reminder comes into my head making me want to jump up. I nearly would have forgotten. "I have a surprise for you. I can't promise it will make our problems go away but it will distract them." I take my bag trying to find it while he looks at me confused as ever. I know that when I arrive home, that I will get this feeling again, the one which doesn't seem to leave me. I hate it. "I hope you do smoke because it would be a shame if you just had to watch," I say, and a smirk comes immediately to his lips.

"Oh, you have no idea darling," he whispers, and his eyes shine full of happiness when I take the bag of joints out of my handbag. "Where did you g…"

"Abby."

"No fucking way. Are you serious?" he asks smiling while take one out shaking my head along with it.

"Deadly. I've been keeping those for about a year now and I've only smoked two of them. I've waited for my smoking buddy," I confess.

"One at Ethan's place where we met Abby and the other one… when did you smoke the other one?"

"There's this one significant bad day that comes every year on the same date and last year… last year it was even more horrible, so I took one, sneaked out of my room, drove away and smoked a joint while playing guitar on a field. It was dark and I could see the stars, it was absolutely amazing."

"Then let us make a new smoking memory," he says, not asking any further.

We lit it and just enjoyed each other's company. *We're like two lonely and broken souls who are lonely and broken together in some way.* It doesn't take long until I start to feel a reaction in my body. No wonder considering how rarely I smoke. My lung feels as if it is burning inside my body, but it feels good. It's a good distraction. By time it becomes harder to concentrate on more serious topics and we're just talking about random stuff like what's the best vegetable. Yes, I know. What I don't know is why he thinks that fucking cucumbers are better than baby corn and peas combined. They are nothing special and the inside of it is just… weird to look at and eat. It feels sort of squishy but it's not. It just feels like that. Many things work like that.

You treat something with much more attention than it deserves instead of waiting for something that deserves this kind of attention. Most people make a thunderstorm out of a cloud. I won't lie, I'm one of those people. I gave it the attention because my sky was cloudy most of the time. The point was always that whenever I thought it became sunnier it didn't take much longer until it eventually started to rain. You think something gets better until it gets worse again. Apparently, that is how life works, don't ask me why. I didn't make the rules. I'm just trying to live with them like all of us. Just because we all live by this, doesn't mean we should be like it though.

"So, you like Ethan?" he asks me with a devilish smile after some time. We have been sitting there for about three hours talking, smoking, and watching the sun set slowly, utterly beautiful and still noticeable.

I laugh at him before replying, "I thought we weren't gonna talk about me or Ethan?"

"Yeah, we said that, but I am high now. We have never spoken about that." he replies. Fair point Jacob, fair point. "So…?"

"I… uhm… yes I like him. He's a good friend," I say and he bursts out in an ugly laugh. Why was that even funny?

"Are you kidding me? I know him better than he knows himself and I'm telling you that he likes you more than a friend, that he does. Did you guys… ya know?" Oh no, we are going down that road. Lord, help me now.

"Do you mean kiss?" I ask as the idiot I am, and he smirks while shaking his head. "Oh. We… uhm why is that even important?"

"Oh Liv, c'mon just answer it I won't tell anyone," he presses me again.

"Okay, chill Jacob. Cheez." I sigh before I keep on talking, giving him the answer, that he was waiting for. "Yup."

"Holy shit, you did? I cannot believe this."

"Is that a bad thing?" I question again. Why would he... is there an issue I missed out?

"Nope, those are good news. I'm just shocked in some way because it was some time ago, he liked someone that much. In fact, I don't think he has ever looked at someone the way he looks at you. I highly doubt that he was... intimate with someone as well for the past weeks..."

"He wouldn't be the only one," I speak up regretting it immediately. Fuck, too much information Olivia. Quick reminder to myself: don't smoke that much with someone because it makes you talkative. Way too much. "I'll take that back."

"You can't just take something back you've just said, you dumbass," he laughs.

Yeah, no shit Sherlock. I stare at the park in front of us, trying to avoid any questions of this... area. I suppose that was the moment it hit him right in the face.

"Oh, no. You were a virgin before him?"

I turn around immediately and see him stuck between a smile and concern on his face. "Good God, no I wasn't. Seriously, can we please stop talking about it, this is embarrassing," I beg him, while he finds it quite amusing. To my uncomfortableness.

"Your cheeks are glowing, I can see that even though it is dark darling," he adds.

"Of course. You're putting me on the spot!" I tell him in a joyful angriness.

"Maybe that will be my favourite thing to do."

"Watch it, if you're choosing to put me on the spot in front of the crew, I will commit murder," I dare him, and he isn't quite taking me as serious as I wish he would.

"We'll see about that Olivia," he says fighting back, knowing that I hate to hear it. Except when Ethan does… I punch him on the arm, and he starts to laugh throwing his head back even more. It's gone that far that he is even holding his stomach with his hands. "I can't breathe," he spits out while laughing.

"Karma's a bitch Jacob," I say before I hear a phone ringing and for once it is not mine. Normally I try to avoid any conversations but most likely the ones on the phone. If someone comes up to me, I at least know who it is or what they want. But not when someone calls, and it is excruciating.

He's looking at the name that has popped up on his phone and sighs. "Speaking of the devil," he tells me before taking the call. "Yes Ethan, it is nice to hear from you as well. Nope… I mean yes, yes, we're all right. Of course she is, I've been watching diamond very well," he jokes while holding the phone further away from his ear. Through his surprised face and the smile, I think Ethan might be screaming at him right now. "Jeez calm down. Yup, I'll take her home. Ethan, just chill out I will tell her. God, damn you need more than just yoga." He hangs up after saying something like 'Yeah, whatever' and looks at me while rolling his eyes.

"Seemed like a nice conversation you two had," I say sarcastically, and he chuckles at my words. I learnt that from Abby, and I am proud of it. Not going to lie.

"He basically yelled into my ear where we were and if you were all right fifty times. We should go home now. He also told me that he would wait there for you."

I'm frowning askin,: "Why?"

"No clue but that is not my problem. I suspect that he will kill me if we continue to do these hangouts and you come home high every time," he says standing up and packing his stuff. Oh don't worry Jacob.

I still have enough joints in that bag. "You know what? He can go nuts, I don't care."

His jokes are simple but very funny and I can't tell why. They just are. No arguments. That is a new rule now.

We climb into the car singing along with the radio while driving all the way back. The drive seems much shorter now and when we drive into the outside of London, I find myself being sad about it. This was something I wouldn't want to stop. He stops in front of my place and I say my goodbye to him. We have also arranged to do it again very soon.

I climb out of the car taking my phone out while walking towards my front door. While doing so I find myself smiling at it more than I expected. Abby has texted me. I know, I know, we had been talking not so long ago but every single time I receive a message from her it just makes my day better in general.

I keep on walking towards my door but I stop when I see a tall frame in front of me. He came here.

"Hi," he says pulling me closer for a hug and a kiss on my forehead while I try to understand. I like this... softness, I really do, but I'm just not used to it.

"What are you doing here?" I ask him while taking the key out of my pocket to open the door. As I said, it's getting colder nowadays, and I have no intention in catching a cold. It might have a slight effect on my ability for feeling temperatures that I spent most of my life in Australia. It does get colder there but just not as cold as it does over here. Most importantly, I doesn't rain like someone is constantly crying in the sky.

"Oh, I don't know… I just wanted to stop by and see you. Haven't seen you today," he says while I give him the awkward smile I'm quite used to by now. It's not that someone would willingly spend a lot of their free time with me normally.

Stepping inside I toss my shoes into the corner. He takes his off like… well, like a normal person would. I neither said nor claimed that I'm normal. Oh, what does normal even mean? I doubt that there is normal in the world we live in, but it took me some time to realize that because I was *half the world away in my head*.

"And besides, is there something wrong in wanting to see your girlfriend?" he speaks from behind me, causing me to stop.

Did I just hear him right or am I losing my ability to hear as well now?

Chapter Twenty-Five

Nope, I suppose I did not get that one wrong.

I turn around to face him again, still confused as hell. "What did you just say?" I ask him to say it again. Maybe I'll get used to it more.

Here's the thing. I really like him, in a romantic way but I'm just not sure if I'm already in love with him just yet. In my life I've only had one relationship… let's just say it didn't end very nicely or fortunately for the two of us but most likely for me. Even then I struggled to stay in a relationship with someone like that. For someone who doesn't really believe that much in true love or soulmates it's actually a challenge to do so. I'm not saying I wouldn't want to be in love with Ethan, he's different, but what I'm saying is that up until fifteen seconds ago I never would have believed that he wanted to be in a relationship with me. God, in his view we are, but he has never asked me, and I don't know if it's that 'natural' for him because it is not for me. I can tell that.

The reason I'm scared to do this step, even if it's something small for others, is that I am scared. I'm scared that he will eventually see me as I see myself. And if that happens, he will run as fast as he can.

I know it sounds crazy, stupid, or even pathetic but in the world that we live in, it is so hard to find your place and yourself. It's becoming harder for people who have suffered from things in the past because they often see what they haven't achieved. As why they have suffered and why they are 'weak'. What should happen instead is being proud when you look back and able to says, 'I did that and I did it myself.' Of course, you can reach out for help, which is a good thing to be sure, but in the end the change that has to happen in order for someone to get better comes from that person. Others can't take that pain away from someone even though they sometimes would. In the end, when the sun goes down, we all get lonely in some way. Some are lonely because of their pain that no one knows about and some try to cope with it in other ways.

"I… uh… unless you don't want that. I've just thought that after what's happened between us that it would be clear… ya know. I'm just not good at all in this relationship stuff, I'm sorry that was stupid of me." Oh Ethan, you're not the only one. After my having said this he turns around in embarrassment. I move towards him making him turn around and I hold his face in my hands. Dang this man is huuuuge.

"Hey. Look at me," I say gently, not wanting to get more emotional that what I already am.

"No, it's okay I get it. I shouldn't…," he begins but I cut him off again.

"Ethan. Look at me," I say, and he finally looks into my eyes. His are swollen and tired looking as if he has just humiliated himself a great deal. "You didn't do anything wrong. For others this would be normal but I'm different. We're different. I'm not saying that I don't want to be your girlfriend, I'm saying that I am not sure if that is the right thing."

"Why wouldn't it be? I like you, a hell of a lot actually and I think you do like me as well," he responds. How do you tell your may-be-boyfriend that you're scared that he will see the truth about how broken you are? Has anyone ever written a book on that, because it would be very helpful.

"I like you a crazy lot believe me, I just… it's not important. I just don't work well with all the relationship stuff as well. Not anymore." I admit, regretting the last sentence immediately.

"Why?" he asks and I stay silent, trying to avoid eye contact with him. He has that thing in his eyes that you somehow cannot lie to and it drives me insane most of the time. "Olivia, look at me now. Please. You know you can tell me everything, right?" he continues holding my face now.

"I... the only relationship I had didn't really end well. I started to fall in love with him more than I ever loved anyone. He made me feel... pretty and I trusted him. *In the end, we were always a losing game. We were never gonna make it.* Some part of me always knew, I was just too dumb to admit it and it was my fault. *We both valued honesty and loyalty, but neither in the same order nor in the same way.*" As I confess this, I hadn't told anyone besides Abby in my entire life, a few tears find their way down my cheek and drop onto the wooden floor. She knows what happened, but she doesn't know how or why. I wasn't ready to tell her back then and I don't know if I ever will be. Besides, she might search for him to do what she's calling 'payback'.

"He misused your trust, didn't he?" he started to build the pieces together and I can only nod. "He cheated on you." Roman was never one to be very open, so I had to find out myself before he blamed it on me. I tried for so long to hate him, but I couldn't. I hated myself for trusting him so blindly after everything that had already happened in my life. I gave him all I could, and still, it wasn't enough for him to stay.

"Yes. It was my fault, I shouldn't have done a few things and I shouldn't...," I try to blurt out but he stops me again.

"Woah, woah, woah. I will not stand here and listen to you putting the blame on yourself. It was his fault and he put it all on you. He made you think it was your fault, so he didn't have to feel guilty. That is what people do, but it's over. He's not here but I am. You are. I hope you do know that I will never do that to you, *I never could.*" he clarifies making me frown.

I manage to say, "What do you mean?" between crying and trying to breath normally.

"I've my eyes on you, and I don't intend to ever look away."

I reach for him kissing him. "I hope you know that a part of me would want to be your girlfriend, but I just need more time."

"Take all the time you need. I'm here and I won't go for now if that's what you want from me," he reassures me and I nod. We head for my bedroom getting rid of our clothes and we lay beside each other without barely speaking a word. And again, it's not an awkward silence, because we appreciate that the other person is here. That's all I've needed for so long. I lie there, staring at the ceiling wrapped in the sheets thinking about all of this. The question isn't if I want to, because I do, it's rather about if I'm able to.

"Olivia?" he mumbles next to me.

"Ethan?"

"I am sorry."

"For what?" I ask him quietly while keeping me eyes on the white ceiling.

"That you got hurt that much and because you don't believe you actually deserve something good. I am not a good person and I know it, but I know that you make me a better one than I have ever been before." He pleads and I turn my head to look at him. His messy hair is mostly in his face, but he looks so confused. I move my body closer to him, and snuggling up against him I put my head on his chest. He takes hold of my back with one of his hands while brushing his fingers through my hair with the other one. I think he makes me a better person too. Not for everyone around me, but for myself.

It sucks. It sucks because I never really had anyone that understood me while growing up. So, whenever someone shows me the slightest bit of attention and I become attached it mostly ends with my getting hurt. Sometimes I'm just too tired to share thoughts. I look at him for a while trying to process my thoughts. His features are so much softer and more peaceful when he's asleep. In a way I can't really express in words. His facial expression makes it even more real. The way he thinks, the way he speaks and the way he makes me feel. He knows what he wants and what is best. However, he will mostly choose to be kind instead of doing what is right. He treats others the way he wishes to be treated. Well, apart from his friendship with Jacob but that is something else.

We fall asleep next to each other and when I wake up, one of my legs is between his. He holds me tight, as if he never wants to let me go. Watching him as he sleeps might get to be the new favorite thing to do for me. I look at the clock next to my small nightstand. It's only eight in the morning but I doubt that I'll be able to fall asleep again. I never do, once I wake up whether it's from a nightmare or something else, I can't fall back to sleep. Up until a few weeks ago I would've used this time to write or play the guitar but now, I use it to clean or write. I love music so goddamn much I just don't know how to bring my words into melodies, in an honest vulnerability anymore. Maybe taking a break will help.

So, I carefully free my leg and then the rest of my body while Ethan turns in his sleep. I get up and take a long shower. I use the time to think as I sit down in the shower while the water keeps running down my body and the glass becomes foggy. I can't even process what my thoughts are about, they're just so quick, confusing, and hurtful. Sometimes it feels as if the most hurtful words are made up in my own head, the different person inside me that I've spoken about.

After what feels like hours, which was only ten minutes, I get out of the shower wrapping myself in a towel, not wanting to get clean clothes out of the closet as I didn't want to disturb Ethan who was fast asleep. Yesterday he looked as if he needed a good sleep. I make my way towards the kitchen pouring myself a cup of tea while opening the blinds. The weather is getting pretty ugly nowadays, but somehow it reflects my feelings quite well. Not always, but most of the time. Grey and rainy.

Grabbing my mug, I take my little journal and the green one of my moms and I take a seat on the couch. I start to write everything down, as I have the last weeks shutting everything around me off. Now there's only me and the empty page that wants to know how I'm feeling and it is an amazing feeling. Every feeling of time disappears along with the acknowledgment of your surroundings.

No perspective.

* * *

He turns in the bed, looking for the one person he fell asleep next to but quickly finds that she is not there anymore. He sits up wiping the sleep out of his eyes his hair messy. He wanted to cut it a while ago, before he met her. But then, he knew that this was another thing she admired about him and he wanted it to stay just like that. Before he met her many things were different. He wanted everything to stay like it was, to stop time and simply enjoy it as long as he could. Just for a little longer. He kicks the sheets away with his feet and goes into the bathroom, looking for her. After not finding her there he throws some water on his face, and makes his way towards the more open rooms of her apartment. He likes the way she decorated it, even though she barely did. In fact, everything she did was one more thing he admired about her. The way she dressed, the way she did her hair, the way she walked and mostly the way she walked through this world. She didn't realize how much she meant to so many people, to him. He enters the kitchen, seeing the rest of the tea she had poured in a tea pot. Opening a cupboard, he takes out a grey mug and pours some tea into it. Even though she wasn't British, her tea was acceptable, but he wanted to teach her how to make it better. He wanted to teach her so many things; how to adore herself the way he did, how to play the drums a bit and how to drive on the other side of the road. *He wanted to teach her how to love.*

He stepped closer to the living room and saw her on the grey couch she liked so much. She was so stubborn, but it reminded him of someone. She was a lot more like he was, before everything started. It took him some time to see it but after all, he does now, and it seems so clear. He stepped closer to her, realizing that she was so lost in her thoughts, that she didn't see him coming. He took a deep breath and sighed, in a good way. "You've been doing that a lot lately. Why do you love writing so much?"

She turned her head thoughtfully towards him. "Because it allows me to escape my own reality. When I'm writing something, I can feel. And when I'm reading her book, I can take myself away from this cruel world and pretend that I'm someone I'm not. I can pretend she's still here." A smile rose to his lips as she continued to focus.

He admired the way she spoke, how she processed her thoughts. He loved that about her. No other words were spoken as he sat down to watch her. No other words were spoken because there was nothing more to be said. But in that moment, he knew it. He knew he loved her.

Chapter Twenty-Six

Heroes and villains. Such a common and still complex expression. What makes you a hero and what makes you a villain?

In our society, the opinions on this are going in one direction and one direction only. In our society, heroes are symbolized as selfless. Perfect creations destined to save and protect others. But that is wrong. Heroes are selfish, they want the fame and the glory, and they will do everything to get it. They will do everything to be seen as heroes.
Villains. The evil and cruel, the dirty and bad. But villains, they are the true heroes here because villains are the most capable of love and have the most compassion. Though they tear down cities, bring kingdoms to their knees, they would drop everything just for one person decent enough to show them love. They are the true heroes because they show us what love is about. They show us what is the most important in life.

That was the first poem I had read and up until this day my favourite one. It has so much truth in it while still being confusing at first sight.

Pumpkins. A fucking orange field full of fucking pumpkins. They convinced me to go to a freaking pumpkin exhibition. Well, convincing is not true because they didn't even bother to ask me if I wanted to come here. They just told me to bring my camera and here I freaking am now.

It started like a normal and harmless day. After Ethan had sat down next to me and observed me the whole time I was writing, which was a bit creepy, Jacob called him in for a plan, which to quote him, would be a hell lot of fun. Little did they know they had brought me to the biggest field of the worst vegetables I know. Yup, that happens if you drag someone with you and decide not to tell them where you're going. Not my fault.

Besides that, Mary and Jacob are trying to find us all 'the perfect pumpkins' while Ethan is feeling bad for bringing me here. Emma and Ben aren't here, and I haven't seen them since the last time and to be honest, I don't think I'll ever see them again, according to what happened. I couldn't even contact them to begin with, I only have the phone numbers of the other guys. However, I would like to know what's happened. I know it's not my place to push Ethan and I won't. If he feels like he wants to tell me something, I'm sure he will. He will tell me, right?

Oh, about that... I kind of tried not to listen to my song a lot or talking to my manager. He said a few times that it was going well, but honestly, I don't care. Right now, at the moment, I don't think I want to release new music. Besides the fact that I can't even write new songs. I am just not sure whether it will make me happy or not. I told everyone before that this was a one-time thing. I can tell that they don't think what I'm doing is right, but they know I need time to think about it. That's a good thing, isn't it?

We also haven't had a studio session in quite some time. We recorded everything Ethan needed for his album, so my feeling is that they have some problems with producing the album. I would help but I am uncapable when it comes to anything involving every kind of technical ability. In this aspect I am fucking useless.

"That is a nice one!" Jacob screams at us from a distance waving to us to come over.

"What's even the point of pumpkins?" I ask Ethan as we walk towards them hand in hand. I can clearly see that people around us are taking pictures of it but for once I don't mind. Because I am very occupied with a pumpkin-talk

"You can make funny faces out of them. For decoration, or you can eat them of course." he tells me chuckling while I shake my head. Why would anyone do that? I am not one for holiday traditions and I know it. Ever since my mom went away, my dad and I stopped doing decorations or anything like that. On every holiday occasion it would just be us with a takeout, not much talking and it mostly ended with him drinking. My mother loved to decorate and bake everything you could think of. Especially for Christmas, whenever I came home from school the whole house was tainted by the smell of Christmas and any music of that kind. I still miss every single thing she cooked and how she danced while cooking and baking or even cleaning. She always had her phone with headphones in her pocket and she danced as if nobody was watching her. She wouldn't have cared if the whole world was watching.

"Since thanksgiving is getting closer, I wanted to ask you something.", he begins shyly.

"And I probably having an answer for you." I joke making him feel less awkward.

"Are you spending thanksgiving with your family? Because in case you aren't, I wanted to ask you if you, you know wanted to stay with the guys. I know it's weird and early but I'm just thinking about…"

"Ethan Murphy, don't get all shy on me now. You don't have to be nervous to ask anything." I reassure him taking a breath.

"So, you're not going home then?" he asks squeezing my hand. Home, I don't even know where that is. I'd like to know, but I can't think of a place that makes me feel at home. And I want to tell him why I don't feel at home anymore with my family, but I can't. Sometimes you want to let something out, to tell someone something so badly. But as good as it might feel to let it out, at one point you will always regret it. *Sometimes I feel as if my pain is not worth mentioning when it is so constant.*

"Uh… nope. I don't know where I would go or if the people would want me." I admit which is the closest thing to being honest I can be right now.

"I hope you know that I feel closest to home with you. I don't spend holidays with my people either. It's just Jacob, Mary, and me this year. Their families live too far away so they stay here." I assume that in the past years it would've also been Emma and Ben. It hurts him, I can tell that.

"I'd like to spend my holidays with you. I really do," I reply, and he is smiling so brightly as we reach the others.

"And…?" Mary asks raising an eyebrow.

"She said yes." Ethan tells them, and they cheer.

"You fucking owe me twenty dollars, you dumbass!" Mary screams at Jacob.

"Wait, you knew? You've planned this all along, haven't you?"

"Absolutely, we have even made a bet. Jacob here said that Ethan wouldn't have enough courage. I, on the other hand knew that he would do it." These little sneaky brats…

"At least we can all have a dance party then," I say giving Mary a high-five.

"No!" Ethan and Jacob say at the exact same time and I smirk, looking at Jacob. He knows exactly what I mean.

"That is a fucking point for me. Three to zero Jacob."

"What is she talking about," Ethan asks confused, while I hold up my camera to take a picture of this iconic moment.

"Oh, nothing important. You'll find out soon enough." I provoke him and his mouth drops.

"Where's that attitude from? C'mon, you can't just not tell me what that's about." Like a little child.

"Ya know, I think it's called payback. You didn't tell me we would go to a field of the world's worst vegetables. Consider this as payback." I reply smirking. Payback's a bitch. "Now, can we please all go? It is cold and I will throw up if I see any more orange today." I beg them and ignore the glance Ethan is currently giving me. Of course, the others think it's hilarious, so do I, but I think I will pay for that as well. *Just play it cool Olivia.*

We walk back to the car. Mary and Jacob are walking a bit ahead of us. Ethan takes hold of my arm leaning closer to my ear.

"So, you think that is funny?" he whispers smirking. *See, I told ya.*

"It's called humour Ethan. Humour is supposed to be funny."

"We'll see about that when we get home."

My eyes widen but before I'm able to respond, we reach the car. He holds the car door open with a smirk, making space for me to get in.

"Hey guys, what's the plan for thanksgiving?" I throw around while Jacob is sitting in the front with Mary. From what I heard, they're also close friends and I am glad they get along as well. It would be awkward if they didn't.

"Since thanksgiving is in three days, the day after tomorrow would make preparation day. I'm hoping you can cook Liv, because these two are shit at it and I need help." Mary answered smiling at me while Ethan rolled his eyes.

"That is not true," he states with his accent clearer than ever.

"Stop lying dipshit." Mary scoffed making him turn his head to me again.

"Do you want to spend tomorrow with me?" That is not a good idea... tomorrow is the day I told Jacob about. The initial sad day. Tomorrow's the day my mom died eight years ago, which also brings me closer to my birthday in the middle of November. Honestly, every year I just cut myself off. My master plan is to sleep as long, as I can to avoid the day. No people, no music for once, just me, tissues, pizza, and the film that Ethan hates so much. I always buy her favorite flowers as well, roses, and eat her favorite food to her favorite film. It makes me feel closer to her. I don't think I'm close to ready to spend this day in a happy way. It's kind of ironic, you think if someone dies that you will get over it in a few months or maybe a year or two. Well, hello there. I'm here, almost eight years later and I'm still not even close to being healed. Back in Australia, I stopped visiting her grave because it didn't feel like her. It's not the funny and loving person I remember. It's just a stone surrounded by dying flowers all over and I hate it. I hate graveyards, graves and everything that goes with it. Most importantly, I hate death.

"Oh... tomorrow...?" I ask like an idiot because I don't know how to turn him down without hurting him. *Come on Olivia Jones, use your language. Words just freaking words.* He just nods raising an eyebrow, not understanding my behaviour. I don't as well, don't worry Ethan. "Tomorrow is not a good day. I'm actually busy. I'd love to spend the day with you but I can't. I'm sorry." Liar.

"That's okay. We've been together a lot lately and I get it. You need some time alone for your things. Just call me if you need something, promise?" *Thank god.*

180

"I will." I tell him, knowing full well that I won't. He can't see me that way on this day. Not even Abby has, she knows about it but that's all.

We don't talk about much more, at least I don't because at the beginning of their conversation I started to zone out, concentrating on the rain drops which are running down the window. With time I can feel how my eyes are starting to get heavier and how I'm struggling to stay awake.

When we reach my place, I tell Ethan to stay in bed because I know for sure he is tired as well. He somehow understands my expression and that I rather want to be alone. I say goodbye and let myself into my apartment as I always do. Opening the door, I take off my shoes and walking into my bedroom, I get rid of my clothing. Putting on my sleeping T-shirt and my pants I go into the bathroom. *Always the same everyday Olivia. It's just a normal day as tomorrow will be. Always the same, nothing to be afraid of.*

After finishing up in the bathroom, I go to the kitchen and pour myself a bit of alcohol. Yes, I am tired but if I'm going to sleep this early, I won't sleep long enough tomorrow. I sit on the floor with my back resting against the wall and I stare at one of my favorite pictures I took of her back then. I wasn't very good but still, she adored it because it made me happy.

"It'll be okay. It has to be," I whisper all to myself trying to focus on something. It's going to be an interesting day.

Chapter Twenty-Seven

Dreams. Something amazing that our minds make up while our bodies try to rest. It's a way of escaping the world when it feels too heavy for us. And still, our minds can be equally heavy.

Our minds can keep us locked in the worst nightmares for hours and even days. Dreams that don't go away and you start to start to fear the one thing that made your soul rest.

When someone would to ask me how I was, my answer always was 'I'm okay, I'm just tired.' And that's the thing, you cannot sleep when the worst things are after you. You can't escape these nightmares because you're trapped in them. When you wake up, you feel like your worlds have collided. A weight falls off your shoulders because this one is finally over and still your chest tightens because you know it will come back. You won't be able to fall asleep again without being scared, and eventually, your soul becomes more exhausted. Dreams show you all the things you're scared of without being aware of it. And most importantly, they hide their true meaning behind the things you know. People who have left you, hurt you, moments you wished you could just forget.

All the time I try so hard to get better. I often find myself trying to find things to do so my brain doesn't have time to speak. Just holding it back, holding it back and holding it back all the time. I try and I try again, but it never seems to work. It looks to me as if I am stuck this way forever and there is no way out.

The reason I don't talk about her as much as I probably should is because I wouldn't know what to say. There are no words that could describe how I feel or how the panic in my body feels every time someone mentions as much as her name. People don't understand how hard it is to ask for help or to tell someone. How they actually feel. To be honest why should I tell people, it will make me feel like a burden and it will make me uncomfortable every time I tried. Ninety nine percent of them tell me when I open up. 'Oh, it's okay. It will get better.' You don't know how many goddamn times I heard that. I learned not to go to anyone because I don't want nor do I need their pity. So, I always keep it to myself until the day I finally break. Today might be the day, at least that's what it feels like to me right now.

It's now a bit after noon. I fell asleep about two hours ago. Yes, I had the nightmare I always have. She came back, all happy tears and the best thing I could want and then, she left. I woke up in a mess and in tears but I'm more used to it by now. It's the day I'm most afraid of every single year because I relive every single thing I felt back then. It's like it will never stop hurting.

I spend the time listening to my sad playlist, cleaning, and wiping away all the tears I bottled up for this year. It's a shame, really. I haven't checked my phone, though I am pretty sure Abby and Ethan have texted me. She always does on this day. I think she probably will call but we both know that I won't take the call. Once in a year, I won't take anyone's call. Because once a year I am fine with being lonely. Now my plan is to get the roses and the pizza. I put my trainers on and big baggy trousers with an oversized flannel shirt. I put my hair into a bun because I haven't showered. On this day I always look like the mess I am inside, it's just more visible than on other occasions.

I put a jacket on, taking a purse, and leaving my phone behind, I take the tube. I observe all the people around me and I try to focus on something else, anything in fact, that doesn't remind me of her. In fact, I had two genius ideas this morning on how to occupy myself. Number one; get a tattoo. I know it sounds crazy, but I always wanted to get one and I thought about this three hundred times. I will do it today. My idea was to get a human heart in which flowers come out of the blood thing (that is the particular reason I didn't became a doctor as my family wanted me to. I just don't get it.) and a phrase underneath that goes like this: *one life for the two of us.* The tattoo will go on my ribs, a bit beneath my heart. Makes sense, right? Plan number two is to get a car somewhere and somehow. I've lived here for a bit of time now and I think it's time for me to get independent from the tube and any uber drivers. Number three is to finally read her journal. I'm not even halfway yet and I really have the strong urge to continue, especially because of today's... well... day...?

Stepping out of the tube I make my way to the grocery store. I am already looking where I can find a serious tattoo studio not too far away from home. Maybe I should wait with the car idea until this day is over and I'm being more... sane? I don't know how to explain, but on this day, I always feel far from being sane or fine. Everything is far from good and normal. I am trying to occupy and distract myself?

Anyway, I put everything that I will need into a shopping trolley. While doing so, I can clearly sense that something makes me feel uneasy. Maybe it's the mass of people or their looks. Maybe it's the day but probably it's all of these three tings combined. More often than not I feel so much at one time, that I start to feel nothing at all. After grabbing my groceries I make my way out of the store as fast as I can. I like to escape terrifying situations like this or certain conversation and I know it. I'm running away from my problems, I always have been. The reason why I do this is because I don't have to be confronted by them again and again. *Running away doesn't solve anything but it makes things seem easier.*

While I'm on my way to the tattoo parlour I realize that I don't have my phone with me... my plan was to Google the place because Google fucking knows everything you could possibly imagine. That is a fact and I won't debate it. It's just the truth, end of conversation. But because I am not Google, I have no clue where the shop is. *Should've considered that earlier, Olivia.* Come on it's a bit ironic, how my mind will immediately consider everything that could go wrong but what it can't consider is important stuff. Fucked up, I'm aware. That plan will need to be delayed. Remember how I said that nothing in my life follows along as planned? That is exactly what I meant and I am to blame again. Not to be dramatic but that wouldn't be anything new.

Instead of going to the tattoo parlour, I will need to go home instead and distract myself with food and movies... after getting my phone to use Google... what a great plan. Stepping into the tube, I wish that I had my phone with me. I have this playlist on it for when I can feel my anxiety rising and sometimes it can be a life saver. It actually has prevented another attack for quite some time. It would help now because the tube is filled with people. I don't mind watching crowds of people but being in one is a different story. Watching chaos is never as bad, as being in one yourself.

When the tube doors open, I rush out through the station until I breathe the fresh air again. And then it hits me. The way it hits me every single year and it feels as if it is a whole new different level of pain every time. She is dead and she will never come back again. I will never see her face again, I will never be able to touch her again, I will never hear her laugh again and neither will I ever be able to hear her voice again. Losing someone sucks but the moment you forgot their voice it is the moment you finally get it. I've actually had people telling me. 'Yes, your mother is dead, life goes on. Just get over it.'

For years I have tried to convince myself that she might come back. A foolish and still desperate wish, made by a naïve teenager that would never ever come true. All over again, I feel my heart aching and my throat being cut. Holding the grocery bags in my hands I rush towards my apartment, hoping that no one sees me or takes a picture of me in this… state of mind, when I am losing my mind.

I know I haven't complained about the taking pictures thing. I chose to go in this direction with people around me who are famous so I kind of knew this would happen. Still, I hate the thought of being watched all the time, it's not really helping my anxiety. Knowing people can look up to you isn't the problem. What is the problem is, is people waiting for you to make the smallest mistake that is my issue. Being watched and judged by every movement. It's difficult to compare, but that is what it's making me feel like.

I manage to hold most of my tears back, until I open my front door and then it hits me again. It's me trying to hold everything together on the outside until I am alone where I finally fall apart. It gets on my bloody nerves. I've always been someone who deals with my struggles alone, but finding the right moment to actually get help is something I haven't figured out yet. To be fair, I don't believe there's a recipe for that either. Like always, it's something individual. But seeking help does not make you weak or small. It shows bravery, a strong will to get over it and a strong heart.

After keeping my off shoes I head towards the kitchen to put my groceries away. While doing so, tears run down my face and I can clearly hear my phone ringing from across the room. Abby wouldn't call me on this day and I am in no mood to talk with anyone else today. So, instead of answering the call I reach for the cell phone searching for the location of the tattoo parlour, turning the incoming phone call down. Luckily, it's only ten minutes away so I can skate there. I missed doing it as well as taking pictures. Such things are always a shame to leave out even for a day. That's what makes me truly happy, not this day or having a mental breakdown. Those things make me furious as well as frustrated every time.

It took me about fifteen minutes to actually calm down and look normal again. After all I did it and that counts. I can hardly believe that this would be what my mother would've wanted me to do every year on this day. She would've wanted me to be happy, live a normal life, do what I love, not to read her diary and to find a person who I can love. If it only were that easy mom… *I probably wouldn't be writing this.* I've been trying not to for years because of the thing I am most scared of to write. The honesty while hiding the true reasons… it just all seems so impossible. When looking back, a year ago I would've been struggling to write an essay and now? Just how fast things are changing. *Hold it back, hold it back, hold it back. You're in public Olivia Jones, people know you now and you can't be stupid in your own mind.*

I find the tattoo parlour to get the tattoo made. The artist who is doing the tattoo is very nice and he tries to calm me down most of the time and we have a nice chat while he's working. I found out that he's got cats and a bird… weird combination for a guy with tattoos on his face. Believe me if I say that the creation he made is looking totally sick and precious at the same time. I realize that I'm not one for pain. It's definitely a distraction, a useful one for once, but I wouldn't want do it again in the next couple of weeks… or months. Perhaps that's because the tattoo actually got bigger than I expected it to, but still it is not one of my favourite things to do. But here I am skating my way back home still ignoring every call I receive. It's new to have so many people worrying about me… not just in a good way.

The time that it takes gives me the needed opportunity to rethink an important matter. The only positive aspect of my mom dying could be that it showed me how precious time is. It showed me that life can be over any second and I do not intend to waste the time with people I no longer love. With Ethan… I appreciate time even more. When we are together, the time flies by but I always know that someday we will have the chance to do it again. And this is something I could live by. I could get used to it. That is what brings me to the relationship topic that I'm thinking about. I don't know what he is making me feel but I like it... most of the time. I like the person he is helping me to become and I like spending time with him. I like being close to him in a way I've never been to anyone in my entire life before. I'd like to have more of it as well. My answer will be, the next time he would mention or ask, that I'd gladly be his girlfriend. I believe so. At least that is exactly what you would've wanted from me, right?

Frankly, I still have a day or two to prepare my answers. Yes, I still do that and no I probably won't stop. Someone once asked me why I put myself through situations before they actually happen that it would be like living through it twice. My answer was that it was partly true, but it's called rehearsal for a damn good reason. As I get closer to my place again, I step off the black board taking it in my hand. For once it's actually nice not to see anyone. It's nice to be on my own again as I used to be every day. It's nice to do things like I used to do them a while ago. The point is no matter how often you do the exact same thing over and over again, you'll probably never feel exactly the same as when you did it the first time. I could watch her favourite film thirty times again, but it would never feel like it used to the first time. Still, most of us humans try to chase after that one feeling the first time. It is like after you finished reading the best book you've ever read, you wish you were able to read it for the first time again because you already know what happens in that book.

That is the exact thing I will be doing now. I got her flowers at the shop, the movie, a distraction tattoo and her diary. What could come closer to how it was before? Right, about every single thing you could think of. Never mind, trying it won't hurt me... well, it will but not as much as her leaving did.

Sitting on my grey couch I turn on the television. After all the times I've watched this ridiculous film I am beginning to know every line of it. That would explain why I would try to read her diary along with it. About that, I'm still not through everything yet but I am getting closer. At this moment, the end of her previous case is coming closer which means the beginning of her last one... the one she gave her life to. Literally.

The second that I am finished with her previous case I feel my body panicking again. It's a sort of feeling that is very hard to describe to anyone who hasn't experienced it as well. It's like losing control over everything you still have left. As if you're trying to hold onto that little bit of water you still have in your hands while it's slipping through your fingers. One thing I've tried to increase over the last couple of weeks is when I feel that it is getting to be too much or when I feel something triggering me, I just stop. I stop doing it or I search for a quieter place. *I'm trying to give my problems more space so that they know that I can hear and see them. So they know that they are valid and heard, so they know that I care when no one else does.*

"This is never gonna get better, is it?" I ask myself, already knowing the answer. As I am about to get myself some ice cream and more tissues, as they clearly are needed, I can hear my door bell ringing. That's the problem when people don't know you well enough. They automatically misunderstand whenever you have something holding you back from being open towards them as usual. To be honest, humans suck. People suck. We all suck, but it's fine.

I slowly move my body towards the door. I am a little afraid to see who is there after reading her diary. I'm not fully at ease a bit more, knowing that I am not alone in this. After having a look through the spy whole in my door I can see Ethan's tall frame. Not good. I slowly open the door resting my body against the door frame not looking into his eyes, as I am focusing on my breathing. Don't show it Olivia, keep your shit together.

"What are you doing here?"

"What am I doing here? Gosh Olivia, you didn't answer any of our calls the whole fucking day. I was worried sick that those people were here! I can see you are here and you're not even trying to acknowledge me!" he states. The touch of anger and concern in his normally calm voice makes me want to close the door. He has no right to talk to me on this day. All I am asking for is one single day a year, is that seriously too much?

"I'm in no mood to have any kind of fight with you Ethan. Not today," I reply looking at his face with watery and puffy eyes from crying.

"What is wrong with you Olivia? All I do is care about you. Why are you pushing me away like this all the time?" he asks me in disbelieve.

And that's it. *That is the moment I'm breaking right in front of him.*

"Because there is one fucking day where I need to be alone. You don't get it, how could you? You don't even know the other half of me and I am not blaming you for that. I am to blame for all of this. I have been alone every time I've wished for someone to be there for me. I've been alone every night when I've wanted to die, I have been alone every time I've wished someone would have cared more about me than themselves for once. So please fucking excuse me if I am acting as if I don't care!" I yell while crying at the same time.

This is the moment. The moment I expect him to walk away because of how broken I am. I've prepared for this. All the time, this is what I have prepared myself for because it has always been like that. What I haven't been prepared for is what he's doing. I haven't been prepared for him hugging me and pulling me out from under the rain. What do I do now?

Chapter Twenty-Eight

If I had to be an animal, I'd definitely be a camel. At least that's what everyone around me says. I actually have been compared to one a couple of times. When you think about being compared to such a… dumb and lazy animal it sounds stupid. If you want to know more about camels, Google knows everything. However, I can see the impact that we have in common. It drinks like a hell lot of water and it makes stupid noises. You know, I'm always trying to understand both sides to arguments. What I have no understanding for is why my laugh is being compared to one. It's not like camels would laugh or anything like that.

The reason I am telling you this, is because Mary and Jacob find it quite amusing to mock me about my laugh. "I do not sound like a freaking camel!" I yell and they burst out laughing. Mary is laughing so much that she has to lean on the counter. At this point she'd most likely not be able to hold herself up anymore. Jacob is doing the same thing while trying to cook the freaking pumpkin soup. Yup, not my idea as well. Since it's preparation day we're all at Ethan's place to prepare most of the food for to-morrow morning. I wouldn't have started cooking the soup that early but since I won't eat anything with pumpkin, that kind of isn't my problem anymore.

Though it's nice being at his place for once, the air between us is kind of… confusing. He pulled me outside with him yesterday and my tears were being mixed with rain drops. He held me tight while I sobbed and he apologized a lot. I could sense that he didn't mean it like that. *However, an apology without a following action is just a useless word.* After he held me so close, we sat on the balcony staring at the rain clouds. It was a good change to sit there even though I felt so empty. The feeling of numbness overtook my body again and I felt like an empty vessel. After a few minutes, when he said we needed to go in before we were going to freeze, I couldn't say anything. I couldn't really look at him either. I was ashamed that he had seen me this way, even though he assured me that it would be okay. He said that he cared.

We walked back inside and got into the shower after getting rid of our soaking wet clothes. He helped me wash myself because I was unable to do anything. I was so lost in my thoughts and still, my thoughts felt empty as well. It wasn't about the physical attraction, thought I am very much attracted to him in that way as well, he didn't want to leave me alone. We got into bed afterwards, not saying much but just holding each other. I might have used him as a pillow again that night, but I think he owed me that. Not long after that, a certain phrase came to my head as it always does on that day when it's finally over. 'I did it. It's over for this year.'

When I woke up my eyes felt swollen, and Ethan wasn't there anymore. For a moment I thought he'd left again until I heard a noise from the kitchen. I went into the kitchen and saw him making me breakfast. All the things you could think of, he thought about it. All my dumb habits such as first pouring milk into a mug before the coffee and the apples I am so used to eating every morning. He also put new water into the vase of the roses I had bought for my mom without asking. This is what I could get used to. He made sure that I was more or less okay, cuddled me and made sure that I was ready to go to his place. I think he felt sorry about the conversation we had yesterday but there is a good thing about it. Through him, I learnt that I don't always have to feel sorry even for things that I didn't do. I didn't feel sorry and I think that is a small process. He once told me that I make him a better man. Well, Ethan, you make me a better person as well. I'm not mad at him. Not at all, I think it's not his fault because he couldn't have known. Yes, it shouldn't have come this far but shit happens and life goes on.

All of that brings me back to the preparations. Mary and Jacob went shopping for all of it and I think they did overestimate my appetite. For a woman of my height, I do eat a lot but not that much. They almost bought enough ingredients for a whole football team. "Your laugh does sound like a camel and I think it's hilarious. Does Abby know that?" Jacob asks me trying to catch his breath.

"I've known her my whole life. If she hadn't said that as well, something would definitely be wrong." I tell them.

Mary and I are continue to focus on some apple pie she insisted on doing. No complaining, I admire apples. I could eat them ever day of the year without getting tired of them. Just like baby corn and peas which I insisted on eating.

"So, what have you been up to yesterday?" Mary asks me. Ethan shakes his head at them starting to turn the conversation away.

"I... uhm... I got a tattoo," I blurt out, that's closer to the truth about what actually happened.

Ethan's head shoots up along with the others. "You did?" Ethan asks for the first time today. He's been quite but I really would want him to know that he doesn't need to worry.

"You're not the only one with tattoos Murphy." I joke seeing his smile for the first time today and God, I missed it. It's as if the sun is shining on a rainy day, breaking through a barrier of clouds. About his tattoos though, he has got a few but they're not that visible and very cool actually. There is a snake on his shoulder, a bow on his arm and a rose on his chest. Seems like she wasn't the only ones to adore these flowers. They're all in black and white and it fits him and his whole style so perfectly. Besides them, he has several small patch work tattoos spread over his arms and even on his legs.

193

"Ethan's got a tattoo?" Mary jokingly asks me now.

"You know he is right here. I'd appreciate it if you ask him." Ethan says sarcastically leaning against the black counters.

"I am sorry, I didn't notice you there since you are literally no help at all. No need to watch your... what is she even to you? You guys are confusing me." *Oh... this won't end well.*

"Mary, I told you that...," Ethan tries to say only to be cut off by me. Life is too short to waste, right?

"Girlfriend." I answer and seeing his face light up a thousand times more than before. He comes closer to me picking me up. While he swings me around in the open kitchen, I yell from shock before smiling and chuckling. These are the things that I missed.

"Oh, am I?" he asks me after putting me down again kissing me right in front of them. A bit awkward, but never mind.

"Mhm." I murmur smiling in the kiss and licking my lips after we broke apart.

"Geez, calm down guys and get a room. That's literally disgusting. We're trying to make some food in here. Get out if you aren't able to help or stop... whatever that is." Mary commands, pointing at us with a knife in her hand while Jacob chuckles again. I hope he's okay with it.

"I think that is our call to leave now. I want to show you something." Ethan tells me taking my hand and smiling.

"Wait, we can't just leave."

"Oh, don't worry. The years before this one I also had to do it alone. Perhaps I should get myself a boyfriend as well then, so I wouldn't have to do this." Mary jokes turning towards the soon-to-be apple pie again.

"Hey, I am here as well!" Jacob says making us laugh.

"You know I love you Jacob, but you're no help when it comes to cooking or baking." Mary scoffs.

"Touché."

"See, they are fine. Now get your shoes on and let's leave." Ethan says rushing to his front door. Before we leave, he tells the others that we will be back in a few hours. Whatever that should mean.

"Where are you taking me Ethan!" I ask him while walking along with him after having put my red Converse and jacket on. Every day for the last weeks it has been raining in tones. I'm glad that Abby made me pack my rain jacket before moving here. She's a goddess.

"Since we're officially dating now, I want to take you on a date. Also, I feel as if I need to show you my apology." He states getting into his black car. As what happens quite frequently, he passes me his phone to control the music. It turned out that he liked my favorite artists as well and that's very good for me. Before I always felt weird because of my taste in music but he accepts that as well. One of his hands is resting on the steering wheel, while he takes my hand with the other rubbing my knuckles with his thumb.

"What about the people and your fans? I thought you wanted to keep it more hidden because… well I don't know if I'm being honest."

"Oh, no Olivia. I want the world to know that you're mine and mine only. I want them to know that I like you so freaking much and that no one can take that away. No matter what happens."

He takes my hand pressing a soft kiss on it. I have to say, for the fact that he's driving on the wrong side of the road he's doing it quite well. I wouldn't feel that safe while driving with everyone. Maybe because I was in an accident once but those are details again. It took me months to feel safe again in a vehicle, but it has gotten better over time.

"Then show me that I am all yours."

"Sweetheart, I won't let you say that twice. So, what's the tattoo that you got?" he asks me and I smile slightly at his statement before.

"It's… uhh it's a human heart with roses and some words that have been marked in my mind ever since my mother died. They also were her favorite flowers."

"That's beautiful, but why especially yesterday?" he asks me and my head turns to look out of the window again. As I do not reply, a light goes on in his brain and he eventually understands my behaviour. "Oh. Why didn't you tell me, baby?" Baby?

"I'm used to not telling anyone. That's just how I am and no one really could have helped me. I didn't want to annoy you with that stuff."

"You are never annoying to me. I am here for you. I care for you and I'm all in with you. *I'm in with you in the long-term Olivia, you just gotta let me.*"

"I think I'd like to be in the long-term with you as well Ethan."

"Then that matter is settled. No more hiding and going through things alone, okay baby?" he asks me with a smile kissing my hand again while the rain pours down the window.

"As long as you'll be open with me as well."

"I'm as open as I can be." He jokes throwing his hands up, making me chuckle. "Since you mentioned not knowing a lot about me, I figured I might show you something before taking you on a date."

"A date?" I frown at the thought of it. Roman never bothered to take me on a date or to even do anything else just sitting around and doing... well you probably know. Nothing that has to do with actually getting to know the other person. He liked to keep me hidden. I don't know if he was ashamed of me, but I only met one of his friends once and then I felt as if they weren't even taking notice of me.

"Of course. In fact, here we are now," he says switching off the engine and getting out of the car. Leaving a confused me behind. While he walks around the car to open my door, I read the headline of the store in front of us. It's a blue shop with a lot of windows and flowers everywhere. In fact, it's an art studio. He opens the car laughing at my facial expression.

"Don't tell me this is an art studio. Your guilty pleasure is painting?" I speak up getting out of the car, standing next to him in the rain.

"It's not an art studio," he says pulling me out of the wet and planting a soft kiss on my lips. "My guilty pleasure indeed is painting and today I'd like to paint you. I need a muse." After his statement I chuckle kissing him back.

"You surprise me every day." I confess, making him shine now. His smile fades after a while looking across the street. I turn around as well, seeing a lot of people with a lot of cameras. See, there we go. "We can go if you don't feel..."

"No. Let them take their pictures and be jealous of me," he declares while pulling me in for a longer kiss now. After that, he takes my hair putting it behind my ear.

"Ethan, are you using me right now?" I joke playfully.

"I might, but I just love kissing my girlfriend," he says and I widen my eyes at the word he used. He seems to realize it as well soon enough. "Uh... I didn't mean it in that way. You know, just like...
He tries to talk himself out of it but he hasn't any chance to do so.

"I love kissing you, Ethan. I really do." I reassure him giving him a kiss while he leans into me.

"Then let's get inside and make this world a little more colour-ful." After saying so, we open the heavy white door and step inside, where he is being greeted by an older woman. He must come here often judging how they're embracing each other and I think it's amazing. However, I am truly shitty at painting, sketching, drawing... do you see, my point now. I am just shit at everything with pencils and colours and being that creative. I'm just not and I know it. There's also another thing that I'm getting to know every day.

Kissing Ethan is not the only thing that I love...

Chapter Twenty-Nine

"You're not supposed to do it that way," he tells me laughing at my actions. See, I am useless in technical stuff *and* creative stuff.

"What are you talking about? There is no wrong way to put colour on a canvas. It's called art for a damn good reason Ethan." I argue back holding my brush up. After we got everything settled, Ethan made me put on an old and colourful flannel, which I love, and we go into a studio just for the two of us. Getting settled I put my brown hair up into a messy ponytail while listening to music in the background. Standing face to face, he observes my whole body for his drawing. He looks absolutely insanely and forbiddingly handsome, well he mostly does, but today is just another level of it. He better draw me pretty. I, on the other hand have agreed to draw him as well. Well, I said I would try to. He shouldn't expect much more than a few ugly lines and colours to make it look better, sort of a cover-up, if you will. The room is full of plants as well, some hanging from the wooden ceiling and others placed around the wooden floor. The walls are full of ideas and colours, ready to be put into art. In the corner of the room, placed on a table near the window, is a bowl with several crystals in it. This old woman must be on the spiritual path of life… I should consider that too sometime in the future. All the time I'm thinking that being able to put your ideas one by one onto a sheet of paper is a superpower. Once I also watched someone draw an amazing painting in a park back where I grew up and since then I've been more or less obsessed with watching people draw. Whenever I could, I would sneak out of the house, sit in the park and watch as many artists as I could. The thing with painting is that you look at the drawing afterwards, but you still remember mostly every line you drew on it. What little steps it took to make something big out of it at the end.

"There is indeed a way of doing it wrong. You're not even watching what you're doing," he tells me laughing even more now.

"That's because I don't want to stop looking at your pretty face."

"You think I am pretty?" he asks blushing just a little bit. Still, he has that same look of pure concentration and focus on his face and in his eyes.

"You always are. No matter what, I think you're about the prettiest person on this planet. Not just on the outside."

"No one has ever said something like that to me. I appreciate it, but I hope you know that I think you're way prettier than me," he says putting yet another colour onto his canvas. The most excruciating thing is that he won't even let me see what he is doing. I just know that it's way better than mine could ever be. Though, I would want to draw a painting of him and hang it on my wall. Maybe then I could look at him just a little longer.

"Nope, forget it right now Murphy. Remember, today is about you, not me. You can tell me such things on my birthday but not now." I joke while his head shoots up.

"Shit, you never told me when your birthday is."

"It is the 13th of November, not so long now. You never told me yours as well."

"Well, mine is the 15th of March," he replies.

"See, now we know. We're even." After saying so, he goes back to drawing while I look at mine and a smart idea comes into my head. As I walk over to him with both my hands behind my back, he gives me a look of confusion. The second before I reach him, he holds his arm out to make me stop. *You won't stop me this time, I'm telling ya.*

"You can't see mine. It's not done yet."

"What I can see from over here is that it needs more colour, what do you think?" I say and smiling like an angel why he looks at his work for a second. *You're just too easy to read.* As he is doing so, I stretch out my arm letting the brush touch his cheek, making it purple. I burst out laughing happily. He makes a grimace and tries to look angrily at me.

"You did not just fucking do that."

I let my paint brush run over his nose now before replying. "Oops, seems like I did it again. My apology." Sarcasm, the best thing ever. As he steps forward, I yell trying to get away from him. "No, don't!" I giggle as he holds me tightly drawing colourful lines on my face.

"I think now we are even," he tells himself more than to me because I can sense that he'd like to keep going. Not with me, though. "Now let's get back to actually working."

I walk back to my canvas attempting to draw something that might look like him.

"Since today is about me, I'd like to tell you a few things that I think I should've told you earlier. I know you don't want me to open up that way, but I want you to know. You deserve to know just as much as I've been blessed to know about you. If I don't push myself to do it, I know that I won't do it," he says making me smile.

"Don't press yourself too much, okay?" I tell him. He nods looking up at me for a second before going back to talking and painting at the same time.

"I'd like to talk about Jacob first. I know I seem different when I'm with him, but he is more like my brother than my best friend.

I'm telling you this because he said he's fine with you knowing and I think it's important in order to understand who I am. His parents died when he was a child and he was placed in foster care. My parents saw it and brought him home to my family because they felt pity for him. In time, they adopted him and he became family. However, my family wasn't as pure as they seemed from the outside. My mother wasn't exactly happy with all of it and so she vanished. Just disappeared in the night and never came back. I don't know where or if she's even alive at this point. The thought of her being happier somewhere else always helped me to be more or less okay with it. Jacob and I kept on going and we helped to heal each other. My father and I never had the best connection, in fact we mostly went our separate ways and we didn't talk more than we had to. We disagreed on most things. I wasn't exactly his favourite child if I can say so. One day, after we had one of our big fights when I was a teen, Jacob got me my first pencils and art supplies. It helped me to heal in one way, before I could even think about doing music. It was the perfect way of drawing your feelings, even if you don't understand them. Along with that, I wasn't always the liked or the popular kid in school. I had my own way and my own bubble and I kept going with it until one day when for the first time I had a guitar in my hand in school and I could actually play. I sang my favourite song and then I knew that this was what made me feel the best. And everything that made feel this way was because of Jacob. He was always there. That's what I actually meant with the 'yee' to my 'haw'." He confesses taking a breath to control his thoughts and also his body.

"When looking back, I am far from being proud of the person I was and the things I did. But with time, the fame came and I realized that I don't need to act as if I was someone I am not especially not for my dad. I told him that it was time for me to go my own way... he... he didn't exactly like it, but he knew he couldn't stop me. So we broke the last straps of our bonding and lost contact. By the time I met you, I was speaking to him again after years and it made me… angry, disappointed and confused at the same time. That's why I was moody and weird at the beginning. Through you, I learned that it's okay though. Because you showed me who I really am. There are still so many more things, but I don't know how you will react. Just know that what I feel for you is true and I would never want to hurt you." It's a beautiful vulnerability. His words and the way he is. The way he thinks and the way he wants thing to be done. He is a good person and his words hurt me because he was hurt, but he isn't alone anymore. *No one is utterly alone, no matter how lonely we seem to be.*

"I am proud of you. I am proud of who you are and what you have achieved. Yes, the things in between might not be to your liking but those are the things that made you the person you are. Not your father nor anyone could take that away from you." I reassure him giving him a soft smile.

"No one knows these things about me except Jacob."

"Don't worry, I won't tell your fans," I joke, making him chuckle. "How do you feel?"

"Relieved. I am glad that you know now, even though it's not everything. However, I feel naked and ugly," he tells me.

"You don't need to. I told you that you're beautiful, but if it makes you feel better, I can tell you something as well. That way you don't need to feel naked and alone." *I can't take his pain away, but I can show him mine, so we can be hurt together. Go Olivia, tell him, you can do it. Feelings are valid, remember?*

"If you're ready to. I'm always listening to what you say sweetheart." He reassures me.

Do it. Do it. Do it.

"I don't write music at the moment. I can't do it. I just don't know what to write in a lyrically way. I've started reading my mother's diary as well. There is much more to be read, but I am working on it. I have this strong urge to know what happened to her. I want to get to know her. All of this made me write my own diary, it's a good way of getting rid of feeling's when they're too much and you're thinking you might be exploding. Writing is a good way of bleeding, maybe I'll try that. However, you're aware that my dad and I don't have the best relationship as well. I moved all the time after her death and I basically had no real friends anymore. There was just Abby and me. I hate pumpkins to death along with pickles, Roman and I hate cucumbers. I hated myself for as long as I could think but I think that is changing. I hate the way you make me feel because after Roman, I promised myself to never let myself feel that again. Here I am, embarrassed but still feeling it. I hate it because you make me believe in love. Because I…," as I start to just babble, he cuts me off, coming closer to me.

"I love you, Olivia." He interrupts me leaving me speechless.

"Are you sure you're not just saying that because I was talking bullshit about…"

"Seriously, I do love you. I've been thinking about this for some time now. I know it seems to be going too fast, that I just fell in love with you so fast. I doubt I'll fall out of it even if you don't like cucumbers. Because I don't like them as well," he says. I laugh, knowing full well that this is the first point for Jacob. Four to one Jacob. I will still win this thing.

"I love you." I state leaning into a long and passionate kiss. The reason I don't use terms like 'I love you too' is because that's what I said to Roman. The particular reason as of why that is, is because it felt as if I had to say it back before feeling the same. However, this way I can show him and myself that I actually mean it. Because I do.

"I think this is the perfect time to tell you that I finished your painting."

"I didn't. I doubt that it will get better anyway, so show me." I confess making him laugh even more. One thing I love about his laugh are his dimples, they're cute and soft, just like him. Of course, it makes him look even prettier. He takes his canvas off the frame and walks back to me with it, stopping a few steps ahead.

"I'm not Picasso but painting you will probably become my new favourite thing." Watching you paint anything will become mine as well Ethan. He turns it around, making me raise my eyebrows in shock. That is delusional. It's a one-to-one copy of me painting with all the gorgeous' plants in the background and the crystal table.

"That is amazing Ethan. I love it, it's so good. How did you do that? Now I am embarrassed to show you mine." I tell him covering my face with my hands. He hugs me planting a kiss on my forehead.

"It's not, you did your best and that is enough." Well, that won't help me. I free myself from his hold, grabbing mine and showing it to him, seeing him raising just one brow and smirking. "Should I feel attacked by this? I hope you don't think I look like this."

"That is not you. An image of a thing is not the thing itself. That is a shitty painting of you," I lecture him feeling smart for once.

"I'll hang it on my wall and appreciate it every day."

"Please don't." I beg him laughing ashamed. He steps forward to me, we're in between the two frames hugging tightly now.

"Oh, but I so will baby. But now let's get clean and have some dinner to make this day even better." It couldn't get better.

We head home to get cleaned up, or more likely making each other wet in his bathroom. Mary and Jacob are still there, laughing at our appearance but not questioning it any further. I'm sure they will know tomorrow anyway, but the rest of the day is just about us. However, Jacob is cheering like a child when I give him the deserved point for the cucumbers. If we're playing this game, we'll play it fair so I can get a fair win. We get dressed me putting on one of his cream sweaters because of the rainy weather. We climb back into the car again as he is taking me to this nice restaurant where we eat the most amazing tacos. A few people notice us through dinner, but after the day and the many times we said the cheeky 'I love you' to each other, I couldn't care less. We arrive home quite late because we were talking about useless stuff and it is hilarious. He tells me how he saw Jacob kissing someone for the first time and it was beyond hilarious.

I wash my face in his bathroom because he has convinced me to stay at his place over night. He said he didn't want it to end. After drying my face I take a glimpse of myself in the mirror, smiling widely as I haven't done so for a long time. I don't know what he's doing to me, but I won't complain because I love this feeling and I love him. God, this sounds so cheesy. Most importantly, I am loved. Not only by him but also by my amazing friends who I think are the closet to family I will ever have. Whenever I look at him, I get this feeling and... and I feel as if I'm home. This feeling, this person and all of the memories... I'd like to believe that this is my home.

I walk into his bedroom. His whole place is a lot different than mine. It's mainly decorated with dark wood and has ornaments, plants, pictures, drawings – you see, my point is that it's just way more decorated and fancier than mine. I like his taste. His bed is also made of dark wood but has white sheets on it, building up a contrast to the rest of the room. His bedroom window has an amazing view over the city and I think I could stare out of it for hours. I climb under the sheets curling up against him. One of his hands is resting on his chest, while the other one is in my hair, twisting and brushing through it. He's one of the persons who never wears a shirt for sleeping... well, never mind. Forget it and act as if I've never told you that.

"Can I ask you something baby? It just has been stuck inside my head...," he whispers, staring at the ceiling.

"Everything and always," I reply watching his face. Just the way he's breathing makes me genuinely happy.

"Do you still think about that thing you told me?"

"You're gonna have to be a bit more specific," I tell him, not sure what he means.

"Do you still want to die?" he asks me, my face turns away from him. Wanting a moment to think and breath. *Oh crap.*

Chapter Thirty

Suicide. Something that isn't talked about enough in the right way and far too much in the wrong way. People who have lost someone to suicide often come up with phrases such as 'I wish the person would've told me', or that suicide is 'selfish'. In fact, that is utterly wrong. Suicidal people try so often to tell someone, to get someone to notice. They try to show it. However, every time they get disappointed or judged, they will shut themselves away even more. *Just because you can see someone in a temporary happy and funny state, does not equally mean that they genuinely are happy.* Over the years this also became one of the things I always wanted to say but never did. The reason was that people suffer, and they die because they think that death is a much better solution than living in something which feels like hell for them. It can't go on like this. This is something that needs to be talked about in order for suicidal people to feel comfortable enough to open up and to get help. Suicide is not selfish. The only thing that is selfish about this subject is the people around wanting someone to stay alive, not helping nor accepting them, even if they'd rather not be alive at all. That is selfish. That is not caring and understanding them. That is they only care about themselves because they 'couldn't bear to lose them'. If you really can't bear losing someone, you will do everything not to lose them. You won't just act as if you never knew or saw anything. No one who hasn't felt this way should judge people who do. They clearly have no idea what that feels like.

The time for watching, judging, having suspicions and waiting is over. It's time for actions and change. And change always begins with people first. All of us need to spread awareness because this is something important and serious. And just because you can't see a mental illness does not mean it's not there. Just because we can't see someone's brain, does not mean it is not there. Well, for most of the people.

Do I still want to die? I doubt that I ever wanted to, I just didn't want to be alive anymore. Does that make any difference? Hardly.

"Hey. I don't want to make you uncomfortable I just need to know because I am worried about you," he says, still laying the same way his breathing becomes heavier. I always get so quickly into my head. Getting out is pretty hard though.

"I… I doubt that I'll be able to give you the answer you want. I never wanted to die. In fact, I hate dying because it's all about death and death is the thing, I hate the most. The point is that I didn't want to be alive. Quite often actually in the past years… I'm… I'm pretty much ashamed of it. It sounds so stupid to say it but if you actually feel it, it's way different. Do I still feel that way? No. not since you made me realize that life can be better. *Maybe I'm one of the lucky human beings regardless.* Still, I'm not perfectly fine, I've never really been and I doubt that anyone ever is." I don't think that I'm anywhere near being over the mountain just yet. In fact, I'm half the world away from that. Nevertheless, I'm currently climbing up and for once I don't intend to fall back down again.

He presses me even closer to him before sighing. "I'm glad that you are here. I'm glad that I met you even though you can be a pain in my ass," he jokes, making me smile a bit.

"I hate you," I state knowing that it's a lie.

"No, you don't. You love me."

"Don't get so full of yourself, but I do. I love you," I tell him.

"And I love you," he says repeating my words planting a kiss on my face. "This might sound a bit stupid, but have you tried talking to someone? I'm pretty sure you can't tell me everything, but I want you to get better for yourself. I want you to feel as happy as you make me every day."

"I did. The issue was that I didn't find the right person and I eventually felt worse every time I went there. So, I stopped. Maybe I should give it another try," I say. Maybe it will help. I want to get better, so much. That's a beginning, isn't?

"I am proud of you baby." I am too. For once, I am proud of what I achieved and what I survived. Even when I hit rock bottom, I still kept going every single day. Most importantly, I did that myself. "If I may say something though. If I were you, I wouldn't read her diary just yet. If you're trying to find out what happened that is fine, and you deserve it. But perhaps you should take care of yourself first and write about what makes you feel a certain way. Write about what you're most scared of and maybe it can be some sort of therapy for you as well."

"Are you proposing that I write a book?" I ask curiously. I've never thought about it in that way... well, I never thought that I was good enough to do so. However, there would be a lot of things I always wanted to say but never did.

"If it makes you happy better than I can. Just remember that no matter what you're doing, I'm always supporting you. Whether that would be music or anything else."

"That might be a good idea," I agree. "But what about your music? I haven't heard any for a while now," I tell him. It's true, the last time he said that they were 'working on some technical stuff'. Whatever that means.

His reaction is a heavy sigh and he moves his hand. "About that... they finished it. I just wasn't ready to release it. There's no particular reason why, I'm just scared it will end. All of it."

"What do you mean end?" I ask, not understanding the meaning of it.

"It's so stupid but I'm scared that things will change once the tour will start. I don't want you to be alone, I can't leave you and I don't want to," he explains making my heart jump.

"You're seriously thinking about not going on tour because of me? Are you out of your mind?"

"No, yes, I mean I don't know. I don't know what you're doing to me, but I know that I don't want to leave you behind. I wanna hug you, kiss you and fall asleep next to you. Every single day. I want to do it all over with you and only you," he states.

"I do too Ethan, I do so much. But I won't let my selfishness take away such a big step of your career and what you love," I explain to him. I can't take away what he loves. Not after people took that away from me.

"Why don't you come with me?" What? He's joking, right?

"Ethan… I'll be useless out there. Not to mention Abby and not one of your crew knows or cares about me. What if it doesn't work the way we want it to?"

"Your wrong. My fans like you and your songs. You just don't know, thanks to the lack of your social media skills," he argues back. Fair point though. "We could sing a couple of songs together, if you feel comfortable. This isn't you being selfish. This is me being selfish and wanting to have you around sweetheart. I can't go longer than a day without you. *I'm obsessed with you baby.*"

Smiling to myself and thinking about this makes my heart beat faster. Music still means the world to me, as he does now. I don't think I could ever go without one of these things. Still, there is so much to think about, such as my work, Abby, and my mother. With time I've stopped asking myself what she would think… the reason I do this is to get as far as I can with her diary, I feel as if the more I read about her the less I knew about her. And the less you know a person, the less you'll ask for their approval. The next painful step of losing someone, I figure.

"I want you to know that I want to say yes if it were only about me. However, there are more matters I need to settle and things I need to consider. I'll think about it," I whisper feeling my eyes getting heavier and heavier every second.

After that, we fell asleep. Yes, I did misuse him as my personal pillow again, but that kind of isn't my fault, okay? Since I didn't have any clothes with me, he gave me his boxers and one of his graphic tees. Let me just tell you that mens clothes are way more comfortable to sleep in. Maybe it's because they smell like he does. Anyway, I had a nightmare again. Not one of those where my mom comes back. No, they seem to have had enough for a few days. I'm talking about the other ones I had. It is me being in this world and with time everyone disappears until I'm alone. The feeling is so… it's as if it is ripping you apart because I hate being lonely as I said multiple times before. I don't really like talking about my dreams because mostly I don't even understand them myself. How am I supposed to explain it to you, if I don't even understand it? The point is, that I woke up and started shaking. I was breathing so fast because in my dream, well towards the end, I was dying. Until I woke up scared as ever. Ethan woke up from this… whatever (how could he not?) and tried to calm me down. He took deep breaths with me and comforted me. Again, he didn't ask, he understood and was just there. After some time, he told me I should go to sleep. Now, as you may know by now, I never do. The reason I can't fall asleep is because I am terrified of what could possibly haunt me in the next dream. So, as I often do, I sort of run away from my problems. How fascinating? Because Ethan was actually there, caring, I could do it. For the first time in years, I fell asleep again and I slept like a freaking baby. After I woke up, I caught myself smiling. Well, it's the day of thanksgiving, which makes this a small kind of family dinner.

A bit of time ago, the time I was with Roman, I used to have these kinds of dreams, but more intense. I used to wake up, shaking and having a panic attack afterwards. It was always the same, but I wasn't used to them as I am by now. In the first few months after Roman and I got together, I had the worst one. He on the other hand cared about nothing more than his 'beauty sleep'. Not that this would have ever worked out for him. Yup, give it to him, he deserved that and every other comment I made about him this far in my life. Anyway, back to the point. What he did pushed me further to the edge, still half asleep, and telling me to be quiet and to just sleep. 'Get over it', he had said multiple times. He never understood nor cared that much about my mental health nor my family in general. I once tried telling him about the stuff with my mother and he just showed not one single emotion. If I'm looking back now, I'm doubting that this man has ever felt anything. This was about the most disappointing moment in my life. Next to the many ones with my dad... yeah, I know. Roman was never one to tell anyone anything. As I said, I don't think there was a lot to be told about him besides his work and his sex life. I didn't trust him just because he earned my trust, I trusted him because he was my boyfriend. That's what you normally do when you have a boyfriend, right? In the end, it was the thing I regret most in my life. When I found out that he cheated on me, for a while if I might add, I wanted to just get away and never talk to him nor see him again. His opinion was, as always, different. He tried again and again to convince me that it was a mistake and that he truly was sorry. Even weeks after I walked away from him, he continued this. He was the first one to point out that I run away from my problems. He wasn't wrong. Looking back, I'm glad I ran away. No, I wish I had run earlier. Or never even met him to begin with. As I said before, *we were never gonna make it. We were a losing game from the start.*

However, Ethan earned my trust a while ago. I think it was the moment at the cliff, our first real moment alone and probably one of my favourites. If I look back to the moment, I promised myself to never fall in love or love anyone again. There was a particular thought in my head, it was the fear that no one would ever be able to love me, despise the fact that I was sick of love and all other emotions. The only thing I can tell you from what happened afterwards our… separation, is that it only went downhill. That's it. Straight downhill.

But I'm glad that I fell for Ethan. He's my daily shot of serotonin.

Anyway, here I am trying to find a towel in Ethan's bathroom after showering. His apartment is so clean that everything seems to be hidden away. At this point, you should've noticed that I'm not quite a confident person. So, walking out of the bathroom without a towel on isn't really an option in my head nor on my plan. As always, nothing goes along with the plan. Not that he never saw me naked but then… that's just something different with a lot of inappropriate details. I swear, those details do hate me.

So, I place my ear against the door, listening for any noises. When I'm sure that there are none, which means he's sleeping calmly, I open the door stepping out of the bathroom. As soon as I do, I realize that the bed is empty. He has woken up. At least he can't see me like this… so, I grab one of his sweaters out of his closet pulling it over my head. Being tall is certainly a plus point for him. No need to buy oversized sweaters anymore. Along with the sweater I pull on my jeans from yesterday. I really need to go and change. But most importantly, I need to call Abby. Every holiday, every year unless we don't spend it together there is this rule. If you don't call the other one you will have to pay for the next five meals, and I do not intend to spend that much money on her vegan stuff. No way, I am supporting her, as these things are often more expensive. Of course, I want to hear her voice again and to check on her. It is not all about me. Especially after the stress she has modeling…

After taking my wet hair out of my face I pick up my phone and click on her contact.

"Hi Liv," she says in a strange voice.

"Hey Abby, you okay over there?"

"What? Yeah sure. It has just been very... stressful, you know," she replies. Strange indeed.

"Want to talk about it? You know that I am always here for you. You've just been so quiet," I reassure her. Once in a while I need to remind her of that. I'll gladly do it every time.

"You've been quiet too. Hanging out with dipshit I assume?" Yep, she's still pissed. No secret that she's not his biggest fan. For the record, if I needed to compare Roman and Ethan, Ethan definitely would be the better guy. Just so you know.

"He has a name, you know. And yes, I have. We've been getting closer with time. However, I would feel less awkward about this conversation if we could have it in person," I suggest. It's always easier to figure out her expressions.

"I know his name. What I don't know is who he is. You haven't known him for long."

"Abby, I know this is a difficult subject after Roman and everything. I just want you to know that he makes me happy," I confess, hoping this will calm her nerves. It's the truth, it really is.

"You said that about Roman as well. Until he cheated on you and screamed at you. Do I need to remind you of that?" Ouch.

"No need to. Thank you very much." Another subject I'm not used to talking about. Abby does know details but not what he screamed at me about or who he cheated on me with. Things that are buried deep down in me for a damn good reason.

"Look, I just want the best for you. Maybe you should focus on something different right now."

"And what would that be Abby?" I ask rolling my eyes. I really do love her but sometimes it's just difficult. I know that wants the best for me but what if he is the best? What if that's what I want? What if that's what I need? What about me?

"On who you are and who everyone around you is. Who your mother was. The only thing you told me is that you wanted justice for her. Whatever that means, I think that it's important. It's clearly still bothering you."

"I'm trying to. I think I gotta go. I'll talk to you later. Please promise me that we'll see each other soon, okay?" *I am basically begging her.* Yes, she is busy but she also is my best friend in the whole world. I deserve some time with her. If I need to fight for that with cloths... I will. Frankly, clothes and me don't have the best relationship any way.

"We will. *Everything will connect eventually.* Not everything is the way it seems, Liv. Love you," she replies. Yes, something definitely is strange.

"Love you too. Happy thanksgiving," I say still a bit confused about her previous statement.

Everything will connect. What's that supposed to mean?

Chapter Thirty-One

I put away my phone frowning, and I start to wonder why she's acting that way. I didn't do anything, right? Besides that she's not really a fan of Ethan.

Back to the topic, I did a post on social media. Crazy, I know. It's just something simple. It's a picture that Ethan took of me while I was painting and it's really shows my current happiness that I get to experience with him. In the mean time I haven't opened Instagram after downloading it, I have a great number of fans on there. I don't know why anyone would follow me, since I don't post anything there. Well, until now. My plan is to not look at it for the next couple of days… or weeks? It's a very effective way of avoiding questions and hate. I doubt that I have done anything against someone, but some humans have nothing better to do. Sadly, that's how it works. I should probably go along with it or try not to listen to it… being a person with low self-esteem that's kind of harder though. No, do not think that way Olivia. You like the picture, you love the person who took it and nothing else is more important.

Leaving his bedroom I walk along the darker hallway. I can hear his voice in the kitchen. He's on a phone call and according to the name he just screamed, it must be Jacob. Poor him.

"Yes, I am well aware of that Jacob… no, no. Yes, I fucking know that. Don't you think I am scared? I care about it and so do you but not in the same way. No, I'm not saying that you don't care about it. I've tried so hard, but I can't, and I don't want to. We both know that. Yeah… we must do something. We'll talk about it in person another time mate. This has to stay between us."

As he speaks to him in an angrier, annoyed and stressed way I walk closer making a noticeable noise when stepping down from a stair that leads to his kitchen. He immediately spins around looking rather shocked and a bit pissed as well. Not sure if he's pissed because of me or because of Jacob but if I'm being honest, I don't really want to know. He holds up his hands, signaling for me to wait. I think he definitely needs some pain killers.

"Jacob, I can't talk right now. Olivia woke up... yes, I will tell her you said hi. Yeah, see you later. We'll talk about it though. Yes, I'll be careful, but you need to be to. Tell Mary what she needs to know for... you know. Right, see ya mate. No shut up Jacob I will not do yoga with you. No, forget it, I will hang up now. Bye. Yeah, love ya too." Bromance, how cute is that? I still want to see Jacob doing yoga poses. Maybe after a couple of drinks I'll get him to do it today... who knows.

Back to the more important things now. I have no idea what they were talking about, but do I even want to know? As I said before, I don't want to push him to tell me anything, but I don't want to put my trust towards him at stake. It's just so confusing. Why is everyone this weird? Is it the weather? I tell you all the rain and the orange is not only affecting me. Pumpkins and autumn should both be a crime. Don't come at me after all it's just a fact. People go crazy in that season. Not to be dramatic but it's the season when the thing with Roman ended. See, I cannot be the only one who sees a dramatic coincidence there. It can't be the only coincidences that is creepy.

"Wasn't too good of a conversation, was it?" I joke stepping closer to the black counter and to him. The dishes that Mary mainly prepared are spread all over. A surprise that there is even a space left on it.

"Not really. There is an issue I need to sort out with Jacob later on. Nothing too important. How did you slept?"

"I took some time to fall asleep again but I did. I slept like a baby and I normally never do." I tell him making him laugh tilting his head backwards. God, his hair looks so good and fluffy. I have no idea how he keeps them curly and messy on purpose, but it looks so hot. Maybe it's not even on purpose, that would make it even more brilliant.

"I'm glad you did," he replies turning around again, making us both a cup of tea. No idea how long he will keep trying to get me to drink tea but I'm just a coffee person. Take it or leave it. My mother used to love tea as well. She drank it every morning and didn't eat. I still have her mugs in some boxes that I hid before my dad could throw them away. I stopped drinking it after she died. Yes, it's a bit pathetic, but it always reminded me of her and that memory still pains me up to this very day. I tried to stop and avoid every memory flashback I could, so it wouldn't hurt that much. Turns out pushing away memories, feelings and things in general that hurt you does not help at all. In fact, you need to feel and go through what hurt you so you can heal. Healing takes time, isn't linear and it hurts like shit, but it has to happen at one point. You cannot just push everything away forever. Believe me, I tried but it simply does not work. Ethan was the one to show me that when we were at the cliff. Again, my favourite moment for us and also for just me. I really need to go there again some time.

"Thank you, Ethan," I say making him turn around, frowning at me. See, even that looks cute with his baggy sleeping trousers and no shirt at all, revealing his tattoos. I'm not sure how long it will take to heal but mine is still a bit sore. Especially while showering or lying on it. However, it's beautiful and it reminds me of her. Good thing, right?

"For what baby?"

"Listening, understanding, helping me grow and helping me learn. *Thank you for making me feel again.*" I admit, making him stepping closer to me.

"Don't thank me. I'm just making you see what you truly deserve. You're a way better person than I could ever be."

"Why would you say that? You're special and kind. I could go on if you wanted me to," I reassure him grinning while giving him a soft peck on his lips, then his nose and his cheek in the end. His hands take hold of my waist and he again has the brightest smile that I adore so much.

"Maybe one day you'll understand why. I'd like you to go on baby. I really do, but we need to get ready for the others. I suppose that will be an interesting day."

"It's not even noon. Why are they on their way now?" It makes no sense to me mainly because I just woke up and my brain is not fully switched on at this time. Again, I am not a morning person at all.

"May I tell you that you're looking absolutely stunning this morning?" Cheeky bugger.

"Ethan, your friends are coming." I laugh while he has that ugly smirk on his face again. Still holding me tightly and not letting go of my waist he puts his forehead against mine.

"No, our friends are coming. But not before we are finished and you'll have enough time to get changed at your place. You might take a few things to stay over at least for that day because neither of us will be able to drive after dinner. You could also call a Uber but considering that you…" he starts to talk trying to turn me on with his talk. Not with me Murphy.

"Shut up Ethan." I interrupt him kissing him. He immediately goes along with it, putting a lot more tension and passion into it as we are slowly making out way back to his bedroom.

"Hey, what about my breakfast coffee?" I interrupt for a second chuckling.

"First off all, we're in England so it's tea. Second off all, you're so hot right now you don't need warm liquid baby." This joke was so bad that it's almost funny again. He's very confident in such things... he can be because he is so good at doing things... well, ya know. Basically everything.

So, I am currently in the car with Ethan, on my way to collect a few things that I will be needing. A huge negative aspect of sleeping with him is that he makes comments all the time. Yes, I am sore, and? It's not even my fault right? Besides that, he left quite visible marks of our... encounter, especially on my neck. That reminds me of the moment he told me that he wanted to show me that I am all his. Well, I might have dared him to, but the point is that he did that quite a bit the last time. I am not complaining at all, it's just a bit embarrassing when someone confronts me.

Nevertheless, he parks in front of my apartment and tells me to get going and to grab all my stuff. Of course, he has that devilish grin on his face as I walk towards my door saying, "Fuck you" to him in response.

"Quite literally." He scoffs laughing again. Next time I'll use my damn braincells and then I'll be aware that something like that has to come next. Stepping up to my front door I take the mail inside again, noticing another blank envelop which causes me to freeze. Not this shit again. Not today and I would prefer never at all. I turn around to see Ethan smiling on his phone... I'll just ignore it. If I don't open it, I won't have to think about it and no one has to know. I just need a break from them. I need to read that damn diary no matter what others are saying. Just not today, I can't do this today. The letter will still be there once I'm back so ignoring it for a while won't hurt. Conclusion, I should take my fucking own advices for once. I hate it.

Regardless, I pick up some clothing and items from the bathroom putting them into a bag. Along with that I put my laptop into the bag and another jacket. England equals rain. Just a fact. I'm making sure not to stay long. If they know my address and things about my mother as well as me, God knows what they are capable of doing wherever they are. I just need to get out of here. I need to enjoy today, reading her diary and then telling Ethan. We'll find a solution. Maybe it's best to get away from here with him which could... no, wait. The tour. They won't know that... the guys are there, and Ethan as well. Abby could come to a few shows, and I would be safe. We all would be safe...

I get into the car when he is putting the phone away, giving me a quick kiss ad starting the engine of the car. "Ethan, I thought about it. Maybe it would be great if I could join you on tour. I could still write and take photos or start writing music again if that is what feels right. It could be good to get away from... them... and we could spend some time and make memories. I don't know, I probably should shut up because I am talking shit and you are looking at me as if you're finding it amusing so I'm shutting up right now." *Words. Built a fucking sentence Jones. It's not that English isn't your* first language. Idiot.

"Oh Olivia, this will need a fucking celebration thanksgiving party. Of course, you can come, I was afraid you'll say no. The guys even made a fucking bet again. Jacob is going to scream once he founds out," he says and smiling while watching the road and mostly the rain in that case.

"Why would he?" I ask raising an eyebrow.

"You'll see."

"Question is do I even want to know?" I joke but actually I am being quite serious. I enjoy his laugh and the music that is playing from my playlist. Good thing about driving with Ethan: getting to play the DJ again. Bad thing about driving with Ethan: the fucking wrong side of the road. Whenever we're getting into a roundabout on the left side, I find myself becoming scared, that we're gonna crash into someone. But I got to admit he's not that much of a shitty driver. He just learnt it wrong so technically it's not even his fault.

We reach his place getting out of the car in the rain. An umbrella would've been useful at this point. As the gentleman he is, he takes the bag off my shoulder opening the door. He even made some space in his closet for me before we left. Nearly too perfect to be real, right? I get dressed putting on a red dress with puffy sleeves and a v-neckline. It ends a bit over my knees and it's the perfect mixture between sexy and adorable. I love this dress very much since it's one of the pieces I have from my mother. The first time I wore it, it even still smelt like her and that was at the end of high school. I try to cover up my neck with tones of concealer but after what this dude did, it's never gonna work. So, I decide to just accept it and use the time instead for curling my hair and doing my makeup. As I said, I like being punctual and on point. Seems, like it works because the second I pull the plug for the hot curling iron out I can hear the doorbell ring. After quickly getting into my black high heels, I walk towards the door to see Ethan hugging them and letting them inside. The second they see me, their faces light up and so does mine. They all have that kind of thing.

"Happy thanksgiving Liv!" Jacob yells hugging me. Shortly after, Mary does the same thing. We all move into the kitchen. They take out bottle after bottle of red wine placing it on the free counter space. Now I know why none of us will be driving later.

"Let's get this party started!" Mary interrupts Ethan's and my critical look opening the bottle they brought while Jacob takes glasses out of the cupboard.

"See, I have to ask you Liv. You're not pregnant, are you?" Jacob asks curiously making Ethan spit his drink back into the glass. I seem to have the same reaction while Mary is genuinely laughing and trying to breath normally.

Yup, let's get the party started.

Chapter Thirty-Two

"What? No! Why would you even assume that?" Me? Pregnant? What the… see, I'm not in high school anymore. Conclusion: I am aware of how to have safe… fun.

"Considering the hickeys all over you and the way you both are acting, I should ask," he states grinning in a very ugly and annoying way. Once again, his hair is in a bun that I have gotten used to by now. In fact, I'm quite fond of it. He's wearing an orange dress shirt, and black trousers made of cotton. For his sake, I hope that he didn't wear that damn orange shirt on purpose. He always looks good, just as much as he is a good person. The only difference is that I'm not really sure how to act with that piece of information that I have about him. Assuming he didn't tell me himself, he doesn't want to talk about it. Which is fine by me, I'm just confused. Mary on the other hand has her long, dark and curly hair put up with a lot of gel as I'm assuming. She's wearing a long and dark green dress made of satin which looks absolutely stunning on her darker skin. Her long earrings are just showing a better symbol of beauty. I must say that my boyfriend still is the most handsome out of them. His black dress shirt is not fully bottomed up revealing part of his chest and his chain with a rose on it. Remind me to ask him about it again some time. Along with that, he's wearing baggier purple trousers. He looks like one of those models with his rings and everything. I really do need to make a photoshoot of him soon.

"No, you do not. You're putting me on the spot and considering that Ethan did the fucking same all day this is so a point for me. Five to one Jacob." I fight back and now I am the one to laugh. Well, at least for three seconds.

"No, what about the tour bet?" Mary argues. Did you have to bring that up?

"I voted that he won't ask you," Jacob says observing our lack of answers. "Assuming he asked and you said yes because you're not talking right now this is so a point for me. Liv, it's five to two right now and I will not let you win that easily."

"What is that counting thing even about? I don't get it." Oh Ethan, little do you know.

"It's about you actually," I explain to him, making him spit his drink back again. Swallowing Ethan, not spitting. Actually, we're all terrible people because the only thing we do is laugh even more. Malicious joy is the best joy. Ask Abby about it. I'm the queen of that matter. However, if someone fell down the stairs I wouldn't laugh because that actually freaking hurts. Believe me, I would know and I do as a matter of fact. "I told Jacob that you and him have a lot in common and he wouldn't believe me. So, the points are me trying to prove to him that you are quite similar. Considering the score at the moment I am right."

"You guys are fucking weird." *Well, yes? Duh. Weird is cool.*

I bring my hand up to my chest and I act as if he has just stabbed me right in the chest. Fun fact, I've been to a couple of theatre classes but I'm clearly no talent. "Ouch. Now why would you say that to your girlfriend? What would people say if they knew about it, Ethan?" I act pulling out Abby's sarcasm. I love it so much I can't even describe it in words.

He steps behind me and hugs my stomach tightly while whispering into my ear. "You're so weird that it's adorable. Another thing that I love about you. Besides that, I haven't had the possibility to tell you how fucking stunning you look baby. I'm proud to call you mine and mine only," he says playfully kissing me right under my ear. Weak spot.

"Watch out Murphy. You're being very possessive today." Truth.

"Am I? Sorry, my bad baby." He's really in a teasing mood today. It's good, it's making me forget even more about the letter. Alcohol will help as well. Nope, I know what you'll think by now, but I am not pregnant. Guess you haven't listened very well in school. Especially when they told you that sex will not essentially lead to a baby. The monthly doses of paranoia when my period was delayed... I think most women know that fear.

"Let's get some food and mainly alcohol into our system, shall we?" I speak out loud and leaving him behind. *If you want to have a game, you sure will get one.*

We collect all the plates and glasses together, and place them on his wooden dining table. Along with that, I convince them to put some fancy napkins and stuff on it. Reason number one, it is fancy, as I said. Reason two, you eat with your eyes as well, and I am hungry. Reason three, I never decorated again since my mom died and this year is the first one, I am finally emotionally stable enough to do it. Mainly because I am not alone.

It was noon after we had finished, I grab my phone and Google some therapist around here. Yes, Google does know everything. I eventually find a lady who seems nice to me, so I contact her. I don't expect anything to big yet but maybe it will work out. I have a little more faith since she seemed really nice on the website but obviously you can write on some internet page whatever you want people to know. The last therapist I had was known to talk a lot. Normally she spoke the whole time and when I finally felt comfortable enough to tell her something she kind of didn't give me the opportunity to do so. It would've been nice if she helped me with her words but since she didn't… it wasn't the right thing. I told Ethan about it and he was very supporting. That was before he started all his teasing and cheeky comments. I'm just hoping that those damn mood swings won't start again. They might be more tolerable but still this time I am in no mood for it. It's all working out so well at the moment. I simply want it to stay that way. The only thing that I would want to change is the thing about the letters and that Abby isn't here.

Back to the dinner. We're putting all the dishes onto the table, and I literally have no idea how long Jacob and mainly Mary must have taken cooking after we went on the date. They made some baby corn salad for me, apple pie, mashed potatoes, chicken instead of turkey, beans, carrots, fucking pumpkin soup and cucumber salad for Jacob. It's like a huge family that is cooking for every single kid on their own. Very funny to think about. We're also celebrating like one. The alcohol does make all of us more talkative and open but especially Jacob. That's the particular reason why I found out that Ethan and Jacob have the same tattoo. A drunk tattoo. Who would've guessed, it's a 'yee' for Jacob and a 'haw' for Ethan. That's about the stupidest thing I heard this whole evening.

"I can't believe you guys. Mary, please tell me that you at least have a tattoo that makes more sense," I spit out in the room while filling my fork with pees and baby corn. This stuff is a life saver.

"Well, I do have one. In fact, we all have the same one," she admits, making me raise my eyebrows in curiosity.

"You have to tell me."

"It's… uh… some sort of stupid band tattoo. Nothing impor-tant," she murmurs looking at the two others. It seemed to me, that they pretty much don't want her to tell it according to their glares. At least that's what I got out of their looks towards her. Ethan coughs slightly before looking at Mary and then back at me.

"Nothing important. Just another stupid drunk idea."

"Yeah, you're probably right. Sorry for… uhm… whatever. Please excuse me, I'm going to the toilet," I state and leaving the table leaving a pissed and regretting Ethan back. I know it wasn't his or Marys intention. Come on, yes I am aware of what you will be saying now. I asked the question but how could I have known? I'm not jealous, truly, but I'm tired of being left out and in the dark like every other time in my life and with my family. With the letter and anything I'm just not in the fucking mood for that shit. They didn't tell me anything about Emma and Ben, about the song, the tour, their stupid band tattoos and almost everything. Seriously, I'm tired of it. I know I haven't been there for long and they have their memories and insiders and everything but it's just getting on my nerves. I'm here, you know? Not only was Abby acting so weird towards me and now they can't even tell me about stupid tattoos. Am I some sort of arm candy to them or what the heck? I never complained to anyone about feeling this way. Normally, I just accept it but right now I am tired of it. This is not what I deserve, even the person inside of me, who is trying to kill me, is telling me that is true… somewhere deep within myself I know that it's not. No one is supposed to feel left out.

I walk into his bedroom, ignoring any calls and just focusing on the silence in my head. It's not even anger, that barely happens, it's just everything and nothing at the same time. I go into the bathroom locking the door. I am sitting on the toilet staring at the shower which is located right across the room. Even his damn bathroom is mostly dark. Don't understand this wrong, I think dark furniture matches very well with mostly everything, but right now dark and empty in my head is quite enough.

Zooming in and out of my mind, I recall every moment I felt like this. Feeling left out before my mother died, feeling left out before even turning eighteen, feeling left out with friends that I had, at every party and mostly feeling left out of my life, feeling left out from living. I swear those zoon-out moments can be like heaven and sometimes they also can be hell. It takes me a few minutes to come back to reality, getting up I throw some water in my face not caring about my makeup even in the slightest. In a matter of seconds, I leave the bathroom and make my way back to the others. This is something that I missed so fucking much. A song idea.

As I arrive at the table their faces turn to me looking worried but soon the looks turn into confusion, when they see my expression. "What is happening?" Jacob speaks up while I casually ignore the question.

"I need someone to write down my lyrics," I tell them seeing Ethan's face lightening up. Jacob has nothing better to do than just opening his mouth. As I am sure they told Mary about my writing problem, it's no wonder that she has the same expression as Jacob. "Right now, guys. Hurry up. Where is the closest piano?"

Ethan immediately stands up walking very fast around his apartment. As I said the first time we were here, in a labyrinth. No wonder this guy is so fast, his legs look like they are twice as long as I am in total. Maybe a little bit hyperbolized, but you're getting the point. No, I am not happy like before, but I need to get this idea out of my head right now, so be a little bit patient, will you? Just hang on a minute or two.

He goes into a room I have never been before. It's not dark, in fact it's more of a wooden vibe. There are a few instruments, such as a bass, and electric and acoustic guitar, drums and most importantly a grand piano. *Note to myself: asking why he didn't fucking show me before.*

"Murphy, I need you to write down the keys and the lyrics, can you do that?" I ask him while sitting down on the chair and letting my hands touch the dark instrument.

"Of course, baby."

"Don't. We're not done yet, but I really need to let this out first." He nods taking a notebook from a table with a laptop on it. He's pulling the chair closer and observes my next moves. I know that Jacob and Mary are right behind us, watching me as well, but for once I don't care. All I care about is the melody and the text inside my head. Zooming out from my surroundings and concentrating on the piano, I start to play. The feeling of it being so easy to move my hands is slowly coming back and I catch myself smiling. God, I missed this so much.

It's not a genuinely happy song. It's a song that sounds happy when the true meaning is so deep. Something, that can only be understood and not judged in that way. It's about the feelings that came with suicide and self-harm. Something I never told anyone. These are the things that hurt the most because I hold them close to my heart. It sounds super awkward, but there was a good feeling that came when I was suicidal. The not caring. Not caring because I knew I was so fucked up. Not caring because I thought I was going to die anyway; because I knew that I was the one who was going to do it.

Now to the other emotions at the same time; pure disgust. Pure disgust when I first hurt myself after trying not to for so long. Disgust of how I was ashamed to walk around in shirts. Disgust of the fear that someone will know and call me weak. Most people realize that someone is hurting, also themselves, when you can only see the scars that are left. They realize it when it is too late to do anything about it. However, with time I didn't even care or feel anything while hurting myself, so, I did it to feel again. To feel something, to feel that I was still there. That's at least what I told myself. In the moment, you think it's the only thing that will help. In the end, it turns out that it just makes everything worse. Another thing that needs to be normalized.

It reminds me of something. The first time someone had pointed out my scars in my family, in front of everyone. This person made jokes, laughed and asked if I fell into a bush with my bike. I sat there and I said, 'Yeah, I fell.' They kept on pushing because they thought it would be funny. I laughed with them. I said that I fell. However, I didn't fall from a bike or into a bush like I told them I did. It still had truth in it. *Because I was falling apart inside. Slowly, and then all at once.* I think no one has the right to point out any scars or similar things to anyone. If someone has scars, they for sure have a story behind those scars that they are not willing to just tell most of the time. It could hurt them more than others could ever understand. They know that it's there, they all know obviously but that does not give anyone the right to point it out or to even make fun of it.

However, back to the song. I sing smiling to it, making the others even more confusion. I have no idea why I'm finding this funny but it's kind of ironic. My humour is fucked up ever since I became worse. Ask Abby, she knows. This song is much more meaningful than any other one I wrote. If I want to record it, I don't want to do it with the piano. I basically recorded every song using a piano. It's just a sad instrument. Besides that, I need some rock and what is better than hiding such a message behind a rock song?

"That is fucking awesome," Mary speaks up after I finished and I turn around to them.

"Have you got everything written down?" I ask him.

"Yes."

"Good, now we can go back to eating." Jacob, Mary and I walk towards the dining table when Ethan walks in rather fast and a little bit pissed again.

"Can we talk Olivia?" he asks me while running his fingers through his hair and placing the other hand on his forehead. Oh, you're not the only one who will have a headache after this evening.

"I'd rather eat now Ethan." I ignore his urge towards me. I'm not some damn doll.

"Come on, you just can't leave out that you were obviously pissed before."

"I am leaving something out. Are you even listening to yourself right now?" I pronounce the 'I' using my arms to hug my body. I am not becoming angry quickly, but I'm at the state of being pissed now. "You never tell me anything. I never pushed you Ethan, unlike the way you have pushed me. I don't want to know everything at once, but a little bit of information would be nice."

"You don't trust me?" he asks me with a disappointed expression.

"I trust you more than I have ever trusted any male person in my life. I just don't like being left out. Ethan, I love you and I trust you, but I don't understand. Why do you love me? Why do you care? Why aren't you telling me everything?" I state feeling my eyes tearing up.

"Because I'm fucking scared! I'm scared, okay?"

Chapter Thirty-Three

Scared? I doubt that there is anything he should be scared of. "Why are you scared? Did I do anything?" As I say this I bring my arms up in front of myself in surrender.

"No. No, you didn't do anything baby. It's because of me. Because of all of us. All the people you met since you came here. Since I bumped into you. It's all because of me," he's basically screaming at me, making me flinch. He never screamed before. If Abby would be here now, she would tell me that I thought the same thing about Roman. It's funny how fast a bad memory can be relived with someone new. He frowns at my flinching shaking his head while laughing. "But you're scared of me."

"I'm scared of someone screaming at me the way you just did. Instead of talking just screaming. Just like Roman did," I yell back for once in my life. Because for the first time in my life, I know my worth. I won't have him screaming at me the way Roman did because I know that he is nothing like him.

"Don't compare me to that ass. I may have done bad things in my life and I may haven't told you everything, but I would never do what he did to you."

"I never believed you would. What are you scared of?" I push further. *No, don't come at me telling me what I said. I know what I said. This time it's different, this is different and I am different. As is he.* We both don't realize that Jacob and Mary are still there. Watching us with open mouths while we're standing about two meters apart by now.

"I'm scared of losing you. Just as I lost everything I loved so deeply," he admits screaming again while his eyes are tearing up. He's speaking from his heart again. I step closer to him and I take his face with my hands. At this point, we're both a crying mess. *We're vulnerable together.*

"Then don't push me away. Don't hide yourself and the things you went through. Don't think that I won't love you because of what you did and who you were. The reason I don't is because all those things made you who you are today. The person I love the most." I assure hugging him tightly, hoping for him to not make the same mistake I did.

"I just can't lose you," he pleads again sobbing in between his words. He doesn't care about the fact that his closest friends are still there. I'm not even entirely sure if he's ever cried before them.

After a while, this one sentence is coming back to my mind. *People who love you will never put themselves in a position to lose you.* Remember that? I do. By the night we promised each other not to promise each other anything (ironic, right?) this was a situation I never thought of. Going on tour with the persons I love the most but also being so scared to lose any of them.

The first step of a relationship or friendship is being glad you have this one person. It's a great feeling because nothing else matters at that point. However, with time going by, you will eventually find yourself wishing for it to last longer. Whether that's because it's already over or because of the more important reason I'd like to talk about. It's because you know what you gained and you are afraid to lose it just as you lost so many other things. Because eventually, with time, this person will become more important to you than anything. Maybe even yourself. I had that twice. And I'm scared he will become the third one. Well, technically Ethan already is but he is still there. Not like the other time when I thought about it. It was the moment I knew that everything was crumbling. The moment before everything ended. Silence. Pure silence and darkness before the storm. The moment I knew that the road and adventure with that person was coming to an end. The first time I realized the feeling of numbness from my toes all the way up to my head. It's something that you feel everywhere and all the time. Something I never want to feel again. Since I met Ethan, I also haven't. Not in a temporary way.

My biggest pet peeve is when someone comes up to me or on that damn social media and says idiotic thing, such as 'Just think positive', 'It's not that bad', 'Talking about it all the time won't help' or 'Yes I know you're bad, but people have it worse. I know how you feel. Yeah, it's shitty but do you know how it is to live with someone who talks about it all the time? A literal nightmare.' See, people who know how it truly feels will never ever say that. They wouldn't dare. Here I am again, talking about the names but you know what? I don't care. I tried to avoid the terms of mental illnesses because I know it's not nice to just be categorized. However, this needs to be said. Even if no one will hear it, I need to say it. For myself and for all of us. Depression is not feeling a bit sad sometimes. Depression is not faking it for attention. Depression is not something that comes and goes or that you can make up. It's there. It's always there and it doesn't leave you alone. Yes, it's an illness caused from your head but if you feel like it, you will never think that this is a sort of technical mistake in your head. You don't believe that a mistake can make you feel that bad. By now most people would say it's annoying how much I talk about it and think about it. It may be but understanding what you feel is just helping me to stay sane.

This is my story and if it is too annoyingly sad for you, I apologize, my bad. You're not the only one to think that, believe me. Understanding the thoughts in my head at that time even if they might be gone in a few hours. The lack of remembering. I couldn't and still can't remember things I thought when I had a panic attack. Or the things that made me happy last week or even from the day before. Everything good is just gone. There is just this empty thing and that aching in your chest and in your throat just once you want to talk about it. You can't think of anything positive because there is just nothing positive that can be thought about. You can slowly feel yourself becoming someone you never wanted to be and you can't even do anything about it because you're physically as well as mentally exhausted. That why 'I'm tired' doesn't always mean they haven't slept much. Maybe they did, maybe they just want to sleep forever and never wake up. Check up on your friends, especially if you feel them pushing you away. They might do it to protect you while they're destroying themselves to achieve that.

As an example, imagine that your head, or more likely your emotional brain part, is made of two containers. One for good things and memories and one for bad ones. While all the water that is in the good container just slowly, day by day, gets emptier. It's likes all the water goes in a magically and not understandable way into the bad one. This goes on and on until it's just runs over. It's not something funny and it's not something you can make fun of. Why would anyone make fun of someone with cancer? The point is, is no one would. While depression, which is one of the deadliest illnesses on this planet, makes you want to kill yourself. Suicidal thoughts are symptoms of depression the final symptom of it. It's nothing more than a symptom but let's be honest, if you had these thoughts would you think about the cause? No. Your head is hurting enough from thinking.

Another short pet peeve before we continue. Jesus, chill out. It's not like the world would be ending while I'm telling you this. Give me a second, would you? Thanks, a lot. Now, let's get this over with so you will be happy, okay? Whenever I was at a party, which was not frequent, I got quite annoyed when they wouldn't let someone play a song or said it was bad and made fun of it. See, I always adored music more than anything on this planet. Music is a way of expressing yourself and your feelings. The words in songs that you can relate to more than you'd maybe like to. Things you can't say and explain that the artist of a song can. It's a way of feeling something when you don't feel anything. So, these 'cool' people would take away the sense of comfortableness and safety in these persons. Most of the time having a 'cool-label' does not help you. It just makes everyone think that you are strong when you're truly very much insecure. Okay, we're back now. Happy?

"Ethan, what are you talking about?" I ask him while his forehead rests against mine and I'm still holding his face. Standing on your tippy toes for that long could count as a workout in itself. Damn these genes that made me small.

"I don't want to put you on the spot. Not for the public to judge you and not for anyone else. I have this feeling that I need to keep you away from everything like that to keep you safe. Not everyone likes me and not everyone is being supportive of me or the person I am in contact with."

"It's not your job to do that. It's not your job to keep me safe, I can do that on my own. You can't keep me hidden from the world for no reason just like my dad did. You need to trust me," I say again. *Not more than two days ago he didn't give a fuck about people taking pictures of us. What changed?*

"You don't know what you're talking about. You don't know things about me. I feel as if you only like the things about me that I show you. The things that aren't that bad." Now it's enough. It's enough of all of this. I'm fed up with this. All I wanted is to have an evening to escape from them. I just wanted to spend time with them and maybe drink a glass or two. Yeah, don't come at me. I know you shouldn't drink if you're trying to escape something, but can you blame me?

I let go of him taking a step back while sighing. My head turns to see two worried faces. I nod to myself before I feel a tear running down my wet face. "You once told me that spreading me open was the only way of knowing me. Now, I am wishing I

238

wouldn't need to do the same thing. I'm wishing that spreading you open wasn't the only way to know you." As I tell him so, I can see him losing it completely. My feet turn around alone while I walk away from this.

"Olivia, baby, where are you going?" he asks shakily and I come to an immediate stop.

"I think we both need a few moments to think. A few moments to be alone and think. Ethan we both know you wouldn't let go of this now. So, I am doing it for you." Don't cry, don't cry, don't cry. I spin around again but before I can even take another step he is speaking up again.

"No. Please tell me you're not gonna leave me."

"I'm not leaving you Ethan. I told you, I'm in the long-term game. However, the right thing to do now is to leave this conversation and all of us alone. That's what I'm doing." I explain giving him a small smile. A small smile of hope. Something to hold on to, as I always found myself wishing for something like this when I was younger. One last smile to know that it'll be okay. In my darkest moments I wished for someone to tell me that it was going to be okay even though I couldn't even have told them anything at that point. Sometimes even if I knew that it wasn't going to be okay, I just wanted to hear it. I'm not talking about the future promises, they seemed hopeless, no, I am talking about someone reassuring me that I will wake up the next morning. To know that even if I felt as if I was dying, that I was still breathing. I was terrified of death, I still am. Death seems like this dark and endless black even ocean that I didn't want to dive into. That I was trying to fight against the person who wanted to kill me in my own body. Sometimes, you can be your biggest opponent. It was the days I wanted not to be alive so badly. There were days where I wondered if I made all of this up for attention as many people on the outside so often like to point out. Nevertheless, when I was alone and I knew, I wasn't going to call anyone or tell anyone, those things were still there. That's when I knew that such bad things just simply cannot be made up for fun or even attention. At least, not for me. Problem with that was that I knew the next day I was still going to show up at school and put on my happy face. I was more afraid of the black ocean than I was of dying. I was too scared to do the thing that seemed to be the only solution.

"Where are you going? You don't need to leave. I can do that."

"No, it's fine. I need to spend some alone time and get things done," I tell him turning around to Jacob and Mary. "Watch out for him, will you?"

"We will darling. You don't need to worry yourself with this dipshit," he whispered in my ear grimacing. He never fails to make me laugh.

"You need to watch yourself too! It's not about everyone else all the time," Mary adds and I find myself nodding. She's right. I need to think and I need to breathe. I just need to breathe and then all of it will be all right. We'll be all right, right?

There are always two sides to everything. To an argument for example. Abby is one of those persons who will listen to both of them and mostly all of the time understand both sides. She's like Switzerland. Nothing against Switzerland, I love cheese and chocolate, but once in a while it feels good to have someone who will just be on your side. Someone who will have your back and worry about you and nothing else in that moment. As I said, once in a while would be nice. I've been that sort of person to many people, but I cannot recall anyone being that for me. However, what I noticed is that at the time I came here I couldn't even have those sorts of conversations with myself. Not even thinking about being able to tell you. I talked myself down for these ideas in my head without even taking a second to understand them, giving them time or even writing about them. Writing is the biggest therapeutic way of healing. That and most commonly for me in songs. I need words. I need to have these things written down because I want to understand them in order to make them stop. I want to make them stop. So, I'm begging you not to complain about me talking about this thing a lot. I'm trying to hold it back, but whats going on in my mind is it my fault.

See, there's the side of mental illness that no one talks about. The side where you have those perfect grades that everyone wants. The side without a messy room. The side without sleeping the whole day and with showering like a normal person would (What is even normal?). The side where you're constantly smiling around people, where even teachers compliment you on being that happy and motivated all the time. The side where no one knows how bad you feel. I think this side deserves more attention. So, shout out to everyone who is there. Because I've been there, and I felt so bad for it because no one talked about it, so it wasn't normalized. If something isn't normalized, you will feel even more abnormal and weird, not a good weird though. Not a good combination, let me tell you. People would call me heather, not to be mean, but it still affected me. They symbolized me as a person who could do almost everything and said they wished to be like me. Little did they know how much fucking effort it took for me to even get up. So, be aware of what you say. Words hurt, more than you'll ever know.

The best way to cope with traumas and depression is to make fun of it. Now, it does sound pretty ironic, huh? Believe me it helps so much. When my mental health got worse, so did my humour. I made fun of things, like black dark humour, and every-one thought it was funny. However, I wasn't even kidding. I just made it sound funny. Nevertheless, making fun of the things that hurt me is the most amazing thing to do. Yeah, they do shitty things to you, but you can get one back at them. I'm aware that you don't believe me but just try it out. It works, I swear on my hate for pumpkins. If you don't try it out and believe me now, there is nothing left that I could do for you. Irony is just one of the most amazing causes on this damn planet. Okay I'm done for this time. You survived this talk. Congrats.

I take my phone and purse not long before walking thought the labyrinth of hallway until I reach the door. See, the smart reason I'm not taking my whole bag with me is to show him that I'll be back. That this isn't the end or anything like that. Because it's not. Long-term game, remember?

"You're walking away from your problem Olivia, our problem." Ethan looks at the floor while shaking his head, almost in disbelieve.

As I step outside the cold air hits me straight in the face. "I know," I say to myself when I'm sure the door is closed. For a few minutes I just stand there breathing in the air to remember that I am breathing and that the earth is still turning around. The sun is still shining, even though it's shining for the other half of the planet at this moment. It's good to remind ourselves how unimportant we truly are to this world. In a way that the sun will still shine even if we aren't around anymore. That is a feeling that I have to remind myself of every once in a while.

Chapter Thirty-Four

I'd like to talk about something for a second or two. About my whole life when I felt as if I needed to please everyone; I still do that about sixty percent of the time. With that, I think I can identify myself as a people pleaser. The problem is that I always give a bigger fuck about what others want and if they are happy. It's okay to tell humans, friends and family to fuck off. In the end this is your own life. Will it make you happy to spend all the energy on others and to let yourself down that much? Certainly not. I can put that to a memory if you'd like me to. I was about eighteen or nineteen. I don't quite remember; all of that time seems blur in my head. Never mind, it was a Monday. A rainy Monday. I hated Mondays more than pumpkins at that time. It was the day after I wrote my last exam. It was supposed to be over. As you can imagine, it wasn't. I still felt like that even though everyone told me that it was going to be over by then. I was very close to doing something stupid. Like very, very close. I didn't tell anyone. I never did. Someone gave me a number that I could call whenever I had those very dark moments and until then I thought I was strong enough to do it alone. As I said, I thought I was. So, I sat there with shaking hands, and I dialled that number. I had no idea how I should explain it or even talk but I knew I had to do something. I let it ring. It took a moment, and, in that moment, I thought I was dead. Until I heard a voice. In that moment I felt so much better. Until the voice said that they had no one available at the moment. Irony. So, instead I laughed and cried at the same time. I made fun of it. Instead, I cried, and I went to bed. Next day I went off to school again as if nothing had ever happened.

A few weeks after that, to be more exact a week after my birthday I ended up in the hospital. Not because of my mental health if that's what you think. It doesn't even matter why. There were a few doctors and whenever they saw my scars, they would ask questions like they've never seen someone harm themselves. Yeah, I get that they needed to be aware of your health as a patient but not in that way. Because I knew they were there. Everyone who saw it knew it. There's no need to make me uncomfortable or to point it out even more. I knew it wasn't really normal nor good, but I never felt understood by them or even by my friends. None of my friends said anything about it when I first started wearing shirts again. Everyone knew they were there, but no one said anything about them. In more than one way I was glad about it. I was glad because I wouldn't know if I had been able to explain why I did it. Did I do it for attention? No. Did I hope for anyone to tell me that it will get better and that they are there for me? Yes. Did that happen? No.

The problem with our society is that people talk about depression as if it's something regular (which it sadly is developing into more and more every day) but as soon as a loved or well-known person has anything like that, they haven't got any clue on what to do or how to act. The idea of having a mental illness is accepted until you actually show signs of it. As a member of this sort of family-connection-thing I can assure you that we do not expect anyone to take the pain or the problems away just so. No, that hope died very soon. We're just hoping for a sort of understanding and love around us. There were times when someone could've screamed at me that they loved me, and I wouldn't have believed it for a single second. That is the particular reason we need to show anyone who is suffering that we love them instead of constantly calling them out. Huge difference. Another red flag; never dare to tell someone that their scars are fading and how good that might be, or how they're 'not deep enough'. Just don't. Some visible scars may fade but internal ones really never do. Words can hurt deeper than any knife can.

See, walking home in the dark can make you think. A lot, actually. I decided to walk instead of taking an uber. It's not too late and not that dark yet. I need air. Not to be dramatic but I am kind of scared to walk around London at night alone. That's a process because at times I wasn't. I wasn't scared because I didn't believe anyone would want to attack me. Funny to look back at that. Another process. I'm aware that I'm still not as scared as I should be of some situations but I'm working to get there. At least I don't want to not be alive anymore. When I was seeking help for the first time, I started to wonder how the healing would look like. Do I suddenly wake up and want to live again? Do I ever want to feel again? Back then, I couldn't imagine being 'normal' again or wanting to live.

Never mind, I walk along the street focusing on my breathing. Whenever I walk home alone, especially when it's getting darker, I listen to music so loudly that I can barely hear any of my surroundings. Another thing that I love about walking home is watching the sky and the stars. Stars have always been something that fascinated me. They are beyond far away and still we can see them as something unmoving and calm. Something natural. About the most calming thing about them is that even if I won't be here to watch them anymore, I know that they'll be there for hundreds and maybe millions of years. As the sun, they don't care if we are here, they are doing their own thing. I'd like to be a star. To watch everything from the distance and being boundless like the ocean. It also has been my dream date ever since I can imagine. I dreamed of such stuff with Abby when we were teenagers. Yeah, what a great term. Teenagers. Children want to be teenagers and get older. Older people want to be teenagers again. Everyone wants to be teenagers except for teenagers themselves. How ironic.

I'm five minutes away from my apartment and I'm about to cross the street. My feet are leaving the walkway when I hear a horn behind me. I jump around holding my chest to realize that I've just been nearly hit by a car. Wouldn't be the first time to ever happen. I say a quick sorry and step out of the way to see the driver shake his head and curse at me. "Holy shit." I say to myself while sitting on top of my stairs as soon as I reach my front door.

That was a fair dose of adrenalin. I won't lie to you, I'm kind of scared to go in there because of everything that has happened but what am I supposed to do otherwise? Ethan needs time to think, I need time to think or just do something to avoid anything to do with the letter and overthinking Ethan and me. It's not something huge or even a fight like I used to have with Roman. I am scared that it will become that. I'm scared that one day I won't have him. That someday with losing him I will lose myself again. Quite earlier I said that I never really believed in love. Well, he changed that. *He changed it because he taught me how to love.* He's the very thing I love most. And Abby. And baby corn with pees. And music and writing- you get the point, right?

After another few minutes I collect myself opening the front door, breathing a sigh of relief. I walk from room to room, making sure that no one is there. After what's happened, no one can blame me for the bit of paranoia that I've developed. As there is nothing to be seen, I turn on the lights, closing the door and locking it behind me, walking to my living room. The empty envelop is sticking in my head immediately. After what's happened, the day couldn't get a lot worse, at least that's what I tell myself while opening it with a kitchen knife. My hands are shaking when I'm on the verge of opening it and pulling whatever there is out. My breathing gets heavier again as the level of anxiety in my body is increasing enormously fast. Again, the little piece of paper is only filled with a few sentences. Like why? Honestly, why me? What did I or even my mum do to piss someone off that much? At this point I'm even too scared to even look at it. What if it's a threat or anything that could hurt someone important to me. What if they will hurt Ethan, Abby, Mary, or Jacob? What if they will do everything in order to... no. *Fucking calm down Olivia. No one is dying, at least not right now. Everything will be fine, we'll be fine.*

It's taken me another five minutes to destress myself. My shaky hands are taking the note out of the envelope to fully read it. My eyes wonder over the words printed in ink a couple of times before I understand what it says. The second I do, I wish I didn't open it. It's a picture of a heart with flowers which come out of the veins. About the exact same pattern that I now have tattooed on my body. Jesus Christ, how? A little further down there is something written. *As green as olives or as green as the forest? Makes no difference, makes it easy. As thick as blood are the connections, full perfection. Everything will connect eventually Olivia...*

What? Green olive green... the diary...? The tattoo which I got... but nobody except the guys saw it. Well, the tattoo artist of course but... the damn tattoo studio. Fucking hell. That's about the perfect Google reviews. I will never trust this damn platform again. They do not know everything... or do they? This is too much for my brain. Dark green for forest... the colours? Blood, thick, connections... as in a blood line for a family? What is that supposed to mean? Of course, at this point I'm aware that they want the diary from my mom – shit. The diary. I left it in my bag at Ethan's apartment. Shit. How can I even be that clumsy? Thanks to the amount of liquid, I already had I'm not getting another anxiety attack. You couldn't blame me either. This would be the perfect time to call someone for advice. Who's the question. Ethan and I need time to think, Abby was acting all weird, Jacob and Mary aren't really involved in all of this drama and my dad... no. Again, I'm here to put myself together alone. Yay. You got this, though Olivia. You did it a hundred times before and you can do it a hundred times again. I'm not alone. She is here with me. My mother is here and she's watching over me. She has to be, right?

I sit down on my comfy grey sofa and I open my laptop to start a new document. While I'm writing my feelings and important stuff down, I can feel my eyes becoming heavier and I close the laptop, promising to just take a nap for ten seconds. It took me a bit of time to calm down enough but with music in the back and a way to tell the document how I'm feeling this will be worth it. What I'm meaning by this is even spending effort in trying to write down what's going on in your head when you don't even understand it.

Chapter Thirty-Five

I'm at therapy. Came unexpected, I know. It happened two days ago, the morning after thanksgiving and my midlife crisis. I got a call saying that the therapist, Susan I think, who I contacted with Ethan had a free appointment because one of her other clients was unfortunately being sent to a psych ward. I texted Ethan that I was going to meet her today, before leaving and it didn't even take him five minutes to respond. He said that he's proud and that whenever something happens, I should just call him. Oh, and I told him that I wanted to talk to him this evening. Okay, that is not true... I'm planning on telling him that. After the appointment, depending on how I am doing by then.

So, here I am in the waiting room of her working... office, space... Is that what you would call it? I'm confused, I'm nervous and I really want to go home to pee. This is just out of my lane and I don't really enjoy this at all. Remember when I told you about my own bubble? Yes? Because I'd really like to be there right now. Am I even sick enough to be here? Again, so many people have it way worse... I have everything that I need so I should be happy and glad about it, right? *Note to myself, taking my own advice for once.*

I don't even realize how my hands are shaking and sweating and how I am running my fingers through my hair at least five times a minute. Yes, I'm nervous. Glad that you did catch up on that. As I was saying, I didn't realize it until I hear the voice of the very sweet and nice assistant I met about ten minutes ago. "Miss Jones?" She knocks on the door giving me a reassuring smile when she sees my state of mind.

"Yeah?"

"You can meet with Susan now. I'll show you the way, just follow along." I nod in response, picking my bag and jacket to follow her. "You don't need to be scared, she's a nice person. It will be fine, I promise." *I promise.*

"Uhm… okay. Thank you." She opens a white door right in front of me, letting me go inside first after saying goodbye. As the art studio I've been to with Ethan this place has a huge amount of plants, making it feel cosier and in some way like home. I should really add more plants to my apartment. New point on the list which consist of things I should do in order to get my life into control. Yay. Will I ever be able to cross things off that list? Probably not. Never mind.

I enter the room sitting down in a brown leather armchair right in front of who I suppose must be Susan. She's a little older than me and gives me a very hippy vibe. I adore it though. We say hello to one another doing a bit of small talk for a bit. It helps me to lower the level of anxiety, so she knows what she's doing. However, the last time I went to therapy for the first time it was even worse. I just started to cry for no reason and it was embarrassing. Progress.

"So, why did you decided to come here Olivia?" she asks the first more serious question placing the pen between her lips. She has curly brown hair, clear glasses and a yellow bandana in her hair. The problem is, is that is the most difficult question that she is asking me right now. Do I know why? No. Do I know what's wrong with me? Definitely not. Why am I here? Good question.

"Well… it's Liv not Olivia. However, to be completely honest with you, I'm not really sure. I can sense that there is something going on with me and it has been for a while. It's not as bad as others have it, so I didn't get any help. People have it worse than me. But with time, my boyfriend thought it could be a good thing. He just wants the best for me and I do want that for him as well." *I would tear my heart out if it meant happiness for him.*

"I see. Can I ask you one simple question?"

"Yeah, sure." I guess? I place my hands on my thighs doing weird movements with them. Another bad habit.

"When was the last time you can recall yourself being happy for a longer period of time?" she asks directly putting her pen aside. Very interesting question Susan, I have to say.

"Depends on what you would identify as a longer period of time…," I reply. Otherwise, I could not find the right answer.

"Let's say for two or three months to begin with," she replies giving me a small smile.

My lips part and my eyes widen in disbelieve.

"People are happy for two months straight. That's possible without being sad," I say laughing in between. Not that fucking humour again. I hate it. "Sorry, I know it's not funny but… it kind of is. Sorry." Awkward. Yay. I'm swearing, and if I could do anything to stop my brain from laughing about the most unimportant things I would. And I tried. As you may be able to tell by now, I failed.

"I think that would be the answer if you're sick enough to get help. *Healthy people, as you would call them, don't spend that much time wondering whether they're sick.* You cannot sick enough to get help. Every person needs that once in a while and now it's your time. So, do you want to get something of your mind? It could be anything that is bothering you or from your past. I'm here and I will listen and try to help as best as I can. I'm aware that it's difficult to open up to a new person but with time it might help you a lot." I like her. She's nice.

Okay, I'll spare you the rest of it. Let's get back to the most important thing. I told her a bit about Ethan and my friends… not about my mom yet. However, she said that maybe I should start on working things out with Ethan. Which gave me get a brilliant idea. We also arranged that I'll be coming frequently every week for now and I hope that it will help me. Because that would be nice.

I walk back to the tube. Taking my phone out I dial Jacob's number. "Hello sweetheart. Are you okay? Is there something I can do for you?" he asks immediately.

"I'm doing… I'm just doing. However, there is something that you could do for me." I find myself smiling and grinning about it. This is going to be fun and special at the same time.

"You're scaring me Liv. Though, I'm listening."

"I need you to get Ethan out of his apartment. Do what you will, you could force him to do some yoga but that's not important. What's important is that I need to get into his place. There is something I need to do." I explain to him hearing him laugh.

"Oh God. That will be fun I suppose. I can do that for you, of course I can. You should just know that you don't always need to apologize for everything that happens. *Not everything is your fault darling.* This time it should be Ethan doing something. Just letting you know. However, you did not hear that from me because I'm his friend and I won't let him fuck up with you for his own benefit. I'm telling you this because you're my friend and I care about you." This is too much for me. I've never been used to having so many people care in a way, that's it is kind of terrifying.

"Jacob you're the best, I hope you know that. It might not be my turn to clear anything but it's my turn to show him something. It's my turn to show him my vulnerabilities. Also, this a good way for you to gain a point for yoga. I'll agree that you're not very similar on that topic." I keep on speaking while scanning my card before going down the stairs towards the tube. It's about time for the car thing. And a lot of other things when we're at it right now.

"That's the spirit. Let's go out and waste one of those perfect birthday presents that you got from Abby."

"Always. You know me, I'm not going anywhere. Do you think Mary would come as well?" I ask out of curiosity. We haven't been able to connect as much as I could with Jacob or Ethan and I'm feeling bad for it. I really am.

"I think she would. But I won't share my special time I got with you. Not even with Ethan. Sorry to say but he's always making you busy. We need to have another recording session for your wonderful song as well. I swear I can smell that this is going to be great like the first one. If you didn't ignore your social media and manager all the time, you would know that for a fact as I know it."

"Good point. Look, I'm getting onto the tube. I'll be over at Ethan's as soon as you text me, okay? Keep him occupied and don't tell him anything." If he tells him then I'll have to smoke those damn presents alone. Which I don't want to do because that would be sappy.

"Yes Ma'am. I'll text you. But please don't make his house explode because then I won't make it to another yoga session. And that will mean that I can't help him to improve and we will all die as yoga losers," he says in one quick sentence, making me chuckle and smile to myself. Yeah, I do realize that people are staring but this is just too funny not to laugh about it.

"Jacob, calm down. I won't break anything. You need to loosen up a bit." Funny that I am the one to say that.

"I am the one who needs to do that? Sure, whatever helps you sleep at night," he replies letting out a sarcastic chuckle. See, told you. I say goodbye before entering the waiting tube. Since it's barely past noon most people are working which makes it less crowded. Just my luck as I'm on my way back home I listen to a certain type of music. My comfortable music. You know that feeling when it seems as if the world is falling apart and everything is shitty but then this song comes on and all of a sudden it doesn't matter anymore. It doesn't matter because when this song or songs in general come on, you know that it will be fine as if nothing else matters because you know that everything else sucks, so you just try to ignore it. You do know that? Good. I don't want to think about how this world would be without music. In my opinion, it wouldn't even be a real world anymore. Because music is my world. Words are my world. *You are my world, even though it's too late to tell you that now.*

I arrive home and start to pack everything that I need. But before packing the rest, I sit down at my black piano for a second to play the chords of the song. Something that has been stuck in my head over and over. I want to work on it, because it... because I don't want to let go of that feeling, of the thought that this could be someone's comfort music, that it could actually help someone except for myself. *To make someone feel something.*

After a few minutes of sitting and tuning the chords of my guitar I pack it. I hope he'll like it because... because it's what I adore doing. Something no one knows about such as he enjoys painting. Today I will show him what my little secret things are. Things that I have kept to myself for almost my while life. When thinking about it, I guess that I just waited for the right person. I know he's the one. Yes, it's messy and confusing with our... well... situation. But this is what makes me feel a certain way. It started on the cliff one night, the night I got to know him and me at the same time. The night everything started and I felt like it never needed to end. The night I knew that he made me feel the most at home I have ever felt. Again, it's not a place for me. It's not a certain emotion because it's him. All the emotions he makes me experience every time I see him. When I stare into his hazel eyes and whenever I hear his voice makes me feel butterflies my stomach. The aching in my tummy when he's touching me in any way possible. And the warm feeling in my heart when he lets it speak for me. That is my home.

When receiving Jacob's text that they're gone, that feeling comes back immediately. I quickly make myself a sandwich before putting on my jacket to leave. With guitar and bag in hand and head-phones in my ears, I find myself smiling so widely that it makes my cheeks hurt. This is good.

Luckily, today it's not raining which is quite fortunate for my plans. Because today, I'm showing him the stars from my point of view. I'll show him the stars, my comfortable music and a song. I won't lie, I'm nervous about it. Not that he would judge it in any way but because I'll be releasing those three things. Things that I hold dear to my heart.

As Jacob had texted me, he hid a key for me. Taking the key out of the spot where he had hidden it, which wasn't too clever to hide it there, I open the front door. To be honest, I would do just about anything to see him struggle with yoga because that must be entertaining as hell. Nevertheless, I have some work to do over here. So, I take my guitar outside together with many blankets and cushions. Comfy is always good. I lay them on the ground just as Ethan did on the night at the cliff. I place my guitar on the blanket taking the few candles I had brought with out of my back. Lucky for me I did not forget the matches this time. You would think I do possess a lighter because of the candles – but I don't. I always lose them, or I burn myself with them. So, I gave up at one point. Last thing is snacks, a music box and a bit of liquid. Not to get drunk and escape stuff, but to have fun and be creative.

As soon as everything is ready I go inside to change. On entering his dark bedroom I see that my bag is still where I had left it on thanksgiving. I pick up my bag to search for the diary. It's still there, which is good. But not today, today is about us in the present with something that needs to be sorted out.

Not long after that, I receive another message from Jacob, saying that they'll be here very soon. Hopefully, Ethan isn't in a bad mood after doing… trying yoga. I sit on his couch, which is made of black leather, scrolling through Instagram. Yeah, I know. Because I've got nothing else to do, I post another picture of the area I created outside while waiting for the others. As soon as I'm done posting, I can hear loud voices outside. What I can hear is the enormously loud giggle of Jacob and a groan from Ethan. Yep, seems like they had a lot of fun. The door opens and they both inside taking off their shoes. Ethan runs his fingers through his messy hair and turns towards Jacob.

"Mate, I'm really thankful that you made me embarrass myself in public, but I need a break. I can't go on with your good yoga energy. It's driving me insane." In public? Sneaky little brat.

Jacob doesn't bother to move and Ethan brings his hands up in front of him in confusion. His face is too gorgeous. It's even funnier that he hasn't noticed me yet. "Oh, don't worry. It was a pleasure. However, I'm not here for you anymore. Liv, he fucked up, I told you he would. That is so five to three," he says as Ethan's head turns around trying to find me. When his hazel eyes meet mine, I can already feel the butterflies in my stomach and a tingling right to the top of my head.

"Olivia, what are you doing here?" he asks walking over to me. I get up standing in front of him while he focuses on his breathing. *He's breathing, everything is fine. It will be fine.*

"Surprise, I suppose. I know you needed time and I did too. I went to therapy and there are a few things that I want you to know.

Well, only if you want to know them of course." I admit and still not fully being able to look into his eyes. At least, not until he places his finger under my chin, making me look up at him.

"You being here is the best thing that could've happen. I was gonna talk to you but then Jacob showed up and made me do stupid poses the whole afternoon. I'm betting they're all over the internet right now," he laughs touching every single piece of my face. I don't know why but it's very intimidating to me.

"Yeah, that was sort of my idea. I'm sorry. But he got a point for it so we're even now."

"Jacob, I think this is your call to leave. We'll talk at the studio tomorrow," he says not turning around even for a second.

"Sure, big boy. I'll see you both. Have fun, but not too much fun," he tells us opening the front door, making me let out a laugh and a weird noise. "Oh, and wear protection!" he yells and before giving us a chance to react he closes the door. Just like Abby somehow I'd like to believe that in another world we were meant to be here.

"So, what about the studio plans?" I ask changing the subject after calming down from chuckling. My hands are now tightly around his neck while his are resting on my waist.

"Soon, baby. First, I want to hear about your plans though," he smirks kissing me softly, asking for my permission in some way. *I would never want to deny that Ethan. Here we go.*

Chapter Thirty-Six

Standing in front of him and slowly moving my lips onto his, all the troubles seem to have just disappeared. "There's a lot we need to talk about, but I think it's time to show you something. A while ago you showed me your secret love for art… so, I want to show you something as well," I say smiling. He raises and eyebrow placing a bit of hair behind my ear which has come loose.

"I hope you know that you don't have to show me anything just because I showed you something."

"That is the point, Ethan. You showed me so much more than you do realize. It wasn't my place to pressure you into telling me anything. I feel as if I had pushed you to tell me things, but that's not what I want to do. It sucks because I know why I am feeling like this is because of Roman. I went to therapy and I figured that out. God, please don't think that I would assume you're anything like him. Because you are not. It's just that after everything he did, I can't…," I try to break through the ice and to explain but he places his finger on my lips, signalling for me to stop talking.

"*Don't blame yourself for the trauma someone else has given you.* I know why you are feeling this way, because I feel the same. I'm scared of losing everything that I have. I'm scared of losing you because you made me who I am and that is who I always wanted to be but never could be on my own. Sweetheart, you showed me the light, the sun and life. You did all of those things," he says interrupting me making my heart beat a million times per minute.

"I'd like to show you the stars as well."

"What?" he asks frowning and chuckling. I take his huge hand in mine, intertwining our fingers passing the hallway until we reach his outdoor space. The space, we first really met with the whole team. To be honest, it seems like yesterday although it has been months. As reach the area his eyes widen.

"You did that? For me?" he asks and I nod, barely standing two feet in front of him I watch his face light up like a little child.

"Of course I did. Why are you so impressed?" *He deserves way better.*

"Because no one has ever done anything like that for me before." I step closer kissing his cheek gently.

"Let's dance under the stars. Those are two things that I love. Dancing and stars. But combined with someone I love would be the best thing I could think of right now." I hope he can dance though. I wouldn't say my dancing is very attractive but I like to do it just for me and then it doesn't have to be perfect.

"You're something else Olivia," he laughs taking hold of me slowly moving to the music in the background. His face is against my neck while I stare at the sky. If she could see me right now, I'm pretty sure she would be smiling as brightly as I am right now. Because right now, nothing else matters. Right now, he is my comfortable music and he is my comfortable person. *Because right now, we're half the world away.* But oh God, I wish he could see everything like I do and see how he means the actual world to me, to see how he looks in my and everyone else's light.

"I have to ask, why the stars?" he asks disturbing the comfortable silence, making me grin to myself before staring into his eyes. They remind me of a planet in the galaxy. Something unmoving and still so permanent. Something that does not care about every single star but still needs to see them around. He's the planet to my stars.

"They're utterly beautiful. They're unmoving and they aren't bound to anything. They're always there, even though we cannot see them all the time. I know they won't leave me. I always wanted to be a star. It's so stupid, but that's just it," I tell him giggling over my stupidness.

"Why are you laughing?"

"It's funny. How it's not even funny, that's funny," I reply and he takes hold of my cheeks, still moving along to the music in the background around the candles.

"If something is important to you, it will never be funny for me." He reassures me kissing me softly, placing one of his hands at the back of my head. "I think you missed out something though."

"What would that be?" I ask in a teasing voice.

"You're wishing to be a star when you already are like one. You're my stars Olivia. The light in my dark sky." *Maybe we can be our own little galaxy together. Half the world away from home, from anything else.*

"But if I am your star, you're my planet because they come together as a pack." I tell him while peaking at the sky above us.

"Then we're our own little galaxy."

"Half the world away?" I ask him in a joking way still needing approvement.

"Half the world away," he replies kissing my forehead. "I still can't wrap my head around the fact that you did all of this for me."

"I care. A lot more than I show you at times. I want to create that space for you and not just for me. That space of knowing it's okay to tell you anything and not feeling pushed to, I'm just not good at doing so," I explain to him my eyes resting on the sky above us. Luckily, I did put those blankets outside because we'll be needing them.

"You already have. The reason I'm not that open is because what I would say would maybe hurt you... hurt us. My past could hurt you and me."

"Once again Ethan, your past is who made you. And still, it is your past and it is over. You can either run from it or learn from it." I love quoting. *It is that bad that it should really be a crime. Ask Abby.*

"Did you just quote from a Disney movie?" He laughs out loud while hiding his face in his hands.

"Of course I did. Duh. Disney is superior."

"So, you love the stars, skating, taking pictures, Disney movies, you're romantic and you hate pumpkins and cucumbers. Those are a lot of things," he chuckles. I love this cute side of him, it's showing his beautiful dimples off even more.

"I am green and I love baby corn and peas. Can't let that out."

"Begging for your forgiveness my lady," he jokes spinning me around to the music. He can dance. That's a good thing. If a man can cook and dance, he's already halfway there. Roman couldn't dance nor cook. Fuck him.

"You're getting it. Only because you can dance. However, I'm tired and I need to sit down." As I say so, he takes my hands getting down onto the ground. Observing is also a thing that I love. I love observing things that make me happy and things in general that I love. I love observing him so much because I love him. Now I'm talking nonsense again, great.

"I never told you my colour," he says suddenly changing the subject. After a bit of talking and me showing him the song I wrote on thanksgiving. It certainly has an emotional effect on people and not just me. That's good. Don't get me wrong, I know I'm very emotional in most ways but knowing that you're not the only weird person to think or feel so is very calming. "The day that you told me you were a dark forest sage green. I never told you what I would be."

"You can still tell me now if you're ready to," I say resting my head on top of his chest which gives me flashbacks from the cliff. It would be nice if it could stay that way.

He places his fingers on top of my chest taking a deep breath. I have that strange feeling that he'll talk from his heart again and I'm not sure if I'm emotionally stable enough to not cry if he does. "I'd be a red. Red as blood."

I find myself frowning at his statement tilting my head back to catch a glimpse of his vision. Sadly, I'm not very good in bending my body in any way so I cannot see anything besides the candles and the night sky. "Why would you think that?"

"Because my told me that I was the reason for everything bad that had happened. That everything was my fault. Everything with my mother and all the bad things he did. He said it was all my fault and that I'm only hurting people," he murmurs his voice is starting to break down. I turn around so that my knees are at the side of his body. I take his face into my hands while my forehead rests against his.

"Don't you ever think that it is true. You did not hurt me. You did not hurt Jacob or Mary or anyone. You're constantly helping so many people with new music that can make them feel something. You helped me in so many more way than you are aware of. You made me feel again and you made me love."

"It's just that I have his voice in the back of my head saying the same sentence over and over again. Just as he said it before... before punishing me for things that I did wrong. He would say it so I knew that it was my fault and that I should've done better. Then he would take me into his room and he would... he would do horrible things to me Olivia," he tells me starting to cry just as I am.

"No, baby. Don't cry. It's over, he will not hurt you anymore. He's not here anymore. Nobody will ever hurt you like that again. *I promise.*" How could anyone do that to their children? How can our world be so messed up?

"No, he won't go away. His voice won't go away every time I'm fucking something up. And every time he said it, a part of me died more and more." I know that. *He's thinking that because someone made him think that it was his fault all over again that is actually it.*

I turn his head slightly from right to left until his eyes are focusing on mine. "Ethan. I need you to look at me. You need to breathe. Breathe with me and for me, okay? This person who made you feel and do horrible things is not here anymore. It was never your fault and it never will be. You need to let go of it. You need to let your past stay in the past and look to the now. You have not hurt me or anyone else. You're constantly helping so many people and now it's time to change that. Because now it's my turn to tell you to be selfish for once."

"I'm sorry I can't get over those things and tell you all about me. I would. I want to spend my whole future with you for as long as I can, but I cannot hide my past."

"No one asked you to do that baby." I reassure him smiling at him. That's my boy. Stronger than everyone would expect and so wise. So wise, soft and warm hearted.

"You're right. Nothing needs to change in that way. I'm aware that we promised each other not to promise such things but I need one from you. I need you to promise me that you will trust me until I'm ready to tell you and you will do everything... do everything to keep yourself alive, even when our worlds could be crumbling," he says softly while kissing my cheeks. I can feel his warm breath on my skin, making all my little hairs stand up. He does have an effect on my whole body not just my mind.

"Don't say anything like that. Everything will be fine. We'll be all right."

"We'll be all right. However, I still need you to promise me that. Promise me that when there is a decision to be made, you will choose yourself over anyone." He pushes further causing me to raise my eyebrows. Why would I need to do that?

"You're scaring me," I confess rolling to sit next to him rather than on top of him. This is confusing.

"Just say it. I need to hear it."

"I promise," I say giving in, giving him the answer that he wants, I know that I'm not entirely sure if I can keep that promise. Don't understand this wrong, I'd love to care about myself first for once but this... this is terrifying me. We have our own little galaxy now, we don't need to be scared anymore, right? It's him and me against the world.

"There's another thing. Since my album will be launching in a few days and the tour and the single, I've been asked to do an interview tomorrow after our studio session. Well, it's rather in the studio with the team because I told them that this isn't just my work. It's our work. As you're one of the greatest impacts on this record, I wanted to ask if you'd be there. It's nothing special but I'm kind of scared and I know that there will be questions and I know that you're not comfortable with that… I wouldn't ask that of you if I knew I could do it alone. I can't do it without you. I can't do so many things without you anymore baby." He goes on changing the topic again. Why are people acting so weird?

And that is the point I was so scared to reach. That is the point that I know I cannot live without that someone anymore. The point where I know that I need this separate galaxy.

"I'll be there. I'll be anywhere where you need me to be."

"I don't deserve you," he confesses kissing me.

"No. You deserve way better than me." I argue pulling away from the kiss. "Come on, we still have a lot talk to talk about but we need get up early in the morning. You don't want to be late when you have your first interview for this one, do you?" I tease breaking the sexual tension between us. Tonight shouldn't be about any of this. Besides, it's that time of the month. So, no. I feel disgusted.

There are also other things that I need to wrap my head around first. His dad. Not only did he do those things to him but he also abused him mentally for probably many years. That's just disgusting on a whole new level. However, it does make sense now. It makes sense how he'd rather suffer on his own and not tell anyone because he doesn't want to hurt anyone. It's because he thinks that if someone is hurting around him that it's his fault. That opinion of the world, not wanting to hurt anyone, is very warm-hearted and kind. It's something good. But not as long as you let yourself get hurt all the time to avoid it. It's painful but it's also the truth. For as long as we are alive, people will be hurt. But just because someone is hurt by you does not mean that you directly did something wrong. Quite a lot of times the people around you make up the most problems that you can't even see.

Chapter Thirty-Seven

You've missed quite a bit. Let me fill the spaces up for you. We went to bed, cuddled and talked about thanksgiving and the interview the next day. I told him that I knew I made a mistake and that I had overreacted and that it wasn't okay. He understood but he also helped me understand that it was a mistake both of us made. We didn't blame each other but rather ourselves. From what I am pretty sure of right now is that we both have a lot of work to do on ourselves. The good thing is that we both have to do it, so we can equally support and remind ourselves of that. It's good to know that I'm not alone for once. Well, I knew that I was never the only one to struggle but having someone right next to you who will understand without having to explain is the best of all. Then we went to sleep. To be more direct he did. I couldn't because the second he fell asleep, which wasn't long given after the long days, he began to snore. Like a fucking tonka truck. Let me tell you I had a grandfather who had a similar problem. He lived a few hours away from us but every single time he visited none of us could sleep. We used to let him sleep in the basement with two to three closed doors but nothing helped. However, he wasn't even close to the tonka truck level that Ethan has clearly reached. So yay, first interview and performance with barely any sleep. Here we go. Please enjoy the show... no, what am I even saying? You're probably smiling so deviously again now. If you are, thanks for that.

Walking next to Ethan holding his hand and hiding my face from the people around us who are taking pictures, I wonder how he can't be on edge at all. For me, all eyes are on me with everyone wondering who I was and what I am constantly doing, would be a nightmare. Luckily, Jacob, Mary, the band member's and Ethan's shoulders are enough to cover most of me. The dress code was casual but with, well, the British side of it. Which means, everyone is so damn hot. Not to be dramatic, but Ethan looks the best out of all of them. He's wearing brown baggy trousers made of fine fabric and a tighter black shirt. On top of that he's wearing a jacket for obvious reasons. As I said, autumn is the worst season. His rings and necklaces match perfectly as always. But for once, he did put a bit of gel in his hair so it would stay there while performing his album for the first time. I couldn't be prouder of him. We pass the huge brown wooden door, as we did so many times before. Ignoring the voices from the fans and everyone around us, I find myself clinging even closer to him. No, I'm not over all those things that make me feel that way but if you would've had the nerve to put me there a few months ago, it wouldn't have ended nicely for you. I'm telling you. He's squeezing our intertwined fingers tighter while planting a kiss on my forehead as soon as we're inside. I, on the other hand went for a matching outfit. Okay, it was his idea. But it's so adorable, right? My baggy trousers are black, while my shirt, a looser one, is the same brown as his trousers. Yeah, I got different accessories but you're getting the point. My hair was a wavy mess after the lack of sleep, so, I just put it into a loose and messy bun. Kind of acting cute today. Am I feeling cute? Kind of yes but also kind of no.

We enter the rehearsal room, which has been prepared for us. The carpets are laid on the wooden floor with all the technical stuff surrounding it. They start off with small talk with the camera team and the interviewers while I rather sit on the a chair a bit further away to gather myself. Nothing to be scared of. I shouldn't be scared. This isn't even about me today. Just don't mess it up Olivia. I take notes and lyrics out of my shoulder bag in order to go through them again because I just cannot mess up today. It's his day, I should show off my best side. Okay, I'm trying to. Until someone in front of me pulls them straight out of my hands, leaving me with a shocked and confused expression.

"What are you doing?" I ask Jacob who is now sitting in front of me smiling broadly.

"You're stressing yourself about something you don't need to. So, you can thank me for I'm helping you."

"Taking away the opportunity to destress myself is not quite helping Jacob. I'm not used to that sort of stuff and I'm definitely not professional as you are." I fight back and trying to get the papers back but he just holds them higher and teasingly raises an eyebrow. God, I hate this.

"Since you've got your own music out there and you're working with us the not professional excuse won't work anymore. You belong with us and you got this. Take a deep breath and enjoy this moment. It's a lot right now, especially now that everyone wants to know you. Show them how badass you are. Show them how strong you are and that you deserve to be here more than anyone else," he motivates me giving me a bear hug. I needed this. Even though I didn't want to allow myself... I need this and I deserve this.

"Thanks you so, so much. I hope you know that I'll gladly give you such motivation any time, okay? You do know that your problems are just as valid as those from anyone else."

"I do. I do, darling," he murmurs into my hear turning around after hearing someone cough behind him. He lets go of me to turn around and sees Ethan standing there. "Don't get so jealous big boy. After how she looks I could guess you were very loud last night. Give her a moment of silence with the best person in this room." He teases earning a glance which is soon followed by a light punch in his upper arm.

"I wasn't loud," he says folding his arms in front of him. Here comes the kindergarten again.

"I wasn't loud." Jacob repeats mimicking his sentence causing me to laugh out loud and to hold my belly.

"Don't make fun of me. I wasn't trying to keep you up all night." Ethan defends himself, facing me now.

"Well, for your sake I hope you weren't. It's okay, you didn't do it on purpose so I'm okay with it. I just wish I knew what to do or how to behave when people are around... people who are judging me, your fans for example, or the people taking the pictures. Because I'm stealing you away from them and I just don't know how to act around them. I mean, I don't want them to accept everything, but I don't want to be mocked by any of them who don't know me." I blurt out touching my head with one hand. He takes my hand away holding it with his own.

"Look, I know this is a lot. I wouldn't want to push you into doing anything you don't want to. But I can tell you my fanbase isn't that toxic and they just want to see me happy. And with you, my sweetheart, I'm the happiest I've ever been. You just need to be yourself then everyone will automatically love you just like I do."

"I love you." I say before kissing him and smiling. After a couple of minutes, they announce that we should get ready. So, we're all line up in front of our mics and instruments. Today I'll be playing a bit of electric guitar and I'll be singing, just like on the record. Sadly, I can't play the piano... that's an ability I've got which is far better than playing guitar. Just like you did before, *it's not that hard Olivia. I wish Abby could be here right now...* Speaking of, we texted again and she's still acting weird. Like, she's not telling me where she is in the world or if she's working at all. *Note to myself: call Abby.*

Not now, now I need to concentrate. So, earplugs in and let the show begin. *Calm down, just a few cameras and people... it'll be fine.* I hear my name being spoken, so I turn around snapping back to reality. Mary gives me a reassuring smile and we begin to count. Let the show begin. In the beginning I'm more quiet and shy, well, I don't need to do a lot in most songs. Just adding a bit of harmony and some notes should be fine. However, towards the end of the first song we wrote when Ethan and I came back from the cliff, my favorite song, there is this high note which I need to endure. It does sound good in the end but while doing it, I'm always nervous to fuck it up. So, when I realize that it's getting closer to that part of the song, my eyes meet Ethan's and he is smiling so widely holding the microphone in his hands. He's just born for this stuff. We work our way up there with our voices when suddenly all I can hear is my voice and not his anymore. My head turns around immediately to see all of the crew grinning and smiling. Especially Ethan. He planned that shit. I can see it now as he deviously smirks to himself before joining in again. That is so screaming for a payback. We end this song and the next two before taking a break and then afterwards we sing the rest of songs. The part of performing is over now at least. One good thing. However, as soon as the cameras are off and my guitar is placed on the stand, I rush towards him hitting the back of his head. His reaction is a flinch and a laugh before turning around to face me.

"You little piece of shit. You had all of this in your goddamn mind. Fuck you Ethan that was so embarrassing. Why would you do that?" I confront him seeing everyone smiling. What the actual fuck? "Why are you all smiling, this is not fucking funny."

"It's quite amusing. You just hit a fucking brilliant high note because he forced you to and now you're hitting him? It's not funny, it's hilarious Liv." Jacob defends Ethan now. How truly amazing.

"Oh no. You are supposed to be on my side in this and not to be just like him."

"I was. I told him not to do it because of you know… but he did it anyway. So, that is a point for me because I wouldn't have done it. Five to four. I'm getting closer every day, I'm telling you," he says making me punch him as well.

"Get away before I kick your butt and you will not be able to do your damn yoga," I whisper at him, so I don't have to scream. *Don't scream, it's over. Everything is okay, no one died.* I push him away and I stand directly in front of Ethan with my arms folded.

"You look adorable when you're trying to be pissed." He teases smirking while leaning down to my level. Great, now you have to bring all the height difference in again? Not fair.

"Don't mess with me Murphy. I am pissed," I speak up not leaving his hazel eyes for as much as a single second. *Staring. I'm good at staring. I can stare all the day and you won't win this contest.*

"All right. But you should thank me." What?

"Begging your pardon? What should I thank you for?"

"Oh, you will see after the interview. When the whole world knows how amazing you sing, and that you're all mine. That everyone can see how perfect you are and that they know that they will never have you," he explains making me chuckle in a sarcastic way.

"Being a little bit possessive again, aren't we?" I tease back still cutting eye contact.

"Not just today, but yes. We are."

"Glad you finally decided to tell me that. Nevertheless, I'd appreciate it if you told me that earlier next time," I add.

"I'll keep that in mind." He reassures me making me roll my eyes. Fuck, staring. "I won the staring thing means you can't be mad anymore"

"Who said I couldn't be mad anymore? Who made that rule?"

"I did," he says with a smirk still on his perfect face.

"Fuck you."

"Oh, we can gladly do that later on. However, there's an interview that needs to be done before that happens sweetheart." He teases making me cough.

"Let's go get interviewed so you can have time to come down to a normal level of cockiness. You're scaring me," I tell him, patting his arm and leaving this conversation. As I said, people are weird. I'm weird too, but I'm used to me being weird.

We're all gathered in the middle of the studio again, where there are a line of chairs placed by now. Fancy. I sit down on the outside on purpose, I don't like being in the middle of this… to begin with I dislike the idea of being in it in general. Did I have a choice? Not really. To my right is Jacob, then Ethan and a few other people. Mostly the producers. On my left is just Mary. I'm hoping that I'm not the only one who feels a little bit uncomfortable. The interviewer sits down in front of us, right next to the camera explaining a few things. For example, what will happen, what subjects he shouldn't talk about and that sort of stuff. I catch a glimpse of Ethan's face which is very similar to a light bulb. He put all he had into this album. This is his heart and his story and I couldn't be more proud to be a part of who he created it with. By about ten minutes into the interview I start to zoom out again. I'm not doing it on purpose, it sometimes just happens. I'm working on accepting it. *Because healing does not mean the damage has never been there. Healing means accepting the damage but leaving it behind with time.*

"So, there have been a lot of rumours as I'm sure you have heard them. People are asking if there is an important person in your life Ethan?" the interview guy, I think his name is Jonas, asks Ethan. Everyone is smirking and that is the first thing to get me back to reality. Snapping in and out of it is not fun, but it's getting less. It'll be fine.

"There definitely is," Ethan answers giving that angel smile towards Jonas.

"Tell us about her then." He pushes further but not in an unacceptable way. I've heard a lot of things about very annoyingly direct interviewers. I get that it's their job to get information but there is a certain point where it's enough.

"She's... I don't think there is even one word that could describe all the things she is and how she makes me feel. I couldn't be more proud to have her at my side that I get to spend time with her. Because just as everyone here has, she has greatly inspired this album, my music and my entire life," he says. My heart feels so warm and all the butterflies are waking up right now. I'm pretty sure that my entire face is probably as red as a tomato but I'm not complaining.

"Oh, so she's in this crew? We haven't seen that much of her?"

"Yeah, she is. To me, she's the very heart of it," he admits looking directly into my eyes. I smile so wide that my cheeks are hurting. Now Jonas and all of them are watching me just as much with a pleasant smile. For once, I don't care if the cameras are filming my ugly nearly crying smile because for once, this shows me how much he cares. How much we both care without having to explain all of it. This man... "Before Jacob got her to work with us, our music was very different. It was good, but something was missing. It just didn't feel right, the sparkling part of it wasn't there. The reason for someone to go back to listening to a song all over again. Her incredible way of writing and playing just changed all of it, she brought the little missing piece that was missing in my music and in my heart. And when she joined us we got to know her... I felt as if I got to know the most important parts of myself and everything I needed to achieve to be happy. Which I clearly am with this, her and everyone else in this room. That is the particular reason as to why I said that Olivia is the heart of it. She opened my heart and turned all the things inside this beautiful piece of art."

"Those are the most amazing news that I've heard in a while. I'm sure your fans will be glad to see how much this all means to you. Now, let's move on. Tell me something about the upcoming tour you've announced a few hours ago." I'm really glad he didn't confront me. I wouldn't know how to explain how I feel about him or any of this. Because I don't know. I don't know what I did to end up here. What I did to deserve him, what I did to feel this way and I still feel as if it isn't real. I'm in a mess of feelings but I don't think I would want it to change. I just want to stay in our own little galaxy. Our own little bubble. I don't want things to connect. I want things to stay. No matter what others think or do. I want this to stay before it is over way too soon.

He explains some details about where we'll start and that he's got some surprises on the way. I haven't thought about it that much, but the tour will be starting in just a few weeks. Well, technically I won't even be here on my birthday which is weird. I hope that Abby will come and visit. The rest of the interview is going by rather uninteresting for me. Much talking about musical stuff that I'm not really understanding fully at this point. Still working on it. However, when everyone is gone and we're still there to record a version of my new song, my phone buzzes. I pick it up answering the call.

"Long time no see Olivia." I hear the voice, I've been so desperate to forget, I can feel my body tensing up and my mouth dropping. Holy fucking shit.

Chapter Thirty-Eight

My hands grab the cell phone tighter while lean against the wall for balance. This can't be real. I must be dreaming. After things ended, I literally ran away as far as I could. By that time, I knew that I could never face him again. That I was gonna get sick if I ever heard his damn voice again. The way he still finds this amusing in some way and that he has the audacity to even call me. Let's not even begin with why he's got my number because Abby made sure to delete it very quick.

"What the fuck do you want Roman?" I ask with a lot of anger, fear and frustration. I thought it would be over. I was getting better; I was forgetting him. Ethan approaches me raising an eyebrow. His face is filled with worry. God, I'm worried to. As a way of safety, he gestures for me to put him on speaker once I show him the name. To be completely honest with you, I've never seen him that angry. He looks as if he's about to rip the phone out of my hands and to beat him up through it.

"No hello for me? I'm disappointed," he says laughing again. I swear he's making my body go into fight-or-flight mode in less than one second. "I saw your dad. We had a lovely chat and we agree on some things. London isn't that good for you, is it? And that little boyfriend of yours… do you really think he wants you? We both know that isn't true. We belong together and your father agrees. I know I made a mistake, but you ran off way too easily. You gave up on us and that was your mistake. I'm giving you a chance to do better now." I need to throw up.

"You and my dad always had similar opinions, that's why I kicked both of you out of my life. I don't know what's going on in your sick head, but this is over. You fucked up and you were never good for me. Face it, you're lonely now because you realized what of a scumbag you are and that no one wants to be around someone like you. It's called karma Roman," letting out everything I had bottled up over time. Karma's a bitch. He's manipulative, sick and he does not deserve to be near me in a radius of at least a hundred kilometres.

"You don't get it do you. He's using you. He's taking you away from your family. He's a fucking cheater, I mean look at his job."

"Even if his job made him a cheater, which it does not, it wouldn't make him any different than you." There you fucking go. Take that.

"Watch your words, Olivia." He threatens me. I hate it when he calls me by my full name. That's originally the reason why I didn't want anyone to call me by my full name. Bad memories. For Ethan however, he replaced the bad memories with good ones. *He gives the bad things a good reason not to be bad anymore.* Suddenly Ethan takes the phone out of my hand, rather forcefully, running his fingers through his hair before he growls back at him.

"Or what you fucking prick? What are you going to do about it? You will not talk to her anymore and you will never ever lay even a single finger on her again. She's done with you, and you deserve to go to hell for what you did. It's over, you asshole."

"There we go, the devil himself. Even if I'm going to hell, I'll gladly meet you there. She might think we're not similar, but we are Ethan. You and I both know that," Roman says provoking Ethan. By now, the whole room has gone silent watching what is happening. They might think it's some psycho- well, it's Roman. Not too far away from each other. But why would he say that? Except for the fact that he's very much not normal in his head…

"I don't hit women," Ethan states making everyone open their mouths in shock. Great, this was definitely not how I planned my day. Again, this is proof that nothing goes along as planned. I face the wall, not wanting to see their expressions. I don't need their pity. I can pity myself quite well, I did, and now I'm done with it. I don't want to be confronted, I don't want to hear from him again and I never want to see him again. I can't relive it all over again. I simply can't. I have no clue why fate constantly decides to remind me of my traumas... sometimes you bleed just to know you're alive.

Since this is enough for me and my nerves, I take the phone back without a moment's hesitation turning the speaker off so none of them can hear him anymore. "Where have you gotten my number from and why are you calling me and why in God's name are you talking to my dad?" I push again, still facing away from them. Ethan steps closer, I think he wants to touch me but I stretch out my arm, signalling for him to stay there. This is enough and I'll need to handle this on my own. I did it once, I can do it again.

"He has the same opinion as I do sweety. He thinks you shouldn't be there to begin with and mostly not with that scumbag."

"You don't even know him! You don't even know me!" I scream at him now. This is good.

"I know both of you better than you think. Your dad's also not too keen on the fact that you're reading your mothers diary. Bad girl, even though he told you not to you're doing it anyway. You should know better Olivia. I taught you better than that. Bad girls get punished," he explains with an awful amount of amusement in his voice. His statement sends shivers down my spine and makes me want to end this call immediately. As I've always hated it and I always will.

"You did teach me something and I'm so fucking thankful for that. You taught me the first bit of self-worth and you taught me the right point when to leave. Because that was the best thing I learned or did from that time on. We were always a losing game and we were never going to make it. I'm sick of you and your games and I will end this call now. I won't be manipulated by you ever again and you can tell my dad the exact same thing. This is my life and I'm happy with it. You should just accept that, jealousy never looked good on you." I fight back and for the first time saying what I am actually thinking.

"All right sweety, enjoy my present then," he adds before ending the call. What present? He has definitely lost his damn mind this time. No wonder. I close my eyes, still not wanting to face the others. Ethan is the first to break the distance and hug me. He doesn't say anything at first, he's just hugging me.

"It's okay baby. Let it out, it's over. I'm sorry. I'm sorry I couldn't protect you, but I am here now," he whispers into my ear holding me close. I hug him back letting the tears finally flow. Feelings are valid, and they the deserve to be felt. It's okay to be vulnerable, none of them will like me less because of it. It's okay. Fighting the inner voices is so, so hard. It's hard because they go deeper than just the surface and making them stop takes about ten times as much effort as just giving in to them. It takes time but it will get better. It has to.

After what felt like hours, I break away from him to wipe away the tears that are still left on my face. "Sorry guys, I didn't mean to ruin this day." I apologize after finally turning towards them.

"You did not ruin anything. It's okay Liv. You don't need to apologize for someone acting that way. Who was that even to begin with? Did he hurt you?" Mary asks from a few meters across the room where everybody is sitting down.

"He's my ex-boyfriend... and yes he did. In more than one way. Up to this day I didn't even know if he was still alive and I didn't care if he was, I never wanted to and never will want to see him again ever." I confess looking at Ethan who gives me a tiny smile before sitting down next to me and placing one hand around my shoulders.

"If I meet him in my life, I will make sure he will never ever get to hurt anyone. Especially not you." Ethan speaks up.

"He's not worth it. Leave him, he's mad in his mind."

"He will be many more things than just mad if he crosses our lives." Our lives.

"Can we just record the song and get it over with?" I ask him ignoring his threat towards Roman. Hurting someone back isn't an option and it seems that I'll be having this conversation with Ethan later on.

"Baby, are you sure that you still want to do it? It's been a long day?" he asks.

"Yeah. We're all here and I'm in a vulnerable state of mind. Perfect for a vulnerable song." It takes me about five minutes to calm down fully and to make myself ready before stepping into the sound prove room to record the vocals with the musical impacts of it. The producers are very easy on me today and I'm glad about it. So, after being done with something that comes closer to a studio version of it, we leave it there and everyone heads home.

Ethan finds out that I haven't eaten anything all day, so he forces me to go to his place to at least have dinner with him. I have no idea how he can still be aware of such things, but it's very heart warming and new to have someone care about that as much. Here we are, waiting for our food to arrive.

I haven't said much on the ride back and I can tell that he's worried. I'm worried too, but I don't think it's that important. I know what's making me feel this way, it's not the first time. I hate it... I absolutely despise it. And the last time I can recall feeling this way for a longer time was when I broke up with Roman. It's as if I've been thrown back in time.

"Food has arrived." Ethan informs me walking over with the bag of food. It smells so delicious but even the thought of putting something into my stomach makes me want to throw up. I force myself to give him a slight smile before helping him set everything down onto the plates. He ordered some burgers and fries. Not that he can't cook, I think he was just too tired. Fair enough, me too. It's not good to always order junk food. Vegetables. Baby corn and peas. That's good stuff.

We sit down and he starts to take bites from his burger while all I can do is stare at it and drift off into the well-known feeling deep down in my guts. "You need to eat Olivia. You've only had liquids and that's not healthy. Your body needs food. Food is fuel." He states watching for a reaction. When nothing comes from me, except blank stares, he gets up kneeling down in front of my chair. He takes my hands in his staring into my eyes. "I know today was a hard day, but you need to do this. Let's eat together, okay? One bite after the other one. Remember when we went to the cliff, we had burgers too there. They were so, so good. Can you remember the view? The most beautiful thing that you get to see around here. We can imagine we are there. Imagine sitting there just like we did last time. We can do it, together," he says smiling hopefully at me. I nod and he sits down again, waiting for me to do something. Even though my body is fighting against it I put some fries into my mouth while concentrating on the memory that we created together. I concentrate on where I felt the most at home. The moment I knew for sure he is my home.

"You're doing so good. Look at you, I'm proud of you and I love you."

"I love you, Ethan. You do know that you don't have to do this, do you?" I say watching how his facial expression changes.

"I don't have to do a lot of things. I want to do it. Just as I told you on that night. *I don't care because I have to; I care because I choose to.* And I would choose to care over and over again. Roman is right. I'm not a perfect match for you because I'm far from being perfect. You're, however, giving me a reason to be better." We continue to eat slowly, and it becomes easier to eat again. It's getting easier because he has brought me back to reality and away from my thoughts for a second. After some more talking, we decide to go to bed and to end this awfully interesting day as you might want to call it.

I lay there while he's still in the bathroom. I watch the window as the curtains are open, and the rain runs down the windows. It's calming because it's predictable. It's a situation that will very unlikely turn into something unexpected and that makes it calming. Again, my thoughts are driven back and I can sense myself getting angry and sad at the same time. Perfect timing because Ethan steps out of the bathroom in briefs only. He watches me frowning before getting under the sheets next to me. His head turns towards me while my vision is focused on the ceiling.

"You can talk, you know that," he murmurs very softly. The rain and his voice are creating a space that I've wished for so desperately every time I was alone. That is the reason why I'm reminding myself that I'm not alone anymore. He is there and I can talk. Talking will help, *you got this Olivia. He won't run off.*

"I feel something and I hate myself for feeling that way. I don't want to but it's not going away," I start to explain as my body goes into panic mode again. My heart beats so fast at this point, my breathing becomes faster and my body starts to feel uneasy again. Since he's aware of what this feels like, he gives me the time to find the right words and the time to feel comfortable enough.

"I hate myself because I'm angry at my mother. I'm angry because she chose to write that damn article that cost her life even though she knew how dangerous those people were. She risked her life for the greater good and I'm so mad for that. I'm so mad because she chose to save others before saving herself. I'm so angry because she left me alone with my dad. With that piece of shit Roman... I know it's so stupid but I tell myself that if she hadn't died that I never would have met him to begin with. Because I met him when I first ran away home after I realized that she will never come back. That makes me so angry because I know she wasn't trying to hurt me, but she did. She did and I will never be able to see her again. It feels as if she chose everything and everyone over her own life and her own family. I hate myself for that and I disgust myself that I wished all the time it would've been me instead of her. It should've been me." I confess crying while holding tightly onto the covers. Right now, I don't want to look at him because I can't bare the way he is looking at me right now. "I hate myself that I can't just fucking move on. I hate it so, so much. Mostly I hate myself that I'm too scared to read that damn diary because I will feel even worse in the end. I would do everything for it to end; for me to finally be normal."

"Shh. It's okay. Breathe sweetheart. Breathe for me." He holds me tightly now, both of us sitting against the wall. He rubs my arms while kissing my head softly and breathing calmly for me as I'm trying to follow along. "You're allowed to feel that way and any other way. You can't blame yourself and you can't take the fall for everyone else. *The reason you're not over it is because you haven't let yourself deal with it.* You've been pushing it away all these years. That's not how it works."

"But I can't take it if it hurts. I just can't take it anymore," I say in a shaky voice.

"You need to let yourself feel it. You need to read the diary in order to let it heal. *You need to let it hurt before it can heal.* Even if that means that things will change and that you will lose some part of you or other things," he states.

It needs to hurt before it can heal…

Chapter Thirty-Nine

People will not always understand. No matter what you do not everyone will support you and be happy for you. Many will be jealous; many will disapprove but the most important thing that I learned is just to go for it. It's scary to create something new when you don't know what people will think or if it's even going to work to begin with. Especially when you're a rather anxious person as I am. Yes, it could go wrong. Yes, it could go sideways and it perhaps could not even happen at all. I had this problem a lot when I was younger and I also had this conversation with Abby before releasing my first song. Yep, I did not tell you that but you're not always around and you weren't in that time so just cut it, okay? As the perfect best friend that she is, she gave me the most precious advice that I'm now willing to share with you. You can convince yourself that everything will go wrong and it might. But what if it doesn't? *What if it turns out better than you could have ever imagined?* Just think about it for a few moments and you can thank me later.

Another thing that has been on my mind for a few days now is that depression is literally deadly. Depression kills your soul and mind before it makes you want to kill your physical being. Because depression leaves nothing from you. All the memories of the good times are gone, any feeling of time is gone. Days don't matter and it doesn't matter how good it used to be because you know it will never be like that again.

It's very early days. I'm sitting on Ethan's couch, which isn't even close to being as good as mine, and I'm writing again. It's great because it's quite, I've got my headphones and nothing else to worry about. Ethan is asleep. He should be because the sun has barely risen. I won't lie to you, I had a nightmare. Not as bad as the others but not nice. And because yesterday was heavy on all of us and because he took care of me, I'm going to take care of him now. I'll let him sleep while I'm letting my thoughts out. And I will text Abby today. I might look into the car thing as well, but I most likely won't. It's like one of those days, where you have it all planned out, but you end up doing shit. Shit is important and not only the poo shit. What I'm talking about is self-care shit. In my case it's writing, listening to music and spending time with loved ones. Although I have always enjoyed a good time alone. Because only if you're able to be on your own, you will be able to be around people and to truly be you then. Writing is therapy in more than just one simple way. It can help you understand, remember and find out amazing things about yourself. You can also find out negative things but everyone has got their secrets, right?

I let my finger fly over the letters on my laptop constantly for about one hour. After that, my head is almost empty and I close the document turning off my laptop. It's still very early and I doubt that he will be awake for at least another hour. I walk over to the bathroom to take shower to get rid of all the sweat and the negative energy in some way. Entering the bathroom, I look over at the sink where my spare toothbrush is in its holder. right next to my boyfriend's toothbrush. He bought me a toothbrush. That is just another level of caring and cuteness. I look at myself in the mirror as I do most of the time. A few times in my life I couldn't bear watching myself because I was so disgusted by it but that's over now. Luckily.

Stepping into the shower and turning on the water, my thoughts are blank again. However, it's not a weird blank. It's an empty blank but not because of worry. Just because it's better. It's not good yet because there still is an empty one once in a while but it's not that negative anymore. I let the warm water run over my naked body while adjusting to the growing warmth in the smaller room. I've always enjoyed showers. Except for the time when I was too tired to even get up. But even then it wasn't the thought of stepping under the water that was exhausting; it was the thought of getting to that point. Nevertheless, that's over for now at least.

I get out of the shower wrapping a towel around my wet hair. I pick up the clothes that I had laid out to put them on. A simple pair of wide blue jeans and one of Ethan's hoodies. Walking towards the dark kitchen, I attempt to make us breakfast since he should be waking up soon. I have no idea where the plates and the stuff is to make breakfast so it will probably take me a little longer than I'd like it to. English breakfast? I think he needs something different for once. Nothing against that, although I'm not really into the heavy breakfast thing, but some fruits are also nice. It's a light start to the day. No, I'm just talking crap. Sorry, I'll stop. Oh, there's another thing that I didn't tell you. I had a very early call with my manager. I stopped avoiding him eventually and told him that there might be something good coming to him. He was very excited and supportive, he's a good guy. Because he's been working in this industry for over twenty years, he has no trouble finding the good stuff that needs to be heard. I'm very proud that I did one song which fulfilled that expectation. It's harder now because since I've released one song, people are expecting something more in a certain way but I plan on breaking that boundary. I want to do something unexpected something very different in the musical way but still with honest vulnerability. However, if there is something I've learnt is that success kills creativity. For example, I publish my song and let's imagine that it went viral and everything around it. Then I'd announce another song, or maybe even an album would be coming out. People would immediately expect me to give them something that is at least as good as the first song. Meaning, I'd be more pressured to give someone a certain kind of music instead of creating my music. Creating what feels best. This all brings me to that conclusion that success kills creativity.

We're always kind of getting back to that aren't we? I might have mentioned to my manager that I'll perhaps be writing something soon, which could be also a subject… as I said he's a good and supportive guy. Okay, now back to breakfast. I put my headphones on my ears so that I can enjoy and have a little dance party on my own without waking him up. That's another self-care thing I'm trying out today. I search through all the cupboards for pans and plates. He's got everything sorted out in one way and it's excruciating. The problem is I'm not even that messy. He's just the polar opposite of it so it's making me feel messy. Not nice, but maybe I should just stop comparing my habits and my way in general to someone else's.

By now, I've got the table laid full of food. I did some eggs, cut fruit, sliced bread and I made him his damn sausage and tomatoes. I couldn't forget the tea as well, so that's what I'm currently doing. The music blasts through my ears, which I'm pretty sure isn't that healthy, but we all die anyway. So what about a little bit of fun? I'm about to pour the boiling water into a mug when I feel two large hands wrapping themselves around my waist and a scream escapes my mouth. I take the headphone off again turning around to see a sleepy Ethan who has his head on my shoulder.

"You scared me," I tell him while he's laughing about it. Of course he would.

"Good morning to you too. I could wake up to this every morning, but I prefer having you next to me."

"I'm sure you do. However, I think it's creepy to watch someone while they're sleeping, don't you think so?" I joke. *Well, it's not a joke because it's creepy. Every time he wakes up earlier, he's staring at me. Don't like that.*

"I just can't help it. You're way too beautiful not to stare at," he replies placing a soft kiss on my cheeks before taking the mug and heads towards the dining room table.

"Let's eat something. It's too early to be flirty baby." I walk over sitting down at the table and I watch his features while he's eating all the food.

"This is… nobody has ever made me a breakfast like this. Thank you, I love it. I love you," he says while I find myself watching him. He's a little fluffy right now. His messy hair and his morning voice with those eyes… he's my favourite planet in my favourite galaxy; our galaxy. We eat talking a bit about yesterday and mainly today. I could get used to this. "Since when are you awake?"

"Uhm… a little earlier than you." I lie. He doesn't need to be worried. I'm fine.

"Olivia. Since when?" he pushes again while seriously watching me. I look towards the ceiling placing my hands on my thigh before looking back at him. I just can't lie when I look into his eyes. It's not possible.

"Pretty much since five or something like that."

"You're supposed to be asleep at five," he says touching his forehead with his hands as if he's getting another headache. I know I should be asleep then and I try to be.

"I know and I tried. I had a bad dream and I never sleep again after those. So, I used my time wisely," I explain as we start to take away the plates and the rest of food that's left.

"You should wake me up. Every time, do you hear me?"

"You need to sleep to. Just because I can't doesn't mean I can take away your sleep as well." I argue washing the dirty plates. Ethan steps behind me taking hold of my waist again.

"You should wake me up. Every time because we're in this together. We're a team and teams don't play alone. Okay?"

"Okay," I say and he places his finger under my chin making me turn around so that he can kiss me. First a single soft one and then more passionate again. "I gotta go home later. I need to clean up and organize some stuff."

He sighs at my comment, not wanting me to leave and not wanting to start an argument as well. "Okay but I'll take you home. Also, I was thinking about a date. I have a brilliant idea and I think you'll love it. Just as much as you love the stars," he tells me and my heart pounds faster again.

Every man that I've been with has never cared about my love for the stars. Or anything else in particular. So, it's something precious that he remembers and that he cares. Something I'm not used to. I could take pictures of the stars for my website and mostly for myself. I'm well aware that they'll never look as beautiful as in real life but that wouldn't be the first thing. Perhaps it's good that it's that way. That the best memories simply always stay in our mind and that no matter how hard we try, those memories will never be the same for someone else. So that we've always got something for ourselves and for ourselves only, memories that no one can take away.

"I'd love that. Our own little galaxy." Shit, did I really just say that out loud? Damn it.

"Our own little galaxy. I like that," he says. Oh, Ethan, I love it. We finish washing the dishes and he goes to take a shower while I pack my stuff. I should really wash my clothes or buy new ones. Since I'm not too fashionable and I don't own that many clothes that actually match, there isn't much left to wear. As I carry my bag to the front of his apartment passing the hallway, he's getting out of the shower and yelling that he'll be done in five minutes. I take my phone out of my back pocket running my fingers through my still wet hair. While opening this damn social media I wonder how people can actually enjoy being so open on social media. Not that I'm open on it, but I'm just wondering how little human beings do not care about their privacy... weird.

"I'm ready if you are," he says from behind. I smile walking towards him, giving a light kiss to him.

We leave his flat and get into his car. Both of us are more than likely in our own thoughts but I'm glad about it since there are a lot of things going on that I need to clear up for myself.

"How's therapy going? Do you feel good with her and in general?" he asks breaking the silence.

Sure, you mean besides the threating letters, myself and my psycho ex... yes everything is good. I'm perfectly fine.

"Yup it's fine." A thing that our society needs to learn is that therapy will not make everyone better the second they go there. It will get worse in fact for the first weeks perhaps. That's because the therapist's job is to bring all the triggering topics up and to talk about them. And talking, whether you feel comfortable with someone or not, is the hardest thing for someone who feels that way. Another thing that I experienced was when my 'friends', and family or even some random doctors saw my scars or found out that I was not good at all to myself was the second I told them that I was seeing someone professional and they immediately went blank. Blank in a way that describes 'Oh, she's psycho but she's getting help so she is fine.' Or anything like that. The second they knew, they didn't care anymore. Not that they ever would have, but you're getting the point.

"You don't seem fine sweetheart," he says causing me to look at him confused and a little bit annoyed. I don't know why but people constantly assume that everything is fine after the first therapy session. It just does not make any sense.

Mental illnesses are different for everyone. Some people can get out, some can't. Some can eat, some can't. Some of them have a messy room and some don't. Some self-harm and others don't. Some people are suicidal and some aren't. It's visible for some people and for some not. Some can shower and some can't. Some people can get themselves to work and others can't. Just as all the others are no way the same, even if they seem so far apart.

"Maybe that's because I'm not fine," I reply staring out of the window again. *Just shut up Olivia you're home soon and you don't want to argue with him now or at any time.* We are both quiet until the car stops in front of my apartment and I immediately get out of the car to avoid the weird situation. He gets out of the car as well... *so, it didn't work. Damn it.*

"Thanks for driving me here. I'm going to get going. We'll text, all right?" I say looking at him for a split second. He's staring at the ground and his hands are once more going through his hair. He does have some habits.

"I'm sorry Olivia. I shouldn't have said it like I did. We know that I didn't mean it that way. I know you're not fine... but I sometimes I just wish you to be for yourself."

"No, you shouldn't have said that. I'm very sensitive to that topic and I won't apologize for it either. You cannot raise your magic wand and make me all fine in an instant. That's not how it works," I reply. *I know he never did that to hurt me or anything, but he could've been more mindful.* "Bye Ethan."

"I'll see you baby. Just know that I'm sorry," he adds walking towards my door. I stop and I take a deep breath. *Let your heart speak Olivia, not your damn mind. He's your boyfriend, you can be honest with him and show him your vulnerability. Communication is key, you learned that in therapy, you dumbass.*

"*An apology without a follow up action is just a useless thing.* I learned that the hard way and I won't let that happen again Ethan." I confess focusing on the apartment door before turning my head to see him standing there frowning.

"But I didn't do anything wrong. I just asked something in a stupid way that I did not mean. I don't get why you're mad at me now. Olivia, I know you've been hurt but I'm not the person who hurt you. Why are you so scared of me doing the same things? It doesn't make sense." *Oh, dear Lord, here we go.*

I bite my lip my eyes watching everything but him. I can't look at him right now, not when I'm close to crying. "Because they said the same thing. They all said they would never hurt me and they did. They said they all wanted the best for me and they did not do what they said. I'm done feeling that way," I tell him with a louder voice.

"You don't trust me," he hisses stepping closer to me. This is the point where I stare at him again. How could he assume that after everything that he knows?

"Don't you fucking question my trust! I told you so many thinks about myself despite the hurt that came with it. I trusted you more than I have trusted Abby with. I opened up more to you than to my best fucking friend. You don't get to stand there and say something like that when we both know it's a load of bullshit. Ethan, don't question my trust or loyalty ever again. I'm leaving now," I yell pointing to his chest. While doing so, tears run down my face. This was supposed to be a good day. We were supposed to have fun and I was supposed to be happy.

I ignore his calls and him saying my name. Even after he follows me and slightly touches my skin. It's like everything around me is blur. As if I can sense there are voices, but I cannot recognize them nor understand them. This is so fucked up.

I take my keys out of my purse with my shaking hands placing the key into the lock of my door while Ethan is still talking. The thing that brought me back to reality and out of that state of mind is when I couldn't turn the key around. I push down on the door handle and the front door opens. I always lock the door. I've locked it. My mouth falls open and my heart beats faster. Please tell me this is not what it looks like.

"I always lock the door," I whisper while my eyes can't move and I'm starting to sweat.

"What? Olivia?" Ethan asks from next to me still pissed.

"The door was open and I did lock it. I always lock the door."

His eyes widen and he pushes me away from the door pulling my behind him. "Calm down baby. Everything is going to be okay. I'm going to go inside after getting help right now. You stay here and you wait for me. Do you hear me?" he asks pulling out his phone after my slight nod. From then on, everything goes faster.

I always lock the door. I always did.

Chapter Forty

I always wanted to belong to something. That is one of the only things that I can recall from my childhood. The particular reason why I'm saying that is because I can barely remember it. As well as how it is to be 'normal' and completely 'happy'. Everything before my mothers' death is just gone. Well, most of it. I'm saying this because I wanted to belong to something bigger. To not feel as if I'm all on my own. To feel surrounded by this feeling that everything is possible together. A little bit like the three musketeers. I didn't particularly want to belong to groups because of the people in there. I was never one for crowds or many unknown children. I was rather on my own. However, I ached for that feeling. It was kind of like power. Power as if nothing in this world could stop us from doing the best thing that we wanted to do. *Feeling untouchable.* On top of the world, unreachable and undestroyable. Those were things that I was aching for.

And right now, I don't feel like I possess any kind of power. No power over my own life and I don't feel as if I'm deciding my own fate. I'm far from feeling untouchable. I'm scared as hell and I'm feeling beyond alone.

I sit on the few doorsteps that lead to my front door. Ethan called someone, I didn't bother to listen to the conversation, and he went inside. That was exactly four minutes and twenty-six seconds ago. And in those four minutes and twenty-six seconds I've listed all the worst-case-scenarios. I'm not even close to calming down. Especially since I know he's in there and having no idea who else could be there or what happened to my place.

As I'm thinking about going inside as well, despise Ethan's commands, I hear a car's engine very close to me. Hoping for the police to arrive, I stand up to see. My eyes must be sore after staring at the bare ground for that long. To my surprise, it's no police car. As my vision becomes a bit clearer, I can see that the car is red.

"Liv! Are you all right?" a well-known voice screams at me from a distance. Jacob. He jogs over to me and hugs me tightly. I can't move, it's as if my body is frozen and my mind is still racing.

"What are you doing here?" I ask him after he breaks the hug to look at me with a worried facial expression.

"Ethan called me. I'm here to help but I can't do that as long as I'm not sure that you're okay."

"Where's the police? We need the police here, someone broke into my fucking apartment," I ask starting to panic again. However, it's a very valid point. I need to get help, I need to call the police. I need to clean my house, I can't sleep when I know someone was in there and touched God knows what. How will I even be able to sleep again?

"We can't do that Liv," he replies and causing me to stop. I stare into his eyes raising my eyebrows. What the fuck is he talking about? As I'm about to say something, I can hear footsteps from behind. It's Ethan.

"Thank the Lord, you're finally here. Come inside and help me, Jacob." Ethan orders him ignoring my looks and the state of mind that I am in right now. Thanks for that.

"What the fuck are you talking about? We need to call the police and I need to see what happened to the place that I fucking live in," I yell trying to get inside but I'm being held back by both of them.

"Stop it, Olivia. That's exactly what they would want us to do," Ethan says.

"Who are we talking about? What happened in there? Let me through I need to clean. I need to get inside to see what happened. I need to…," I start to list all the things that I need to do while being cut off from the guys.

"I'm talking about the people who were after you a couple of weeks ago. Olivia I'm not fucking stupid I saw the other threatening letter right on top of your counter. You should have fucking well told me. We'll talk about this later but right now we have other things to worry about." He starts to explain taking a deep breath before sighing. Excuse me? What is going on right now? "Everything in there is a mess. Someone was clearly searching for something important. If you ask me it's for that damn diary. We can't call the police as they won't be able to do anything about it and it's exactly what they want. They want us to panic but we can handle this. Where have you got the diary anyway?"

"I took it with me. It's not a damn diary. It's one of the only things that I own of my mothers who is dead if I have to remind you again. It's the only thing that can tell me what happened. It's the only possession that will tell me something about my past. The only possession that will make it all clear in my head."

"Do you really fucking believe that finding out who killed your mom will make the pain just disappear like dust in the morning? God, Olivia, this is not a joke. Those guys are dangerous and you made them fucking furious. They're after it for some reason and since you haven't read it yet, there's still a way of getting out of this mess," Ethan says still holding onto me.

"I will not give the only thing away that I still have. I will not be scared anymore and I will not hide anymore. I'm done having people taking away from me what is mine and not leaving anything for me. How do you even know how dangerous they are to begin with? It doesn't make sense."

"Because we've been involved with those guys before." Jacob confesses standing on the other side of Ethan. Ethan gives him a very dangerous look.

"Keep your mouth shut J."

"She deserves to understand the danger that she's in. That we're all in right now. We're going to your place now mate. Then we'll have a little chat," Jacob says but it is directed at Ethan than at me.

"I'm not going anywhere. I need to sort this out and call the police. I need to clean my home or I'll never be able to sleep in there again." I decide to try to get past the door, but my boyfriend is holding firmly onto my left arm. His face is now closer to mine but more likely my ear.

"Baby, listen. What you'll find in there is not your home anymore. They took away that feeling for you. I won't have you sleep in there again, before this is sorted out. I'm going in to grab a couple of clothes and your stuff and then you're staying with me. Enough is enough!" He demands. Even though he knows that I hate this, he's still doing it and it makes me boil this time. Like he's pressing all my buttons without actually wanting to press them. "Olivia, look at me. Please look at me," he says in a calmer voice. "You know that I love you so, so much. I love you and our own little galaxy my love. You also know that I would do anything to keep you safe, right?"

"Yes, I know that," I reply giving in.

"Then please come with me. Let me keep you safe and let me love you and tell you things. The ugly truth about my past." He holds onto my face with bis hands leaning his forehead against mine. Our noses touch briefly and I could swear that I heard his heart racing a thousand miles per minute. He's scared. He's scared that I won't trust him or won't choose him. I don't have a clue what is going on right now, but what I do know is that he's the calmness in my storm. He's the one spot of light when the rest of the sky is dark. He's the one holding the sky back from falling on my head. He's the one to keep me together. He's the one to save me. He's the one putting all the pieces of my broken heart back together. *He is my hero.*

One day I'll tell my children about you, your strength and your music. The only one who was able to save me from myself.

"I trust you." I tell him leaning into him, not being able to handle any more of this situation. I trust him. No matter how angry I would be at him, I would never abandon him or end things with him. We're in this for the long haul. Not because we're prefect for each other, we're far from that, but because we can make each other the best version of themselves. I hope that one day he's capable of providing himself the same love he gives to others. Remember how I explained to you the feeling of home at the cliff? The first night, we actually connected and the first night I gave in. I said that for me, home would more likely be an emotion than a place. I know better now. Because now, I'm beyond sure that Ethan feels like home.

"I need to get away from here Ethan. I can't do this," I sob into his shoulder hiding my face. It's as if I'm hiding from the truth and from reality.

"You can do this. We'll get you away from here. Jacob is going to take you in his car while I grab your things. I'll be right back, okay?" he explains kissing me on my head.

"Okay."

I step away turning around to face Jacob. He places one of his arms behind my head, so his arm is resting on both of my shoulders. We walk back to the car not saying anything. To be honest, I don't think I would be able to. I don't know what I should think about them knowing God knows what and not telling me or about them being behind my mother and now me. *Should I just give them what they want? I can't do that since it's not the right thing to do for everyone involved and not for my mum. She deserves justice and I deserve to know. I deserve to know what I've been crying about my entire life. At least, that's what it feels like.*

After a couple of minutes Ethan also joins us. He is constantly watching me from the front seat since I'm seated in the back row of Jacob's car. The whole ride, my thoughts are running so fast that I develop a headache. I'm scared. Scared of the truth and scared to lose the game that I intended to win so badly.

To be completely honest with you, I am more terrified about the thought of losing Ethan. At this point in our relationship, he's everything. He's not just my boyfriend, who I love from deep down in my heart, but he is also a huge part of me. Of whom I have become and who I feel I want to be. Because every single time I look into his gorgeous eyes and see him walking towards me I know it. Because every time I'm closer to finally under-standing that he's the one. I just know it. And if I were able to, I would tell my mum every detail that I learned about him and every little aspect of who he is and why I love him. Of whom he made me be. I feel safe in his arms, like nothing could hurt us or our galaxy. *I feel untouchable when we're together.* The problem with that is that no matter how much I am happy with him, I have this strong fear of losing everything. Of losing him. And I doubt that my heart can take another fall like that.

I don't realize that the car has arrived until my door is opened and my head turns towards it and the rain outside. God, I hate this weather and I do hate autumn. We walk inside and I'm still quiet and they are whispering things to each other. They're probably discussing our little talk which I am not looking forward to if I'm being honest. Ethan walks towards his bedroom with my bag, probably throwing it in there. While he is doing so, I sit down at the table and Jacob is carefully watching me.

"Why didn't you tell me? I thought we were friends Jacob. I told you about my personal stuff just as I opened up to Ethan about my mother. Nevertheless, both of you chose to lie to me about this," I say without looking at him. My hands are intertwined under the table and I'm sort of playing with them trying to calm my nerves. I really should talk to Susan again. Maybe she has some advice for this situation... or not. That would be a good question to ask oneself.

"Liv...," he says but something is keeping him from continuing. It's almost as if his voice is shaky and close to crying. I should be the one doing that Jacob, no offence. I can hear footsteps and counting on the way they sound, it's Ethan. Not that anyone else would be here. With time, I can tell by the sound of footsteps who it is. Weird, but helpful in most situations.

"Jacob, I think we should sit down as well. There are a couple of things to discuss from our side but first I have a question and I want you to answer honestly." Ethan demands while taking a seat across from me on the other side of his dark wooden table. He's so intimidating, he has always been.

"Do I even have a choice here?" I ask him because I'm pissed. I am pissed and I have the right be pissed. *Olivia, you've got to concentrate on your feelings for once. Yours, and only yours.*

"You always have a choice Olivia. But you won't make it easier for all of us if you're not talking honestly. We'll be honest with what we have right now and we're asking the same back from you. It's only fair."

"Fair?" I question laughing out loud. This is hilarious. I continue while they stare at me irritated. "You're speaking of fairness when both of you chose to lie to me and to keep things from me. Important things which include my life and my mother's. One of them has been lost and I intend to find out why. So, Ethan, do not speak of fairness in that matter." I won't let this go and I won't let the death of my mother be forgotten. If she gave her life for something, I must have been important for the world to know.

"You're right and we're wrong. I'll give you that. However, I do not fucking understand why in the world you did not tell me about that stupid letter you found. When was that? Why didn't you tell me?" Ethan asks again placing his folded hands on top of the table. Something about him has changed. His eyes don't show the same amount of calmness anymore. They're darker, more violent and still scared at the same time.

"It was before thanksgiving. I didn't tell you because I didn't know how to and I didn't want to kill the mood. I thought it was a joke or something like that. Your concern would've been irrelevant. This is my fight. I cannot ask any of you to fight it for me. I can't and I won't do that."

"I will always come and save you Olivia. Fucking hell, you know that. I would leave everything behind in an instant to come and save you. You need to stop caring about everyone else for once in your life. I told you before and I will again. Start being selfish."

"See, that is the problem," I reply looking deeply into his eyes without changing my serious facial expression for once.

"Why in hell would that be the problem?" Jacob asks.

"I told you that not every person is meant to be saved. I was saved by you Ethan, by you and all of the band. You saved me from myself, but I can't ask you to save me again. That's not how it works."

"Don't say stuff like that. Don't push me away. That's not normal and it's not true either. Baby, come on. You need to stop believing things like that." Ethan tells me.

"Don't act as if I'm some psycho or shit like that. Don't act as if I'm the only person in this room who has mental issues!" I blurt out without thinking, immediately regretting it. I should keep my mouth shut again. "Sorry, I shouldn't have said that," I add shaking my head in disbelief at all of this. Myself, my place and the two of them. While doing so, I can feel an aching pain in my chest. The thing that I'm most scared of; someone breaking what's left of my heart. Not that they're doing that… but it feels like I am. Like I am destroying myself more than Roman has and more than my father ever will be able to. Like I'm destroying my home.

Chapter Forty-One

"It's okay. You're upset and that is normal. It's human." Jacob reacts to my apology and I find myself wiping away a tear that found its way down my cheek. I can't explain to you why I'm crying right now because I honestly don't know. I have no clue why I constantly tend to be so emotional and it upsets me.

"Jacob, the others and I have had certain dealings with those guys. As you might know by now they like to destroy other people's lives when they don't get what they want. In fact, Jacob and I were working for them after we ran away from my dad for... for obvious reasons. We thought it was a good thing to get some money for a place to live and to start our own musical career. We didn't know that they were like that. We've never met the leader, just only the lower class as you might call them. It's like a club of cruel and evil people who will trick others into contracts and promises while never keeping their own. They always make sure of that. So, they tricked us into this. We had to do a one-time-delivery to a person a few hours away from London. We had no idea what was in the van when we were driving there. We just had our orders to deliver it to someone else. And we did. We earned a shit ton of money for it, since it most likely was illegal drugs. We had enough money after the third time delivering because we were stupid enough to think that two times more won't hurt anyone. We were young and stupid and we weren't thinking clearly. I mean, how could we have known that?" he explains taking a break to look at both of us with a desperate look now. I'm not able to say anything since my head and thoughts are a mess. Jacob goes on while Ethan focusses his eyes on me the whole time.

"We were going on with our lives because we had a promise from them that it would be over after the third time. Of course, we were naïve enough to trust their words. As we went on, a couple of months after, we received certain letters. They wanted us to pay them money or they would recruit us again and use us as their fucking transport guys. They said that if we refused, they'd send footage of us delivering that illegal stuff to the police and we would've been fucked. Everything that they didn't want to do, or get their hands dirty, would've been our job. Since we had a bit of money by then, thankfully after working on music and doing concerts and such things, we could pay them back. Since then, we never heard nothing from them. Until we met you."

"That makes no sense. Why didn't you tell me earlier?" I ask both of them.

"Because we were ashamed of that past. It's a part of who we are and what made us who we are... still, it's nothing nice to talk about. Besides, I didn't think it would be necessary. They were onto you because of your mom, not your connection to us and I assumed that you didn't need more stress and chaos... so I... we, didn't tell you," Ethan says. I roll my eyes. *How can men be that stupid?*

"Ethan, I love you, but you are so stupid. To assume things that involve me and all of that. You can't just always handle things on your own. A relationship involves two persons which equals two heads and if I need to remind you; two heads mean two functional brains. Idiot."

"One would assume that Liv. When it comes to our Ethan, I'm not sure his is entirely functional," Jacob jokes and Ethan hits him at the back of his head in annoyance. And I had hoped several times for this kindergarten to end. Don't get me wrong, I enjoy it and it's hilarious. However, it's leading away from important topics.

"Shut up J."

"Make me," Jacob dares him, smirking like an idiot at the same time.

"Stop. The two of you are acting like toddlers again. We're discussing important matters and I'm too mad and emotionally unable to watch your damn shit show!" I yell and causing their heads to turn to me in a split second. Like you just caught two children doing something forbidden which is hilarious to me.

"She is feisty. I'm really regretting that I didn't make the first move mate," Jacob tells him instead of listening to me which makes me cross my arms in front of me. *Is no one listening to anything I'm saying?*

While Ethan glares at him and is about to talk, I interrupt him. "I am right here, you know? I'd appreciate it if you stopped talking as if I wasn't present. Now, what are we going to do? Something that will actually prevent something worse from happening. Something to expose them or such things."

"You'll stay here with me and I won't leave you alone again. I'll make sure that they don't hurt you," Ethan says immediately and I reach for his hand looking at them. Our holding the hand of the other person and feeling their skin it's always like fireworks which goes through my whole body starting from the place we touch and always ending in my chest. *You truly found your way into my heart, didn't you?*

"Ethan. We both know it's not possible for you to always be around me. We also need our own space. We can't live in constant fear and we can't let the fear control our lives'. I won't risk yours over mine baby."

"This is not something to discuss. I love you so much, but I don't care whether you agree with this or me right now but I am doing what is right to protect you no matter how much you like it or not. Therefore, you're going to stay with me. If they went into your place, they certainly won't stop searching for that damn diary any time soon." He debates with me.

This time it's different. When I met him, he did what was right for others and not for himself. Right now, on the other hand, he's doing what is right for him and not in general. Because he can't bear to lose me as well as I can't do that when it comes to him. *We both would destroy ourselves in order to keep the other one safe.* I don't think that it is healthy but what can we do about it?

"For the other thing... Liv with all due respect... those people are far more powerful and dangerous than you think. You can't win them over. You need to give them what they want before they come and get it. Because if they do come for it, they certainly won't be very friendly." Jacob is trying to convince me and I nod along to follow his game. Deep inside I know that I can't do this. It's not the right thing. My mother wouldn't want that and I don't either. Besides, if I give them her diary, how could they be sure I haven't read it? How could they be sure that I won't tell what is written inside there to the whole world?

"I can't think clearly right now. I'm exhausted and I need to sleep." I tell them knowing that it's not true. I might be a tiny bit tired, but my brain is turning so fast that it feels as if it's about to explode. I just can't have them know my plan.

"Let's get you into bed then. We'll talk tomorrow if you're ready," Jacob says gesturing with his head towards the long hallway and Ethan. He stands up holding out his hand for me which I take. I murmur my goodnight to Jacob before walking behind Ethan into his bedroom. He helps me to find my pyjamas and undresses me putting my hair up into a bun while I brush my teeth with his spare toothbrush for me. I have no idea where he had learned to do a woman's hair but it's nice to know and I'll gladly come back again. We walk towards his bed and I lie down, hiding myself in the sheets while he tugs them around me. He cares. He brushes his finger through my hair.

"Don't worry baby, I'm here and you're safe. I'll talk to Jacob for short while and then I'll be sleeping on the couch. I get that you're angry, but you don't need to worry. We'll be all right," he whispers with his soft and calming voice. After looking at each other, he stands up closing the blinds.

He is walking towards the door when my mouth says, "No. Wait." He stops turning around immediately.

"What's wrong?"

"I'm still mad but I don't want you to go. I'm scared. And never leave like that again. Never leave without kissing me goodbye again. Not in this dark world, where you never know what's going to happen next," I tell him and he's smiling. I can tell even in the dark. He steps closer giving me a soft kiss onto my lips, which I return. *We never know how long it will take until the sky crashes down onto our heads.*

"I won't do it again, promise. I'll be back soon. Try to get some rest," he murmurs planting a soft kiss onto my forehead. Before walking out the door he asks me if he should leave the door open. After what happened today, I'm glad if it's open so a tiny bit of light can come through. So I can hear better when his footsteps are getting closer to me. The second he has disappeared, I turn my body towards the left side of the room his side of the bed where the window is. I hide myself even more in the sheets not caring how hot I'm getting under there. Normally, I don't really need that many sheets because Ethan has a shit ton of body warmth to offer.

To be honest, I miss the old times. In a way of not being scared as I'm right now. Not needing to worry about any tour or fans or even paparazzi. Not worrying about what others will think of me. That doesn't mean that I didn't worry about it back then because I did. It means that in a way, I was worried about what people on the streets thought about me but not that much because I knew that the chances of seeing them again were very low. Because they didn't care about me. Now on the other hand, they care about Ethan. It doesn't matter in what way, but they do. And since I'm on his side and he cares about me and loves me, they immediately turn their side to me. I'm not too fond of that. I wish it would be just like in the past but with him there. With him and all of his crackly sides and friends. All of my friends and Abby of course.

Speaking of, I'm in need of her advice and to hear her voice. I miss her and I wish she could be here. All the time, in fact. I'm aware that she has a lot to do and that she's been sort of avoiding me because she's still pissed that I'm with Ethan. She despises him. Frankly, I don't care because she can't deny that Roman was the worst of all my... let's call it acquaintances. He's the best out of them all and it's painful to see that she's not accepting it in that way. So, I think it's about time for a late-night call. I sit up again reaching for my phone on the nightstand which Ethan plugged in. He is sweet. You can't deny that. I dial her number, which I know by heart as I should, and I wait for her to reply. I wait for a solid minute until her voicemail takes over. So, I call again and again until I start to cry after the sixth time. The sixth time after the call is ended I leave her a voice message hoping that she listens to it as soon as she can. You don't need to tell me that I'm emotional, I'm well aware of that, but I really needed to talk to someone. I really needed that right now. However, we can't always get what we wish for. However, she's never acted like this around me and it's putting me on edge.

I have a strong fear of endings. In fact, it's the very thing that haunts me in my dreams. Whether it is because the limited time with my mom is over again or just simply the thought of having to go back to reality. I'm scared of endings because on one side I want certain things to end but I don't want to have to miss them. I don't want to miss them because in my head and in my heart I know that I never enjoyed it. I never did. What follows after the end is what scares me. The unknown. The unknowing and the not knowing if there's going to be an after. When giving your whole heart and soul into something and it's coming to an end… what happens after that? It's as if you have given everything that you had to offer and that there's no purpose for the rest of your life anymore. Like there's nothing left to your life and to yourself as well. When something that kept you alive is ending. Those thoughts are triggering me so much lately. What comes after life? What happens when we're dead? Will someone remember me? Will the project that I gave my all into go forgotten?

The truth is we don't know. I don't know and you don't either. No matter how bad we might want to know we can't know that. Humans in general are terrified of the unknown. We're scared when we can't figure something out. We're scared when we don't know what dark creature might be hiding behind those bushes. We're scared of unaccountable things, but what's most important is that we're scared of each other and of ourselves. Scared that someone else might do better and that they might be faster, prettier, more intelligent, more famous and more likeable. We are so petrified that we tell ourselves that we can't be better than this one person. We talk down to ourselves because the thought of what might happen if we were the most intelligent, prettiest, fastest, most famous and most likeable person in the room or in the world is even more petrifying than thinking someone might be better because we've been used to it our entire lives. This behaviour is one thing that we humans must make ourselves aware of. It's because our behaviour when not knowing it will hold us back from doing the absolute best that we can.

We need to work on our goals. And by working on our goals I don't mean extra shifts or earning more money. No, it's not all about money or things you can possess. By working for our goals, I mean working on ourselves. How to treat ourselves and how to be nice to one another and us. How to work through the shit that every single person on this planet has to go through. How to ignore the opinions of others and listen to our thoughts instead of the ones around us. We've all got a lot of work to do when it comes to self-care, self-love and the right amount of self-confidence. We need to hear to our hearts, our minds, our souls and the ones we hold dear to us. We need to talk less and listen more and we need to believe. *Because if someone tells you something that would make their lives a lot harder by telling you… believe them.*

It's good that I have this way of telling someone how I feel when others can't listen to me. Thank you for letting me talk to you. *Even though you're not actually here to listen to me now.*

I can't let myself go down that road again today. Especially not after what happened before. I need to focus, calm down, and sleep. As I try to calm my breathing down after plugging in my phone again, I can hear footsteps again. I don't think I need to tell you who it is. He's getting closer and I try to mute my breathing and crying while I lie there as still as possible. I can't have him think that I'm weak. I can't have him, nor others look at me in the same way as I see myself in those dark moments when I look into the mirror. He's not moving from what I can sense for about thirty seconds. I can feel his stare. It's something about those eyes, because every time they lay their gaze on me, I immediately get goosebumps. He takes off his trousers and hoodie before walking over to crawl into his side of the bed. He is still looking at me. When he pulls me into his bare chest, I can't hold it in anymore. I hold onto him letting everything out. All the tears, and the heavy breathing is coming back while he holds the back of my head.

"It'll be all right. We'll be fine, just like the stars always are. Remember, they can't be taken down by any force. We have our own galaxy Olivia, nothing will hurt us nor destroy what we have," he whispers into my hear leaving a soft kiss there.

"What if it won't be? What if we won't be all right? What if they take down our stars?" After asking that, he's quiet for a brief moment while I snuggle closer to him. I'm trying to get the feeling of nothing can hurt us again.

"They can't. They can't stop us from feeling the way we do about one another. You can't think like that baby." He's not giving me my answers but instead, he is opting encourage me. "We need to sleep. You need and deserve to rest. Mind and body. We can worry another time. There's always another day."

Another day, another surprise.

Chapter Forty-Two

I can remember when I was a little child that I was so excited to finally grow until I was able to see my full head in the mirror in the bathroom. I was so excited to grow taller and to finally see the world as adults do if you want to say so. If you ask me, I strongly believe that most children do think in that way. They don't want to be treated as children, they want respect and responsibility. They want to belong. We all spend most of our time wanting to become something or someone else, just as teenagers and everyone else did. We wasted our time wondering who we could be instead of enjoying who we were for as long as we could. That's the thing I regret the most when looking back. I regret not enjoying my childhood because now, I'm constantly wishing for it to come back.

I've had a few more flashbacks than I'm used to if I'm being honest with you, I'm not too fond of it. It's a wonder that I even get them, considering how much I have forgotten about my past and just things in general. I don't like them because they remind me of how good I felt back then. How naïve I was. I was naïve because I thought that things were just going to stay that way forever and that everything would stay perfectly fine. Surprise, I was wrong. I'm jealous of the little girl in those memories, I really am. I wish I could go back to that feeling and to the people that I used to be around before my world began to crumble before I could even see the whole world that I had. That's what it felt like. Nevertheless, I learned that I need to accept the fine line between living too much in the past or in the future and finding the balance. The balance, in my point of view, would equal the focus on the present and equal balance with focus on the past and the future. It's a part of who we are but it's not what defines us. The past leads us on the track to who we are but it's not the very thing we consist of. It will never be and we need to remember that. I must remember that.

I get up to take a much needed shower since my hair is oily and disgusting. After getting out of the shower, I braid it so that I don't have to bother with it throughout the day. I have a feeling that it's going to be a long day. I go back into the dark kitchen once more, wondering how long it will take for me to finally feel at home in here. I brew myself a coffee before sitting down on the coach with my phone, diary and coffee. I take one of the green blankets and I'm cosying myself into it. At least it's not orange.

Abby hasn't called back or texted yet. Well, for her it's still night, but I'm guessing she wouldn't ignore me. I scroll through social media for a little bit, before bringing myself to finally open the damn diary again. Honestly, I wouldn't be surprised if it gave me the next couple of nightmares. Ethan and I have tried to keep our heads down in social media, but as his manager and mine said, it's blowing up. I can't blame his fans for wanting to know more but considering our situation, we can't give anyone else anything besides ourselves – self-care. Maybe we can show others a tiny wee bit of our galaxy when the world around us has calmed down. However, I'm doubting that I will want to share what I hold dear to my heart.

I open the diary to the last page I was on; which is the beginning of her newest and also last case; the case that changed hers and my life; the last thing she did on this planet. Am I ready to look into this? No. Will I ever be fully ready? No, probably not. Am I going to do it anyway? Hell yes! Since the moment I got this diary, I constantly feel the need to smell it. Call me weird but new books just smell so good. I can't get rid of the thought that she actually touched it, that she perhaps smelt it and that maybe I took this weird habit from her. I would feel flattered if I did. I'm reading the first page when my phone buzzes next to me. It's Abby. Thank the Lord.

"Hi Abby," I say first.

"Oh my God Liv, are you okay? I was worried about you! I heard your voicemail and I'm sorry that I didn't reply. There's no right excuse for it. I was just exhausted so I went to bed."

"Don't apologize. I'm sure you needed a break after all your hard work and it's okay to take one. It's okay to be selfish once in a while," I reassure her while still reading. It's definitely harder to do so while talking to someone, but it's working. I am guessing it's another thing that I got from my mom. The love for words, definitely; but not much of the multi-tasking ability. Whether it's in song texts or books… just the love for words – words that can describe so many beautiful things and don't even expect to be spoken out loud. They can also turn something so painful or some warming, breathtaking and beyond-believable thing.

"We're not talking about me. We need to talk about what happened. Where are you? Have you called the police? Where was your mister boyfriend at that time?"

"I'm at his place. He didn't let me go home and he wanted me to be safe. I swear he's so overprotective," I tell her with a slight laugh.

"He'd better be. I'm not a fan but if he had left you there, I would have had to kill him," she explains to me and from what I can hear in her voice, she's deathly serious.

"Calm down tiger. Where are you and what are you doing?" I ask; to loosen the atmosphere.

"I'm home. Australia is getting warmer over here. I bet you're freezing your pretty ass off over there, aren't you?" she asks jokingly.

"Very much so. You know I'm not a fan of autumn or the cold," I say.

"You're also not a very big fan of Halloween and pumpkins, I know Liv. I know you. But are you okay? What are you doing right now?" she asks, questioning my more silent behaviour since I'm trying to focus a little bit on reading. As she asks, my eyes stumble across a sentence in that book which makes my heart stop. My body is going into instant freeze mode and my mind is racing. This doesn't make sense. This cannot be true; I must be going blind and crazy. Since I no longer trust my eyes, I get up and walk rapidly towards the window, trying to get a better light from there. As soon as I arrive there, I read the sentence over and over again. But it's not changing in any way. The truth is not changing, and, in my head, a thought is taking over. It's all lies!

"Olivia? What's going on? Why are you breathing so heavily?" Abby pushes me but her voice sounds distant to me. My hands can't hold onto the book, so it slides out of my hand. My remaining hand is going through my hair stopping to hold my head in a certain way. Like I need to hold it, so it won't explode at the thought of this being true. I was aware that life wasn't always nice to me, but this didn't have to happen, did it?

I follow the line that is now marked in my head like a fire in the woods. Murphy. An Irish businessman. It's making sense now while it's still not.

"No!" is the first thing to escape my lips in a state of disbelief and shock. "This can't be true. No, no, no. God dammit!"

"Olivia fucking Jones what in God's name is happening?" Abby yells into my ear. She's probably scared.

"Ethan. His name is Ethan Murphy. And his dad, his dad is the one… one of my mum's last cases. His dad was t-the one who killed her. I-I, please tell me this isn't true Abby. I can't take t-this!" I cry into the phone letting myself slide down along the wall, hugging my arms around my body. She's not saying anything.

And that's when the light bulb finally comes on in my head. *Everything will connect eventually.* As she's not saying anything, my mind hurts from thinking until it becomes clearer and clearer that there isn't another option for this.

"You knew it, didn't you?" I whisper my voice full of utter pain. When she doesn't reply, I finally realize it. A part of me wished, desperately, for her to deny it. But now, there's nothing she can say anymore to make it better. "I trusted you. I trusted you my whole life Abigail," I hiss into my phone and for the first time in about seven years I'm using her full name. The room is turning around my head, as my chest aches and I feel a sharp pain in my throat. My hands are shaking and my eyes are swollen at this point from all the tears. I probably looked like a mess the whole time. Honestly, who cares? My life is a lie. Everyone lied to me. I fell heavily and deeply in love with the son of my mother's murderer.

"I promise I wanted to tell you. I wanted to tell you all this time but I couldn't. He told me he would hurt you if I told you. I needed to protect you Liv. I needed to save you. I'm so, so sorry."

"Don't tell me you're sorry, feel sorry for yourself. Who told me that?" I said, turning down her apology.

"I can't tell…," she's begging to talk herself out of it but I cut her off.

"Who fucking told you? Don't even think about lying to me again!" I yell before another heavy cry escapes my dry mouth.

"Roman." What the fuck? Can this even get worse?

"Why? Why would he do that. This doesn't even make sense." My head can't wrap around all of it; and some part of me knew exactly, that this was how it would end. Not the whole story of illegal stuff and murder, but the unbelievable pain and betrayal.

The feeling of not having known better and being mad at yourself more than at the other people who were guilty. I was betrayed by the person whom I trusted and who I told about all the things that hurt me the absolute worst. The person who I opened my heart to, only for him to break it worse than anyone else did; the person I loved and valued above all others.

"I don't know. He just told me that he's friends with Ethan's dad and that I should make sure you don't continue to read that fucking diary and hand it over to him. He wanted me to make sure you stayed put or he would hurt you. I know you currently hate me; but Liv I love you so much. I was trying to protect you," she says, while trying to apologize and explain herself again all at once.

Honestly, I don't care. Because despite all the hurt from a moment ago, I don't feel it anymore. My heart and my mind have closed in order to protect me from another chunk of hurt that I couldn't carry.

"Well, you failed!" I tell her with no emotion in my voice. She knows this and she knows how fucking dangerous it can be for me.

"No, Liv, you need to focus and listen to me. You need to let it hurt, don't cut yourself off again." She begs me to continue trying to get through to me. Abby, you destroyed your path to get through.

"Frankly, it's neither your place, nor your job to worry or care about me anymore. Goodbye."

"No, don't do this. Please, Olivia, don't…" she says, but I end the call before she can even say another thing. I throw my phone onto the floor next to me, not caring about it in any way. It's not as if there is any person who I would want to call or even text. I stare in front of me with just blankness on my mind.

The day we met… he knew it. He must have known me. All of the band fucking knew who I was and no one bothered to say anything? I trusted every single one of them. What about Ben and Emma? Were they thrown out because they wanted to tell me? Were all of the things that Jacob and Ethan talked about yesterday straight lies? They knew who went into my house because they didn't even fucking bother to call the police. But why would he want to take me home with him? Why would he want me to go on tour with him? Why would he lie right to my face and tell me that we would be all right when we'll clearly would not be? Not me nor him. Not in this world and not in our own galaxy. What about Roman? Did he know from the start when we dated? Was this all some sort of fucking master plan? Are they all friends? Was my mother trying to warn us before she died?

It's all a mess, isn't it? My whole life. I was never going to make it. Roman and I were never going to make it. We were always a losing game. But Ethan? Ethan and I weren't always a losing game. We were going to make it. We would have if *we were half the world away.* Perhaps, we would've made it then.

As all of these thoughts go around in my mind at a hundred miles per second, I was not concentrating on what was going on around me. Maybe that was the reason I didn't hear anyone coming. Or maybe, maybe this whole thought clearing thing had caused me to not notice his footsteps as they approached me.

He's coming rather fast towards me, not sure what's going on. Yeah, go on and play the innocent. When he reaches me, he crouches down in front of me and tries to touch me but I flinch away.

"Don't come near me," I whisper as the tears and the pain kick in again. Seriously, I liked it better the other way; when I only felt numb. A while ago, I told you that going into the numbness could be something good, but coming out of it, on the other hand, is very scary. Honestly, I don't care about it anymore. I don't care because it doesn't feel like there is any part left of me that will survive this. There's no part left of me that will survive without him at my side and we both know that. Everyone knows it.

"What happened baby? What's wrong?" he asks me with a worried and honest expression until he sees the open diary on the floor just a few steps away. That's when his eyes go wet as he falls to the ground.

"I can explain. I can explain everything."

I knew that this was going to happen. I knew that I wasn't one of the lucky ones to have such a life. I just wish I could've known and prepared for the fall. Because I fell much deeper into the trap that was set for me, compared with the speed with which I fell in love with him. I just wanted to go home.

Chapter Forty-Three

Rain – rain is a comforting thing, as I've told you before. But rain can also be scary; when there's so much rain that it feels as if the sky must be about to fall; that our world can't take that much coming from above. It is as if I can't take much more rain from our sky after I've loved it for what feels like an eternity. Because it feels as if my life only began when the first few raindrops touched the top of my head, when I began to find it comforting and I trusted the rain. I trusted the rain because it felt like it couldn't destroy me. It's just water drops from the sky, isn't it? But who thought that you could be drowning in it and that your sky could be breaking down caused by water? That's what it feels like.

Eventually, the rain will turn into a storm and thunder starts to sound from the clouds above as well. Your comfortable drops will turn into a scary mess; and eventually, you'll lose your comfort in it, along with everything else you saw in the rain before.

During my life, I ran away from many storms. I lived through many storms. But this one… this one is something different. *Because this one could actually take down whole galaxies.* My galaxy – and it did; in less than a single heartbeat. But perhaps I was attracting the storm in some way. Maybe it was meant to hit me, no matter how hard it was then. Maybe we're meant to grow – driven by storms. Perhaps this is the way of fate to protect us from what's coming next. Maybe it isn't. Who knows?

"Why? Why did you have to do this? Did you know who I was?" He looks at me with puffy eyes as he nods and I break out in another round of ugly sobs. "Why?" is all I can think of asking right now; but in this very second, the front door opens harshly, and I hear a couple of footsteps. When I turn my head to see who's there, I can see Mary and Jacob standing there looking at both of us. There's no need for Ethan to explain to them that I know, I'm guessing it's quite visible. At this very second, I would gladly throw anything at them. The anger is boiling up inside of me, ready to take over every emotion I've got; but I won't give that to them. It could be the only thing they want to achieve. No, I'm smarter than that. So, I push the anger away, turning it into something else. As many times before, in a desperate attempt to cope, I make fun of my problems.

I find myself laughing and crying at the same time about this. How fucking ironic.

"Great. Now that the whole party is here, I think after what happened I deserve some consideration. So, tell me, what were all of you thinking? What kept you going? Was this all a stupid game to you?" I ask, while the hurt turns into anger. I don't even bother to stand; but instead I glare at each of them in turn. *Push the anger away, Olivia.*

Mary and Jacob are both looking rather pale, as if they've just seen a ghost. To be honest, I should be the one doing that, but for some reason I'm not. I'm not even terrified enough to just vanish. I'm not scared because there's nothing of my life left now. Every single person I've cherished with all my heart has betrayed me in some way. So, I feel that at least I deserve a bit of an explanation and for Jacob and Mary to listen to what I had to say.

Jacob and Mary step closer sitting down on the ground. Ethan speaks first. "I... we both knew who you were. My dad... he... my dad had us trapped in his service for some time. Just as I explained to you yesterday. It wasn't just me and Jacob. No, it was all of us. We met because of those circumstances and we wanted to try and solve the problem together, once we realized how fucking nuts he was and still is. We ran away and we broke contact. All of us did. We got through it all eventually and we were okay with that; until one day, one of his little bitches showed up and threatens us. They threatened me and Jacob, saying that if we didn't do this one job for my father he would hurt my mother. He would torture her or even worse, kill her; and because I hold her close to my heart and she was the only thing I had left, we all agreed, because we were together and we were a team." Ethan murmurs rather than speaking; but making sure not to lose eye contact with me once; but it didn't make sense. Of course his mother was very important to him, but she didn't care about him. Neither did his father, from what I had been told. I don't have a cold heart, but him protecting his mother by putting his own life in jeopardy was definitely not fair or logical.

"And I was the job?" I whispered and they all looked at the floor, making it quite obvious to me.

"The job was to watch you once my dad found out that you had come out of hiding with your dad. We didn't know about your mother back then. We just had our job and no other information. It was either doing what he told us to do or he would hurt my mother. I swear Olivia, we didn't know. We should have just kept working with you and the plan was to get to know you and find things out about that fucking diary." He was taking a break to calm his breathing before continuing.

It's still too fucking early for this. Too fucking early to wrap my head around the fact that I slept next to this man not even two hours ago. It was too fucking early for that to ever happen.

Ethan continuous. "When I approached you, I ran into you, I didn't know you were Olivia. We were in that restaurant after getting the first bit of information and that was when I wanted to refuse doing the job. I couldn't hurt someone I didn't even know. When Jacob met you, we didn't know it was you until you told him your name and that you liked music and all that stuff. We knew by then that it was true because a few hours later we got the first few pictures of you from my father. That was why I was so cold and pissed-off at you the first few times. I wanted to scare you away. I wanted to protect you by scaring you away. But I didn't think that even after I had scared you away, my father would make us go all the way to get back with you again. I'm giving you my word on that."

"Your word doesn't mean anything to me anymore."

A few tears escape his eyes after those hurtful words and somehow; very strangely, I had started to feel sorry for him. I was sorry for what he had been through, but that pity wasn't even comparable to the pain that I was feeling because of what he and the others had done to me.

"My father wanted to push you away and he did; until his father found out and took his mom. He took her and threatened him. But this time, it wasn't just words, it was action. So, he got closer to you. We all had to."

Mary then joined in, saying, "And with time, you grew closer to every one of us Ben and Emma wanted you to know what was going on. But we knew that there was no way we could protect you, Ethan's mother and Ben and Emma at the same time. We needed to protect you because once his father found out that you meant something to him, he started to make threats against you. He's a sick bastard who finds happiness in seeing others suffer. Not even his son can get him to feel any other emotion. He simply does not care about anyone. So, we had to kick Ben and Emma out for their, our, and your safety. We met and we tried to find a plan to get all of us out from under Ethan's father's threats and actions."

"And what is the plan?" I ask them folding my arms in front of me. No one replies and only Ethan looks at me. "There's none," I say, crying again. "Why couldn't you have fucking pushed me away as you wanted to? Why were you so selfish? Why didn't you think for even a split second about how this would end for me? I opened up to you and I told you everything. I trusted you. I fell in love with you. I did all those things with you after I felt as if I would never be able to do anything worthwhile or feel ever again. For what? For you to betray me even worse than everyone else?" I say demanding an answer from Ethan.

At that point, we were both a mess and the need for me to leave is coming up fast, while my body is still in utter confusion. There's a weird pressure on my chest that I've come to know over time. *Not here, not in front of them!* My fingers are numb and my head is pounding while my heart is racing and my chest is rising way too fast!

"No! I couldn't!" Ethan responds, "because I was so selfish; and after that fucking night on the cliff, I was a goner because every candle in a room, every song I heard, every ocean, every sunset I saw, every planet I thought about, every star in that fucking stupid sky, has always been about you. Always; but it's never been just about me. All those things I wished someone felt about me or even how I felt about me, I felt about you. Everything I saw about you was just… there isn't even a word to describe it. It's never been about me because it's always been you. And I wanted to keep you and everything else. I tried to stop the world from crumbling down. I tried to protect our galaxy and I failed," he admits to me almost spitting with emotion, while the veins in his neck are bulging. He's speaking from his heart again. I can't take this!

"What about Abby and Roman?" I have been avoiding his statement because I can't say anything about any of it. I can't say anything that sounds like a goodbye because I just cannot say goodbye to him.

"Roman is a fucking cunt. I worked with him before, before I even knew he was your ex; and at one time, I met him and my father explained the situation through him to me. He told me that he had threatened Abby but that was all after the cliff meeting we had. I couldn't do anything because you were in the middle of it. If I had taken as much as a single step, the whole thing would have exploded," Ethan was telling me and, in some way, I knew he was not lying. His eyes were speaking for him. I could feel what he was feeling so clearly, because I had come to know him so well in the last few months.

"And my mom?" I ask, dumping that huge question into the pile of questions already there. I had been asking myself that last question throughout my entire life and I had come to think that my whole life came down to getting that single answer. I'm looking around and Mary is shaking her head while looking at me with tears in her eyes. That was when I shook my head and went into a whole new level of crying. There had always been a small part of me that hoped that she was still alive. However, that part had just died. Another part wanted to know how, but my rational mind stopped me from asking that question. I had a feeling I would regret that.

"Baby, you need to calm down for me," Ethan says, trying to calm me down by moving a bit closer to me. I flinch at his movement and move further away from him.

"Don't you come any closer to me! and don't baby me! I'm not your baby, I'm nothing to you!" I hiss at him and the others, while pointing my finger at him in anger.

"I would never hurt you; you know that. I love you. Please, you need to believe me."

"But you did hurt me; worse than any physical thing that could've happened. I gave you the million pieces of my heart and you said you were going to put them back together, not throw them onto the ground and step on them as if it meant nothing." I confront him with that while leaning forward, because now my stomach had decided to ache as well.

"Baby, please. I can't do this without you. We need to fight for this."

"You can't do this without me? Do what? Spy on other people? Lie to them? Trick them? Hurt them? There is nothing left to fight for, Ethan," I say and before he says another thing, I turn my head towards Jacob, who hasn't said a word yet. He hasn't even looked at me, which is almost worse. "And you? What about us being friends? What about trusting me? You know what Jacob? You're getting a point because only one out of the two of you had the nerve to look at me. That would be five to five. However, there is another point to adjust because both of you lied to me. Five to five Jacob. I won. You're more alike than you'd like to confess," I tell him while crying a tiny bit less now, although I'm utterly disappointed in him. From the look on his face, which has finally turned towards me, I can tell that he's getting it.

"Liv…" Jacob begs but he soon stops because of a lack of words. I nod towards him with tears, signalling for him to stop; saying that I'm tired of all of it, and that I don't want to go any further.

I turn to Mary. There isn't even a word to say to her. I wasn't the closest with her, but I thought she was my friend. She was one of the nicest persons I knew. "When were you planning on telling me that then?"

Our surroundings are still rather dark since it's morning and it's all rainy outside. What a perfect coincidence. I'm not able to see their faces completely, but I'm glad it's that way. It's easier to do these things when I can't see and remember it so well. I have no idea where this is going to go. I wish I knew, but I don't. I can't even think of another day right now.

"No. We were going to figure it out and you were never supposed to know. We wanted to spare you this. We wanted to protect you and we failed. We failed and I couldn't be sorrier for that. I'm so sorry Liv," she replies, in a small terrified voice, while her lips stay slightly open. I can't reply to that. I just feel empty. As I look around the room again, I get up, leaving them staring. I pass the hallway, leaving them confused, and adjusting every little thing around me for the last time. I need to leave.

As I go into his bedroom. I take my bag which is still mostly full and I throw my stuff into it. When it's done and closed, I take it with me and walk back into the main area. They're still there, but all of them are standing now looking at me the second I enter the room again. God, I will miss those faces, despite everything they did and every pain they caused. I will miss this place and every place I've been to where I created those perfect memories. I pass them to grab my phone, ignoring the ten missed calls from Abby, and the diary. I throw my phone into my bag, throw the bag over my shoulder, while still holding the little book in my hands. I turning around to face them and walk towards Jacob, handing it to him. He looks at me in shock shaking his head. Since he's not grabbing it, I put it into his hands.

"I won't need that anymore. It will solve your issues and let you do whatever you please. I haven't read the ending and to be honest, I don't want to anymore. I don't want to know what those cruel people did to my mother and it's best that I don't know what she gave her life for. But I realize that after today, no matter what's behind this, trying to expose the whole story was still worth doing."

I step one foot closer to Mary, who is on the left side of the group and I look into her eyes. "Goodbye Mary."

One step to the right, there's Jacob with the diary in hands, looking at me as if he's in need of a huge hug from me. *Sorry to disappoint, I can't give those to you anymore.*

"You're a good person Jacob. You don't need to hide your emotions. Everyone will still love you the same. Even the strongest people need help sometimes," I say and he nods, still not able to say anything; but he whispers a quiet 'I'm sorry' to me. And one step to the right, there he is. The man who made me feel and get past my boundaries and fears; the man who made me who I am now.

Out of all of us, he's crying the most at this point. I'm not crying. There are no tears left anymore. "Please don't go. Please don't leave me. I can't do this without you. I don't want to because I love you the most out of this whole universe baby," he tells me. I smile at him slightly.

"I know. I still love you Ethan and I don't think I'll ever be able not to love you. But this… this can't go on, no matter how much we want to see each other. I won't be gone. Remember how we talked about our own galaxy? How you were saying that I was the stars and you were the planet?" I ask him and he nods in response. "Stars don't move, do they? They're always there. So, every time you look up at the stars you'll know that they are still there. That's how you'll know that I'll be there. Because I always will be. I won't forget you, I couldn't; *But stars can't shine without the dark.*"

"Please don't go," he begs again taking hold of my hands. His hands are cold and sweaty at the same time.

"Ethan, whenever I look at you, I feel it and I know it. I know I'm home, and I'm not ready to let that feeling go, but I have to. We both have to. I'm with the one person that I want to spend my life with, but fate doesn't want that. Our future does not always keep the things for us that we wish for. Now it's my time to protect all of you." A slight tear leaves my eyes, as my mind replays all the moments we had together. I couldn't be more grateful for them.

I step closer to him and leaning into him, I leave a slight, soft wet kiss on his cheeks. God, how I'll miss those perfect dimples, his messy hair and especially those eyes. Those eyes, that could explain more than words. Those eyes aren't speaking about anything at the moment as they're watching every single inch of my face. It's as if the light in his eyes has burnt out. I step back, while biting my lips fighting the urge to kiss him; the urge to just forget about what had happened and move on; to forget the unforgettable things. Sadly, that's not possible. I take in another view of them.

All of us are crying again, and I turn around on my heel to leave this place. I put my shoes and my coat on before opening the door for the last time; for the last time I look at them; for the last time smelling the whole house like he did. I'm seeing them for the last time and breathing in for the last time before another piece is ripped out of my heart. It's being ripped out because it belongs to him. It always has and it always will. No matter whether our paths lead separate ways or not, a part of our hearts will always be meant to be together. I'm glad that there's even a tiny bit of it left. As I leave his apartment, the cold wind hits me straight in the face, bringing me back to reality; and there it is.

But what now? I don't have anyone or anywhere else to go. I'm on my own again, but in some way it's a good feeling despite the utter pain I feel. I can't let him go... but there is this one thought coming into my head... *some people are not meant to be in your life forever.*

Just because things could've been different does not mean they would've been better.

Chapter Forty-Four

Standing here feels so weird. I wouldn't have ever thought of actually ending up here. It's been a week; a week since I found out about all of it, my mom, Roman, Ethan, Abby and of course all my friends. It's been a week of hiding away and ignoring everything coming from them, which was a lot. Abby called as much as the others, but one text got stuck in my head. She came here. At some point in this week, she flew over to talk to me. Probably, she met with the others first. It wouldn't be a surprise after everything that happened. To be honest, I'm the most disappointed with her and secondly Jacob. I thought they were different and I had hoped that I meant something more to them. And Ethan? For him, and me for that matter, I'm feeling pity; but we'll come to that later. So, it's been a week of ignoring and moving around to different motels and hotel rooms.

You don't need to tell me that ignoring my problems will solve them. It won't and I'm aware of that. That's the goal. See, this is another one of my toxic traits. I just wait and ignore everyone until the storm has gone away. But this time, unfortunately, the storm won't go away. So, I'm running away from everything again. I'm running away from my problems. I'm running away in hope that his father will accept the diary and my word, that we all can move on and most specifically; that I will be able to let go at some point in my life. I'm aware that it's going to take ages, but even if I have an opportunity to see them again or even talk to them, I won't be able to do it. I need to save myself from that, and I will, at any cost. So, no! ignoring is not the best solution but it's the only one I have in mind now, where I won't end up getting hurt even more – not that I think that's possible, but you're getting it, right?

Even my dad called me once or twice. That was just the cherry on my cake. Since I'm no idiot, most of the time, of course I didn't answer. I felt good after ignoring him as a matter of fact. Therefore, I will name this as the best event of last week's episode. Not that anyone would care besides you... thank you for staying this long, by the way; for listening and for making me feel. Thank you, Ethan.

After I left Ethan's apartment a week ago, I went to mine and got the most important things out of it; my guitar for example. Then, I went to the first hotel room. Come on, did you really think I was stupid enough to stay there? With Ethan's dad and the whole group looking for me? Nope.

The next thing I remember, after endless sessions of crying, nightmares and lying in bed, is that I bought a car. A black one. I bought it so I could be independent, and I am. I'm now an independent woman who can do whatever she pleases. That brings me to where I am right now. A week after I left the group I took my car and I drove here – to the place where everything seemed to have started. I drove to the cliff, and when I arrived, I took my guitar, notebook, blankets, and every other thing with me and I sat down on the blanket at the same spot where I sat with Ethan months before; so, here I am.

To be fair, I had to ask a few people for the way, but I ended up here and that's the most important thing. I'm sitting here and I'm watching the sun. Don't get me wrong, it's freaking cold but with blankets and lots of clothes it's fine. It has to be. Because today is one of the first beautiful days and I need to see that sunset again. Just for once, I need to remember how I felt. How you made me feel, Ethan. I need to get that little piece of happiness back. Just to know, that there was one.

This has all been for you. It has been for you the entire time, Ethan. It's always been you. And it will always be just you; in my head, in my soul and mostly in my heart. You own a piece of my heart. My story started when I met you. When my heart became at one with yours.

I feel untouchable. As I told you before, I feel untouchable. I don't feel like that because I'm with you, or because everything is perfectly fine, because it's far from being that. I feel that way because I'm at the starting line of one of the greatest adventures of my life. Every story, every adventure and every fairy tale must come to an end eventually. I feel that way because there's nothing in this world that could take anything away from me right now. Nothing can take anything because I don't possess anything anymore. I've got nothing left but myself; and nothing could hurt me more, than I already am; because at the end of the day, or at the end of the story, we all are alone.

But this story, is something I'll forever hold close to my heart. Sadly, Ethan, your chapters in my story are over, but I'll never forget the days that we thought we could live forever in that story. I'll miss you. Your chapters are over Ethan, But I can't keep rereading the book, hoping for another ending.

But one day; one day I'll tell everyone that I hold dear to my heart about you. I'll them about your laugh, your smile, your gorgeous eyes, your messy hair, your dimples, your music and how you were the only one to save me; because you were the calmness in my ocean, that kept me from drowning. You scared my storms away. You saved me.

Music, well. I haven't been able to write anything. I told my manager that I'm okay with publishing the last song we wrote and worked on but that this will be the end. I told them that I'm okay with publishing the song called 'Our own galaxy'. He knows that I'll be gone, and he does understand. Otherwise, I haven't even been able to listen to it. Because every song I hear, every song I write and every melody in my ear, always comes back to you. Every single piece reminds me of you, Ethan; because you were my music. Whenever I tried, I ended up like the sobbing wreck I am, and I had to shower to think I was washing it off. How pathetic, right?

However, no matter how much I tried to rinse it off, all the memories about you, the voice never leaves my head. No matter what I do or where I go, you always follow me. You laughed next to me when I finally cheered up after three days. I think I might be going insane at this point.

I didn't just go insane. I also got addicted. I got addicted to a losing game. Loving Roman was a losing game because we were never going to make it. We were always a losing game. Loving Ethan gave me the best time until we also lost the game and it became the worst thing in my life. Either way, I lost. God, how much I hate this man.

As I'm thinking about all those things, a few tears escape my eyes again. So, I'm taking the few crystals that I got from Sandra, my therapist if you forgot, and I'm holding onto them. I'm sure all of those have a certain meaning but I'm not smart enough to get it just yet; but the longer I hold onto them, the warmer they are in the end. They get me closer to a real hand to hold or a real person to hug. Speaking of Sandra, I visited her almost every day, because I couldn't end the day without having someone to talk to. Evening and nights were the worst. Normally, I would have just crawled into your arms… and I missed that every single day. Sandra, I'm pretty sure it must have been exhausting to have me around that often, but you helped me and I finally opened up to you. Like completely opened up. It was horrifying but I did it any anyway; and I felt a lot better afterwards.

It's really interesting to look at that. First, I was terrified of the thought that someone might know too much about me; but in the end, it felt as if I had the most power after I opened up. I had power because I didn't give my hurt the chance to have power over me. I got power because either way, I won the battle. It's a lot like finally escaping a prison I built on my own over time.

I said at first that I like being alone, but I don't want to be lonely; and in these days, I've been the loneliest of my entire life. I never want to feel like that again. I don't want to be lonely again; but what we humans often forget is that there are periods of your life where you will be alone. It's just inevitable. We can either make the best out of it and learn something new about ourselves or drown in self-pity. I need a fresh start. I need new people who know nothing about me. It will be the hardest thing, opening up, trusting again and trying to get over it, but I'll have to start some time. Sandra says the same. She's an angel.

No matter where I go on this planet, there's one angel who I know for sure is following me. I started wondering if my mother had the same struggles when she was younger. If she ever felt left out or alone; and from the bottom of my heart, I wish I could ask her. What I'm saying here is there are things in our lives' that will never make sense and that we will never find out about. Perhaps it's better that way. Grief and pain are unique for every human being. It's difficult and unique but we need to go through it. There are no rules on how to do it, or how long it will take because our own unique mind doesn't know. All we can do is be brave enough to go on this journey and hold on until it gets better; because it will getter, it has to. Life's not supposed to be that hard.

For the first time in my life, I'm thankful that I got and still get to see her in my dreams. I'm thankful that I'm able to see Ethan, my mom and all the others. It might not be real but going a whole lifetime without seeing any of them again would be so much worse. So, last night, when I had my most recent dream, I woke up and I felt relieved. I was thankful for it. That was when I decided to take those kinds of dreams away from my nightmare list. They are not nightmares. That's my brain showing me the wonderful people I met, the memories we made, and how much I miss all of it. Although I'm sad that it's over, I'm also thankful that it happened.

Right now, while watching the grass sway in the wind and hearing the sound of the ocean, that's all I can think about; about this feeling that your heart is warm and it holds the warmth leading from your chest through every vein going through your body. I believe that you can have several homes. One of them is, or was in that case, Ethan and the other will be this place from now on. I haven't been here often, but it feels like a strong connection. The roughness of nature combined with its beauty and all the small things stuck in between. If I had to spend the rest of my life somewhere, even my after life, I would choose this place. I would choose to have it all again, just as I would choose you all over again. Because it's always been like that.

Don't ask me why I brought my guitar with me. Perhaps a part of me was hoping that being here would bring me closer to music again. Perhaps I was wishing for someone special to come here and play it for me; for someone to take away all that pain; or perhaps it was all of those things combined.

I'm far away from being good or all right. I'm far away from the end of this journey. I am far away from finding my true self and also loving some particular person. I'm far away from accepting my past. I'm at the beginning of it because I was thrown all the way down again every time I climbed until now. All of us have a lot of work to do on that journey. Ethan, Abby, Jacob, Mary; and let's not even get started on Roman. I have no idea what I'm doing most of the time. I'm just doing it; and sometimes it's better to go ahead without thinking about where you could end up. Sometimes, it's important to take the first step without planning the journey. It could lead you to much greater places that you could have ever imagined. I learned that the hard way, but I did learn it.

If someone came up to me and asked me if I'm okay, saying yes would be a lie. I'm not okay, but is anyone really okay though? I don't mean that in a bad way, I'm just refusing to believe that there is a person who is perfectly fine, with everything in their lives all the time. We're all messed up in some way, but that's what makes it special. We can always be perfectly messed up with someone else, can't we?

There's a huge difference between feeling untouchable and actually being it. I wish for myself, deeply from my heart, that I'll experience that; though I'm guessing I already did.

What I also learnt about love is that it's only for the brave; because the chances of us getting our hearts broken are so high and yet, we still try to find it. Most humans do. Love doesn't hurt you. A person who doesn't know how to love right does; and as I said, I don't believe that there is anything like soulmates or persons who are perfectly made for each other. No. But you can develop a bond which will be much stronger and even harder to break. Because if you build up everything from the ground and don't just rely on and settle for what's already there, you will see the ground of it and aim to build it up higher and higher; until you can touch the stars. When you are that far up, you'll have to ask yourself how on earth you were able to do that just by working together; and then, you will be untouchable.

As the time goes by, the sun is setting, just like last time. The sky is tainted in the greatest colours of pink until yellow. That's how I define beauty; the undeniable beauty of nature itself. That's all I need at this moment. I just need a sign that the sun is still shining and that another day will come, no matter what. No matter what will happen, some things are always certain. It's a must to remind yourself of that every once in a while; how truly unimportant we are. We're unimportant to the sun, the stars, this world and to the whole galaxy.

A while ago, I told you my first and favourite poem I ever read. The one about heroes and villains? Shall I explain it again to you? All right, I will.

Heroes and villains. Such a common and still complex expression. What makes you a hero and what makes you a villain?

In our society, the opinions say; go in one direction and one direction only. In our society, heroes are symbolized as selfless; perfect creations destined to save and protect others; but that is wrong. Heroes are selfish. They want the fame and the glory, and they will do everything they can to get it. They will do everything to be seen as heroes.
The villains are the evil and the cruel, the dirty and the bad. But villains, they are the true heroes here because villains are the ones who are the most capable of love and they have the most compassion. Though they tear down cities, or bring kingdoms to their knees, they would drop everything just for one person who is decent enough to show them love. They are the true heroes because they show us what love is about. They show us what is the most important in life.

Ethan's a villain. You're a villain, Ethan; because despite everything that you tore apart and destroyed, despite how much you hurt me, you did it to keep me safe; and after all that, you showed me the most important thing in life. Ethan taught me how to love. You did that, Ethan. I will forever be grateful for that.

I stand up, taking something well known out of my backpack. Abby's birthday present for me. I take one out and I'm lighting it before stepping closer to the end of the cliff. I'm inhaling it and letting the filled air go deep down to my lungs before breathing it out again. I wish I didn't have to do this alone. I stretch my arms out in front of me and the cold wind blows past me. I'm inhaling the fresh air through my nose and letting it out through my mouth. I'm repeating it all over again while smoking my joint. My eyes are looking down at the ground and at the edge of the cliff. It's a beautiful view, to be sure, but I should be more scared. The average human being wouldn't even step that close. I'm standing here, with open arms and I'm not scared to fall. That's what is terrifying.

Seeing life from my point of view is weird. I could tell you a lot of things that you should be doing, what humans are in fact doing and all that stuff. However, I can't tell you specific things about me in such a short time. I can't tell you if I'm doing things wrong or right because I don't know if they are the right things to do. What I'm trying to show is that your life or things in general might look a lot less difficult from the outside. Just as a tornado looks almost peaceful from a distance, inside it, there is hell going on. Just because someone else tells me that my life is not that hard or that I should just 'suck it up' does not mean that person is right. It's not true; and people who have never experienced hard things will be the first ones to joke about it. So, whenever someone comes to me and says something like, 'Yeah, I know how you feel, but just think positive' I know that they have never felt the way I do. Because someone who felt like that would never dare to come up to me and say such things.

If I could leave something behind in this world, I believe it would be kindness and listening. In many ways, I'm not perfect either, but I often dream about a world where everyone would listen a little more than they speak or think. Where everyone would be just a bit kinder towards others but also to themselves. That would be the world I would like to live in.

Just as these thoughts are leaving my mind, my joint has also come to an end. I'm staring at the view in front of me which consists of the ocean. The sun is setting on the horizon where all the colours seem to be displayed. I'd like to have this memory painted, so I could look at it a little longer. So, I have another option than just reliving something that isn't in dreams.

I know that I'll probably talk to Abby first out of the group; and I believe that I will do that one day, I kind of have to. We lived our whole lives together, so I owe her that. Nevertheless, until then, there are a lot of things to do. I'll be leaving London and England; the city and the country I fell in love with a long time ago. My love for it isn't gone. It's just time to find something else to admire. After all, there's the whole world left to explore. There are adventures yet to be experienced and new acquaintances and friends to be made. I've got the rest of the whole world to discover; I don't need to feel any more that the precipice is waiting to swallow me.

It's time to stop settling for what's already there and to reach up higher into the sky. I'm keeping my eyes focused on the bright light as I'm whispering to myself; "This isn't the end."

Maybe I'll see you again. Maybe we'll meet and forget about all the pain. Perhaps things will feel just as they felt before. And perhaps we will just not; but until then, I won't forget any of it. I'll hold onto it and I'll fix the million pieces of my heart on my own. It was never my position to have to hand them over to be glued back together by someone else. Some things in life need to be done by ourselves because it will help us learn and grow.

I believe with all of my heart that this could have worked. I have to believe that because it felt too good to just be over. Perhaps it would have worked better. If we were *half the world away*; closer to our own galaxy, closer to my home.

I step away from the edge of the cliff walking back to the pink blankets on the grass. While gently and slowly walking I turn around and look up at the sky. I could get addicted to this feeling. Who knows, maybe I'll be coming back again. I doubt whether I could go without it for a long time. When I reach the blankets, I sit down again and lie down on them for a few minutes, just watching the sky which is slowly getting darker. It's almost as if time has stopped out here; like nothing else is important.

One part of me feels very guilty about just going MIA because I feel like I have to make sure they're okay and that everyone I left behind isn't hurting too badly. But it's just hard to take care of others when you can barely take care of yourself. I have to stop being there for everyone else before thinking about myself first. After what happened; after our story, I for sure have a lot of work to do on that. So, let's start with it right now. I open my backpack taking my grey laptop out of it. After laying it down in front of me, I watch the sun and I close my eyes to focus on the noises coming from the ocean. *Breathe Olivia, you've got this.*

Things have changed, but I'd still like to be the ocean. Some combination of the stars and the ocean, that's who I would want to be. Once more, I open a new document and taking a deep breath before letting my fingers, which are covered in rings, float over the letters until the first sentence is there. Ethan, there's a piece of you in who I am. The first sentences, are dedicated to something unknown and to a new start.

Where everything ends and begins; where everything will connect, eventually.

You said it's never been about you; but that's wrong, because this story, has all been about you. So, Ethan, this one's for you. Here's to us!

There's one, first sentence and thought that's not leaving my mind after typing it. I have no idea what's going to happen or what this will become, but that doesn't matter right now; because this is something I'm doing for myself and it's something that's been overdue for so long; and just like my mother, I've always had a connection to words. First it was books, then there was music. God, how much I loved music. Nevertheless; maybe it's time to open my heart to a new chapter and to a new beginning. Perhaps words in the form of stories might be the next thing. Maybe it's time to follow another path and to see where it goes... So here we go...

She loved reading. It allowed her to cry over someone else's sadness when she could no longer identify her own...

Credits

A credit to all the talented human beings I have quoted is inevitable. You are all amazing and I thank you for continuing to be every day. If you have time, check out their works.

Hero and Villain Poet by @loserpoetry on TikTok

Cigarett Metaphor by Sophia Gaslighter Petikas

The Lion King by Walt Disney

'always you' a spoken word by iz, @isabelladortax on TikTok

The author

Lisa Krämer was born in Aarau, Switzerland. Lisa
first discovered her passion for writing in 2021. She
has been reading and writing short poems since
she was a child. For her it meant letting out her
thoughts and escaping the world to create a new
one where she was the one in control. Throughout
the years Lisa has realized that the genres she most
enjoys are a mix between fiction, non-fiction and
subjects regarding mental health. Lisa is single and
still a student.

The publisher

> *He who stops getting better stops being good.*

This is the motto of novum publishing, and our focus is on finding new manuscripts, publishing them and offering long-term support to the authors.
Our publishing house was founded in 1997, and since then it has become THE expert for new authors and has won numerous awards.

Our editorial team will peruse each manuscript within a few weeks free of charge and without obligation.

You will find more information about novum publishing and our books on the internet:

www.novum-publishing.co.uk